Praise for The Wildwood Chronicles

"A richly satisfying weave of reality and fantasy."

—*New York Times Book Review*

"Meloy's debut is the kind of delicate, elaborate fantasy that is so well versed in classic Narnian tropes that it is destined to be enthusiastically embraced."

—ALA *Booklist* (starred review)

"Meloy has an immediately recognizable verbal style and creates a fully realized fantasy world. Ellis's illustrations perfectly capture the original world and contribute to the feel of an instant timeless classic."

—*SLJ* (starred review)

"Meloy's storytelling skills, honed on his epic ballads for the Decemberists, translate well to prose. Ellis's precise, detailed style evokes a folksy charm that is just right for the overgrown natural world of Wildwood and its inhabitants."

—*The Atlantic*

"This book is like the wild, strange forest it describes. It is full of suspense and danger and frightening things the world has never seen, and once I stepped inside I never wanted to leave."

—Lemony Snicket

"*Wildwood* is an irresistible, atmospheric adventure—richly imagined and richly rewarding."

—Trenton Lee Stewart

"A satisfying blend of fantasy, adventure story, eco-fable, and political satire with broad appeal."

—*Kirkus Reviews*

UNDER WILDWOOD

THE WILDWOOD CHRONICLES, BOOK II

COLIN MELOY

Illustrations by

CARSON ELLIS

BALZER + BRAY
An Imprint of HarperCollins*Publishers*

Balzer + Bray is an imprint of HarperCollins Publishers.

For information address HarperCollins Children's Books, a division of HarperCollins Publishers, 195 Broadway, New York, NY 10007.
www.harpercollinschildrens.com

Library of Congress Cataloging-in-Publication Data

Meloy, Colin.
Under Wildwood / Colin Meloy ; illustrations by Carson Ellis.
p. cm. — (Wildwood chronicles ; bk. 2)
Summary: "Prue and Curtis are thrown together again to save themselves and the lives of their friends, and to bring unity to the divided country of Wildwood"— Provided by publisher.
ISBN 978-0-06-2024718 (trade bdg.)— ISBN 978-0-06-202473-2 (pbk.)
[1. Fantasy. 2. Animals—Fiction. 3. Portland (Or.)—Fiction.] I. Ellis, Carson, ill. II. Title.
PZ7.M516353Und 2012 2012019040
[Fic]—dc23 CIP
AC

Typography by Dana Fritts
18 19 20 PC/LSCH 10

First Edition

For Steve Malk

CONTENTS

PART ONE

PART TWO

PART THREE

LIST OF COLOR PLATES

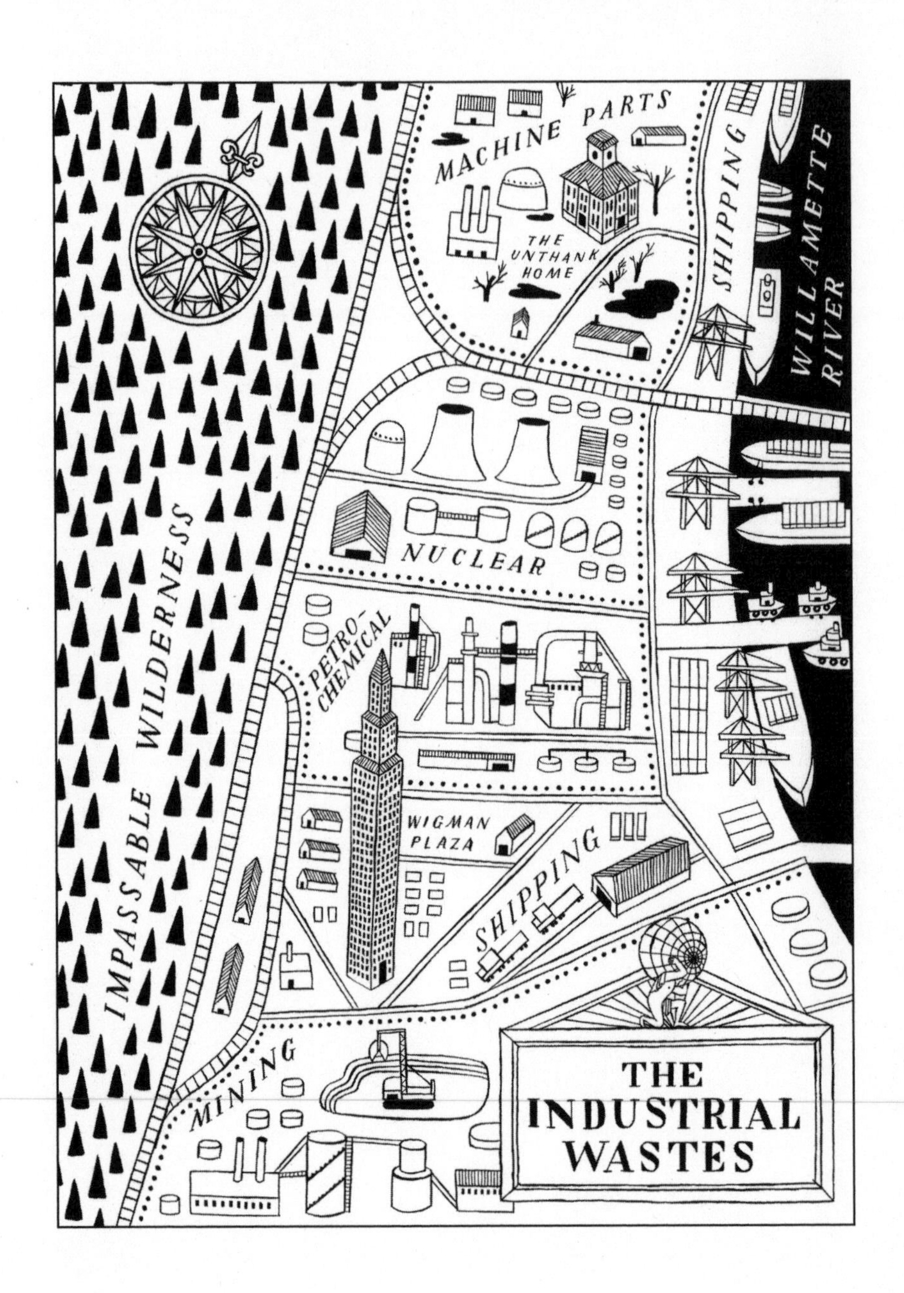
MACHINE PARTS
THE UNTHANK HOME
SHIPPING
WILLAMETTE RIVER
IMPASSABLE WILDERNESS
NUCLEAR
PETRO-CHEMICAL
WIGMAN PLAZA
SHIPPING
MINING
THE INDUSTRIAL WASTES

PART ONE

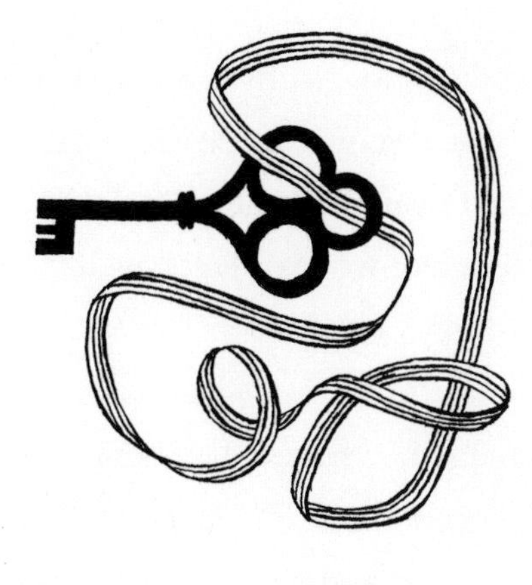

CHAPTER I

A Boy and His Rat

Snow is falling.

Snow as white as a swan's feather, white as a trillium bloom. The whiteness is nearly blinding against the dark green and brown of the surrounding forest, and it lies in downy heaps between the quiet, dormant clutches of ivy and blackberry bushes. It is heaped against the bases of the tall fir trees, and it carpets the little trenches in the shallows around the wide cedar roots.

A road carves its way through the deep forest. It, too, is covered in an untouched shroud of snow.

In fact, if you didn't know there was a road beneath the snow, if you didn't know there were centuries of footsteps and hoofbeats and miles of weathered flagstones beneath the snow, you might just think it was a fallow stretch of woods, somehow left untouched by the forest's teeming greenery. There are no wheel tracks, no tire treads on this road. No footprints mar the delicate white of the snow. You might think it was a game trail, a stretch of ground where no tree could take root because of a constant traffic of silent walkers: deer, elk, and bear. But even here, in this most removed area of the world, there are no animal tracks. The more the snow falls, the more the road disappears. It is becoming just another part of this vast, unending forest.

Listen.

The road is quiet.

Listen.

A distant clatter suddenly disrupts this placid stillness; it is the sound of wagon wheels and the whinnying of a horse, pushed to the limit of its strength. The horse's hooves beat a mad rhythm against the earth, a rhythm dulled by the mute of the snow. Look: Around a bend comes flying a carriage, two of its four wheels lifting from the ground momentarily to make the turn. Two sweat-slick black horses are harnessed to the coach, and plumes of steam blow from their nostrils like smoke belching from a chimney. Perched above the horses is the coachman, a large man piled in black wool and a tattered top hat. He barks gruffly at the horses at their every stride, shouting,

"GYAP!" and "FASTER, ON!" He spares no strike of the whip. There is a look of deep consternation on his face. He spends the brief moments between the snaps of his whip eyeing the surrounding forest warily.

Look closer: Below him, in the simple black carriage itself, sits a woman, alone. She is dressed in a fine silk gown, and her face is covered in a shimmering pink veil. Rings studded with bright jewels glint on her fingers. In her hands, she holds a delicate paper fan, which she opens and closes nervously. She, too, watches the flanking walls of trees surrounding the carriage, as if looking for someone or something within them. Opposite her sits an ornate chest, its sides decorated with gold and silver filigree. A lock holds the chest's twin clasps closed, the key to which hangs at the woman's throat by a thin golden cord. Antsy, she raps at the ceiling of the carriage with the fan.

The driver hears the rapping and spurs the horses on, raining even more blows from his whip down on their heaving flanks. A sudden flash of movement on the road ahead catches the driver's attention. He squints his eyes against the blinding white of the falling snow.

A boy is standing in the middle of the road.

But this is no ordinary boy. This boy is dressed in what appears to be an elegantly brocaded officer's coat, like some infantryman from the Crimean War. His hair is black and curly and sprouts from beneath the coarse fur of an ushanka hat. He is idly swinging an emptied sling. There is a rat on his shoulder.

"STOP!" shouts the boy. "THIS IS A STICKUP!"

"You heard him!" shouts the rat. "Rein it in, fatso!"

The coachman hisses a curse under his breath. With a quick turn of his wrist, he has dropped the whip and has taken the reins in both of his hands. He snaps them eagerly, and the horses lean into their gallop. A cruel smile has appeared on the coachman's face. "HYA!" he shouts to the beleaguered horses.

The boy's face, formerly buoyed with confidence, falls. He swallows hard. "I—I'm serious!" he stammers.

The coachman's cracked lips have pulled back to reveal an astonishing row of yellow teeth. He is not slowing. The lady in the carriage gives a slight shriek as it careens along the snowy road. The boy quickly reaches down and pulls a rock from the ground. He wipes it clean of snow on his trousers and sets it into the cradle of his sling.

"Don't make me do this," he warns. It's not clear whether the coachman hears this; he is barreling toward the boy and the rat at an alarming rate.

With a casual expertise—he's evidently been practicing—the boy lets loose the stone from the sling, and it flies toward the coachman, who ducks just in time; the stone sails over his head to fall into the deep, snowy bracken of the forest. The boy does not have time to pick up another; the coach is so close that the boy can smell the sweat coming off the horses.

The rat gives a little *ulp!* and dives into the gully at the side of the road. The boy follows him, and they tumble into a pile together. The carriage roars by. The horses, spooked at having so nearly missed hitting the two brigands, whinny noisily as they pass.

The veiled woman in the carriage clutches at the key at her throat. She gives a high-pitched warble of fear. The coachman, somewhat chuffed at his bravado, throws a look over his shoulder at the boy and his rat. "Better luck next time, suckers!" he shouts. His attention thus diverted, he does not see the cedar trunks as they fall, domino-like, in a crash of splinters to block the road ahead. Three of them. One after another. *Bam. Bam. Bam.*

The woman screams; the coachman swings his head to face forward and gives the reins a violent yank. The horses yawp. Their hooves scramble desperately against the slick surface of the road. The carriage tips and shimmies and emits a shuddering groan. Thinking quickly, the driver hollers an impassioned *"HYA!"* and deftly navigates the horses and carriage through the obstacle course of the fallen trees. Bodies, male and female, are appearing from the woods; they are dressed similarly to the boy, but their uniforms are mismatched. Some wear tattered shirts; some have bandannas covering their faces. They are all children. The oldest might be fifteen. They are staring with disbelief at the coachman's ability to thread the cumbersome carriage with its two panicked horses through their trap. Within moments, the coachman has cleared the obstacles and has returned to his whip, urging the horses on.

In the meantime, the boy and the rat have picked themselves up from the roadside ditch and have brushed the clinging snow from their clothes. The rat leaps back up to the boy's shoulder as the boy puts his fingers to his lips and gives a shrill whistle. From the dense scrub of the forest comes a horse, a dappled brown-and-white pony. The boy throws himself astride the horse, the rat holding tight to the boy's epaulet, and kicks it into a gallop. Arriving at the fallen trees, he leaps the horse and clears the three cedars. A spray of snow and mud flies up when the horse makes landfall. The children in the woods have shaken themselves from their shock and are calling their mounts; soon the road is filled with galloping

riders giving chase to the fleeing carriage.

The coachman, ahead, marks this. He curses the bandits' temerity. The wind is lashing at his face; the snow is now driving, icy.

Of the pursuing riders, the boy with the rat is clearly among the fastest. Many are unable to keep up the pace that the carriage is setting and fall away. Within minutes, only four remain: the boy, another older boy, and two girls. They draw closer to the speeding carriage and split apart, two on each side of the vehicle. The rat, holding tight to the boy's shoulder by a flap of his furry hat, issues a warning to the coachman: "Give up your gold," he shouts, "and you can go free!"

The coachman responds with a hair-raising curse that makes the

boy blush, even in this most hectic of moments. He is now level with the carriage. He can see inside: the veiled woman, the key at her neck, the clasped ornate chest. The woman watches him curiously, her large brown eyes glinting from above the shimmering cloth at her face. The boy is momentarily distracted by the scene. The rat shouts, "LOOK OUT!"

In an effort to unseat his pursuers, the coachman has feinted the carriage to the left, and the boy nearly runs his pony directly into the coach's traces. He catches a shriek in his throat and veers the pony off the road. The pony's hooves hit the soft underbrush of the roadside and it falters; the ground drops away here and slopes down to a rushing brook far below. The boy braces for the fall, but the pony is nimble. In a flash, the boy's steed has righted itself and finds its footing again on the road. The boy whispers a word of thanks in its ear. They are back in the chase.

The carriage leads them now by several horse lengths. The three other bandits are struggling to keep up. One of the riders, a girl with straw-blond hair, has grabbed hold of the roof of the coach and is attempting to climb aboard. It is a risky ploy; the girl's face is set in concentration. The other two bandits, a boy and a girl, have managed to spur their mounts to ride parallel to the coach's horses. The blond-haired girl grunts loudly and vaults from her horse; she barely manages to grab hold of the latticework that runs along the top of the carriage. Her horse veers away; her body swings against the carriage-side, eliciting another high-pitched scream from its passenger. The girl steadies herself and climbs to the top of the carriage, giving a triumphant whoop. She turns her head to the boy with the rat, who is still several horse-lengths behind.

"May the best bandit—" she begins. Her sentence is cut short when the carriage plows underneath a low-hanging bough and the girl is lifted from her perch in the blink of an eye. The boy with the rat must duck to avoid the girl's dangling feet as he gallops his pony toward the carriage.

"Win," finishes the girl, suspended from the limb of the tree.

The boy nods to the rat and grits his teeth in determination. There is now only he and the other girl. The other boy has fallen away from the chase, his mount limping into the underbrush.

"Aisling!" the boy shouts. "Get the horses!"

The girl, now parallel with the right-hand horse, has heard him. She is trying to get her hands on the horse's bridle, but the coachman's whip is foiling her every attempt. "Away, vile brigand!" shouts the coachman. The girl winces as the whip's leather tip leaves a red welt on the back of her hand.

"Septimus," hisses the boy to the rat, "think you could help out?"

The rat smiles. "I think I could do a little something." The boy is now even with the carriage. He can hear the mewling of the maiden within. The rat leaps from the boy's shoulder and lands on the nape of the coachman, who lets out a bloodcurdling scream.

"RRRRRATS!" he shouts. "I CAN'T STAND RATS!"

But the rodent has already crawled down the coachman's shirt and is busy practicing a kind of Irish step dance between his naked shoulder blades. The coachman hollers and lets fall both the whip and the reins; the coach's horses, confused, lose their gallop, and the boy and the girl are able to pull up even with them. With a quick glance at each other, the two bandits leap astride the carriage horses and pull them to a scrambling stop.

The coachman jumps from his seat and stumbles away down the road, his hands desperately clawing at his back. The girl and the boy watch him, laughing, before turning to the task at hand. The girl beckons graciously. "After you." The boy bows and walks toward the idle carriage, radiating confidence. He swings the door open.

"Now, ma'am," he says proudly, "if you wouldn't mind turning over . . ."

His words falter. Inside, the woman has removed her veil to reveal a shocking, tangled nest of auburn facial hair.

Also: There is the barrel of a flintlock pistol pointing at him.

"I don't think so," says the passenger, in a husky (and very unladylike) baritone.

The boy is crestfallen. "But—" he begins.

"Bang," says the passenger. He gives the boy a scolding rap on his forehead with the pistol barrel.

The boy stares and scratches at his temple, as if replaying the entire scene in his mind. He kicks his boots in the snow. The winter term of Bandit Training has begun. And Curtis has just failed his first test.

❧

In what might seem like another world from the one in which this scene was playing out, but was in fact only a handful of miles distant, Prue was staring out of a second-floor window, watching the snow fall and disintegrate against the lawn of George Middle School. *Typical Portland winter*, she thought, *falling slush*. With every dropping clump, she felt her chin bore farther into the palm of her hand. A couple walking along the sidewalk gingerly avoided the gathering puddles along their way, their coat lapels folded up to cover their exposed necks. Cars, dusted with a layer of brackish gray snow, splashed rooster tails of icy water from potholes as they swished along the wet streets. It looked positively miserable out.

"Prue!"

The voice sounded in Prue's mind like someone calling to her over a vast distance; like a lighthouse keeper hailing a ship in a gale. She chose to ignore it. It came again:

"Prue McKeel!"

It was sounding closer. More present. A master of ceremonies beckoning the star performer to the stage. She began to lift her chin from her palm.

"Earth to Prue McKeel!" This time, an explosion of laughter

followed the voice. The noise abruptly brought Prue back to her present circumstances. She swiveled upright in her chair and scanned the room. Life Science, third period. The entire class was staring at her, pointing and laughing. Prue felt her face go deep red.

"Sorry," she managed. "I was . . . distracted."

Ms. Darla Thennis, olive skin, floral dashiki, stared on from behind a lectern at the front of the room. She adjusted her wire-rim glasses and smoothed her crow-black hair. She then silenced the class with a wave of her hand. "Your project, Prue?"

The following images flashed in quick succession through her mind: her mother digging a canning jar from the top cupboard; Prue shoving a leftover piece of baguette into the jar and setting it on the windowsill; her father mentioning, that morning, that he'd gone ahead and thrown away a jar full of disgusting mold-covered bread, and why on earth would there be a jar full of mold just lying around?

"My dad," began Prue. "My dad threw it away."

More snickers erupted from the class.

Ms. Thennis peered at Prue from above her glasses. "Uncool, Prue," she said. "Deeply uncool."

"I'll let him know that," replied Prue.

Her teacher studied Prue for a moment, clearly trying to gauge whether the response was meant as a kind of slight. Ms. Thennis was new this quarter—Mrs. Estevez, the class's normal teacher, had unexpectedly resigned, citing health issues. Darla Thennis was from Eugene and clearly prided herself on being cool, being at the kids' level. She never failed to remind the students that she loved pop music. She made strange growling sounds every time the principal, Mr. Bream, left the room, and walked the halls engulfed in a dense cloud of patchouli. She pushed her glasses back up the bridge of her nose and scanned the classroom.

"Bethany?" Ms. Thennis asked. "I don't suppose you'd be ready to exhibit your project, considering that Miss McKeel's father has made it impossible for her to exhibit her own?"

Bethany Bruxton, relishing the moment, shot a condescending glance at Prue before standing to attention. "Yes, Ms. Thennis," she replied.

"Please," corrected the teacher, "it's Darla."

Bethany smiled shyly and said, "Darla."

"If you wouldn't mind, then . . ." Darla Thennis waved the student to the front of the room.

Tugging at the hem of her black turtleneck, Bethany walked to the far side of the classroom, where a long table held a variety of students' projects. Opening the door of a lamp-lit greenhouse, Bethany removed a tall, flourishing tomato plant and walked it to the front of the class.

"This semester, I'm working on grafting," she said, cradling the plant in her arms. "The idea is to create a more disease-resistant plant, and one that will produce totally delicious tomatoes."

Ugh, thought Prue. *What a showoff.* They'd been class partners the fall semester, and Bethany had gone out of her way to sideline Prue in all their experiments. She'd taken full credit for the leaf collage they'd made, even though Prue had collected all the ochre-colored oak leaves herself.

Ms. Thennis nodded along with Bethany's speech. "Rad," said Darla Thennis. Prue glared.

"Thanks, Darla. I'm happy to report that it's doing really well," Bethany continued. "And the graft seems to be taking. And while there's no fruit to report as yet, I expect in a couple of weeks we'll start to see a few nice blooms."

"Very cool," prompted Darla, inviting the class to join in. The seventh graders in third-period Life Science murmured a collective, but decidedly unenthusiastic, *ooh* at the teacher's behest. Prue stayed silent.

She was listening.

The tomato plant was issuing a low, angry hum.

Prue scanned the room to see if anyone else heard this. Everyone was staring listlessly at Bethany.

The hum was getting louder; it quavered as it hitched upward in volume. As it grew, it became clear that it was a hum of discomfort and frustration.

Sorry, thought Prue, directing her thoughts to the plant. She could certainly sympathize; it wasn't even the plant's proper season and here it was: being grown in a science class hothouse. And she couldn't imagine having had a fellow tomato plant's limb grafted onto your stalk. It was positively barbaric!

The tomato plant seemed to heave a sigh.

Prue had an idea. *You know what would be funny?* she thought.

RMPPH, hummed the tomato plant.

Prue laid it out.

Suddenly, Bethany flinched her head backward, crinkling her nose. The students gasped. It had appeared, for a split second, that the top leaf of the tomato plant had actually slapped Bethany in the nose. It was evident that Ms. Thennis had not seen it; she shot a glare over the classroom. "Now kids, c'mon," she said.

Gasp! the classroom heaved again. It had happened once more; the topmost limb of the small, green tomato plant had feinted upward and undeniably given its holder another swift swat across the nose. A look of bewildered terror had spread across Bethany's face, and she began holding the plant at arm's length. Following the students' gaze, a very confused Ms. Thennis turned to watch Bethany as she inched toward the little greenhouse.

"M-maybe it needs a little more time," managed Bethany, her face grown perfectly pale. She gingerly placed the plant back in the glass confines of the greenhouse and backed away. "It was totally healthy this morning."

A low, satisfied whistle had replaced the tomato plant's unhappy hum.

Ms. Thennis's eyes swiveled to Prue; she stared at her with shock and disbelief. Prue smiled and returned her gaze to the window, to the falling slush beyond the glass and to the gathering puddles in the rain-swept streets.

❧

FROM THE DESK OF LEE BREAM, PRINCIPAL
GEORGE MIDDLE SCHOOL

Date: 2/15/—
Anne and Lincoln McKeel
Parents of Prue McKeel
Dear Mr. and Mrs. McKeel:

Since your daughter's admission to this school last year, she has proved herself to be a bright and independent thinker. Her promise was judged to be very great.

It saddens me, however, to report that this promise has been somewhat clouded of late. Since the beginning of last term, her grades have fallen precipitously, and her behavior in class has been reported as being—across the board—uncharacteristic. She has shown little of her former interest in her schoolwork and has taken to exhibiting a very unbecoming attitude to her teachers. The bearer of this note, Ms. Darla Thennis, has kindly volunteered to speak to you on this subject, and we hope that her involvement can lead to a happy resolution.

We understand that the crisis your family underwent earlier in the school year, the disappearance of your young son, must have been incredibly difficult. We are aware of the effect that such trauma can have on the minds of our children. However, we would wish to get to the bottom of any unfortunate backsliding and nip the problem in the bud lest it should become insurmountable and lead to a promising student being suspended, or worse—expelled.

Sincerely,

Lee Bream

Principal, George Middle School

Prue lowered the letter from her eyes, allowing the faces of the three adults in the kitchen to rise over the page like the orbiting moons of some distant planet. The room was silent, save for the regular *sproing* coming from Prue's little brother Mac's doorjamb-mounted bouncing chair.

She shrugged. "I don't know what you want me to say," she offered.

Sproing.

Her mother and father shared a concerned glance. "Hon," said her mother, "perhaps you should . . ."

Sproing.

Prue's dad looked away from his wife to the dashiki'd teacher, the third of this celestial triumvirate. She was leaning against the refrigerator.

"Ms. . . . ," began Prue's dad.

Sproing.

"Please," said the teacher, her gaze transfixed on the little boy in the bouncing chair, "call me Darla." She seemed to be waiting for the next loud—

Sproing.

"Darla," continued Prue's dad, "I have to say this comes as a complete shock to us, I mean . . ." *Sproing.* "It's been a difficult few months, for sure, but we feel like this is inevitable, considering the kind of . . ." *Sproing.* "Craziness that we'd all been through at the beginning of the year and . . ." *Sproing.* He paused, noticing that Darla's attention was being forcibly diverted to the bouncing child in the baby seat with every contraction of the seat's spring.

"Sweetheart," he said, finally, to his wife, "would you mind taking Mac out of that thing for a second?"

Once Mac had been removed from the bouncing chair and Prue's mother had returned to the kitchen, the discussion recommenced. Darla Thennis: "Listen, I know what you're going through—this is all very normal for a child of her age—we just don't want her to fall too far behind."

Prue remained silent. She studied the three adults intently. They were talking about her as if she weren't even in the room. It made her all the more disinclined to include herself. She kicked her Wellies against the cork-tiled floor and attempted to imagine her three interrogators away. She envisioned an earthquake sending a jagged crack through the middle of the kitchen, consuming the adults in one swift tremor.

Darla evidently caught on to Prue's disconnectedness and began speaking directly to her. "Hon, your final exams last semester were dismal; it's like you're not even there in class, like your head is just somewhere else—in some faraway place."

It is, thought Prue.

"And don't even get me started on your absences," said Darla, looking over at Prue's parents.

"Absences?" This came from Prue's mother. "What absences?"

Darla fixed her gaze on Prue. "You want to tell them?"

"Well," said Prue, looking up from her boots, "there have been just a few days . . ."

"A few days?" sputtered her dad, staring at his daughter in disbelief.

"A few days where I didn't quite make it in time and I thought, Well, that means I miss homeroom, and if I miss homeroom, that means I won't be ready for World Studies, and if I wasn't ready for that—how was I going to manage in math?" She waved her hands in front of her face, as if conjuring the disorienting mists of a dense fog. "It was like a long line of dominoes falling. I decided to just bag it and read at the coffee shop."

Prue's father smiled sheepishly and looked at Ms. Thennis. "At least she's reading, right?"

His wife ignored the comment. "And this . . . this . . . domino thing—happened on several occasions?" she asked, her eyes boring into Prue's bangs, which were now conveniently covering her downcast face.

"Five, to be precise," answered Ms. Thennis.

"Five?" pronounced Prue's father and mother, in unison.

"FITHE!" came Mac's voice from the living room. "POO! FITHE!"

"Ugh," said Prue.

But the truth was that she hadn't been reading at the coffee shop. And she hadn't really even "not made it in time" to school. The truth was that Prue McKeel, twelve years old, would sometimes wake up in her comfortable bed, in her comfortable house, with her comfortable family, and feel a very sudden and very sharp *tug*. On those days, she'd pull herself out of bed and try her best to go through the repetitions of her daily life—to ignore this mysterious *tug*—but sometimes she'd get as far as her bike and she'd feel compelled to pedal it in the opposite direction of her school. And this *tug* would be guiding the way. It would *tug* her down Lombard and *tug* her past the opening shops and *tug* her down Willamette and *tug* her past the college until this strange *tug* would deposit her, bike and all, on the bluff, overlooking that vast fabric of trees across the river that was the Impassable Wilderness. And that's where she would spend the better part of the day, just staring at that wide field of green. Remembering. On those days, the thought of going to school seemed perfectly out of the question.

The snap of a finger. "Hellooo?" chimed her mother. "I swear it's like your brain's been abducted by aliens or something."

Prue calmly looked each of the three adults in the eye, one after another. "Mom," she said, "Dad, Ms. Thennis—I'm sorry, Darla. I appreciate you bringing these concerns to my attention, and I'm sorry for any disappointment I might've caused. Excuse me, but I'd like to go on a walk right now. I will meditate on everything you guys have said."

And with that, she turned heel and walked out the back door, leaving a flummoxed huddle of grown-ups watching her depart.

CHAPTER 2

The Messenger; Another I.W.

They were an odd assemblage: the two young boys, the two young girls, the large man in a top hat, the skinny bearded man in a dress, and the rat. They stood in a line in the middle of the wide, snow-covered road, watching as two riders approached on horseback. When the riders arrived and had dismounted, the man in the dress stepped forward from the line.

"Brendan," he said, in greeting. He was visibly shivering; the chiffon of his frayed gown rippled in the chill breeze. His posture was hunched, his arms folded across his chest.

"William," replied the man, serious, nodding a chin that was forested in a deep tangle of red whiskers. He wore a fairly dirty officer's coat and a pair of riding britches, patched at the knees. A blue-black tattoo snaked up the side of his forehead. He studied the salmon-gowned man for a time before a smirk rolled out across his mouth. "The pink," he said, "really . . . brings out your eyes."

The top-hatted man stifled a laugh. Curtis, standing just behind the bandit William, joined in on the laughter; he was rewarded for this by a penetrating glare from Brendan.

"Who said this was funny?" he shot at Curtis, again serious. The smile abruptly disappeared from the boy's face. A wind had picked up, blowing the remaining flurries of snow sideways across the road, and the little flakes clung obstinately to the fur of Curtis's hat.

"Henry, William. Back to camp." The man in the top hat and the man in the dress scampered away, the latter doing this with some difficulty until he'd hiked the hem of his skirt above his pale, hairy knees. Brendan returned his gaze to the remaining bandits. "Colm: Mind your horsemanship. You were pushing too hard. You've got to have a better feel for your mount." He held his leather-gloved hands out to model his words. "Let up on the reins; feel the strain of the horse. Only urge on when you've got the power to do so."

"Aye, Brendan," responded Colm.

"Now, back to camp. Get ice on that pony's shin. And it's two more weeks of horsemanship for you." Brendan watched as the boy jogged away toward a limping horse in the distance.

Looking back at the line of four: "Carolyn, solid job. The hard work you've been putting in—it shows. Quite an improvement from last week's drill. As for you, Aisling." Here he smirked a little—Aisling was the pursuer who had been clotheslined by the cedar bough. There were still bits of twig and moss in her hair, and her face was smeared with tree sap. "Not so cocky next time, eh?"

"Aye, Brendan," responded Aisling, chastened.

"Now back to camp with ye." The two girls sprinted from the line as if they were running a dash and had just been waiting for the starter pistol. Only Aisling hazarded a look backward. She gave Curtis a quick, reaffirming smile—a moment that he barely had an opportunity to enjoy before the wiry whiskers of Brendan's beard were inches from his forehead. They smelled like wet dog.

"As for you," began Brendan, drawing out the words in a low growl. "As for you: I've lost too many good bandits who made that same move. They think it's all in the bag, everything's taken care of, and BANG." His hand, shaped like a pistol and pointed at Curtis's forehead, gave a little recoil. "Dead. All because of what?"

"They didn't consider the passenger."

"They didn't WHAT?"

"THEY DIDN'T CONSIDER THE PASSENGER!"

"Right," said Brendan. "Biggest mistake you can make. Not only is the passenger just as likely to be armed as anyone, he's likely to be the most dangerous—in my time, I've seen more than one jumped-up banker come out of a carriage with pistols blazing, all panicked, and take out more of his own armed guards than bandits. Never open that door—don't even approach it—till you're sure whoever's inside isn't going to come out fighting. Got it?"

"Yeah, I got it," responded Curtis, nervously adjusting his furry cap. Brendan reached up and gave the ushanka a firm pat, pushing the brim down over Curtis's eyes.

"Good," said Brendan, his voice softening. "I'd hate to lose our most promising recruit."

Curtis beamed. It was the first time he'd heard such praise from the Bandit King during these many weeks of intensive training. It had been hard initially; for some reason, even mounting the pony without nearly toppling sidelong to the ground took a good two weeks to master, and Brendan hadn't passed up a single opportunity to hector him for it. But he could feel he was improving; he knew that Brendan did not give such commendations lightly.

Septimus cleared his throat. "Um," inserted the rat, "what about me? Did you see that move? Straight down his back!"

Looking down at the rat: "Very good, Septimus. But an easy target; you know Henry's squeamish about rodents. He's going to be traumatized for weeks."

Septimus cracked his knuckles. "It's a joy to have such an effect on a man."

The Bandit King laughed before saying, "You two will make fine coach-robbers. I have no doubt." His voice went steely as he continued, "Though I can't say that you'll have a chance to practice on the real thing."

This much was true: For the past few months, the rustling parties that had been sent out from the camp had been coming back empty-handed. There were fewer and fewer carriages on the road these days, and those travelers that did brave the frozen path were rarely carrying anything more than a few bushels of dried onions and wilted winter greens. It was severe enough for Curtis to notice; the elder bandits were all grumbling how it had been among the worst dry spells they'd ever seen. They said it was a herald of bad times.

The wind picked up, and a new front of falling snow moved through the trees. Winter was in full sway, and the light felt ever dim, even at midday. But now, at the first breath of evening, a dark mist was settling over the branches and obscuring the distant bends of the Long Road. Brendan shivered in his coat and gestured to the two remaining bandits-in-training. "That's enough for today—let's get back to the camp. There are many more points to review, and we have to be ready for tomorrow's . . ." His voice dropped away as they began their walk toward the awaiting horses. Something had caught his attention. He brought up his hand. "Hold," he said. "Something's coming."

Curtis and Septimus froze; they hadn't heard anything. Septimus sniffed the air briefly before scrambling up Curtis's pant leg and coat to arrive at his shoulder. Again he sniffed the air. "Bird?" he said.

Brendan, his hand still an open palm, nodded. "A big one."

Suddenly, a crashing noise exploded from the canopy of trees above them, sending a flurry of smaller birds twittering away. A shower of broken branches toppled to the road below. The horses in the road spooked and whinnied. Brendan's hand went instinctively to the saber hilt at his side. Out of the sky fell the crumpled form of something blue and gray and feathered. It slammed into the ground with a pained squawk; a spray of dirt and snow erupted at its landfall.

Silence followed. Brendan: "Who's there? Name yourself!"

The lump of feathers quivered slightly where it lay. Finally, its long neck rose from its body, like the articulating antenna of a lunar rover, at the top of which was the stately beak of a heron. The bird shook its head and picked at the dirt that had sullied its wing.

"Are you okay?" This was Curtis, having recovered from the surprise.

The heron's response was unexpected; it was defensive, embarrassed. "I'm fine, thanks," it said acidly. "Just fine."

"Who are you?" called Brendan. "And what business do you have in Wildwood, waterbird?"

As if ignoring the Bandit King's demands, the heron took its time pulling its long body from the snow. Curtis was awed by the majesty of the creature; by the time it had bloomed to its full height, it was like a metamorphosis had taken place. What had been a dirty gray lump on the ground was suddenly the towering, graceful form of one of the most striking birds Curtis had ever seen: a long, slender-beaked head topped an S-curved neck that led to a great egg of a body, covered in long, lashlike, white and gray feathers, all supported by two spindly legs. Stretching its neck to its full height to take in its new surroundings, the bird stood easily as tall as Curtis.

"My name is Maude," replied the heron finally. "And I've been sent by the Crown Prince of the Avians." The bird swiveled her head to look directly into Curtis's eyes. "I've come for you, boy. Your friend, the girl McKeel, seems to be in grave danger."

By the time the car's wheels had left the familiarity of the pavement and began crunching along the wet gravel of the artery road, the passengers had grown silent. Elsie Mehlberg, nine years old, fiddled with the shoulder strap of her seat belt and watched her parents as their faces grew progressively more sallow and concerned. She could tell they were struggling with the decision they'd made—but what choice did they have? Elsie didn't blame them. And while her older sister, Rachel, had put up more of a fight when the plan was initially presented to them, in the end she'd begrudgingly agreed.

The snow had given way to a heavy, cold rain, and the drops made thick streaks down the car's backseat window, distorting the already imposing metal buildings into bulging and fractured shapes. They'd crossed the boundary into the Industrial Wastes some time ago. It was a place Elsie'd never been; it was cold and ominous. The rusted white chemical tanks that lined the gravel roads, with their winding staircases and wiry tresses of plumbing, looked almost science fiction in their otherworldliness. Somewhere, deep inside this nest of clattering machinery, she imagined bearded dwarves at work, long removed from the sunshine of the above-world—only instead of broadswords and battle-axes, they were making refrigerator doors and motorcycle camshafts.

Elsie looked back again to her father in the driver's seat as he navigated the family sedan through the Wastes' narrow roads. There were filigrees of gray hair at his temples; Elsie was sure they hadn't been there the summer before. And those deep creases that made a kind of canyon landscape on his brow—certainly those were new as well.

All since her brother's disappearance.

The initial shock had been tremendous; a fog had descended over the house. Whatever joy had previously lived under that roof had all but disappeared. And Elsie hated her brother for it. First had come the police. They squatted down on the living room furniture like elephants in polyester and scribbled down little notes while her mother and father tearfully repeated everything they remembered since the last time Curtis had been seen. Then came the reporters, the news cameramen, the rubbernecking neighbors walking by the picture window and peering in at their broken, desperate family.

Finally, Lydia, Elsie's mom, had drawn the curtains to block out the inquisitive, and the windows remained that way for months. The living room, all through the fall, stayed as dark and shadowed as their hearts. Elsie's dad, David, became withdrawn and spent hours on end in his home office, standing vigil on a variety of internet message boards, imploring anyone who would listen to help him find his son. Elsie would sit up at night in her bed, listening to her parents' hushed conversations in the room next door, and would alternately curse her brother and plead for him to return. "C'mon, Curtis," she'd whisper. "Just quit it already. Come home."

So when Elsie's dad came running into the kitchen from his office one day, announcing he'd gotten a lead, that someone in Istanbul, Turkey—of all places—had seen a young American boy who fit Curtis's description on the streets of this ancient city, the entire family erupted into a fit of unbridled celebration. It wasn't until they began investigating the cost of airfare and lodging that it was decided that the two girls, Elsie and Rachel, would have to stay in Portland while the elder Mehlbergs flew to Turkey to search for their son. And where would the girls stay? Without a suitable family member in town to take them in, the only option was the local orphanage, where, for a reasonable price, a desperate parent could board his or her children for however much time was needed.

"The Jamisons did it with their kids when they went on that scuba vacation," was all the reassurance the two younger Mehlbergs were given.

And so here they were, slowly winding the labyrinthine byways of the Industrial Wastes, to arrive at the Joffrey Unthank Home for Wayward Youth. A neon sign shone in the dim light ahead of them, advertising as much—with the helpful addendum below it, a flickering string of words that seemed to be at the mercy of a lesser power source: AND INDUSTRIAL MACHINE PARTS.

Rachel, who'd remained silent the entire journey, looked up and gasped when the building came into view. Her pale face appeared briefly from between the twin curtains of her long, straight black hair, and her thin shoulders shuddered beneath her threadbare Corrosion of Conformity T-shirt. "I can't believe this," she said quietly. She fiddled with the little tangle of dark bands that encircled her left wrist.

"Now, honey," said Lydia from the front passenger seat, "we've been through this. We just don't have any other options." She craned her head to look at the two girls in the backseat. "Think of it this way: You're doing your part in helping to find Curtis."

"Right," responded Rachel glumly.

"Whoa," said Elsie, staring ahead through the whisks of the windshield wipers. "That place looks creepy."

Silence followed as everyone in the car gave tacit agreement. The gravel drive the car was following finally cleared the rows of windowless metal buildings and chemical tanks to arrive at an open space, fenced in by a wall of chain-link fence. In the middle of the clearing stood a drab building, seemingly transported to the spot from another era. Its slate-gray stucco walls were stained by lichen and soot, a surface broken regularly by tall mullioned windows. The roof, shale shingles sporting an impressive growth of positively iridescent moss, sloped up to a crest topped by a clock tower. A heavy oak door loomed just beyond a jumble of untidy blackberry bushes. The neon sign pulsated noisily just above this door, a strange modern juxtaposition to the building's decidedly nineteenth-century appearance.

A wave of nervousness overcame Elsie, and she reached down between her feet to undo the top zipper of her backpack. From within, she peeked the head of her Intrepid Tina™ doll from the bag and attempted a warm smile.

"It's okay, Tina," she whispered. "Everything's going to be just fine." Intrepid Tina was made of hard plastic, and her blond hair was cropped in a bob at her neck. Elsie snaked her fingers down the back of Tina's beige "Safari Sass" outfit to find the little button nub nestled between the doll's shoulder blades. She gave it a push and was calmed to hear the following affirmation, muffled as it was, coming from the little recorder in Tina's chest: "INTREPID GIRLZ NEVER SHY AWAY FROM THE PROMISE OF A NEW ADVENTURE!" Tina's voice had a kind of tough rasp to it.

Elsie heard her sister sigh and looked over to see that Rachel was watching her askance through the strands of her hair. Elsie waited for

HOME for
WAYWARD YOUTH

a snarky reproach, Rachel's usual response to having been within earshot when Elsie activated Intrepid Tina's voice box, but none came. The situation really was so bad, Elsie thought, that even Rachel was inspired by Tina's words.

Easing to a stop in front of the building, the Mehlbergs' sedan idled for a moment before David turned the key and the engine sputtered into silence. The whistling of the wind, blowing down through the corridors between the Wastes' structures, sounded through the car's windows. David craned his head and looked at his two daughters in the backseat. "Just two weeks," he said, attempting reassurance. "That's all. Two weeks. And then we'll be back for you."

Elsie ran her fingers along the plastic flaxen hair of Intrepid Tina. Two weeks had never seemed like a longer span of time in her life.

CHAPTER 3

The Secret Language of Plants; North Wood Ho!; The Janitor's Warning

With her long knitted scarf wrapped high around her face, Prue pretended momentarily that she was a Bedouin nomad, braving the vast expanse of some Saharan range, when in fact she was only walking aimlessly down Lombard Street. Given the circumstances, it did really seem like a preferable way of life. She wondered if Bedouin kids were forced to go to Bedouin school and memorize stuff like who invented the cotton gin and where penicillin came from. She guessed not. She supposed that Bedouin kids mostly just had camel races and learned how to find oases in the wild desert. She decided that she would Google Bedouins when she got home and see if there wasn't any way she could volunteer to be one.

In the meantime, she found herself wandering the cold streets of St. Johns, her home neighborhood in this northernmost part of Portland, Oregon. It was February; even at this hour—barely four o'clock—the light was really beginning to fade. The streets were wet from the previous morning's fall of slush, and Prue kicked idly at the puddles as she walked. It was too cold to ride her bike, she decided, but she had desperately needed to get out of the house. All this talk of expectation and promise and disheartening behavior was really driving her crazy. It almost drove her to fall further away from what her parents and teachers wanted. For the first time in her life, she was feeling the nagging pull of adulthood, and she did not like it one bit.

She cut a corner across an empty lot, heading west, and suddenly she found herself where she'd often been finding herself, these many long, listless weeks: standing on the bluff overlooking the Willamette River and the Impassable Wilderness just beyond.

She laughed to herself; the Impassable Wilderness. A thick blanket of towering green trees covered this long, ambling expanse of land, stretching out in either direction. A haze of low clouds settled amid the branches, and a wind blew chilly through the gorge the river made. From this distance, their voices were too far off to make out. The trees' voices.

That had been a change; on returning from the Wood, after that great adventure she'd been thrown into at the beginning of the fall, she'd expected her life to return to a level burble of normalcy. Mac was home, their family reunited—all should be fine, right? It wasn't long, however, before she began to notice the murmuring. The voices were familiar; they were the same timbre and pitch as the voices that had come to her at that frenzied moment, those months before, as the Dowager Governess had held Mac in her hand and had come so close to ending his life and beginning the ravage of the ivy. They were the mumblings of the natural world around her. The chiming voices of the trees and the plants.

She'd expected to leave this incredible new insight behind, once she'd left the boundary of the Wood, but she soon found that even her family's most dormant and unassuming houseplants, when appropriately provoked, were happy to speak to her—even if their "speaking" was totally unintelligible. They were half-throated, wordless whispers, these voices, and they seemed to originate deep within the recesses of her ear canal. And while the voices did not codify into understandable words, after a time Prue found she was able to intuit a kind of emotion in the noises. A quick census of her house's many leafy occupants showed a dizzying array of personalities: the succulents gave a kind of grumpy and standoffish *PHHHT*; the palm in the bathroom, an ebullient *KRRRRK!* The sword fern in the living room had a sort of lonesome whistle, while the potted vinca that sat on top of the bookshelf in the dining room was always snippy (*VRT! VRT!*) when approached, though Prue chalked that up to the infrequency with which her parents remembered to water it. Much to her chagrin, Prue's mother brought home a basket of ivy over Christmas, and the stuff had positively hissed at Prue.

All in all, however, the plants mostly kept to themselves, and it didn't take long for Prue to go from feeling almost certain that she was going crazy to a kind of surrender to her new (and much weirder) reality.

She nestled her scarf to her cold cheeks and watched the mist filter down through the weave of trees on the far side of the river. That would be Wildwood, she thought. She wondered what had transpired since she'd left, what incredible shifts and changes had occurred to forward the fate of that miraculous place. Her eyes followed the snow-dappled ridgeline down, across a field of chemical tanks in the Industrial Wastes, and over the river to a tawny field directly below the bluff. There, she saw something very strange.

Initially she thought it was just a weird shadow, cast from a puff of smoke or from a high-flying bird. But as the mists curled and cleared, she could tell the shadow was in fact the form of an animal. Yes: The more she squinted, the clearer the thing came into view.

It was a jet-black fox.

And it was staring right at her.

A violent noise suddenly exploded in her ears, the unmistakable sound of the rackety fauna. It came from the thicket of Scotch broom that sprouted from a rocky outcrop below the bluff's edge. No words formed; the noise was abstract, a deafening raspy shushing, and it seemed to wipe out all hearing, like a crashing wave or television static pushed to its highest volume. Prue's hands went instinctively to her ears, though it did little to lessen the sound. She stumbled backward, feeling her mouth issue a muted scream, her every nerve shocked by the intensity of the noise as it grew louder and louder. Something caught her heel, and she was pinwheeling downward, footless. A jolt of pain shot up her spine as her tailbone made contact with the rough ground.

The noise blotted out everything; Prue promptly lost consciousness.

All was darkness.

❧

All was darkness.

This was because Curtis had his eyes squeezed as closed as they possibly could be. His mouth was fixed in a rictus grin, so great was his effort to keep any visible sunlight from getting past his eyelids. That way, he stood a chance of pretending that he wasn't flying. He could more easily pretend that the wind that was currently ruffling the fur of his chin-strapped ushanka and whipping at his clothing and chilling his cheeks was not from flying; no, it was just a heavy wind blowing—it was February, after all. And that feathery texture that he had gripped in his fingers so tightly? Perhaps it was a pillow—a cozy, goose-down pillow—giving up its dander. And that bit of turbulence? That certainly wasn't from flying. It was . . .

He peeked his eyes open.

He was flying.

"RAMMING SPEED!" hooted Brendan as his mount, the long, lithe egret who'd accompanied the heron, took a sudden dive to buzz Curtis's furry hat. Curtis panicked and gripped his fingers tighter to the heron's neck. They were far above the trees now; those towering Douglas firs looked like leafy, snow-covered toothpicks from this height. The vista stretched on into the distance; the sun, setting low behind a deep veil of clouds, graced these high flyers with the day's last light.

"Ouch!" shouted Maude, the heron. "Not so tight around the neck, please."

"I'm s-sorry!" Curtis shouted back, tears streaming down his face. He couldn't tell whether the tears were from the wind or from his very genuine fear. "I'm just not that good with heights!"

"Why didn't you say that before we left?" the exasperated bird replied.

"It didn't seem appropriate!"

"It didn't seem what?" The wind was very loud. It made for difficult conversation.

"It didn't seem . . . ," Curtis began, but he was cut off by another of Brendan's loud, celebratory *WOOPS!* The egret and the bandit had flown ahead by several bird lengths and had just executed a terrifying-looking loop-the-loop; they again fired directly over Curtis's head, causing him to bury his face into the down of the heron. "I wish he would stop doing that," said Curtis.

"Just relax!" said Maude. "You're too tense! It's throwing off my pitch!"

A clutch of song sparrows erupted from a mist-shrouded piece of the canopy, causing Maude to bank sharply to the right. Curtis squealed.

"GAH!" he cried. "Can you not do that, please?"

"You mean this?" asked Maude. She banked again, this time more severely. They were now just skimming along the highest tips of the trees. A sputter of snow sprayed across Curtis's clenched face.

"YES! THAT!" he responded.

The heron, tired of the game, ascended to a more comfortable cruising altitude and began to glide. The turbulence passed, and Curtis was able to relax his grip on the bird. "So where are we going again?" he asked.

"To the Great Hall in North Wood," replied Maude. "A clandestine meeting has been called."

"A meeting with who?"

The bird sighed. "If I knew that, it wouldn't be terribly clandestine, now would it?"

"But why us?" asked Curtis, perplexed.

The egret pulled up alongside the heron. "Yes, waterbird," called Brendan, "why have we been summoned? Why should bandits be called to a secret meeting among the North Wooders?"

The heron looked over at Brendan. "How quickly you forget the lessons of the Battle for the Plinth!" she scolded. "Are you not still a Wildwood Irregular?"

The comment piqued Brendan's temper. "Don't talk to me about the Battle for the Plinth!" he roared. "I don't recall seeing you there, staining the ground with your bird blood."

"Calm yourself, Bandit King," replied Maude. "I mean no disrespect." She cleared her throat and continued, "The Elder Mystic has called for representatives from each of the four provinces. Since no one technically 'rules' Wildwood, it was assumed that an envoy from the Wildwood Bandits would suffice."

Ahead, a snow-dappled peak distinguished itself from a chain of surrounding hills, its tip lost in a haze of clouds. "Cathedral Peak," said Maude, disarming the tension. "Not far now." A lazy road carved its way in switchbacks through this range of high hills, leading down the lee side, where the mountainous landscape gave way to a gentle valley. The forest below the flyers began to thin, and intermittent meadows and fields supplanted Wildwood's thick fabric of trees. After a time, Curtis began to see small cottages on the margins of these clearings, their squat stone chimneys blowing white smoke into the misty air. A man and a woman, stepping out onto the porch of one of these hovels, shielded the dim sun from their eyes with their hands and watched, curiously, the two birds and their riders.

The farms, however, seemed desiccated and gray. No crops grew; great farm fields lay fallow amid the dun of winter that lay over the land. The heron swooped low, and Curtis could see a gang of children, shoeless in the road. He caught a glimpse of their faces; they looked hollow-eyed, tired.

Maude guessed at Curtis's observation. "All is not well in the North Wood," said the bird. "We are more affected by the distresses of our populous ally to the south than we expected. There is no call for our exports; what's more, the winter has been very harsh. Even our well-kept stores had not prepared us for this dark season."

"I had no idea," said Curtis over the whipping wind.

"And should you?" asked the bird. "Since when did Wildwood Bandits keep tabs on the welfare of North Wooders?"

Curtis thought for a moment. "I mean, I've heard people talking about fewer shipments—we've all been stretched a little thin. The elder bandits called it a dry spell."

The heron laughed coldly. "That, bandit Curtis, is an understatement. Many children will go hungry tonight. Many parents' cupboards remain empty."

"But why?"

"All will be revealed. In time. In time." The bird ascended, saying,

"We are growing closer. Look: the Council Tree."

At the bird's invocation, the canopy of a great, gnarled tree could suddenly be seen in the distance, towering above this patchwork of fields and thickets. Curtis gasped; a constellation of small birds created a kind of halo over the tree's array of leafless branches, wheeling and diving in play. A crowd of animals and humans milled around the fat trunk, as minuscule as ants compared to the grandeur of the incredible tree. Beyond this scene, Curtis could see a high, barren hill, topped by a wooden fire tower. Farther, past a stand of gray maples and tucked into a narrow defile created by the meeting of two small hills, sat a long wooden building. Seeing this, Maude stretched her long neck and shifted her wings. She began to descend.

As they came closer, Curtis studied the building they were approaching. Its long roof, white with snow, supported a large central chimney, and the dark wood of its slatted siding appeared stained and weathered by age. The tip of a massive beam jutted from beneath the framework of the roof, just above a set of wide wooden doors that were hatch-marked with iron struts.

Maude swooped down in a graceful figure eight to land on the snowy clearing that stretched away from the hall's entrance. A robed badger, sweeping snow from a slate-stone path, paused from his labors and watched as Curtis and Brendan dismounted. Curtis's feet met the ground unsteadily; his legs wobbled and the earth seemed to undulate as his equilibrium reset itself from the long flight. The badger returned to his sweeping.

"Inside," said Maude, panting a little from the exertion. "The meeting is just now being called to order." She gestured with a wing to the great doors of the hall.

Uneasy, Brendan surveyed the surroundings. His hand rested reflexively on the saber hilt at his side. Maude saw this and said, "You'll not be needing that, Bandit King. You're in peaceable country now."

"I'll be the judge of that," responded Brendan tersely.

Curtis felt a squirming in the canvas knapsack on his back. Pushing open the top flap, Septimus nudged his snout into the fresh air.

"Are we there?" he asked.

"Yep," said Curtis. "Enjoy the ride?"

"Yes, thanks," said the rat. "But I was thinking we might take the ground route on the return journey. What do you say?" He pushed one of his paws out and smoothed back the fur between his ears. "Don't freak out, but I threw up in there. Just a little."

"What?"

"Just a little. Mostly into this pouch." The rat's other paw brought up a leather satchel, loosely tied at the top with leather cord. He tossed it casually to the ground. "Don't open that."

"Septimus! That was my lunch!"

The comment was ignored. "So where are we?" asked the rat.

Curtis grumbled under his breath before responding. "The Great Hall," he said. "A clandestine meeting. We've been called."

Just as he finished speaking, the great doors of the hall were thrown open with a clatter. Standing on the threshold was none other than Owl Rex, a massive, bespectacled great horned owl and someone Curtis hadn't seen in many months—not since they'd parted ways at the Mansion earlier in the fall. A smile crept across his face as the owl, his wings extended, walked down the pathway toward the three new arrivals.

"My bandits!" he boomed. "My good bandits! I hope your flight was not too taxing."

"Owl!" said Curtis, beaming. "What are you doing here? You're a long ways from the Principality."

Brendan's hand fell away from his saber, and he walked proudly up to the approaching bird. "Dear Owl," he said, giving a slight bow, "it's a pleasure to see you again."

"And you, King," said the Owl, inclining his head. He threw his massive wings around the two bandits' shoulders. "I did not know when we three would be reunited."

Septimus cleared his throat.

"We *four*," corrected the owl, winking at the rat. He then frowned as he spoke again: "And to answer the question of my bandit friend Curtis, I did not relish the idea of leaving my home province so soon after my time of incarceration. The Avian Principality is quite beautiful this time of year, all the nests gilded with snow." He sighed and continued, "But the fate of the Wood seems to be in the balance; a new threat faces us all." He looked at Maude and the egret, who were still picking debris from the undersides of their wings. "I trust you were not followed," he said.

Maude shook her head. "No, my prince," she said, bowing. "We've come alone."

"Very good. Now"—Owl Rex turned about and began guiding Brendan and Curtis toward the Great Hall—"the meeting must commence."

❧

"Mehlberg," said Elsie's father. "I called earlier this week?"

The light from the ancient-looking computer monitor cast a strange glow across the garish features of the woman at the cluttered desk. It made the layers-thick smear of makeup on her face appear all the more ghoulish.

"Mehlverg?" the woman drawled.

"No," corrected David. "Mehlberg. With a *B*."

The woman turned her attention from the computer screen to give Elsie's father a withering glare. "It is what I said," she intoned, icily, "Mehlverg." English was clearly the woman's second language. To

Elsie, crowded against her father's pant leg with her Intrepid Tina doll embraced closely to her chest, the woman's voice carried the echoes of a far-off kingdom, one populated by onion-domed palaces and kick-dancing Cossacks.

David, chastened, smiled politely. "Oh," he said, "I'm sorry. I didn't hear your accent." He cleared his throat. "Yes, Mehlberg. Lydia and David. We're here to drop off our daughters? Elsie and Rachel?" Getting no reply, David squirmed uncomfortably in his loafers and, looking down at the name placard on the desk, attempted

to pronounce the name written there. “Miss . . . Miss Mudrak?”

The woman still did not respond. Her composure was lazy, languid. She studied the Mehlberg family for a time before setting her long-nailed fingers against the edge of the desk and pushing her chair back. She unfurled the great length of her body and stood, suddenly towering over the family before her. David, who Elsie always thought to be incredibly tall, only came up to the woman’s collarbone. The woman wore a shimmering, slender gown, and her fingers were studded with a rainbow spectrum of gemmed rings. She reached out one hand blithely to David, those long fingers splayed in the dramatic fashion of a countess receiving a suitor.

“Please,” she said, the words issuing from her ruby-red mouth like a slurry of molasses, “call me Desdemona.” The flicker of a smile appeared on her lips.

David’s words of greeting came in a rush of sputtering, blather and nonsense. He began to reach his hand to meet Desdemona’s, but Lydia’s hand beat him to it. Glaring, Elsie’s mother shook the woman’s hand firmly.

“How do you do, Miss Mudrak,” said Lydia, loudly. “We’re here to board our children. We’ll be back for them in two weeks’ time.”

Whatever lightness had appeared on Desdemona’s face in that moment fell away as she turned her attention to Mrs. Mehlberg. She pulled her hand from Lydia’s and slowly eased herself back into her chair. “I see,” she said. “Let me find wot is on computer.” Her face was again illuminated by the screen's glow as she slowly began tapping on one of the arrow keys of the keyboard. "Ah yes," she said finally. "I see it here. Two girls. Elsie and Rachel." She turned her head slightly and made sharp eye contact with Elsie, who froze.

"And you are . . . ?" asked the woman.

"I—I'm Elsie."

"Very nice to meet." Without moving her head, she looked at Rachel. "And this?"

Rachel only glared at the woman from beneath her hair, saying nothing. She held her arms across her chest defiantly. The mohawked skull on her shirt was all scrunched up.

Lydia interjected. "This is Rachel," she said, frowning at her daughter. "She can sometimes be very rude."

Miss Mudrak smiled, and a long row of teeth appeared between her lipsticked lips. They were nearly perfect, Elsie observed, save for a single golden tooth, third from the center, which glinted in the light of the computer monitor. "This is no a problem," said Desdemona. "We are accustomed to such things."

Elsie swallowed loudly.

"Well, *famille* Mehlverg," said Desdemona Mudrak, turning back to the computer and stabbing her fingers at the keys. "Let me be the first to welcome you to Joffrey Unthank Home for Wayward Youth." (Here she thrust a single polished fingernail at a framed picture on the desk; a toothy man with a goatee and greasy hair smiled out from inside a loud argyle sweater—Mr. Unthank, Elsie presumed.) "Founded 1985. We are full-service orphanage and reformatory academy, boasting a population of one hundred fine children in the various unfortunate circumstances." The woman droned this recited speech with all the enthusiasm of a veteran flight attendant talking about seat cushion flotation devices.

As Desdemona continued on about the administrative details of the business, her eyelids lazing at half-mast all the while, Elsie's attention was drawn to the decorations on the office's walls. She had always assumed that dust could only collect on a horizontal surface, but the Unthank Home's drab green walls proved otherwise—a thin sheen of gray dust seemed to nearly act as a second coat of paint. The grime covered a sprawling collection of what looked like old movie posters, though Elsie couldn't make out the titles—they were all written in what looked like an alien language. Handsome leading men in tuxedos, smoking cigarettes, lounged against white balustrades on these posters, sharing meaningful glances with tall, striking women. In one faded broadside, the lips of a man and a woman were poised inches apart, their eyes smoldering. Above the photo, in tall, eye-catching text, was written the following Martian glyph: Ніч в Гавані. Looking closer, Elsie was shocked to recognize the woman on the poster as none other than Miss Mudrak herself, just a little younger. Aghast, Elsie looked down at the woman behind the desk, still talking, and back to the poster. The resemblance was there, but the spirit was missing from the woman's eyes. Elsie couldn't help but spout out, "Is that you?"

Jolted from her monologue, Desdemona looked to where Elsie was pointing and smiled weakly. "Yes," she said, "it is me. Old movie, *A Night in Havana*. Do you know it?"

No one spoke.

Desdemona frowned and dismissed the silence with a wave of her hand. "It is old movie from Ukraine. No in English. That is Sergei Goncharenko, great Ukrainian actor. He is cab driver now in San Francisco." She blew a snort of air through her lips. "It is way it is. We come to America. It is better, no?" She pushed back the chair and stood again from the desk. "Come, I give you tour of facility."

Sliding out from behind the desk, she gestured for the family to follow her into the hall. A long corridor stretched out before them; plaster stucco walls painted the same pale green-gray as the office. The paint flaked away in great chips near the ceiling. Several doors presented themselves on either side of the hallway. A young boy, Elsie's age, stood mopping the checkerboard tile of the floor. He stopped to look up at them and smiled shyly.

"This is central hallway, this is door to cafeteria, and this one to common room." She shoved each of the doors open following their description, though they swung closed too quickly to give the Mehlbergs more than a few seconds' glimpse into the rooms they hid. "This is closet. This is to game room, this is bathroom, this is

Edward." The boy with the mop smiled again and waved. "And this is stairway to dormitories." Here she paused and slouched against the open door, waving the family forward. She studied the Mehlbergs as they walked through the doorway and began ascending the stairs.

"Miss Mudrak," spoke up David as they climbed, "what's this about industrial machine parts? I saw it on the sign outside."

"Side business," said Desdemona.

David waited for a further description, but none came.

They arrived at the top of two flights of stairs, and Desdemona pushed open a pair of doors to reveal a gymnasium-sized room filled with cotlike beds, neatly arranged in four long rows. The beds were empty of sleepers; each was neatly made, their woolen blankets pulled taut across thin mattresses. A potbelly stove at the rear of the room provided what little heat there was. "This is where you will sleep," said the family's tour guide. A series of tall, dirty windows let the afternoon's gray light into the chamber.

"Where are the other children?" asked Lydia. A concerned grimace had been developing on her face.

Desdemona smiled as she ran her finger along the edge of one of the cots. "They are out." She turned to David. "Now, all I need is deposit and we will say good-bye."

Rachel, breaking her silence, turned to her parents. "Please don't do this," she said. Elsie hadn't seen her sister act so vulnerable before.

What's more, she'd pushed the twin veils of her hair aside and was looking them directly in the eye.

"Two weeks, darling," consoled David, though his face betrayed his worry. "That's all. And we'll be back for you."

Elsie felt the urge to step in. She knew there was nothing they could do; her parents had a flight to catch that afternoon. She turned to her sister and smiled. "Two weeks, Rach. That's nothing, right?"

In a moment of inspiration, she pushed on Intrepid Tina's voice-box button, hoping for a pertinent slogan. "DON'T FORGET YOUR BINOCULARS! YOU NEVER KNOW WHEN YOU'RE GONNA SEE WILDLIFE!" *Doesn't quite cut it*, Elsie thought. She did, however, notice that the look of concern had left her sister's face; Rachel was instead glaring at Elsie with an annoyed frown. That, at least, was a small improvement.

"What is this things?" asked Desdemona, looking down her nose at the doll in Elsie's hand. It was like she'd seen a dead mouse. "Is it always talking?"

Elsie pulled Tina to her chest protectively.

"That's Intrepid Tina," explained Lydia. "You know, from the TV show?" When the reference didn't seem to register, she continued, "Elsie's really attached to her—she's been a sort of comfort blanket for her since she was five."

An unmistakable look of scorn was drifting across Miss Mudrak's face. "It is not good when one child has thing other childs will desire. We do not advise childs to come with toys from home."

Elsie felt her father's hand massaging her shoulder; a feeling of terror was creeping up her spine. Would they try to take Tina from her?

"Miss Mudrak," asked David, "can we make an exception, just this once? They'll be here for such a short amount of time; I can't imagine it'll be a problem."

Silence. Desdemona ruminated. "Very well," she said at last. Elsie let out a breath of relief. "Just this time."

A wave of Desdemona's lithe arm ushered the family from the dormitory and back down the stairs to the corridor on the ground floor. The boy, Edward, was still mopping. He didn't seem to be making much progress. As the group passed him on the way to the front door, Elsie heard him clear his throat. She paused and turned to see that he was holding a small, folded-up piece of paper in his hand. "Excuse me," he said to Elsie. "I think you dropped this."

Elsie looked to see if anyone else had heard him; her mother and father were lost in conversation with Miss Mudrak, parsing out the finer details of the payment due. Rachel was staring at her Converses. Elsie turned back to the boy. "Me?" she asked.

The boy nodded.

Strange; she didn't remember carrying it in. At a loss, she reached out shyly and pulled the paper from the boy's fingers, just as she heard her mother call, "Elsie! What are you doing?"

Elsie smiled a confused thank-you to the boy before stuffing the paper into the pocket of her skirt. She skipped back to stand at the ruffled hem of her mother's dress, listening to Miss Mudrak say, "And I will leave you to say your good-byes."

David knelt down and took his two daughters in his arms, clutching them tightly to his shoulders. His voice was quiet, choked. "My girls," he said. "My girls. We're going to find your brother. We're going to find him, so help me God. And we're going to bring him back so we can be a family again. A whole family."

Rachel began to cry. Elsie stood with her face plastered into the fabric of her father's corduroy sports coat, smelling his musky aftershave and wondering why she wasn't crying too. She felt her mother's hands on her shoulders. Lydia Mehlberg didn't speak, but Elsie could feel her begin to sob; the convulsions sent little spasms down her arms.

"Be good, girls," was all she managed to say.

Then, David and Lydia began to extricate themselves from their daughters' arms and make their way back to the car. Rachel was the hardest to leave; she tore desperately at her father's clothes, trying to hold on. And then they were gone, the family's black sedan crunching down the gravel drive back into the dark, snowy corridors of the Industrial Wastes. Elsie and Rachel stood on the landing by the building's front doors, watching them go. Their breath made little plumes of mist in the air above their heads. Remembering, Elsie reached into her pocket and pulled out the piece of paper the boy had given her. Slowly, she unfolded it and read the words that were scrawled on the yellowed surface:

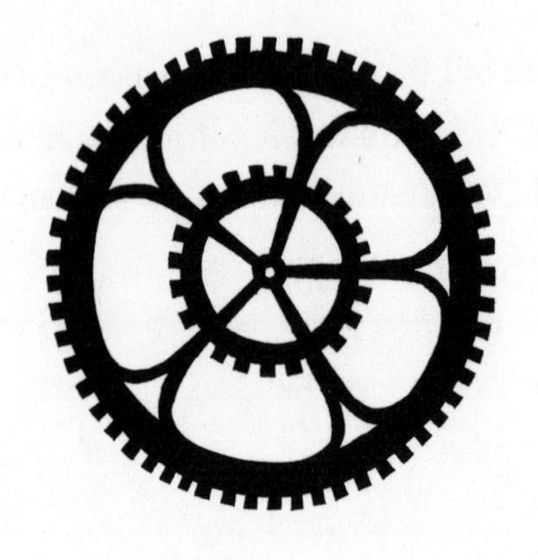

CHAPTER 4

The Corporal's Story

"Prue!"

...

"PRUE!"

Wind. The rustle of leaves.

"Prue McKeel! Can you hear me?"

It was a woman's voice, a voice that Prue recognized, but only slightly. It was like hearing the sound of a familiar song over the loud thrum of a noisy restaurant. The voice made her think of safety. And cell mitosis. And patchouli.

It was the voice of Darla Thennis, her Life Science teacher.

"Are you okay?" asked Darla, her face blocking the dark sky.

Prue groaned. "I—I think so," she managed to say.

The teacher helped Prue to a seated position on the snowy ground. Prue's legs felt numb; her pants were icy cold and wet and clung tenaciously to her legs. She guessed she hadn't been lying there long; the day didn't seem much progressed. She began to piece together the events that led to her passing out: the walk to the bluff and then the noise. But she'd seen something, hadn't she? Something startling. It came back to her in a sharp vision: the black fox. And then the screaming, deafening hiss. Prue craned her neck to look over the precipice of the bluff and scanned the ground below. The fox was gone. She looked over at Ms. Thennis.

"What are you doing here?" Prue asked.

"I'd ask you the same," replied the teacher, rubbing her bare hands together. The tips of her fingernails were black with mud. "Interesting place to come walking." She searched the horizon. "Just having a nice gander at the Impassable Wilderness?"

"I was just wandering," said Prue. "And then I . . ." She paused, unsure of how much she should reveal to her teacher. She hadn't mentioned anything of the plants' voices to anyone—she was sure she'd be seen as a lunatic. "And I just became really light-headed."

"It's been a tough day," said Ms. Thennis, standing up from her squatted position. There were bits of dead grass clinging to her skirt, and she wiped them away before she offered her hand to Prue. "Come on, I'll buy you a steamed milk. You need to warm up."

They made their way to the coffee shop on Lombard and slid into the opposing chairs of a table at the front window. The server brought a cappuccino for Darla; the steam from a mug of honey-sweetened milk warmed the air in front of Prue. They talked for a while about the snow, the dreary Portland winters. Darla sketched out her childhood for Prue, her love for books and music, her military dad who kept moving the family around. She talked about being a "real hippie" in high school and how she followed some jam band around the country, selling hemp jewelry in the parking lot during the shows.

"Do you like music?" asked Darla.

"Yeah, I like some bands. I don't know. I'm kind of nerdy when it comes to music. Like, I've recently started listening to a lot of Cajun stuff. Do you know it?"

"Like, accordion music?"

"Yeah," said Prue, feeling herself blush.

"Wow, kid," said Darla, taking a hit off her coffee. "You are nerdy."

They shared a fit of laughter together, which died away to a calm silence. They both looked out the window and watched the cars *shshing* by. A man struggled to open a newspaper box. Prue turned her head to watch her teacher across the table silently; the woman raised her mug to her lips with an almost inhuman grace.

The truth of the matter was that Prue had long kept the secret of her adventures in the Impassable Wilderness from her Outsider peers—only ever speaking of the harrowing events that unfolded there to her mother and father, who tended to greet mention of the place with a saddened frown. The entire incident only dredged up memories of lost children and sleepless nights for them. Mac ended up being the best and only confidant for her, someone who would appear to listen without judgment as she wondered what events continued to transpire beyond the wooded wall—and he was barely receptive, babbling "Pooo!" every time she took a pause in her speaking. It often occurred to Prue that it was a tremendous weight to be carrying about; she longed to share her secret with the world.

As if reading Prue's mind, Darla set down her mug and fixed her companion with a look of wide-eyed confidence. "Do you ever wonder?" she asked.

Prue knew she was speaking of the Impassable Wilderness, though she thought it was too weird how matched their thinking was. "About what?" she asked.

"The Impassable Wilderness. Like, what's beyond it?"

"I guess so." Prue could feel her heartbeat speeding up.

"I used to hang with these kids, back when I was just out of high school. My parents lived in Hillsboro, and we used to stand at the edge of the I.W. and just . . . stare. And wonder. Just like you were doing, I suppose. Back on the bluff, there. This old boyfriend of mine—he was a little loony—he used to swear up and down that he'd seen things in the trees. Like, animals—but ones that walked upright. He even said that one tried to talk to him once." She waved her hand dismissively, miming the boyfriend's crazy mental state.

Prue couldn't take it anymore.

"Can I tell you something?" she asked finally.

Darla looked at Prue quizzically. "Yeah, sure."

"This is going to sound really weird, I'm warning you."

"That's okay."

"And you're the first to hear this, other than my parents."

"That's what teachers are for, Prue."

A deep breath. "I've been in there."

Darla's eyes widened.

"Into the Impassable Wilderness."

"Really?"

"Yeah," said Prue. "And you wouldn't believe what happened."

Prue felt an enormous weight lift from her shoulders.

A blast of hot air greeted Curtis as he walked into the enormous hall, and his glasses immediately fogged up. He stumbled forward a few steps, feeling the stone floor beneath his boots, until he stepped on something soft.

"OW!" came a voice from below him. It was Septimus. "Watch where you're walking!"

"Sorry!" said Curtis, yanking the glasses from his face. He opened his coat and began wiping the lenses clean with the hem of his shirt. His vision was intensely blurred without his glasses on, but even so he could see that a massive conflagration in a central fire pit provided the long hall its warmth and light. It glowed in the center of the room like a sun. He could make out the misty silhouettes of figures around the fire; they began to move toward him. He fed his cleaned glasses back onto the bridge of his nose. What he saw made him smile.

"Iphigenia!" he said, recognizing the approaching figures. "Mr. Fox!"

"H'lo, Curtis," said the fox, a toothpick hanging jauntily from his teeth. He stuck out a red paw, and Curtis shook it happily.

Iphigenia watched the exchange, and when Curtis turned to her, she grasped him by the shoulders. Her gray hair hung strawlike to touch the rough weave of her sackcloth robe. Her eyes, mottled green and deep, quickly sized him up. "I'd say you've grown a bit since last I saw you, Bandit Curtis," she said, "but how can that be?"

He felt a hardy slap on his back; Brendan stood behind him, smiling. "That's what a few months of rigorous bandit training will do to a lad."

"Welcome to our province, Bandit King," said Iphigenia, her eyes still searching Curtis's. When she appeared satisfied, she turned to Brendan and bowed.

"Hrrmph," said Sterling Fox gruffly. "If my grandfather Chester had lived to see this day; Wildwood Bandits in North Wood." The slightest wisp of a smile played on his face.

"Indeed!" exclaimed Brendan, his arms akimbo. He made a show of surveying the interior of the long hall. "Hope you made a careful log of all the valuables that you've got stashed about," he said. "I don't intend to rob ye blind, but I can't speak for my comrade here." He nudged Curtis playfully. "An ace on the pickpocketing, this one. Could steal the lip ring from a sultan's concubine!"

"He's joking," explained Curtis, embarrassed. "We won't take anything." He paused, then corrected himself. "But yeah, I've gotten fairly good at that."

"Very impressive, my boy," said Iphigenia. "You've taken to the bandit way of life with gusto."

"Still needs help with his horsemanship, I understand." This was Owl Rex, folding one massive wing around Curtis's shoulders.

"How do you know that?" Curtis asked, chastened.

"We have eyes," said Owl. "We are the creatures of the air, after all."

Brendan looked down on his recruit proudly. "He'll get there, I have no doubt."

"But come!" said Iphigenia, taking Curtis's hand. "To the fire pit. We have much to talk about and very little time to do so." There was a new sadness in her eyes, Curtis couldn't help but notice; she seemed to have grown impossibly old since he'd seen her last. Her fingers felt like fragile twigs in his hand; they felt as if they would dissipate into ash at the slightest pressure.

Iphigenia guessed at his concern. "Rationing, my boy," she said sadly. "Takes a toll on old bones." She waved a gaunt hand to the surrounding hall. "*'Tis the winter of our discontent.* I believe one of your Outsider poets penned the line. Hard times are upon the North Wood. And we are not alone in our misery."

"That's what the heron—Maude—said. She also said Prue was in danger. What's happening?" Curtis ventured, his curiosity getting the better of him.

A frown was set on Iphigenia's wizened face. "Indeed," she murmured. "That is a chief concern. But it is a symptom of a much larger problem."

The group walked toward the heat of the central fireplace, a circular stone hearth surrounded by a series of low benches. The warm glow of the fire sent shadows flickering through the darkened hall, and Curtis could see spectral figures hovering just beyond the reach of the light.

"What is this place?" Curtis asked as he felt Owl's wing guide him to sit at one of the benches. One of the shadowy figures glided into view, carrying a glass and a pitcher of water. It was a young boy, and he wore a robe similar to Iphigenia's. He silently handed Curtis the glass and filled it with the clear liquid.

"The Great North Hall," answered Owl Rex, finding his seat on the far side of the fire pit from Curtis. "In my grandfather's time, it was a gathering place for Woods folk from all provinces who wished to share ideas beyond the reach of the Mansion's many ears and eyes."

"And so it must be again," said Iphigenia, waving another robed attendant, his arms filled with chopped wood, to the fireside. At the Elder Mystic's command, the attendant fed the logs onto the fire and the flames grew, licking at the large copper hood that was suspended from the hall's wooden rafters. The explosion of light revealed the true size of the hall, its corners reaching far away from the central hub of the hearth. The vaulted ceiling towered above the building's milling occupants, and Curtis could make out the sprightly motion of a few swallows diving and twisting between the rafters.

"All present?" asked Sterling, eyeing the gathered figures as they murmured approval and found their places on the wooden benches. Curtis counted the ones that had stepped forward: He, Brendan, Owl, Iphigenia, and Sterling all sat equidistant from one another, facing each other over the curling tendrils of the fire. There was only one figure Curtis didn't recognize; he'd joined the circle last, issuing from the darkness like a ghost from the ether. He was a gray wolf, and he wore the colors of the South Wood Guard: a smart khaki officer's coat, all natty wool and brass buttons, with a sash attached at the shoulder displaying the tricolor of the South Wood Reformation: green, gold, and black. The wolf wore two chevrons on his left shoulder, which seemed to indicate a high rank, and on his right lapel, oddly enough, he'd pinned a brooch that appeared to be a small, toothy bicycle sprocket. A black eye patch reduced the wolf's usable eyes to one, and his left ear appeared to be half chewed off.

Iphigenia spoke. "My friends, it is dire times. Dire times, indeed. The winter has taken hold of our poor, embattled country and has refused to let go. Even now, as we speak, the gentlefolk of North Wood line up for their rations and hoard what little food they have in their stores for the worst of emergencies. In my time as the Elder Mystic—alas, even since I was a Yearling—I have not seen a time of such despair."

Curtis eyed the figures present. Owl nodded gravely while Sterling Fox took a long, ponderous drag off his clay pipe. The strange wolf stared silently into the glow of the fire.

"What is to blame?" continued the Elder Mystic. "I have spoken with the tree, and as yet I have no satisfactory answer. Certainly, the winter is unforgiving in its harshness. But I feel I would be remiss if I did not voice my suspicions: that there is a disease in the land that goes deeper than the whims of weather. The unrest in South Wood is a poison to us all. And it must be removed at its root."

"Unrest?" Curtis spurted out. "What about the revolution? Wasn't that supposed to fix everything?"

The mysterious wolf coughed up a withering laugh at this remark. Everyone's eyes fell on the figure by the fire.

"Curtis, Brendan," said Iphigenia, "meet Corporal Donalbain.

He's risked his life to be here; I'm sure you'll find what he has to say very interesting."

The corporal huffed a greeting and took a long final draw from a wooden pipe clenched in his teeth. Wisps of smoke drifted from his gray snout as he tapped the contents of the pipe into his paw and scattered it on the ground. "How do you do," he said. His voice sounded like a metal rake being dragged across loose gravel. "Call me Jack." He leaned forward and placed the pipe on the edge of the fire pit.

"Corporal Donalbain has come directly from South Wood," explained Iphigenia. "He has traveled those many miles secretly, and by foot. His commanding officers do not know he is here; he has placed his station—indeed, his very life—at risk to bring us this information. His good conscience has impelled him."

"Is this the boy?" asked Jack, lifting his snout to Curtis. "You're friends with the girl—the half-breed girl. Prue?"

"Yes," said Curtis, feeling himself moving forward on his bench seat. "Is she okay?"

The wolf was silent for a moment before speaking. "She'll be dead before the evening. Of that, I have no doubt." He scanned the attending circle of listeners. "They've sent an assassin."

Curtis felt all the muscles in his body tighten in a quick jolt. His mouth went completely dry. Brendan, sitting at his left, growled angrily.

"Who would do such a thing?" asked Brendan. "And I thought

you South Wooders considered her to be some sort of hero—the Bicycle Maiden or some such hogwash. Did she not, with this lad here, bring on your great revolution?" The ire was rising in his voice. "And did we not, we Irregulars, cut our flesh and spill our blood for your precious safety while you were all about throwin' them birds into prison for nought? And this is how you choose to move on?" In his anger, he had nearly tipped off his bench. He steadied himself on the lip of the rock hearth.

"Easy, Bandit King," soothed Owl Rex. "Your sacrifices have not been forgotten." He waved a wing in the direction of the corporal, who was listening, disinterestedly, to Brendan's rant. "He is a friend. The good corporal is an ally." When the room had quieted, the Owl continued, "Please, Corporal Donalbain, tell our bandit friends who 'they' are."

"Well, that's the tricky bit, ain't it?" said the wolf dryly. "No telling who's the responsible party, really. I mean, I've got a fairly clear idea, but there ain't no way of proving it. They've come to be pretty handy at passin' blame, they have. Ever since the Emergency."

Curtis moistened his lips and spoke: "The Emergency? What's that?"

"I spoke of poison," interjected Iphigenia. "This is the poison."

"It's what's left of the government in South Wood, ever since you lot left us to our own devices," continued the wolf. "Though most folks don't call it that; it'd be seditious, they say. But me? I'll call it as

I see it. And it's as good a description of the cock-up of that formerly great province as any."

"What happened?" asked Brendan, regaining his seat.

"Nothing. That's what happened," responded Jack. "Too much of nothing. Lots of people comin' forward demandin' reparations, and no one willing to take the blame. Once the workin' people got over the romance of the thing, this Bicycle Coup, they started realizin' there weren't no government for to take care of 'em."

"But what about the interim government?" asked Curtis, remembering the charter that he had signed himself, along with many of the people who were present around the fire, that had established the temporary structure of government.

"It's still there, all right," said the wolf, "just gettin' more and more like a congregation of snakes every day. Almost straightaway, after the Owl Prince and the Bandit King and the Elder Mystic left"—here he looked each one in the eye, intoning their names as if they were only words from a storybook—"folks in the government got down to what they knew best: backstabbing and palm greasing. Suddenly, so-and-so weren't so patriotic as he was before, according to folks in the Mansion. Then this so-and-so counters by sayin' that at least he weren't the one taking bribes on those poppy beer shipments or what-have-you. Which invites another so-and-so to discredit the lot and bring all the attention on himself. Suddenly, you've got a 'interim government' that ain't as concerned about runnin' things as they are makin' sure their backsides are covered. Things get heated; suddenly so-and-so's not only unpatriotic, according to his enemies, but he's a collaborator from the Old Regime, and maybe he's not done such a good job in his palm greasin' and—boom—he's in the prison. So the prison starts gettin' fairly filled up, as you might expect. And suddenly, there's a new 'patriotic sentiment' in the province, and everyone's trying to out-patriot the other one, and people start gettin' all misty eyed about the 'legacy of the Coup' or some such piffle. And now we all got to start wearin' the sash of the revolution, and we all get stuck with these badges." He thrust a claw at the sprocket brooch at his chest. "To remind yourself of the Great Bicycle Coup and all the good it done people. But this ain't ordained or nothin'—no, no—no one's tellin' anyone else what to do, right? 'Cause it's the New Society, right? We're all free now." The wolf laughed a little under his breath and held his arm straight across his chest in a severe salute. "But if you don't be walkin' around with one these brooches, well, 'Citizen Donalbain is a Svikist and a counterrevolutionary!'

"So I keep my head low and I do as I'm told and I wear the sash and badge and I sing 'The Storming of the Prison' and '*Le Vélo Rouge*' when everyone else is, even when I'm sick to death of those damned treacly numbers. And I do all right for meself, don't I? But now: With law all coddly-wobble and such, there's hellions on the loose, and it ain't safe to walk the streets at night so much." The wolf coughed into his paw; he looked at Iphigenia imploringly. "Don't suppose I could importune you for another mug of that fine North Wood poppy beer, could I? All this talkin' brings up a mighty thirst."

The Elder Mystic nodded and called forward one of the milling attendants. The corporal was given a large mug of frothing liquid, which he lapped at thirstily before continuing.

"But this ain't the worst of it. Nah, not by a long shot. So this prison, you know: the one from the tune? The one that we stormed to free all those unjustly imprisoned bird citizens? Well, it's just gettin' all filled up again, ain't it? But that ain't a worry, 'cause all the name-calling and backstabbing has got to such a pitch that the real detractors, the real collaborators and Svikists, well—they're just: *skkkkkrrrk*." He made a kind of tearing noise with the back of his throat while he dragged a claw across his neck. "That makes things awfully tidy, don't it?

"But the worst of it—oh gods, the worst of it—is the Synod." After saying these words, the wolf took a long pull off the mug of beer, as if to settle his nerves. "The council of the Caliphs, religious zealots pushed aside during the rule of the Svik dynasty in favor of a more secular society, now back in full force."

Curtis glanced over at Iphigenia and noticed that a very worried look had come over her face.

The wolf continued, "Suddenly, everywhere you went you saw those hooded clowns on the street corners, jangling their little bells and reading their tracts on sanctuary and salvation, and when folks've got no food in the larder, well, those pamphlets and all their starry promises seem awful attractive. So then the congregation's growing at the Blighted Tree and then you've got the Synod themselves, all hooded and masked as they are in their dark robes, walking through the streets of South Wood, bangin' their gongs and swingin' their smoky censers, and everyone's out all starin' and listenin' to them carry on. And before you know it—and I swear to this, as I've seen it with my own eyes—I seen a few of the Caliphs wanderin' the halls of Pittock Mansion itself, glad-handin' with the pols and having closed-door meetings with commissioners and councilmen and what have you."

Curtis heard a groan; it came from Brendan, who now had his head in his hands.

"Their influence is growing," said Iphigenia solemnly. "We've known this to be so for a time now. The Council Tree has made us aware. This poison works at the root of the plant, my friends. If it is not cut out, our present circumstances will only be made worse."

"But what about Prue?" asked Curtis. "Who's sent this assassin? The Caliphs?"

The wolf knocked back the remaining poppy beer and set the emptied mug down on the hearth noisily. He licked his chops clean of foam. "Could be, could be," he said. "Though it's just as likely to be some faction from the Mansion—a real Old Regime Svikist. They still have a scrap of power, though they're forced to scheme in secret."

"How do you have this information, then?" asked Brendan, his chin resting in his hands.

"Like I said: I've made a good name for myself. I've kept my noggin intact." A black claw tapped three times at his temple. "Kept my head low. Got a job in the Mansion intelligence service. Pushin' paper. Tidy office job, right? So what if I watch a few reams of paper go by that might condemn a man to imprisonment or death? I'm watching out for myself. Anyways, they've got these Intuits working in the Mansion, folks who have the way to listen like the North Wooders—you know, can hear plants talk and such—and they're just sittin' out in the garden all day, listenin' to the chatter among the leaves and trees for information. And they report to my office every day with what they've heard. Well, comes down from one of them—an awfully good Intuit, this one—that there's word of an assassin, a Kitsune, no less, who's been sent to murder the Bicycle Maiden. Seems like a big deal, right? I mean, she's the hero of the revolution! But no sooner do I report this to my betters than they're stampin' the thing confidential and throwin' it in a archived box to molder away in the deepest depths of the Mansion basement."

"But why?" asked Curtis.

"Beats me," replied the wolf. "And I don't have much time to think about it; things start getting tense in the office, and suddenly I see another report come through from the Intuits sayin' something about cleanin' out the intelligence office, and I figure that means me; that they're wipin' out anybody who's seen that bit of intel about the Bicycle Maiden. That's what I guess anyways, so I finish my afternoon's work—say I'm goin' out for a quick bite to eat and I'm out of there, scramblin' north as fast as my paws can carry me. You wouldn't believe my feeling of relief when I managed to get across the North Wall and into Wildwood. Pure relief to be out of that cesspit." The corporal reached for his mug again, forgetting he'd downed it, and attempted to take a long swig. He looked forlornly at the empty pewter mug and gave a pleading smile to Iphigenia.

"In time, Corporal," was her reply.

Owl Rex spoke up. "Were you discovered? Does the Mansion know you've left with this information?"

The wolf shrugged. "Dunno. Managed to slip the gate without too much hassle. Got roughed up one night in Wildwood, by the Ancients' Grove. Some coyotes. Did this to me." He pointed to his torn ear. "But otherwise, who knows?"

"It's not safe for you to return," said Iphigenia. "You must stay here. In hiding." She looked at the assembled circle and concluded, "As must we all. We are the face of the Bicycle Coup to the people of South Wood. If they—whoever 'they' may be—intend to go after Prue, they're likely to go after all of us."

"And what about Prue?" asked Sterling.

"We need to get her to a safe place," replied Owl. "And quickly."

"Where's safe?" pressed the fox.

Owl Rex looked over at Curtis and Brendan. "In the farthest redoubt of the wildest province. To the newfound camp of the Wildwood Bandits, in the deepest crevices of the Long Gap. If you will take her."

"Of course!" shouted Curtis. "She should come to the hideout!" Even though the prospect of Prue being hounded by a vengeful assassin was making him queasy, Curtis felt a jolt of excitement travel through his body: to think that he'd see his friend again!

"Hold up, boyo," interrupted Brendan, before turning to Iphigenia. "How did you know where the camp is?"

"There are no secrets to the North Wood Mystics," answered the old woman. She added: "While you may be beyond the ken of the Intuits, the tree knows all. It is important, should you take the girl, that we know where she is hidden. We are all brethren here."

Brendan seemed to take in this information with a certain amount of resignation. "Speaking of brethren," he said, "there's no sense bringin' this all down on the bandits; they've not got a say in it. She'd be a dangerous fugitive. We'd be puttin' the whole camp at risk."

"She's got nowhere else to go," said Iphigenia quietly.

A silence came over the hall. The fire crackled noisily. Brendan deliberated while the eyes of the gathered attendants stayed on him.

"Very well," he said finally, reluctantly. "We'll take her in. Gods know she saved my life once; it's the least we can do to repay." Here he wagged a finger at the Elder Mystic. "But if that Katchoony catches wind of our camp and comes sniffin' around . . ."

"Kitsune," corrected Owl.

"Whatever. As soon as it comes around—it's time for one of you lot to take the 'Maiden' in. Agreed?"

The Elder Mystic and Owl Rex nodded in unison. Curtis scooted forward and turned to Corporal Donalbain, who was by now looking as if he were about to nod off in his chair. "Jack," he said, "what's a Kitsune, anyway?"

"Hmmph?" asked the wolf, clearly having been startled from a nascent stupor. "A Kitsune? Well, it's a creature from the Shrine Groves at the edge of the Wood. A shape-shifter."

"Shape-shifter? What do you mean?"

"Some folks say it's an ancient aberration in the Woods Magic. Some say they're demigods. But either way: A Kitsune is a black fox," replied the wolf. "With the very incredible ability to transform itself, at will, into human form. The damndest thing. The damndest thing." And with that, the wolf's words trailed away, his snout coming to rest on the fabric of his coat, and he fell into a deep slumber.

CHAPTER 5

Enter the Assassin

A braided barista excused herself while she stretched her arm over Ms. Thennis's head and pulled the cord to the neon OPEN sign in the café's front window. It flickered a few times before turning off, and Prue looked up at the girl apologetically.

"Sorry," she said. "We'll get out of your hair now."

The barista smiled and waved her hand. "Nah," she said, "don't worry about it. Looks like you two are having a serious conversation. I got a ton of cleanup to do, anyway. Take your time."

Out on the dark avenue, a red traffic light changed green, and the shine of passing headlamps flashed the front window. The last of the fading, dim light was rapidly disappearing behind the wall of trees just beyond the river's ravine. Prue glanced up at the clock on the wall above the café bar: It was five thirty.

"Shoot," said Prue. "I should really get going." Ms. Thennis was sitting beneath the taxidermied head of a moose. Prue hadn't noticed it until that moment.

"Yeah," said Ms. Thennis, dazed. "Yeah." She hadn't touched her cappuccino; the milk foam had begun to look like Christmas tree flocking.

Prue waited for her teacher to say something else, but nothing was coming. "I'm sorry to, like, burden you with all this. I know it sounds so crazy."

"Yeah," repeated the teacher. She shook her head a little and rubbed her chin with a finger. A bracelet made of small wooden beads clattered against her wrist. "So, again: Curtis. Your friend. The one who went missing. He's still there."

"Yeah," said Prue.

"With a band of bandits."

"Yeah. I mean, he's a bandit himself now."

"Uh-huh," replied Ms. Thennis. "Right. What about his parents?"

"They don't know."

Ms. Thennis seemed to blanch. "Okay."

"You swore yourself to secrecy, Ms. Thennis," Prue reminded the teacher.

Darla squirmed in her chair. "Yeah, well, I didn't know your story would involve a missing child." A pause. "So Curtis is just there? In the bandit camp?"

"Yup. Totally safe. I'd even go so far as to say that he's probably totally happy there."

"And where is this place? Like, where's the camp?"

"Doesn't matter," said Prue, scraping a fingernail at a little of the foamed milk residue on the edge of her mug. "Like I said: You wouldn't be able to go in there anyway."

"Right. Magical barrier."

"Mm-hmm."

"But he's safe?" Ms. Thennis leaned forward in her chair. "And this so-called Bandit King, this Brendan—is he in the hideout too?"

"Yeah—that's his home."

"Well, I can tell you I'm going to definitely have to let all this, well, settle for a bit. In my mind." She sat back in her chair and wiped her hands on her gauzy, floral-patterned skirt. The room's quiet was disturbed only by the occasional clacking of the barista and her juggled fleet of pitchers and mugs.

"Sure," said Prue. "Listen: I know that's a lot to take in, but I can't tell you how nice it is to have someone other than my parents to confide this stuff to. It's been driving me crazy."

Darla allowed herself a smile. "No problem. But you have to get going, right? Walk you home?"

"Yeah, thanks."

They walked in silence down the wet sidewalks, their shoulders hunched against the cold. The torrent of words and emotions that had positively poured out of Prue at the coffee shop haunted her; like an overly rich dessert you'd devour without a thought, the regret kicking in only once the last spoonful had been consumed, Prue was now wondering if confessing her wild adventure in the Impassable Wilderness had really been the best idea. Without turning her head, she glanced sideways at Darla, who was walking lost in her own thoughts, and inwardly cringed. What was going to happen now? Would Darla respect Prue's wishes to keep this revelation to herself? Would she tell the police? Or Curtis's parents? Her nose stung at the frigid wind, and she pulled her scarf higher against her cheeks. Maybe that was for the best, after all. Maybe Prue had been the one at fault here, not telling the Mehlbergs and letting them despair over the loss of their son.

Curtis. What had Prue brought on him? What kind of wild life among bandits would he be leading? Would they be sufficient parents for a kid? Was Brendan really the right father figure for a boy to . . .

Suddenly, something occurred to Prue. It revealed itself to her like the answer to a puzzle you'd contemplated for hours without seeing the easiest solution. And it made her spine go cold.

“Hey,” she said. “Darla.”

“Yeah?”

“When we were talking back there, in the café, you said his name.”

“Whose name?”

“Brendan’s. The Bandit King.”

“Uh-huh. So? Isn’t that his name?”

Prue dug her hands deeper into her peacoat pockets. “Yeah, but . . .”

“But what?”

“I don’t remember telling you his name. Before.”

Quiet. A car passed. The muffled sound of a syncopated bass track reverberated from within.

“You must’ve,” said Darla Thennis.

“I don’t think I did.”

Darla laughed a little. “Oh, Prue. You’ve been through a lot. You’re just confused. It’s totally understandable. Here, isn’t this your house?”

The familiar front porch loomed on the sidewalk ahead.

“Yeah,” said Prue. “Maybe you’re right. Maybe I need to just chill out or something.” She looked into Darla’s eyes, black and empty in the streetlamp-less dark, and reached out her hand. “Thanks,” she said. “Thanks for listening.”

Darla, grasping with both hands, holding tightly, saying: “Of course. See you tomorrow.”

Pulling from the handshake, Prue mounted the steps to her front door. Light from the living room descended from the house onto the yard, and a weave of leftover Christmas lights winked on the steps' banister. Prue felt unsettled as she climbed; reaching the front door, she paused at the handle and turned. Ms. Thennis was still standing on the sidewalk, her face obscured in the blank dark. The figure waved. Prue waved back and walked into her house.

Whatever uneasiness she was feeling disappeared immediately as she stepped into the foyer of her family's home. Instead, she was overcome by a scent so pungent and all-consuming that it seemed to dispel all other thoughts from her mind. Pickles. She crinkled her nose and shouted, "What is that?"

Her dad appeared from the kitchen, wearing long rubber gloves and holding what appeared to be a mossy clump of greenishness. "Oh, hi, honey," he said. He quickly slipped back into the kitchen. Prue shed her peacoat, kicked off her Wellies, and followed her dad. "What's that smell?" she asked.

In the kitchen, her mother and father were staring at a large brown crock in the middle of the cork floor.

"Pickles," her mother explained. "Forgotten pickles."

Her dad smiled sheepishly. "Remember those cukes we got at the farmer's market at the end of September? Kinda forgot about them. Now they're either the best pickles known to man, or totally poisonous." He held aloft the weird green mass in his gloved hand. "Wanna try?"

"Blech," said Prue. "When can we fumigate?"

"Immediately," said her mother, grasping the crock and pouring the remnants into the disposal unit in the sink. Her father acted downcast.

"Good-bye, magic pickles," he said mournfully.

"Lemme help," said Prue, reaching under the sink for the spritzer of lemon water. She began spraying it about the room.

"How was your walk?" asked her dad as he peeled the rubber gloves from his hands.

"Good," she said. "Fine. Weird."

"Why weird?" This was her mother, wiping the counter clean of some of the pickle crock's brackish liquid.

"I ran into Ms. Thennis. Darla."

"Really? That's funny; she left just after you did. Said she had to head back to school."

The bluff would not be on the way to the school; this was odd. "Yeah, I ran into her, and she bought me a steamed milk at the coffee shop," said Prue. She didn't mention that she'd passed out—that seemed like too much to reveal. And it would require mentioning the screams from the Scotch broom, which would be downright weird.

"She seems like a very cool teacher," said her mother. "Is she new this semester?"

"Yeah," replied Prue, staring fixedly at the lumpy pickle her dad had left on the counter. "From Eugene, I guess."

The strange wolf stared silently into the glow of the fire.

"Well, that explains it," said her mother.

"So what ever happened to Mrs. Estevez?" her father asked.

"Dunno. Retired. Health reasons. Someone said we all drove her crazy."

Her dad made a face. "Ooh."

Prue swiveled and began walking upstairs. "Anyway, I'll be in my room. Let me know when dinner is."

"Soon!" hollered her mom after her. "It's lentil curry! Your favorite!"

Her father couldn't help but interject, "And don't think we haven't forgotten about that note from school." Pause. "Because we haven't!"

Prue closed her bedroom door behind her and found herself blessedly alone. The patterned rug on the floor, littered with the contents of an overturned laundry hamper, was only barely made visible by the yellow light from the terrarium on her desk. Following the glow, she leaned over and tapped on the glass. Her box turtle, Edmund, moved inside, the half-chewed remains of a leaf balanced on his small head. She reached over and turned on the swivel lamp and assessed the few textbooks strewn about the desk's surface. She halfheartedly grabbed the slim paperback at the top of the pile and flipped it open to its dog-eared page. She read for a moment, trying to worm her way into the world of Atticus and Scout Finch, but found, after a time, that she was merely reading the same paragraph over and over. Defeated, she set down the book and launched herself into the folds of her bed.

Lying on her back, she stared at the strange shadows cast on the ceiling by the neighbor's house lights through the bared branches of the trees in the yard. The wind had picked up, and the branches appeared to be long, spidery fingers lashing at one another. As she watched, a large blot darted over the display, blackening the shadows completely for a split second.

What was that? Prue mouthed. She hopped from her bed and ran to the window. She arrived just in time to see something dark disappear into the neighbor's juniper hedges. She pressed her forehead to the window, studying the ground below; the glass was icy cold against her skin. Her mother called from downstairs.

"Prue!" came the voice.

She turned away from the window and stuck her head out of her door. "What?"

"I screwed up the naan bread," her mom called, sounding defeated. "Can you run down to the take-out place and just pick some up?"

Still absorbed with the thought of the dark shape in the backyard, Prue marched down the stairs. In the kitchen, her mother was studying the back of a packet of instant yeast. "Did you call it in?" asked Prue as she dipped her feet back into her Wellington boots.

"Yeah," said her mother. "Here's ten bucks. Grab some chutney while you're at it."

"I don't know why we didn't just order it all from there," murmured Prue, pocketing the cash.

“Hey,” scolded her father, reading a magazine in the living room. “Home-cooked meal. Your mother’s specialty.”

Mac was sitting on the floor at his feet, chewing on the frayed end of a chopstick. “Poooo!” he said.

“Be right back,” said Prue, rolling her eyes.

As she’d witnessed from her bedroom, the wind outside had picked up considerably. The temperature felt like it had plummeted several degrees, and Prue was back to experimenting with different, more efficient ways of wrapping her scarf around her neck. None of the options seemed to block out the chill satisfactorily, so she found herself just knotting the massive knitted thing at her chin and shoving her hands deep into her coat pockets. The Indian take-out place was eight blocks away, but the distance felt unfathomable with the brittle wind and frozen drizzle beginning to descend from the sky. Prue guessed it to be only six thirty, and yet the dark was everywhere. She eyed the underbrush warily as she walked, searching for movement. Pausing for a moment at an intersection, she focused her listening at a line of oaks to gauge their thoughts. The sound she heard was not unlike the noise made by a colony of bees, if you were to catch them in a sympathetic mood and swimming in a large, thick puddle of mud. It came in lazy waves. For whatever reason, it inspired in her the necessary confidence to continue on her errand. But it occurred to her then: Had the Scotch broom screaming been a warning? But a warning of what? The fox?

A *crack* from above. Prue jerked her head upward. A tree bough, weighted with what little heavy snow remained, had broken from its trunk and fallen into the branches below. The tree gave an audible groan. An electricity radiated through Prue's limbs from the surprise, though, and it took another half block of walking before she was able to shake it.

A pitch darkness preceded her. The streetlamps lining the last few blocks between her and the restaurant (she could see the warm, lit windows in the distance) appeared to not be working. Pausing momentarily, she took a deep breath and stepped into the veil of shadow. And that was when the trees started screaming.

HHHHHHHHHH!!!!!!!!

PHHHHHHHHHH!!!!!!

Prue's heart leapt. Instinctively, she began running in the direction of the restaurant. Something had crashed through the low bushes of a vacant lot and was now running after her; she could hear panting and frantic footsteps. The thing barked at her angrily—though she did not allow herself to look back to identify her pursuer; she kept her eyes on the safety of the restaurant's lit windows. The trees were still hollering at full throat, and their voices kettled in her mind like barely containable steam. The sound overpowered her thoughts, like it had at the bluff, and it was all Prue could do to maintain consciousness. The trees, if they were trying to safeguard her, were unaware of the power and presence of their voices.

She flagged; she fell.

The thing was on her in a flash.

It pinned her to the sidewalk; it was a black fox, its fur matted from the cold precipitation in the air. Its muzzle snapped at her face. It smelled of moldering leaves.

And patchouli.

"Got you," hissed the black fox. The voice was feminine, familiar.

"Ms. . . . ," Prue wheezed, her breathing hampered by the weight of the animal on her chest. "Ms. Thennis?"

The thing smiled, if it could be said that a fox can smile. "Please," it said, its voice calm and insidious, "call me Darla."

The trees were still screaming.

"Sorry to have to do this to you, kiddo," said the fox. "I'll try to make it painless."

Prue squeezed her eyes shut. The moment seemed to last for an eternity. She waited for the teeth to sink in, the claws to bite.

Just then, there came a terrific gust of wind. The trees quieted, as if surprised. A yell from above: "GAAAAAAH!" The weight was instantaneously lifted from Prue's chest, and her breath came roaring back. Glancing over, she saw that the black fox had been knocked across the sidewalk. Gasping, she scrambled to her feet while the fox desperately tried to right herself.

"What was that?" cried the fox angrily. The words had scarcely left her snout, though, before another thing had descended from the sky and knocked her rolling out into the empty street. Prue, her hands on her chest, watched as two giant herons alighted on the sidewalk before her.

"Prue!" shouted a boy's voice. It was Curtis, astride one of the large gray birds. Prue could not speak.

"Watch it!" called another voice. Prue looked over to see that it was Brendan. He, too, was mounted on one of the herons. "She's coming back!"

The fox had pushed herself up and was about to make a running leap at Prue. Stumbling backward, she threw her arms up to cover her face and felt the full weight of the fox come down on her shoulder, knocking her sideways. A row of ivory-white teeth snapped noisily, just inches from her ear. As she fell, however, she managed to get a foot under the fox's haunches and kicked hard; the fox yelped and tumbled away to the concrete.

"Run, Prue!" This came from Curtis. Prue glanced up at him—he was clinging to his heron's neck as the bird launched itself aloft and dove toward the prostrate fox. Both of the bandits' mounts pounced on the back of the fox while it was briefly incapacitated; the fox howled in pain as their claws dug in. Her energies renewed, the fox spun and struck Brendan's flying mount hard across the beak. Prue pushed herself up and bolted down the darkened street. She could hear behind her the sound of the fox breaking away from the skirmish and giving chase.

Brendan swore; a bird squawked. Prue felt the fox growing closer. She wasn't sure if she'd be able to survive another attack. She felt something sharp digging into the fabric of her peacoat and screamed. And then her feet began to lift from the ground.

She looked up and saw that she was in the talons of one of the herons. The bird was straining under the weight, and its wings were moving in long, powerful beats. Prue could see Curtis's face just over the wing of the bird. The fox leapt and swiped at Prue but only caught the hem of her pant leg. The heron let out a loud, mournful call—a kind of gravelly howl—and Prue found her feet touching back down on the pavement.

"Come on, Maude!" shouted Curtis from the heron's back.

Prue kept up the bird's frantic pace, the soles of her Wellingtons smacking the pavement like a runner on a treadmill gone wild. She could only hope that the heron would have enough thrust to get into the air again. She glanced behind her and saw that the fox was close in pursuit. Just as it was about to leap, the other bird, with Brendan astride, appeared from the darkness and struck the fox hard against its rump, and it tumbled sideways. Prue's feet once again left the ground, and the street below began to diminish. A brief tussle ensued between Brendan's mount and the fox, but on seeing Prue's escape, the bird gave the fox one final swipe across the snout and took to the sky. The fox howled, but the sound was soon lost as the two massive birds climbed above the treetops and disappeared into the low-hanging clouds.

Prue finally managed to speak. Her hands clasped tightly to the heron's claws at her shoulder. "Where are you taking me?" She found she had to holler it above the whipping wind.

Curtis's yelled response was, "To Wildwood!"

CHAPTER 6

The World Waltzes to Wigman; Welcome to the Unthank Home

The man was sitting on the sofa. A squat fedora was balanced on his knees. In his hands, he held a green bottle of Lemony Zip soda, which he sipped at politely. An array of magazines was laid out on the coffee table in front of him; he scanned the titles: *Industrialist Weekly*, *DUMP!*, *Modern Mining*, and *The 1% Journal*. None of them piqued the man's interest, except for *Industrialist Weekly*, which he had a subscription to; but the issue was from October of 2006, and he'd read it cover to cover already. On the front, in block letters, it read: "Cigarette Holders: Are They Really Necessary?" He sipped again at the soda and looked out the wall of windows opposite the couch. He was on the top floor of a very tall tower, one that overlooked a vast landscape of smokestacks, warehouses, and chemical tanks. A thick layer of haze made a kind of translucent veil over the view that rendered the world almost dreamlike. One could imagine this landscape stretching on forever into the distance, but it stopped abruptly at a great, blank wall of green just at the edge of the man's vision. Seeing this, the man's stomach gave a turn. It was a view that he saw daily, and yet it never failed to dismay him.

A *ding!* sounded, and the man looked up to see the elevator doors on the opposite side of the room open and disgorge a plump man in gray coveralls. He walked over to a circular desk in the center of the room (it stood as the only obstacle between the sofa and the two giant ornate bronze doors on the far wall) and signed his name to a piece of paper handed him by the secretary. He then walked over and sat in one of the chairs near the other man's sofa.

"Unthank," said the plump man in greeting.

"Higgs," said the man, Unthank, on the sofa.

They both sat in silence. Higgs picked up the copy of *Modern Mining* and began flipping through the pages. He smelled like pavement. Unthank sipped at his Lemony Zip.

Ding! Two more men walked into the room. They were both very, very tall. Unthank supposed they might be described as "willowy." One wore a white lab coat, while the other was encased in a baggy yellow hazmat suit. They, too, signed the sheet of paper given them by the secretary and found seats near Higgs and Unthank.

The four men all nodded to one another. They greeted each other in a litany of surnames: "Higgs." "Tumson." "Unthank." "Tumson." "Dubek." "Higgs." "Unthank." "Dubek." Dubek wore the hazmat suit, Tumson the lab coat.

Joffrey Unthank sipped at his soda and stared again out the window at the dark green lump of vegetation in the distance. It continued to bother him. He twisted his wrist slightly and took a quick look at his watch; it was getting on nine forty-five a.m. He'd told Desdemona he'd be back by eleven. He glanced up at the giant golden doors on the other side of the room. The copper-cast relief of a massive shipping barge straddled the gap between the two doors, and Unthank briefly marveled over what the cost of the doors must have been. No sooner had he done this when the crack widened, the ship broke in two, and the doors flew open. A large, muscle-bound man in a tight-fitting three-piece suit walked proudly into the room.

"Gentlemen!" he boomed. He was flanked by two hulking men wearing identical maroon beanies.

The four men in the various chairs and sofas all stood up in unison. Joffrey's fedora fell to the floor, and he stooped awkwardly to pick it up. Standing again, he realized he was still holding his Lemony Zip soda; he set it down on the coffee table. The man in the suit watched the action with a bemused smile on his face.

"H'lo, Mr. Wigman," said Joffrey.

"Please," said Mr. Wigman, "come in."

Opulent was the only word that could describe the huge room on the other side of the double doors. One wall was entirely made of windows; the other walls were covered in various advertisements for Wigman Shipping, as tall as the tallest men in the room, interspersed with framed magazine covers featuring Mr. Wigman himself, smiling widely in the vicinity of proclamations like: "Industrialist of the Year!" and "The World Waltzes to Wigman!" Short columns made of shiny metal provided a kind of obstacle course throughout the room; on top of each was some award that had been given to the great industrialist, as well as a few ancient-looking pieces of art that Joffrey imagined had been acquired unscrupulously. In the center of the room sat a very long conference table, hewn from what could only have been a massive, ancient tree; the highly polished surface was lined with the tree's gnarled grain. The four men waited for instruction; Mr. Wigman waved for them to sit as he stood at the head of the table. Joffrey set his hat in front of him and smoothed the front of his argyle sweater. When everyone was seated, Mr. Wigman turned his back and gazed out at the view beyond the windowed wall. The landscape was similar to the one seen from the foyer—a wide plain of multihued buildings spewing multihued clouds of gas, smoke, and fire—except the outer limits gave way to a wide river and, across it, the city of Portland.

"Darn it!" shouted Mr. Wigman.

The two attendants, the maroon-beanie-cap-wearing apes, jerked to attention. Wigman sounded angry.

"I said, DARN IT!" he repeated.

The four men at the table sat forward in their chairs.

Mr. Wigman took in a deep breath through his nose; his broad shoulders heaved inside the taut suit. "Isn't it *beautiful?*" he whispered.

Everyone in the room gave a sigh of relief.

Mr. Wigman turned around dramatically. His hair was crisp and black and parted perfectly on the right side of his scalp; his jaw was cleanly shaven. His teeth were long and bright, and his chin jutted from his skull like a cliff-face promontory that would pose a challenge to the heartiest of mountaineers. "And it's all ours, gentlemen."

Mr. Dubek rapped his fist on the table. "Hear, hear," he said.

The rest of the men voiced their approval as well.

"Stevedore!" yelled Mr. Wigman, and one of the beanied attendants snapped to attention. Mr. Wigman clapped his hands, and the stevedore drew from his pocket a blue squash ball and threw it at Mr. Wigman, who caught it easily with one hand. He began to squeeze it mightily.

"Let the meeting of the Five Titans commence!" announced Mr. Wigman. "Our quarterly review, shall we, gents?"

At the command, the men at the table produced individual leather

briefcases from the floor and set them on the table; they snapped them open and began to sift through their contents. That is, all the men but Joffrey. He looked around uneasily as he reached into the inside pocket of his corduroy jacket and retrieved a single folded-up piece of paper. He opened it gingerly and studied it; written there in smudged pencil were the words *Eggs. ½ n ½. Arugala (sp?). Lightbulbs.* Meanwhile, the other men had pulled from their natty briefcases thick, neatly bound volumes of documentation; they began flipping through the pages while Mr. Wigman spoke.

"Nature, fickle nature, created the seasons. For centuries man was imprisoned by these seasons. He could only eat certain things at certain times. Certain activities had to wait till the appropriate season arrived. But then came the great, golden industrial age, and seasons were nothing to man. Incidental. A piffle! Instead, we count our time by the passing of the great Fiscal Quarter—and we do what we like, when we like. We eat whatever we want to eat. And we eat well, don't we, gentlemen?"

A murmur of agreement followed.

"For here, we Titans have created the ideal state! They call it the Industrial Wastes, don't they? Pshaw! I say. Pshaw! I call it an Industrial Wonderland! The industrial ideal, made whole. A century of dreamers—Whitney, Edison, J. P. Morgan—and they never achieved half of what we've done here. The Quintet: four powerful industries under the watchful control of one dominant one—Wigman

Shipping—and we've shown the world a force to be reckoned with! A city-state is what we've built here. The great Corporatocracy!"

He was really getting into it. His face was beet red, and a smile was plastered on his face from ear to ear. "Now, my good fellow Titans, what've you got for me? I want the headlines." He glanced over the table. "Mining!" he yelled.

Higgs, in the coveralls, pushed his chair back and stood. "We've increased yield twenty percent, sir!"

"Fantastic. Petrochemical!"

Tumson stood as well, holding the lapels of his lab coat proudly. "The South Korean market is ours for the taking, sir."

"Outstanding. Nuclear!" Mr. Wigman was really giving the squash ball in his hand a good working-over.

"Regulations be damned, sir, we're free to dump in the river." This was Mr. Dubek. His hazmat suit rustled noisily as he stood.

"Music to my ears!" Mr. Wigman rounded on Joffrey now. "Machine parts!"

The room was silent. Joffrey cleared his throat as he went to push his chair back. He accidentally hit one of the many levers that protruded from the underside of the chair's apparatus and suddenly, with a hiss, the seat lowered dramatically. Joffrey felt his face flush. His fingers searched for the lever to raise the chair again; what proceeded was not unlike a child's carnival ride, with Joffrey jerkily being dropped and raised as he attempted to get the chair back in position.

Finally, he gave up and just pushed himself up from his seat.

"Well," he began. He looked at the other men in the room; they were all standing proudly and staring at him. He cleared his throat. "I think I'm closer to getting in there." He jerked his finger to point toward the foyer, toward the vast treed hills.

Silence.

Joffrey thought he heard one of the other men snicker.

Plump Mr. Higgs was the first to speak. "What, the Impassable Wilderness?" He looked at Mr. Wigman for an explanation.

"Joffrey, Joffrey," said Mr. Wigman, dolefully shaking his head.

Joffrey slammed his hand on the table. "Listen to me: I don't care what people call it—I don't care what people say about it. There's got to be a way!"

Willowy Mr. Tumson shifted uncomfortably in his chair. "It's the Impassable Wilderness, Unthank. It's impassable."

"Better left alone, I say," said willowy Mr. Dubek.

"What is it with you, Unthank?" injected Mr. Higgs. "It's like some weird obsession."

"But don't you see?" cried Joffrey, pleading. "If we could somehow get in there, raze those trees, level some of the hilly bits, why, we'd be able to at least triple—quadruple—our holdings! Think how many chemical tanks you could get up on that hill, Mr. Tumson! And water! Enough water to cool a forest of reactors! And Mr. Higgs, dear Mr. Higgs, can't you just taste what kind of minerals those hills must be sitting on? I mean, the copper veins alone have got to be—"

Wigman interrupted this tirade by saying simply, "Unthank, sit down."

"But—"

"Sit down."

Chastened, Joffrey did so and proceeded to ride the hydraulics of his chair for a few more moments before settling on the appropriate height.

"Where's your quarterly report?" asked Mr. Wigman.

"Pardon?"

"The quarterly report, Machine Parts." You knew Mr. Wigman was serious when he began referring to the individual Titans of the Quintet by their industry.

"Oh, of course," said Joffrey. "Right here." He gave the piece of paper before him a final ironing with his hands before sliding it toward Wigman. Mr. Wigman nodded to a stevedore, who marched to the table and delivered the piece of paper to his boss.

"This is it?" asked Mr. Wigman, holding the paper as if it were a used Kleenex. He glanced at the writing. "This appears to be a grocery shopping list, Machine Parts."

"Just down there, on the bottom." Joffrey wagged a finger, and Wigman looked closely at the few lines above the bottom margin of the paper.

"It says, 'Third quarter: looking pretty good.'"

"Mm-hmm," said Mr. Unthank. "Not much to report, really. Things are pretty much as they were last time. Mixed sales. Up and down. That's what I like about machine parts. No big surprises. Steady as she goes, right?" He looked at his fellow industrialists, expecting nods of understanding. Everyone was staring at Mr. Wigman. Mr. Wigman, for his part, was beginning to develop a facial tic. A loud *POP* suddenly sounded, and everyone in the room jolted in their chairs. Mr. Wigman calmly opened his hand; the shredded remains of the squash ball fell to the floor.

"Mr. Unthank," said Mr. Wigman very steadily, "I don't pretend to know exactly what goes on in that machine shop of yours. And I don't really care. Using orphans for labor? Good move. More power to you."

Joffrey smiled and displayed his hands to his fellow industrialists. *Small fingers,* he mouthed as he wiggled his digits.

"But if I don't start seeing growth . . ." Here Mr. Wigman's voice became louder.

"Growth!" he repeated, even louder.

"GROWTH!" Wigman slammed his fist on the table. "And soon, I'm going to come on over to that little section of yours and I'm going to bring some of my buddies here"—nodding to the stevedores—"and I'm going to make some GROWTH HAPPEN, GOT ME?"

Joffrey was plastered to the weave of his chair. A little line of sweat appeared at his brow.

"Now, you do what you want in your free time. But it better not interfere with your contribution to the Quintet; e.g.: I don't want to hear anything more about this Impassable Wilderness. Is that clear, Machine Parts?"

"Yes, sir."

"I said, is that clear?"

"Yes, Mr. Wigman. Sir."

"Good," said Wigman, sitting back down in his chair. He clapped his hands at one of the stevedores, who dutifully threw him another blue squash ball. "Now, I'm going to spend some time with the other Quintet members who have some real numbers to show me. Come back when you've got some too."

Joffrey felt his chair jerk backward; one of the maroon-beanied stevedores had yanked it out from the table. Submissively, he stood up and, nodding to those present, walked from the room. Entering the foyer, he placed the fedora back on his head and tried with all his might to avoid the view out of the room's large windows. It wasn't until the elevator doors were slowly closing in front of his ruddy face that he caught a glimpse of that wall of green, just barely visible through the haze of the Wastes. And it made him heartsick.

❧

Once their suitcases were unpacked and their belongings stowed in the little gray lockers that sat at the foot of each of the beds, there wasn't much for Elsie and Rachel to do. Initially, Elsie was chagrined to watch Rachel wait for her to pick a bed in the giant dormitory room and then pick a bed for herself as far from Elsie's as possible. This caused Elsie to sit on her bed with her knees to her chest and whimper quiet sobs until Rachel had grabbed her green duffel and marched back to the bed adjacent Elsie's. Several hours passed; they barely spoke three words to each other. Occasionally, an ancient-looking loudspeaker above the dormitory's door would squawk some unintelligible babble, and the two girls would start at the noise.

"What's it saying?" Elsie asked her big sister.

"I don't know," replied Rachel.

After a time, Rachel lay back on her bed and, tucking the thin pillow behind her head, listened to her iPod through little white earbuds. Elsie knelt at her bedside and made a volcano-topped island out of the blue blanket for Intrepid Tina to explore; the tinny distant sound of crash cymbals, struck repeatedly, issued from Rachel's headphones. This was their joint activity for nearly an hour until Elsie, bored, reached over and tugged on Rachel's pant leg.

Rachel popped one headphone out. Music blared. "What's up?"

"Where are all the kids?" asked Elsie.

"Dunno." The headphone went back in.

Elsie tugged at her sister's hem again. Rachel rolled her eyes and pulled the headphone out. "What?" she asked, clearly annoyed.

"I mean, isn't it weird that we're here all alone? I thought this was, you know, an orphanage." Elsie looked around the dormitory.

"Where are all the orphans?"

"Just us orphans," said Rachel caustically.

Elsie stuck out a lip. "I'm not an orphan."

"Whatever. You're kidding yourself if you think Mom and Dad are coming back. They're gone."

"Don't say that."

"Curtis left, and after they were all sad at first, they were, like, hey: This is pretty cool, not having so many kids. So they ditched us. Easy as that." She pressed the white bud back into her ear; she slapped her hands against her knees to the barely audible drumbeat.

Elsie glowered. Without thinking, she leapt up and grabbed the headphones from Rachel's ears and yanked the silver iPod out of her hoodie pocket. It clattered to the floor, and Rachel yelled.

"Take that back," howled Elsie.

"You're crazy!" yelled Rachel. "What's wrong with you?"

"You take that back about Mom and Dad." Elsie reached up and grabbed a handful of her sister's black hair and tugged, eliciting a yelping scream. Rachel was about to retaliate with a strong punch to Elsie's shoulder when the speaker above the door whistled into life. A string of abstract barks preceded the only five words the two girls could make out:

"NO AGGRESSION IN THE DORMITORY!"

The sisters froze. Elsie let Rachel's hair fall from her fingers. Rachel dropped her arm to her side. They both stared at the loudspeaker. It crackled a few times, ominously, before falling silent. Elsie edged over to her bed; she grabbed Intrepid Tina and pulled her to her chest. Rachel, in a clear spirit of defiance, walked over to the doors and stood beneath the loudspeaker, studying it. She looked around the room, marking the four corners where the walls met the ceiling.

"What are you doing?" whispered Elsie.

"Looking for cameras," said Rachel. "How else can they know what we're doing?" She tried the handle of the door and found it was unlocked. She peeked her head into the hallway beyond before turning and gesturing to Elsie. "Come on," she said. "It's clear. Let's explore."

As they toed quietly onto the linoleum checkerboard of the hallway, Elsie hissed to her sister, "Did you see any cameras?"

"Can't tell. If there are, they're super secret."

The hallway was quiet and dimly lit by a line of grim fluorescent lights on the ceiling. To their left was the stairway down to the first floor; to their right, the hallway ended in a closed door. They listened intently for footsteps. When none came, Elsie followed her older sister as she walked toward the door to their right. She held Intrepid Tina pressed tightly to her chest. The door opened with a loud creak and revealed a set of wooden stairs leading up. Taking them, the sisters found themselves in a vast attic room decorated similarly to their dormitory: a matrix of perhaps thirty beds occupied the wooden floor. The ceiling of the room followed the contours of the building's roof, all angles and low overhangs. Dangling lightbulbs, contained in small metal cages, hung from a central beam and provided what little light there was. A chill pervaded the room. The threshold of the entryway had a sign hanging down that read HERREN. Elsie pointed to it. "What does that mean?" she whispered.

"Boys," responded Rachel, "I think. Or girls. One of the two. I get them mixed up."

"It must mean boys," Elsie puzzled out, "because we were put downstairs. And we're girls. So this must be the boys' dorm."

"Way to go, Sherlock," said Rachel.

"Thanks," said Elsie, missing the sarcasm.

A noise startled them. It was a metallic clanking, coming from the far end of the room. They walked toward the sound, Rachel in the lead, Elsie following close behind. They arrived shortly at the noise's source: a metal grate covering an air duct in the floor behind the farthest bed. The clanking, intermittent and distant, was being amplified through the vent from some other place in the building. Listening closer, Elsie could tell that it was actually many smaller metallic noises, sounding in chaotic syncopation. It creeped her out. She squeezed Intrepid Tina; she wished they'd never left the other dormitory. And so she was relieved to hear her sister whisper over her shoulder, "C'mon."

They padded back down the stairs to the hallway they'd left, and Elsie, on seeing the door to their dorm, began walking more quickly. Rachel stopped her. "Where are you going?" she whispered.

"Back in here," said Elsie, pointing to the girls' dormitory. A sign reading DAMEN was affixed to the jamb.

"I thought we were exploring. What about that noise?"

"Rachel!" pleaded Elsie. "I don't care about the noise. I just want to . . . I just want to . . ."

"To sit and wait for Mom and Dad to come home? You've got a long wait, Els."

Elsie folded her arms across her chest.

"C'mon," said her sister, smiling beneath her wiry hair. "What would Intrepid Tina do?"

The green commercial carpet of the staircase's runner was deeply worn in the middle, and the wooden steps creaked at the girls' every footfall. Rachel moved ahead of Elsie to the landing where the stairs took a 180-degree turn; arriving there, she directed her sister to freeze with an urgent wave of her hand. A woman was speaking on the floor below. Her tone was firm and castigating. Elsie joined her sister, pressed against the banister at the landing, and listened.

"Edward," the woman said. This was undoubtedly Miss Mudrak. Her accent was as thick as a particularly chunky borscht. "You finishing just now? It is almost end bell."

"Sorry, ma'am," replied a boy's voice. Elsie assumed it to be the boy she'd met mopping. "I'll be quicker next time, promise."

"You will, or back to the shop for you."

"Yes, ma'am."

The sound of a large door opening and swinging shut interrupted the conversation. Then: footsteps on the ancient boards of the downstairs hallway. Elsie and Rachel heard Desdemona usher the boy Edward away. She spoke now to the person who'd just arrived. "Darling, you seem to me exhausted."

The man's voice was weary; he needn't have said a word to affirm Desdemona's assessment. "Long day," he said. "Don't even ask me about it."

"And you spoke to Mr. Vigman?"

"Well, honey," said the defeated-sounding man, "Mr. Vigman didn't really want to talk. Let's put it that way."

"Joffrey, Joffrey." Elsie and Rachel made eye contact; this had to be the proprietor of the orphanage himself. Desdemona continued, "Please. You must relax. Let me take your coat." A rustling of noise, a large coat being draped on an obliging hook. "But you mentioned to him the film, yes?"

There was a pause. "Oh, the film," said Joffrey. "No, I didn't."

"But darling, if we are to make this change in life, we must be . . . we must be . . . preactive?"

"Proactive, Desdemona," said Joffrey. "The word is proactive. And I'm being as proactive as I can."

The voices moved down the hall, forcing the Mehlberg sisters to edge their way along the banister toward the bottom flight of stairs. Elsie, peering between the railing posts, could see the two adults, Desdemona and Joffrey, making their way slowly to a large door at the far end of the hall. Desdemona's long arm was stretched over Joffrey's bowed shoulders; he was easily six inches shorter than his companion.

"And what of the visa?" asked Desdemona. "When can we procure?"

"Visa?"

"For Bozhek."

"Oh, right, Bozhek. The esteemed auteur. Tell me again: Why can't he get one himself?"

Desdemona's voice dripped like cherry syrup. "Darling, really. You remember. He make art film and drop a bucket of glow paint on Liberty Statue. It is most beautiful; he is deported. But it is America's loss; he is great artist. He is Ukrainian Spielverg."

"Oh. Right."

"You said you would approach Mr. Vigman about this. He has pull at immigration office."

"I did, yes. It's on my list."

They arrived at the door. Following, Elsie and Rachel found

themselves on the bottom step of the staircase. They watched, partly concealed by the banister, as Joffrey fished his hand into his pants pocket and procured a large key chain. Selecting one of the keys, he undid the lock on the door and opened it. Elsie could just make out the room beyond: it was an officelike chamber, lined with ceiling-tall shelves. Strangely, there were few books on these shelves; rather, they were filled with odd-sized jars and receptacles of multicolored liquids and powders. The couple faced each other in the doorway.

"On your list," repeated Desdemona, clearly unimpressed. "Darling, this is your chance. Put this machine parts thing behind you. Become your dream of childhood: producer of movies. Yes? This is prize to keep eye on, yes?"

"Yes, Desdemona," said Joffrey.

"Who needs Titan of business? Be Titan of movies!"

"Yes, Desdemona."

"So you will speak to Mr. Vigman?"

"Yes, I'll speak to Mr. Vig—Mr. Wigman."

"And you will procure visa?"

"Yes, I will."

"Give me kiss, my little *kapusta*."

The man did as he was instructed. Desdemona patted him affectionately on the cheek when she pulled away. "Now you have to work to do, yes?"

"Yes. Closer every day."

Miss Mudrak paused as she turned from her partner. "Did not last tincture work?"

"No, it did not," said Joffrey. "It didn't work at all."

"Oh," said Desdemona. "A shame. And the specimen?"

"Gone."

Another pause. "Oh. A shame. Well, get back on the chicken, Joffrey love."

"Yes," said Joffrey, turning and walking into the room with the bookshelves. "Back on the chicken." The door closed behind him.

Elsie and Rachel froze as Desdemona turned toward them and began walking down the hall; they'd been so rapt listening to the two adults' conversation that they'd neglected to plan their escape. If they made any sudden movement now, they'd undoubtedly be detected—and yet it seemed that Miss Mudrak was heading directly toward them. Elsie didn't have a sense of what sort of punishment was handed down in the orphanage for eavesdropping, but she guessed it would be fairly severe. She could feel her sister tense behind her. "Rachel," hissed Elsie, "what should we—"

The last word of this sentence was rendered unintelligible; a very loud bell suddenly sounded, and the hallway was full of its metallic clanging. Elsie and Rachel could see it; the bell was installed high on the wall in the middle of the hallway. Even Desdemona started at the noise. It rang for what seemed like an interminable amount of time, and Miss Mudrak stood looking at it with her hands planted on her hips, as if willing it to stop. While she was thus distracted, the sisters Mehlberg managed to make their escape, dashing up the staircase and back into the girls' dormitory.

They barely had time to climb onto their beds and act inconspicuous (Elsie with her Intrepid Tina doll back atop the blanket mountain; Rachel with earbuds firmly in place) before a rhythmic tramping startled them: It was the sound of a multitude of feet pounding up the stairs. The dormitory doors flew open, and in walked a congregation of haggard young girls, their hair disheveled and their faces marred with black streaks of grease. They varied in age—some looked to be younger than Elsie, while the oldest were clearly teenaged—but they all had the carriage of weathered adults: Their shoulders sagged, and their brows hung over sallow faces. They all wore identical gray jumpsuits, which were similarly streaked with grease marks, and their hands were soot black. They paid no attention to the two new occupants in the dormitory, but rather marched straight to their respective beds and sat down heavily; they each carried little metal lunch boxes, which they slid underneath their bed frames. Several lay down, fully clothed, and appeared to fall immediately to sleep. Some sat with their heads in their hands. Others spoke in hushed tones to their neighbors. The footsteps in the hallway continued unabated; Elsie could see a long line of boys, dressed in the same kind of coveralls, file past the doors toward their upstairs dorm. Rachel and Elsie shared a look; it felt like the room had been invaded by ghosts.

"Psst."

The hiss had come from the bed next to Elsie's; an Asian girl, Elsie's age, was pushing a pair of plastic safety goggles from off her eyes to rest on her forehead, leaving a pale strip where the pitch-black grease hadn't reached. Her hair was slightly matted from sweat and bunched beneath the elastic straps of the goggles. "What's your name?" asked the girl.

"Elsie." She instinctively offered a handshake. The girl smiled and shook her head, holding her hands up: There wasn't an inch of clean skin on them. Elsie withdrew her hand.

"I'm Martha. Martha Song." Her voice was tired, but assured. "Welcome to the factory."

"You mean the orphanage?"

Martha laughed. "Oh, right. I forget they call it that, too."

"Are you one of the orphans?" asked Elsie, puzzled.

"Orphan? Ha. Ain't no adoptions happening here."

"Really? But I thought—"

The loudspeaker above the doors barked into life: "BZZT CHVVVK XZZZT SILENCE IN THE DORMITORY."

The girls complied; a hush fell over the room. After a short squall of feedback, the noise from the loudspeaker continued, but this time a new voice had taken over. It was Desdemona: "Attention to girls' dormitory: We have today new members. Meet Rachel and Elsie Mehlverg. Beds twenty-three and twenty-four." A loud click sounded, and the speaker fell silent.

Everyone's eyes fell on Rachel and Elsie. Rachel scowled beneath her hair; she fiddled with her earbuds nervously.

The click came again. Another squeal of feedback. "Please give them best of Unthank Home welcome." *Click*. Silence.

Elsie looked around her. The surrounding crowd of girls gave them both a feeble, exhausted wave.

The loudspeaker howled into life again. "It is brought to attention that quarter yield in shop must improve. As of tomorrow, we must reinstall extended hours."

A collective groan greeted this announcement.

"And now some words from your host, Mr. Joffrey Unthank."

The girls waited; the quiet extended into the room. Elsie felt a tug on her shirtsleeve. It was Martha. "Hey," she whispered conspiratorially. "You should tell your sister to knock it off with the headphones during announcements. That's an Unadoptable offense, for sure."

Elsie looked at her, confused. A click came from the loudspeaker, threatening another burst of information. Before it began, Elsie managed to grab the headphones from Rachel's ears. "We're supposed to listen," she hissed. Rachel glared but complied with her sister's instruction.

The voice from the loudspeaker was now distinctly male. "Hello, boys and girls," it said. "Residents of the Unthank Home, I understand you are looking forward to a moment of rest. And I understand how distressing it must sound to have your hours extended again. However: I ask you to remember all the good men and women—all those potential fathers and mothers—who are relying on your labor for all the machines of convenience on which their lives depend. Without you, dear children, there would be no washing machines, no alternator assemblies, no digital watches or electric fresh pasta makers. The very things that make our society work. The more convenience we allow into citizens' lives, the more they are able to consider the idea of caring for children."

A click. The voice paused; it seemed to Elsie that his line of reasoning required a good deal of careful thought.

"And the more these citizens consider the idea of caring for children, the likelier it is that you, boys and girls, will find a place in a comfortable, warm home with a caring family, a family surrounded by every amenity that modern life can afford. And now, before you're given clearance for showers and supper, I'd like to ask that you put as much spirit into the Recitation as you can muster. The childless mothers and fathers of America are relying on you."

The dormitory girls straightened their backs and spoke as they were prompted by the faceless voice, repeating each line back to the gray-green loudspeaker.

> *"MACHINE PARTS MAKE MACHINES.*
> *MACHINES MAKE CONVENIENCE.*
> *CONVENIENCE IS FREEDOM.*

FREEDOM IS FAMILY."

"Very good, children," said the voice gently. "I will speak again with you tomorrow."

The loud click, the disengaging of a handset, sounded. It was followed by the brusque voice Elsie and Rachel had heard earlier—robotic and terse.

"BXXG ZZZGT STRIP AND BATHE. SUPPER AT EIGHTEEN HUNDRED HOURS."

A burst of energy filled the room as the girls in the dormitory shed their soiled jumpsuits, revealing identical red woolens beneath, and dashed toward a door at the other end of the room, presumably leading to the bathrooms and showers. Elsie and Rachel sat in shock. In a few short moments, the large room was emptied of its occupants and a noisy commotion could be heard echoing from within the tiled walls of the bathroom. At that moment, a figure entered the room and approached the two Mehlberg girls. He was an old man, dressed in the requisite gray coverall, and he was carrying what looked to be two packages, wrapped in transparent plastic. Arriving at the girls' beds, he wordlessly dropped the packages at their feet; he then abruptly turned and walked, stooped and crooked, from the room. Elsie watched as Rachel picked up the package and tore into the plastic. Inside, neatly folded, were two items of clothing: a starched gray jumpsuit and a pair of red long underwear.

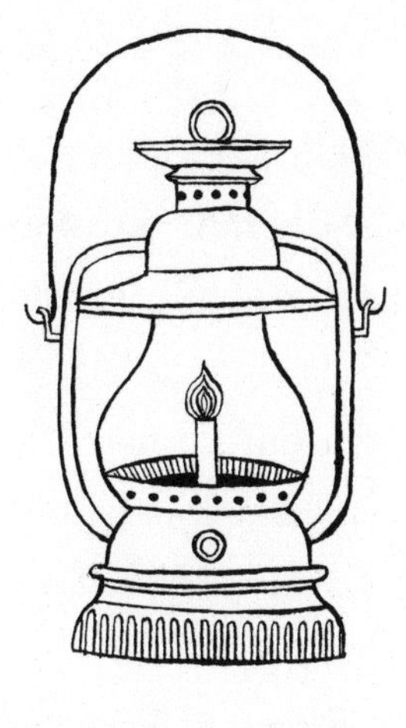

CHAPTER 7

Return to Wildwood

Prue was still in shock by the time the heron wove through the deep, snow-shrouded canopy of the trees and touched down on the forest floor. She'd barely uttered five words to Curtis, whose midsection she'd hugged tightly during the flight. They'd flown high enough to break through the low-hanging clouds, and she'd been awed to see the pinpricks of stars shining through the darkness of the night sky. But her heart was frozen; the attack had left her numbed, and her mind was spinning with unanswered questions. Why had she been targeted? Who was Ms. Thennis, after all? And more important, how was she ever going to explain another disappearance to her parents? The heron's breathing was labored as its two riders dismounted; Curtis turned to Prue and thrust out his hand.

"Hey, partner," he said.

It was the first time Prue had been able to smile since the scuffle in the street. She and Curtis shared a handshake that collapsed into a long hug. Pulling apart, Prue searched her friend's eyes. "What's going on, Curtis?"

The other heron had deposited Brendan near them; they were standing in a snowy glade, surrounded by tall fir trees. A little moonlight was peering through the shifting clouds, dappling the white snow opalescent. The Bandit King approached Prue and set his hand on her shoulder. His red beard was flecked with frost.

"For your safety," he said, "you've got to stay with us."

"Who . . . what was that thing?" Prue asked.

"A shape-shifter," explained Curtis. "This is all going to sound totally crazy. It was sent to kill you, Prue."

"By who?"

Brendan spoke. "We don't know. Important thing is you're kept hidden. We gave that thing a good thrashing, but I don't expect it to stay away long."

"But what about Ms. Thennis? What happened to her?"

Curtis and Brendan shared a look. "I don't think Ms. Thennis really exists," said Curtis. "She's a Kitsune—a black fox who can take the form of a human."

Prue absently massaged the nape of her neck, thinking back on the previous few weeks: Mrs. Estevez's resignation, the sudden arrival of her fresh-faced replacement, Ms. Thennis, at the school, the dirt beneath the teacher's fingernails after she'd found Prue on the bluff. In the face of these strange events, "Why?" was all Prue could manage.

"Too much to tell," said Curtis. "Let's get to somewhere warm."

Bidding farewell to the exhausted herons, the three travelers marched beyond the clearing's looming underbrush. Curtis and Prue followed Brendan closely as he wove his way through the dense knot of trees; as they walked, Prue peppered her companions with questions.

"Your family should be safe," responded Brendan to one of Prue's most urgent queries. "We're told that Kitsunes, while being vicious, deadly creatures, rarely waver from their mark. She was after you, not your parents or your brother." Prue imagined her mother and father watching the lentil curry simmer on the stove, fretfully eyeing the clock. They'd have guessed her disappearance by now.

"I'll need to let them know I'm safe," said Prue.

"It's done," said Curtis, lifting the dangling boughs of a vining maple so that Prue could walk underneath. "Owl said he'd take care of it; he promised to send a messenger."

"Oh, that'll be just great," said Prue, envisioning her mother's surprise to have a starling alight on her knee and explain to her that her missing daughter was okay, she'd just been abducted by bandits and taken back into the Impassable Wilderness. "But I guess nothing my family isn't kind of accustomed to by now."

"Exactly," said Curtis. "Weirdness abounds in the McKeel family."

A massive cedar bridged the gap of a narrow defile in the landscape, and the trio carefully walked across the tree's snowy bark to arrive at the other side; a rushing creek babbled below. "So where are we going now?" asked Prue.

"To the camp," replied Brendan. "You'll be safe there."

"And what then?"

"We wait them out."

Curtis jumped in: "Maybe you could get in on some bandit training!"

Brendan grumbled. "It mayn't be safe for her to venture past the boundary of the camp. In fact, it might not be safe for any of us."

"Right," said Curtis. "That was another thing the wolf said: that the Kitsunes might be targeting all the important people in the—what do you call it?—Bicycle Coup."

"The Bicycle Coup?" asked Prue, nonplussed.

"Yeah, you missed that bit, the naming," said Curtis. "That's what they called the overthrow of all the South Wood government when—after the plinth—we freed the birds and got Lars Svik out of the Mansion. I didn't think much of it at the time, but I guess a lot of people are really attached to the whole thing—the bicycle and all. They call you the Bicycle Maiden, supposedly."

"The Bicycle Maiden," Prue repeated quietly, trying out the words. The label seemed pretty appealing, actually. Suddenly, a thought occurred to her. "Wait a second. If these shape-shifters are after people who were part of the coup, what about Iphigenia? And Owl? Won't they be targeted too?"

"Aye, perhaps," said Brendan. "We don't know the details of these assassins'—or their masters'—intents. We don't rightly know if there's more than just the one. Maybe they're after everyone. Maybe they're just after you! In any case, we've been tasked to keep you safe, Prue, since there weren't nothing to guard you in the Outside."

They walked in single file along a game trail that seemed to Prue indistinguishable from the wild forest floor; Curtis told her everything the wolf, Corporal Donalbain, had reported at the clandestine meeting in North Wood: the patriotism surrounding the Coup, the rise of the Synod, the marginalization of the interim government, the deprivations brought on by the unrest and the harsh winter. It was enough to make Prue's head spin.

"I can't believe how much has changed in only a few short months!" exclaimed Prue as they skirted the boundary of a grassy meadow. "I mean, what happened? They're getting it all wrong!" She abruptly stopped and planted her hands on her hips. "Why don't we just go down there—I mean, I'm the Bicycle Maiden, after all. Can't we just go march into South Wood, to the Mansion, and just get things going again?"

"Not safe, Prue," said Brendan. "Our instructions are to keep you away from the watching eyes of whoever is trying to have you done in. Come on, let's keep moving. We're nearly there."

Within fifteen paces, they arrived at a dense tangle of high salal bushes, which created something of a wall that seemed to extend in either direction endlessly. Brendan paused and studied it. "This is fairly new," he explained. "Still getting used to . . . Where . . . aha!" Tucked inconspicuously within the hedge's greenery was a weblike piece of fabric that Brendan pulled aside to reveal a passageway. Prue walked in first and ducked low to avoid the low-hanging tendrils of leaves that batted at her hair. Clearing the massive hedgerow, she suddenly felt the ground slip away beneath her. She yelped and scrambled backward. The moon had disappeared behind a cloud, and the ground before her was veiled in blackness. Brendan appeared, carrying a lit torch. "Careful there," he cautioned. "Watch your feet." The Bandit King swept the torch out before them, and Prue saw that she was standing at the edge of a rocky cliff.

"Where are we?" she exclaimed.

"The Long Gap," said Brendan. "Our new home." Handing the torch to Curtis, he reached behind a nearby rock and produced a large spool of rope that had been hidden there. Giving a quick, shrill whistle, he tossed the rope over the edge, where Prue heard it patter against the cliff wall. He then looped an oxbow of the rope through a metal ring attached to his leather belt and tried the strength of the line; it held firm, anchored at the base of a large tree. He gestured to Prue. "Climb on," he said. Prue threw her arms around Brendan's neck and felt her stomach plunge as he began descending, backward, down the cliff face. The rope supported them; he fed it from his gloved hands as he easily walked his way downward. Prue nuzzled her face into his shoulder, her eyes shut tight; the bandit smelled of sweat and evergreen needles.

After a time, as the mouth of the giant cleft swallowed the cloudy sky above them, the two rappellers alighted on a wooden platform that was affixed to the cliff wall. A small red lantern provided a dim light. Brendan set Prue down gently and then gave two hard tugs to the rope. Prue looked around her, getting her bearings. The bottom of the rocky fissure was still obscured by impenetrable dark. Leading from the platform was a rope bridge, which crossed into the darkness. A few flickering lights could be seen in the distance, like a swarm of fireflies. Curtis joined them shortly on the platform; he detached the rope from a figure-eight clasp at his belt. Prue looked at him with amazement. "Where'd you learn to do that?"

"Rappelling," he said, smiling. "Third period."

A whistle sounded from across the chasm; Prue could see someone on the other side of the rope bridge swinging a lantern. Brendan

whistled twice, quickly, and the three travelers began crossing. The wind whipped through the gorge; the bridge bowed and shivered as they reached the midway point. Prue, her hands fixed tightly to the rope that served as the handrail, concentrated all her powers on not looking down. Arriving at a platform on the far side, they were greeted by a bandit.

"Eamon," said Brendan.

"King," replied the bandit.

Prue now recognized what had been those elusive, dancing lights she'd seen from the other side of the bridge: All along the steep, jagged wall, lanterns dotted the cliff face, illuminating deep recesses in the rock where crude structures had been built of knobby tree limbs—door frames and vestibules, covered here and there by deerhide flaps. More rope bridges could now be seen, linking these many cave openings together—several crisscrossed the gap farther along, where other lanterns could be seen shining; wooden steps led down deeper into the chasm, and Prue saw that this dizzying constellation of lantern light continued on downward beyond the range of her vision. Having heard their whistle, faces began appearing from within the fissures in the stone—the hardened faces of the bandits could be seen peering down at the newly arrived travelers.

"You moved," was all Prue could manage to say.

"Yeah," replied Brendan. "We change hideouts when the assembly determines that the camp ain't safe. We'd been compromised by the coyotes; we had no choice but to move." He stood on the platform and proudly surveyed the entire camp, extending out as it did in all directions along the cliff wall. "It was a doozy to set up, but I think we'll be able to stay here a while."

Prue looked over the edge, trying to make out the farthest lights and the cave entrances they illuminated. Beyond was total blackness. "How far does it go down?" she asked.

"No one knows," said Brendan. "We found some sign of ancient settlers, cliff dwellers, farther below, but the way gets harder beyond that. So don't be droppin' anything you might value, 'cause you won't see it come back."

A rickety wooden staircase led farther down the face of the wall to what looked to be a launching area of some kind: a long platform that extended out into the chasm, surrounded by a wooden handrail. At one end of the platform, a hole had been routed to allow a gnarled tree that had grown out of the cliff face through the planking; the stout tree anchored a cable that bowed out into the distant dark. Attached to the cable was a wheeled pulley assembly, which in turn supported the weight of a large box, big enough to support four or five people. Brendan waved the way forward, and Prue gingerly climbed in. "Hold on," instructed Brendan as he and Curtis climbed into the box beside her. Curtis undid a line that was holding the box in place and the vehicle took off, zipping down the cable past a dazzling array of lantern-lit hovels and cave entrances, platforms and walkways.

The box stopped sharply at a lower platform. As another bandit attendant greeted them, Prue could see beyond to a massive opening in the cliff face, where throngs of colorfully clad bandits gathered around a large fire pit; the smell of cooked venison hovered in the air. As soon as Prue arrived on the stone floor of the cave, everyone's attention immediately swiveled to the new arrival.

"Prue!" one said.

"The Outsider girl!" said another.

Brendan swiftly allayed their curiosity. "Fellow bandits: Please welcome back to the camp our friend and ally, Prue McKeel. We've been asked to give her asylum; her life is in great danger."

There followed a murmur of consent. Prue heard someone mumble something about another mouth to feed, but the voice was quickly shushed. One voice rang out above the rest: "What's the danger?"

Brendan addressed the assembled bandits, telling them everything he'd been told; he explained in detail their desperate flight from North Wood, the skirmish on the street in the Outside. After the story, a hush fell over the crowd; more bandits had arrived, and Prue could see the dirty faces of young children peering at her from behind their parents' legs. Finally, one bandit stepped forward. He was a younger man, dressed in a kind of ratty sashed coat; Prue didn't recognize him. She guessed that they'd needed to recruit a whole host of new bandits since the war with the Governess.

"But Brendan," he asked haltingly, "what if it comes for us?"

Another voice chimed in, a woman's voice. "Yeah," she said. "We've only just got settled here. Will we have to move again?"

"It ain't going to come for us," said Brendan. "It won't even come close. This is the best-hidden camp we've had in a generation. I don't expect to leave it till the babies born here are old. But if it makes everyone more at ease, we'll post extra watches—tighten security. Even if a Kitsune does get in here, it won't survive the fight. Clear?"

A litany of "ayes."

The Bandit King continued, "To many of you, this may be just another body to feed and clothe. That's a reasonable concern. I know the stores are thin. I know the robbing ain't bringin' in what it should. But we're a strong band, and we've weathered worse. My great-grandfather, Ben, survived the Bandit Wars with his people eatin' naught but grass and moss tufts and still came out the victor. We're made of that stock. We can weather this."

The crowd talked among themselves; after a time, consensus was reached: Prue could stay. She smiled warmly at the crowd. "Thanks, everyone," she managed, though her voice was hoarse with exhaustion; it'd been a very long day. Curtis guessed as much and nudged his friend with his elbow. "C'mon," he said, "I'll take you to the trainee barracks."

The two friends bid their good nights. They followed a wooden walkway that snaked along the cliff wall away from the common area; Curtis carried a red lantern, lighting the way. Prue studied him as they walked, a dusty halo from the lit wick revealing a Curtis she didn't think she recognized from before. His face looked longer, older. It seemed to her that his shoulders filled out the raggedy uniform he was wearing in a way she hadn't remembered. The left lens of his wire-framed glasses had a hairline crack in it, just at the nose. The eyes behind them seemed somehow more worldly.

He noticed her looking. "What's up?" he asked, smiling embarrassedly.

"Oh, I don't know," said Prue. "You look changed, is all."

"Well, I am a Greenhorn Bandit, first class."

She laughed at the terminology. "Oh, Curtis. Who knew this was how you'd end up?"

"It's where I belong, Prue. This is my life now."

A rope bridge split off from the walkway, leading across the gap. They followed it.

"What about your parents? Your sisters?"

"They're fine. I convinced a migrating crane to do a flyby recently, just to see how things are. He sent word that he saw them packing bags for what looked like a vacation or something. So I think they're getting along just fine without me."

Prue nodded, placated, though she sensed that her friend was not entirely convinced of his own story. "Think you'll ever tell them?"

"I dunno," replied Curtis. "Maybe someday. It's complicated. I wouldn't want them to try coming in here to find me; they'd get lost in the Periphery."

"Though you're a half-breed," suggested Prue as she stepped off the rope bridge and followed Curtis down another wood-plank staircase. "Like me. Wouldn't that mean that your parents can cross over?"

"Who knows where that blood comes from?" said Curtis. "Maybe one has it, not the other." He thought for a moment. "I suppose my sisters are probably half-breeds, huh?"

They arrived at the end of the staircase. Another wooden promontory stretched out into the chasm. A wire, looped around the top of a tall post, disappeared into the blankness before them; a flickering campfire could be seen in the distance. Curtis put his fingers to his lips and gave a shrill whistle. Within moments, a noise could be heard, the sound of something sliding along metal. A wooden cross, fixed with copper wire to a pulley assembly, came down the zip line and loudly thunked against the pole. Curtis grabbed it. "You want to go first?" he asked.

"Okay," Prue said, with some trepidation. She positioned her hands along the wooden handle.

"Just hold tight," instructed Curtis.

"You think?" said Prue, laughing. "Listen, I'm a natural-born bandit. Maybe I can teach you a thing or two." And with that, she lifted her feet from the ground and was carried at a breathtaking pace across the Long Gap. The wide rift's cool wind whisked up and bit at her face and hands; she could feel her face flush from the cold. Once the initial fear had fallen away, she found herself smiling so widely that her cheeks hurt.

It seemed to Elsie that she'd barely closed her eyes, barely drifted into a half sleep, when an alarm bell rang loudly in the dormitory, followed by a renewed round of distorted barking from the loudspeaker: "MORNING BELL! AEROBIC REGIMEN, COMMENCE!" Immediately, the room was filled with the complaining voices of sleepy girls and the cumulative rustle of thirty woolen blankets being thrown aside. Elsie followed suit; she noticed that not only had Rachel managed to ignore the command from the loudspeaker, but she also seemed to have slept through it. Elsie whispered loudly to her sister, "Rachel! Wake up!" There was no response.

A short, aged woman in a gray housedress entered through the double doors. Using a long wooden dowel, the woman pulled down a white screen that hung on the east wall. She then walked to the far side of the room and removed a shroud from a short pedestal, revealing an ancient-looking Super 8 projector. She turned it on, and a shivering ray of light fell on the screen, showing grainy black-and-white footage of a woman in a leotard. The film looked very, very old. As the figure in the film began to move, so did the girls in the dormitory, imitating the woman's every action. Elsie did likewise: The woman touched her toes, so did Elsie. The woman executed a series

of jumping jacks, so did Elsie. This routine lasted about ten minutes, with the wooden floor of the dormitory vibrating with every shift and jump of the roomful of girls. Rachel managed to stay sleeping. Between activities, Elsie tried to wake her by kicking one of the legs of her sister's bed frame, to no avail. Finally, the program came to an end and the projector shut off with a series of noisy clacks. The loudspeaker sparked afresh: "BED TWENTY-THREE."

No response. Elsie shuffled over to the bed and discreetly kicked the frame again. "Rachel!" she whispered.

"Hmmph?" answered Rachel, her face burrowed into her pillow.

"BED TWENTY-THREE! RISE IMMEDIATELY!"

Rachel's hand snaked out from beneath her thin blanket and began feeling around the side of the bed, presumably for the nonexistent alarm clock. "Mom!" she mumbled. "Ten more minutes." This elicited a chorus of giggles from the surrounding girls.

"MISS TALBOT?" squawked the loudspeaker.

The gray-haired woman who'd been manning the projector tottered over to bed twenty-three and, taking a deep breath, lifted the metal bed frame, spilling Rachel's dormant body onto the hard wood of the floor. Rachel scrambled to her feet, trying to reorient herself to her bizarre reality. The girls around her had ceased their giggling and were looking at their feet.

"MORNING REPAST, OH SEVEN HUNDRED HOURS. THEN ALL WORK CREWS REPORT TO MACHINE SHOP."

An army of compliant souls, the girls in the dormitory began slipping their grease-marked gray coveralls over their woolen long johns. Some spoke in hushed tones to their neighbors; others prepared for their day in silence. Rachel and Elsie watched in awe, unmoving, until Martha kicked at Elsie's footie'd foot. "Get your work clothes on," she hissed.

"What, these?" asked Elsie, pointing to the coveralls she'd been given the night before; they were still shrouded in their plastic wrapping.

Martha rolled her eyes. "Yes," she said, before adding, "Do I have to hold your hand through all this?"

An older girl, sitting on the bed next to Martha's, spoke up out of the side of her mouth as she carefully laced a pair of black steel-toe boots. "Bein' awfully charitable with the newbs, eh, Martha?"

"I'm a gracious person," said Martha snidely.

"Are we supposed to go to work, too?" Elsie asked.

The girl in the boots stifled a laugh.

Martha: "Yes, you're supposed to work. We're all supposed to work."

Elsie cast her eyes around the room, perplexed. "But I've never really worked before. I mean, I help out with chores around the house and stuff. But I've never been to, like, a job."

"Well, welcome to the working week," said Martha.

Rachel, still half-asleep, was taking this all in wordlessly. "Hey, goggles," she said finally.

Martha gave her a look.

"I don't know who's told you what, but we're only here for a couple weeks. We're not officially 'orphans.'" Here, she made air quotes with her fingers. "So I don't think we're going to be doing any work, thanks very much. 'Specially not in a machine shop."

"That's what they all say." This came from the girl next to Martha, who'd just finished stringing the last eye of her boot.

"That's what who say?" asked Rachel.

"Newbs. Newbies. Newcomers. They're all like: 'I'm not going to work; my parents are coming for me any day.' Or: 'I might get adopted today! I'm not going to muck around in some machine shop.' It's all the same. You'll break. Trust me, you'll break." The girl's voice seemed to have been long hollowed out, like a dead log.

"Or what?" challenged Rachel. "What if I refuse? There's, like, laws against this stuff."

Martha chimed in, "You'll get a demerit."

Rachel laughed. "Oh no! A demerit?" She held the back of her hand to her forehead, feigning horror. "What'll I do then?"

"What's a demerit?" whispered Elsie.

Martha ignored the younger sister, focusing her increasing annoyance on Rachel. "Well, you chalk up enough of 'em, and you're Unadoptable."

"Una-what?" asked Rachel, her hand falling from her face.

"Unadoptable. You know, like you. And no adoption," answered the girl.

"But what does that even mean? I'm not an orphan! I'm not even up for adoption!" Rachel had abandoned her snarky tone and was instead beginning to sound genuinely upset.

"Everyone is an orphan, here," said Martha. "It's not like anyone ever comes for us. But if you're Unadoptable, then you're sent to the Mister's study. And then we never see you again."

Elsie stammered, "R-really? Never?"

"Never," said Martha.

Rachel, still shaking the sleep from her head, looked back and forth between the two younger girls. "That's ridiculous," she said. "They can't do that. We're just boarding here. Mom and Dad are coming back in two weeks."

"You said they weren't, Rach, before," offered Elsie.

Rachel shot her sister a glare. "I was joking. That's not for real. Of course they're coming back."

Martha began slipping into her gray coveralls. She wiped some grease from the lens of her goggles and slid them over her hair. "Hey, then you're fine," she said, sounding indifferent to the sisters' plight. "Just don't rack up any demerits."

Rachel's temper was growing. Her face was turning the shade of a ripe, late summer tomato. Elsie had seen this happen before—a similar hue had risen to her sister's cheeks in the wake of her mother sneaking into her room to throw away all her black lipstick; Elsie cradled Tina close to her chest, as if protecting her from the inevitable explosion.

"They . . . can't . . . do . . . this," said Rachel, enunciating every word, each one louder than the last, until she capped the phrase at the top of her lungs with: "We're . . . Americans!" With that final declaration, she marched toward the front of the room. Her red woolens were a size too big, and she had to hike up the leggings as she walked. Positioning herself below the loudspeaker, she addressed the disembodied voice angrily.

"Hello?" she called. "I'm a, you know, temporary resident here. My sister and me. We don't belong to the orphanage. And we're not going to be working in any machine shop."

No response.

"And for the record, I don't think kids are being treated properly here. I don't think it's legal to make kids work in a factory. I'm pretty sure."

Still, silence.

"This is not fair. I'd like to get a phone call or something?"

A pair of girls could be heard whispering discreetly in the back of the dormitory.

"Okay, then," Rachel said, stepping up her air of defiance. "How about this: I refuse to work at your stupid machine shop." Then she stuck out her tongue and walked proudly back to her bed. Everyone in the room was watching her silently. Martha had frozen in place, her hands still on the goggles at her forehead. At a loss for what to say, Elsie pushed the button on Intrepid Tina's back. "A GOOD DAY ALWAYS STARTS WITH A BALANCED BREAKFAST," said the doll helpfully.

Before Rachel had reached her bed, the loudspeaker sputtered alive. She stopped abruptly at the noise. "BED TWENTY-THREE," came the voice, and then: "ONE DEMERIT." If a robotic voice could sound unfazed, it did so now.

Everyone gasped at the speaker's denunciation. Rachel's facial expression went from pride to shock back to anger in the span of a few seconds; Elsie witnessed them all. But before Rachel could turn and shout a damning retort, Elsie grabbed her by her arm.

"Please, Rach," she pleaded, "don't do anything! Just . . . be quiet!"

Rachel stared at her sister's hand, her muscles twitching beneath the grip. Finally, like a dissipating cloud, the anger vanished from her face, and her eyes retreated again beneath her bangs. Elsie could feel the muscles in her arm relax; she let go her grasp and looked at her sister squarely.

"Just two weeks, remember?" asked Elsie. "Let's just hold on."

"Okay, Els," Rachel said. "Okay." She slumped down on her bed, defeated.

It was minutes before the aura of drama had dissipated from the dormitory; Elsie felt everyone's eyes on her and her sister as they both obediently slipped into the gray coveralls. Miss Talbot was on hand to receive the clothes they'd worn on arrival, which they would be allowed to have back during adoptee visits—though there was no indication that these visits would actually occur. The Mehlbergs then fell in line with the rest of the girls and made the slow march down to the cafeteria, where a meal of soggy pancakes and watery orange juice awaited them. They were soon joined by the other dorm; a dour gang of gray-coverall-clad boys poured into the cafeteria and silently tucked into their breakfasts. Elsie and Rachel sat apart from the rest of the kids, across the laminate top of a long table, by no choice of their own: No one deigned to sit near them. Rachel picked at her food; she barely had two bites before she set down her fork resignedly. The spark Elsie'd seen in the dormitory was long vanquished; back was the Rachel she knew from before: maudlin and silent.

Once they'd finished and had deposited their metal trays in a dirty bus tub, a barked instruction from another loudspeaker in the cafeteria had the collected kids line up against one wall. From there, they marched single file out the door and down a wide staircase. Elsie could hear a hissing noise sounding in regular intervals, somewhere off in the distance. The stairway led to another long hallway, and the line of workers followed it, their syncopated boot-falls echoing along the walls, before finally arriving at a tall set of double doors. They must've been triggered automatically, because as soon as the first in line had arrived at the doors, they swung open with a hydraulic wheeze, revealing a sight that made Elsie's stomach plummet.

It was a large room. A very large room. In fact, Elsie couldn't remember seeing a building that could enclose such a large room when they'd first arrived at the orphanage. But it did exist, beyond doubt, and it was filled to the brim with what could only be described as contraptions. Small contraptions. Big contraptions. Copper and bronze contraptions. Wooden contraptions. Contraptions that spit steam from buglelike orifices. Contraptions that belched smoke and fire. Kettle-looking contraptions, with dials and gauges dotting their sides; square, boxy contraptions with tentacles of iron and copper piping sprouting from their sides. Spinning contraptions, static contraptions, contraptions that whistled, contraptions that farted. And all of them interlinked with a mesh of multicolored wire and electrical cable that gave the giant room the distinct aura of a dissected television set, like the one Elsie's father had let Curtis dismantle in his bedroom, and which, once its myriad screws had been unscrewed, revealed an entire byzantine cosmos of unknowable circuits and wires. Oddly enough, the room smelled of raspberries. A long conveyor belt snaked around the room's many machines, and it was along this belt that most of the kids assembled, wiping their hands in preparation for the day's labor.

Joffrey Unthank stood in the center of the room, cast in the light of a few caged bulbs hanging from the vaulted ceiling. He held a mug in his hand and sipped at it absently as the kids took their places along

the conveyor belt. When Elsie and Rachel arrived in the room, he approached them.

"I understand you're the new ones?" he asked. "The Mehlbergs?"

Before Elsie could respond, Rachel stepped forward protectively. "Yeah," she said. "You're the owner, huh?"

He sipped at his mug before answering, "Joffrey Unthank. Mr. Unthank to you. Owner and chief operator."

"Well, this is illegal, I think," said Rachel.

"You'd be surprised, dear," said Joffrey.

"I'd like to make a phone call," said Rachel.

"Not with a demerit on your record," said Joffrey. "Would you like another?"

Elsie jabbed her sister with her elbow. Seeing Rachel retreat, Joffrey spoke. "Hands, please."

"What?" asked Rachel.

"Can I see your hands, please?"

Dutifully, Rachel held out her hands. Joffrey inspected them. "Conveyor belt, third station." He pointed to a section of the belt over which hung a wooden sign marked with the Roman numeral III. "Your neighbors will get you up to speed."

Rachel gave Elsie a withering look and slouched away. Joffrey turned to Elsie. "Hands, please?" he asked.

Elsie did as she was told; her hands felt empty without Intrepid Tina, whom she'd left safely stowed in the lockbox at the foot of her bed.

Joffrey's eyes widened. "Beautiful!" he exclaimed. Setting the mug down, he began inspecting Elsie's hands. "So . . . small!" he breathed. He looked at Elsie. "My dear," he said, "you are the proud owner of hands that were positively meant for machine parts. I haven't seen hands like these in years!"

Elsie, despite herself, murmured, "Thanks."

Joffrey put his arm around her shoulder and walked her over to one of the contraptions, a glossy aluminum barrel-like object, set on its side, with a series of red and blue plastic tubes leading from it. There were three gauges on the front of the machine, one labeled ACK, another labeled UZ, and another with a glyph that looked to Elsie like an upside-down ice-cream cone. "This little baby," Joffrey said, patting the side of the machine, "is the Rhomboid Burnishing Oscillator 2.0. RBO for short."

"What does it do?" asked Elsie.

"Why, it oscillates. And burnishes. It burnishes while it oscillates. The 'rhomboid' bit is anyone's guess."

Elsie didn't know what *oscillate* meant. But she didn't say anything.

"Now," said Joffrey, "the operation of this machine is fairly simple. A huge improvement over the 1.5, let me tell you. You hit this button here, wait ten seconds, and then pull this lever here and you'll hear a little clanking noise." Joffrey walked her through the various steps; a clanking noise, followed by a gentle spinning sound, came from the machine. "Once you hear that, you just open this panel here and . . .

voilà!" Inside the machine, just beyond a little door in the chassis, Elsie could see a small octagonal metal nut—like one you would see threaded on to a very small bolt. "Grab it, please. And quickly," he instructed Elsie. Doing as she was told, she slipped her hand into the small opening, grabbed the nut, and handed it to Unthank. Holding it between his thumb and forefinger, he continued, "Very good. This here is a High-Alloy Rhomboid Oscillated Bolt Nut. There's one in every automatic daiquiri machine. Now, for all the manufacturer's improvements over the previous iteration of this machine, the way I see it, it's not enough. And so I've taken it upon myself to do some tinkering of my own. Cherried the thing up, so to speak. Needless to say, it voided the warranty."

The machine made a loud noise as a set of what looked to be metallic teeth chomped down on the space where the nut had been. Joffrey smiled. Elsie stared at him.

He cleared his throat and continued. "Thing is, in order to maximize the efficiency of the machine, I've had to lose some of the . . . how would you put it . . . safety measures in place. So, instead of the machine just spitting out a new nut into this tray, someone with *really* small hands has to remove the piece manually. Like you just did."

"Okay," said Elsie. "I see, I guess."

"Now, one thing you should know . . ." He paused here and looked at her, a blank look on his face. "Sorry, what was your name?"

"Elsie."

"Lovely name. One thing you should know, Elsie dear, is that if your precious little fingers happen to be inside the machine when it recalibrates the dispenser, the greater machine parts community will be deprived of one of a pair of the greatest set of hands to come along in a generation."

"What?" asked Elsie, trying to ferret out the meaning of the man's last phrase.

"Or a couple years, anyway. Top ten, for sure. Beautiful, tiny hands."

"It'll cut off my hand?" she gasped.

Again, Joffrey cleared his throat. "Yes." Smile. "BUT: You've got easily five, six seconds to get in there and grab the nut before it comes down. A girl with your gifts, you should be in and out of there in two, maybe three."

Elsie was still imagining the consequence of delayed action; at that moment, she became acutely aware of how much she valued the fact that she had two hands. She tried to imagine life without one of them—she saw herself in some future kitchen trying to make a peanut butter and jelly sandwich with a hook for a hand. Even in her imagination, it was no simple task.

Joffrey snapped his fingers. "Stay with me, Elsie dear. The other thing you should know is that these nuts are so very valuable. So very, very valuable, that if one should be destroyed—and trust me, the machine will destroy it if it gets stuck and is not removed before the assembly continues—we, the factory, the orphanage, the greater community, are left with a world where there is one less High-Alloy Rhomboid Oscillated Bolt Nut in existence, and, by extension, one less satisfied automatic daiquiri machine owner. And that is bad. Very, very bad. Is that clear?"

"Yes, Mr. Unthank," said Elsie.

"And so I'm sorry to say that if you do happen to let one be destroyed and do not retrieve it with these world-class machine-part hands before the assembly continues, I'll be forced—by no fault of my own—to give you a demerit."

A spike of fear ran through Elsie's chest. "Yes, Mr. Unthank," she said.

"And you know what happens if you get three demerits, don't you?"

"You're Una—Unadoptable?"

"Exactly," said Joffrey, beaming a little. "You learn fast, Elsie. I think you're a very astute girl. And very astute girls often prove to have a very long and happy career in machine parts."

"Thank you sir, Mr. Unthank, sir."

"Well then, I'm going to turn this little baby over to you. Remember: press button, wait around, pull lever, cranking sound. Yeah?" He repeated, stressing the rhythmic pattern of the rhyme, "Press button, wait around, pull lever, cranking sound." He walked away from Elsie, repeating the mantra in a singsong voice, his fingers bobbing as if he were conducting an orchestra. Arriving in the center of the room, he surveyed the morning's production. The machines were all going full steam, creating a symphony of metallic clanks, buzzes, and moans; the kids were hard at work, some attending to the controls of machines like Elsie's, while others, like Rachel, were picking over minuscule bolts, nuts, and cogs on the long conveyer belt.

"Music to my ears, children," called Mr. Unthank. "Music to my ears. Remember: Machine parts make . . . what?"

"MACHINES," the kids called back in unison.

"And machines make . . . ?"

"CONVENIENCE."

"And what does convenience make?"

"FREEDOM."

"And freedom makes . . . help me here, children. On the count of three. One, two, three . . ."

"FAMILIES," finished the kids, with Joffrey joining them.

"That's right: families," he said. "Now, if any of you need anything, I'll be right up there"—he pointed to a wide window looking onto the factory floor—"keeping an eye on my little busybodies. Ta-ta!" He then exited the room, sweeping his coffee mug along in a deft gesture.

Elsie turned to the RBO 2.0. The twin gauges, ACK and UZ, seemed to be two eyes, glaring at her. Repeating the rhyme that Unthank had taught her, she began operating the machine. Within a few simple processes, a little clank could be heard, and a tinsel-bright nut dropped into the small inner chamber. Elsie's heart leapt into her throat, and she shot her hand into the hole, removing the nut just before the machine's teeth descended onto the space where her fingers had been. She whispered a benediction of thanks before placing the nut onto the conveyor that led away from the RBO. Elsie saw that Martha was manning the neighboring machine, her goggles covering her eyes as she pulled what looked like a fluorescent lamp on an articulated arm over the newly made nut. She saw that Elsie was looking at her and waved. "Keep 'em coming," she shouted over the factory's din. She flashed Elsie a thumbs-up and returned to her work. Elsie did likewise, pressing the red button in the middle of her machine, eliciting yet another ringing *clank* from the belly of the metal thing.

CHAPTER 8

A Dream Remembered; The Great Race

Iphigenia sat on the edge of her bed and rubbed at her ankles. They were very sore; they seemed to be getting sorer by the day. Age was throwing its heavy mantle over the Elder Mystic's shoulders, and she did not like it one bit. The lit wick of a kerosene lamp cast wavering shadows across her simple bedroom; the dark of the morning blackened the windows. The old woman took a deep breath and finished pulling on a pair of woolen leggings beneath her gown. A chill racked her frail bones. She heard a noise come from downstairs: the door thrown open, the stomping of feet in the entryway.

"Hello?" Iphigenia called. There was no answer. She groaned as she pushed herself up from her bed and hobbled to the landing. "Who's there?" she called again.

A grunt preceded the response. "Sorry, Elder Mystic," came a voice. "Just getting the fire going."

Iphigenia sighed. "Good morning, Balthazar," she said, recognizing the acolyte's voice. She walked to the edge of the landing and watched as the acolyte brought an armload of logs to the fireside. He dropped his load in a metal stand with a relieved sigh and looked up at Iphigenia on the landing.

"Shall I get water on for you, Iphigenia?" he asked.

"Yes please, Balthazar," said Iphigenia, padding back to her bedside. She pushed a pair of worn slippers over her feet and stretched. Her back gave a long, mournful crack; she smiled and shook her head. *Things are not as easy as they once were*, she thought, *especially waking up in the morning*. She moved to the stairway.

"How did you sleep?" asked Balthazar as Iphigenia made her way slowly down the stairs. He was holding a long match against some bundled-up kindling in the hearth; soon, a warm glow exuded from the fireplace.

"Not well," responded Iphigenia. "Not well at all. But that's to be expected. I don't find I'm a strong sleeper anymore; it is not my forte."

"I'm very sorry to hear that, Elder Mystic," said Balthazar, watching the flames grow. A black iron kettle hung on the hob, and he swiveled it over the burgeoning fire. Iphigenia eased herself into the chair before the hearth. While the water boiled and the acolyte ran to fetch more wood, the Elder Mystic was able to reflect on the dream she'd been having, the one that had woken her from her sleep. The tangled and unreachable narrative of her deep-sleep dreaming had deposited her, somewhat disoriented, in the midst of a forest clearing. She was cupping something in her hand, though she was not inclined to see what it was; she was keeping it enclosed in her hand for some urgent, yet elusive, reason. There were dark shades in her periphery, just on the other side of the clearing. She was being followed. Gifted with the speed and endurance of a child, she began running through the woods, holding the treasured item in her hand close to her chest. She came up short, arriving at a narrow defile in the hillside. The shades were coming closer, but the darkness of the tight ravine seemed ominous, full of danger. Suddenly, her rational self had inserted itself into the dream: She had a desperate longing to look at what she was holding against her chest. Uncupping her hands, she saw that she'd been carrying what looked to be some sort of bright metal ring, impossibly tangled inside itself. It was the size of a small pebble, and little ridges ran along its edge. The figures behind her grew close, and she shut her hands again and threw herself into the darkness of the ravine, following a rocky path that led down, down, until all was blackness.

That was when she'd woken. Sitting in the chair in front of her fireplace, she wondered at the dream. The chasing shadows required no heavy unpacking to understand; she knew full well what spirits pursued her. What was baffling was the significance of the defile, the hole into the earth she'd entered. Her understandings as a Mystic taught her to never underestimate the power and wisdom of dreams, to find the meaning within every symbol. In her own teachings on dream reading, the appearance of a hole in the earth was clearly an allusion to death. One's own death. She shivered at the notion.

But what of the strange object in her hand? What had it been? Like a word one has forgotten yet hangs on the tip of one's tongue, the thing was naggingly unrecognizable. The tall clock near the bookshelf gave its sullen chime and the door creaked open; Balthazar had returned with more wood. As he began setting the load on the stack by the fire, Iphigenia's eyes lit up. "Of course!" she exclaimed, her eyes fixed on the clock and its innards, a lattice of wheels, chains, and chimes.

Balthazar was caught by surprise. "What is it, Elder Mystic?" he asked.

"A cog!" she said. "A machine's cog. That was what I was holding!"

The acolyte stared at her, confused. Iphigenia waved away his confusion apologetically. "In a dream," she explained. "It was only a dream."

"Yes, Elder Mystic." He seemed relieved to hear the kettle boiling; he pulled it from the hob and poured the hot liquid into a teacup, which he then handed to Iphigenia. The fire was beginning to take, and the room was filling with warmth and light.

"Balthazar," said Iphigenia, after taking a hesitant sip from her tea, "I'll be needing to confer with the Council Tree today; please let the other Mystics know. At noon."

"Yes, Iphigenia," said Balthazar. He hurried from the room.

The Elder Mystic remained, staring at the lazy flames as they licked at the logs in the hearth. The dream, while having been somewhat elucidated now, was still a mystery to her. It seemed to her that the tree would have insight. She felt, in a way, that the tree had had a part in sending her the dream. It must have something very important to relate, Iphigenia decided, very important indeed.

❧

It surprised Prue very much, but nevertheless there it was: The camp did, in fact, have a library. She had stumbled on it, some five days into her quarantine among the bandits, while wandering the labyrinthine walkways and rope bridges that made up this precarious cliff-face encampment. It occupied a tall, narrow cave and was made up of about five makeshift bookshelves. The librarian, a heavyset, kindly-faced man with dark skin, sat at a wooden table and read. A potbelly stove had been installed next to him, and he occasionally broke from his book to stuff the thing with logs.

When he saw Prue enter, he lit up.

"Ain't you the Outsider?" he asked.

"I guess so," Prue responded. "Though I prefer Prue."

"Well, Prue," said the librarian, "welcome to the Bandit Library. Browse at your leisure."

"Where did these books come from?" asked Prue.

"Oh, you know," said the librarian. "Here and there. We don't typically rob folks for their books, but occasionally a volume will catch a lad's eye. You get the idea. Though a lot have been furnished legally. When we've got enough scratch up, there's a bookseller comes through, and we can get some new material that way." He paused, frowning. "Though it's been a time since we got new stock. Hard times for all. Even librarians." Remembering himself, he looked back to Prue. "Anything in particular you be looking for?"

"Oh no, just wandering," said Prue. She ambled over to the short row of bookshelves and began studying the spines. She'd always been most comfortable in libraries ever since she was a small child, and even though this one did not resemble any library she'd been in previously, it still managed to inspire a kind of solace in her. The books sat on their shelves in lazy patterns, some stacked on their backs, others neatly filed in a line. Some looked fairly new, with bright lettering on glossy paperback stock, while others looked as if they'd survived generations and generations of readers, their leather-bound covers worn down in places to reveal wooden boards beneath. Prue began studying the titles and found she didn't recognize a single one: *The Rule of Trees*, *Mr. Slipshod's Arcania*, *Ten Badger-Friendly Activities in South Wood*, *A Woodian in the Outside*. This latter volume, a well-thumbed paperback, caught Prue's attention, and she pulled it from the shelf. To her best guess, it looked as if it'd been published decades before, judging from the black-and-white photograph on the cover: An older gentleman in a gabardine suit and a porkpie hat stood smiling in front of a clearly Portlandian city street. A few cars could be seen in the background, and they looked to be models one would see in a movie from the 1950s. Intrigued, Prue flipped it open to a random page and read:

quite different from what one comes to expect in the more affluent burgs of our own South Wood. It would seem that many of the residents of these central districts don't so much rely on their arborous neighbors as use them for decoration. I stopped a young man on a bicycle and put to him: Why does the Outsider, in general, choose to remove so many of the healthy, thriving native vegetation in favor of more of these obscene concrete structures? Well, dear reader, I can scarce begin to describe his confused stare; he merely named the thing a "parking structure," a title which I came to understand as meaning a windowless building, some many stories tall, explicitly used for the parking of automobiles. I thanked the young man for this information and hurried on my way, my poor stomach growling for its afternoon chocolate mousse, which, you'll kindly remember, I'd refrained from allowing it since its "troubles" the night before.

Prue set the book back on the shelf and was just about to reach for another volume, this one enticingly titled *The Lost Letters: Lewis and Clark in Wildwood*, when a noise disrupted her from her browsing.

"Prue!" It was Curtis's voice.

Prue turned to see her friend, his face flushed and smiling, standing at the opening to the cave. They'd parted ways early that morning when Curtis had left for Bandit Training. She'd not been allowed to go along, not having taken the oath, but it didn't bother her. She had listened to the other kids in the barracks moan at the morning bugle and had quietly thanked heaven for the opportunity to sleep in a little. They'd arranged to meet back at the barracks for afternoon recess; since her arrival, it was how their days had typically been shaped.

“They let us out early,” explained Curtis, waving to the librarian, “and I heard you were here. Figures, bookworm.”

“This is amazing,” said Prue. “This whole library here—and it’s all books written and published in the Wood. I mean, look at this.” She pulled the last title she’d been eyeing from the shelf. “Lewis and Clark! They were here!”

Curtis grabbed the book from her hand and looked at it momentarily before setting it back on the shelf. “Yeah, whatever,” he said. “C’mon, they’re running the ravine!”

“They’re what?”

“Running the ravine,” explained an impatient Curtis. “It’s a race. Happens every Thursday. Trainees do it; it’s like an obstacle course. It’s starting!”

Curtis grabbed Prue’s hand, and they darted from the library. Prue gave the librarian a last, quick wave before she was dragged out into the light of the day. Back out in the hazy sunlight, she had to squint until her eyes adjusted. An early morning snow squall had left a thin carpet of white on the many wooden structures of the bandit camp and the shallow nicks and gullies in the jagged rock of the cliff face. The wind blew brittle, and Prue turned up the collar of her peacoat as she followed Curtis up a zigzagging flight of stairs.

Atop a circular tower built into the rock at the western end of the encampment, about a dozen young bandits-in-training had amassed; Brendan stood in the middle of the group. By the time Prue and Curtis had hiked the staircase that wrapped the tower, the Bandit King had nearly finished with his instruction.

"You're late, bandit," said Brendan curtly.

Curtis, out of breath, spoke haltingly. "I had to get Prue; I wanted her to see this."

"What, see you get your butt handed to you?" This came from a girl a few years older than Prue and Curtis, who was leaning against the crude wooden rampart of the tower. She wore her blond hair back in a leather clip and had on a grenadier's coat, crisscrossed in the center by twin sashes.

"No, Aisling," said Curtis defensively. "Though I'd consider looking out for stray tree limbs, if I was you."

This seemed to curb the girl's attitude; the rest of the trainees laughed softly under their breath, braving Aisling's glare. Brendan cut them off: "I'll repeat the rules for the new arrivals. Green flag is posted at the East Tower. Follow the waymarks. No fighting allowed. Let's keep it clean. Otherwise, it's every bandit for themselves. First one to grab the flag is the winner. Clear?"

"Yes, Brendan," said Curtis.

"And, as host to our young guest, it would be unbecoming if I didn't extend an invitation for her to join the race as well," said Brendan, turning to Prue.

"What?" asked Prue. The eyes of the crowd were on her. "No, I couldn't."

"A week off kitchen duty if you win," put in one of the trainees, a younger boy in a frayed top hat.

Having not yet experienced kitchen duty, it was hard for Prue to judge whether this was reason enough to engage in what looked like a life-threatening activity. She hemmed uncertainly.

Curtis's eyes had lit up. "C'mon, Prue!"

"Listen, I appreciate the invitation," said Prue, "but I don't really think I'm up for it. It's been a while since I did any real sprinting, and I feel like I'd just hold people up. I'd prefer to spectate, if that's okay."

"Fair enough," said Brendan.

"Yeah, fair enough," repeated Curtis. "That totally makes sense. I mean, I didn't really think you meant it when you said you were a natural-born bandit or anything."

Prue said nothing; Curtis took it as an invitation to move in. "I mean, I realize it's tough being an Outsider. It's easy to get soft when you've been away from Wildwood for a bit."

Prue crossed her arms, refusing to bite.

"You might be a half-breed and all," said Curtis, "but I'm not sure which side of the half has all the guts, if you get me."

Finally, Prue broke. "OKAY!" she shouted. "I'll run your little race. I'm not afraid."

The congregation on the tower top burst into laughter. Brendan slapped Prue on the back. "Good on ya, Bicycle Maiden. But let me warn ye: The wood on these platforms is awful slippery this afternoon. You take one wrong step and you'll be flung halfway to who-knows-where in the flick of a sparrow wing. Now mind me: The course is waymarked by red flags; some in plain sight, others not so easy to spot, 'specially with this new fall of snow. It takes a bit of intuition to run this one, I'd say, but intuition is a bandit's first and only friend sometimes. Got me?"

Prue nodded, suddenly worried. She tested the wooden floor with her boots; the rubber squeaked and skidded a small smear on the snow.

"Okay," announced Brendan, now addressing the rest of the gathered bandits. "When the sun rises to its noontime height, I'll give the starting word." Pulling a dagger from his belt, he held it in such a way that the blade cast a dark shadow on the ground at his feet. Prue watched interestedly; she couldn't quite figure out how he could manage to tell time in such a rudimentary fashion, but nevertheless, within moments he said, "Noon. Prepare yourselves: The race begins."

❧

The Council Tree, it was said, was the first tree in the Wood. In fact, many believed that it was the first seedling to sprout when the world was still awash with fire; likewise, it stood strong when the world was covered in ice. And when the great flood had come, the giant ice dam having broken, and the Columbia basin was covered in water, the tree had survived and prospered. It was the lone steward to the explosion of life that occurred around it: a deluge of species, all imbued with magic. Magic that, it was believed, sprang from the woody muscle of the tree itself. Iphigenia never failed to meditate on the tree's origins when she prepared for a council, though much of the story was still shrouded in mystery and myth. Even the tree couldn't speak to its actual beginnings, the events having happened so long ago as to have burrowed themselves too far in the tree's memory for extraction. Complicating matters, the tree did not speak in words, like much of the younger flora of the Wood; rather, it spoke in impressions and images, metaphors and symbols, its ability to communicate having predated language. It was Iphigenia's task, as Elder Mystic, to interpret these sense-images and relay the message the tree wished known.

Arriving at the clearing, she saw the solemn figures of the other ten Mystics surrounding the tree. She greeted them warmly. They, like her, spoke of unquiet dreams in the night, though none were able to describe them; the images had been too fleeting and abstract. Their inability to recall the dreams seemed to parallel their understandings of the Council Tree's way of communication; this, to Iphigenia, was further evidence that the dreams had been sent by the tree. She looked from the gathered Mystics to the Council Tree's giant, gnarled limbs. They were like skeletal limbs, the branches, all bereft of leaves.

What do you want? she asked. The tree was giving away nothing. *Why have you called us?*

There came a sound of laughter; Iphigenia looked over to see a group of younger acolytes—Yearlings, as they were called—on recess from their training, playing in the snow. They were throwing snowballs at one another, dodging and weaving in a hail of these white missiles. The sun, breaking through the gaps in the cloud, had reached its highest point. The Elder Mystic turned to the other ten and said, "Let's begin."

❧

At the starting call, the bandits-in-training, with Prue McKeel in unsure pursuit, took off down the circular staircase around the West Tower. Prue, in the crush, was nearly pitched off the side of the staircase but was caught by a friendly arm. She looked over to see Curtis, smiling. "C'mon now," he said. "You're off to a rough start." Once she'd been righted, he let go and sprinted the rest of the stairs, skipping steps as he went. Prue took a deep breath and ran after.

The racing scrum had arrived at a platform, its outside members searching the area for a waymark. Prue shoved her way into the crowd and began searching as well. Someone hollered, "There it is! On the other side!" Sure enough, across the span of the gap could be seen a red flag, snapping in the breeze, affixed to a wooden stake. A group peeled off from the whole, running toward a zip line farther along the platform. Others, including Curtis, sprinted for a rope bridge in the other direction. Prue, not wanting to be seen aping her friend's choices, followed the group to the zip line. There was some illicit shoving happening, which allowed Prue to make it to the front of the crowd. Just as she was reaching for the handle assembly, she felt a push from behind.

"Out of the way, Outsider," came a voice. It was the girl, Aisling. Before Prue had gained her bearings, Aisling was on the zip line and lifting her legs to cross.

"That was mine!" shouted Prue, and she, despite her best judgment, grabbed onto the girl's legs as she left the platform.

The cable sagged under the weight; Aisling screamed. Prue stared, terrified, at the great maw of darkness below them as they crossed the chasm at a wicked speed. Arriving at the far side, Prue let go of the girl's legs and found herself, tumbling to stand, the first to reach the waymark. She slapped the post and looked to her right; Curtis, in a pack of scrabbling bandit trainees, was just making his way down a staircase from the rope bridge. Prue hardly had time to revel in her initial success before she was searching the chasm for a sign of another waymark. She couldn't find it; she heard the other kids approaching, and her desperation grew. "Where is it?" she hissed to herself.

"Try looking down!" This was Curtis, who, from above, was able to see that the red flag was on a small platform at the bottom of an iron ladder, directly below them. He ably leapt past her and managed a neat slide to the bottom of the ladder, his legs acting as brakes on either pole. The crowd followed him, one after another, and it was this way that Prue found herself dead last in the race.

The racers then sprinted a winding walkway that snaked through a section of jagged rocks emerging from the cliff side like giant teeth. Prue tried to keep pace as best she could, but the young bandits-in-training were clearly more cut out for this sort of activity than she was. She'd been slacking in PE lately; a sympathetic gym teacher had been letting her do equipment inventory during class, and she was dearly out of shape. Groups of bandits, children and adults, were starting to appear from the little cracks and openings in the rock along the course, cheering on the racers.

"There!" shouted a runner; across a smaller break in the rock, spanned by a short rope bridge, was another fluttering red banner. Two boys had broken away from the pack in the sprint and had managed to cross the bridge before the others; they stood grinning by the waymark. Each pulled a knife from their jacket and proceeded to saw away at the ropes holding the bridge in place.

"Hey!" shouted a girl near Prue. "That's not legit!"

"Anything goes!" shouted one of the cutters. One rope broke away.

"Every bandit for themselves!" shouted the other as the bridge came unanchored and fell with a noisy clatter against the rock.

While most of the pack pondered the crevice, perhaps ten feet wide, Curtis came rushing through. "On your left!" he yelled, and without giving it a second look, he leapt the small gap, landing with an *OOF!* on the other side. Taking his lead, several other racers backed up and made the jump as well. A few trainees flagged, winded, unable to make the leap. Prue was not to be deterred; if a schoolmate whom she'd personally witnessed being held back in elementary school gym for not being able to do a single pull-up was able to do it, so could she. Thus energized, she took a running jump.

Her foot slipped as she left the ground, and she, cartwheeling, plummeted into the crevice.

❧

Iphigenia saw a hole. A black hole; a fissure. After a time, she recognized it as the hole she'd seen in her dream: a split in the hillside, it led down into the deep, unfathomable dark. In her mind's eye, her vision was blinded; and yet she still sensed the things that lived and breathed and grew inside the void. Creatures small and large who had existed there for untold centuries. The dark beckoned her. She followed.

In the black of her vision, a light glimmered. A glowing grain of sand. She held out her hands to it, touched it. Three rings folding into one another, cycling and spinning about a central axis. Light flooded in; her vision was returned. She realized that this thing, this glowing, radiant thing, was the clockwork cog from her dream.

Iphigenia then saw that the golden object was in the center of a larger pattern, and suddenly her perspective shifted: She was no longer the watcher, the observer, of this object, but was now commanding the center of a luminescent mandala. She sat, cross-legged, with the object held in line with her heart. Orbiting this center were four objects. Iphigenia, in her mind's eye, immediately recognized three of them: They were the Three Trees of the Wood. The Council Tree, with its warm-grained woody trunk, stood to her left; to her right was the Blighted Tree, its limbs crooked and wizened. Above her was the Ossuary Tree, the tree to which all Mystics ascended at death. A soft light pulsed from its canopy. Below her was a thing she did not recognize; it, too, was a tree, but its identity was a mystery to the Elder Mystic. A length of bright golden filigree connected each of these objects in the mandala, one to the other, a sign of the interconnectedness of the Wood. And at its core, Iphigenia realized, was this thing she held in her hand. Like in her dream, she uncupped her palms. But the cog was gone; in its place she saw that she was holding a living, beating heart.

The heart of a boy.

Just then, darkness filled her vision again. The mandala dissipated, and in its place she felt shadowy forms encroaching, forms that would seek to destroy the thing she had in her hands—or worse, use it for their own evil ends. The forms swirled about her and snapped at her, attempting to distract her from her vigilance. Using all her power, she summoned herself from her vision and began striving to swim for the surface of her consciousness.

The darkness followed.

❧

Prue screamed; her arms flailed.

She managed to grab hold of a frayed piece of rope that was

left dangling from the anchoring structure of the bridge. Within a fraction of a second, she was slammed hard against the side of the crevice. She howled loudly at impact. Her arm felt as if it was being yanked from her shoulder socket. She clenched her eyes, refusing to look down at the swirling pit below her dangling feet. She reached up her free hand and grabbed at a chink in the rock; it held firm, and she scrambled to the lip of the crevice, where she saw a hand being proffered her. It was one of the younger bandits-in-training, a boy. She took it gratefully, and together they tumbled to the safety of the wooden platform.

No sooner had they done this than the boy was up and running, tearing after the diminishing pack of racers. Prue slapped her hands together, freeing them of rocky grit, and gave chase.

The remaining pack of racers—there were perhaps six now, with Curtis in the middle—were leaping between a series of platforms that served as the open-air vestibules for a number of bandits' homes in the rock. The runners who were best able to get ahead were the ones most willing to risk their lives by bypassing ladders and leaping from ledge to ledge. Prue was winded at this point; her near fall had really taken a toll on her spirit. She had just climbed to the third in a series of platforms, watching the pack disappear around a rocky corner, when she heard someone whisper.

"Pssst," came the voice.

She looked over; standing in the shadow of a long arch was a little girl, perhaps six. She gestured to Prue to follow her. Guessing she didn't have anything to lose, Prue trotted after the girl. The arch proved to be an opening in the cliff face, the entryway to a short tunnel—so narrow that Prue had to walk sideways to get through—that let out on the other side of the rock. The little girl, reaching the end of the passage, pointed to a wooden pathway against the rock wall that led along a sliver of fissure to a distant stone staircase. Atop the staircase, Prue could see something fluttering in the wind: the fourth waymark! She thanked the little girl and began gingerly stepping out onto the walkway.

She had to walk carefully, step by step, as the path was really just two planed boards set next to each other, their ends balanced precariously in the little crooks in the rock face. They appeared to be older than many of the structures of the bandit camp; they were covered in a slick layer of moss and they bowed deeply, with a worrisome moan, at her every step. Arriving at the other side, she dashed up the stone staircase—a series of winding steps etched into the rock—and was happy to see that she was the first to arrive at the fourth waymark. The rest of the racers were clambering, one by one, up an impossibly tall ladder to arrive at the same spot. They were far enough off that Prue was able to stop for a moment, to catch her breath and take in the view.

The Long Gap, from this height, could be seen for what it was: not just a straight, open chasm in the earth, but a kind of waterless, bottomless river, complete with stems and tributaries and little inlets where hazy smoke from campfires could be seen drifting. She was nearly at a height where the ravine wall met the mossy ground of the surface, on top of a kind of pinnacle in the rock. Looking down, she noticed that the stone walkway she'd followed led down the other side of the rocky tower in quick switchbacks. It occurred to her then that the stone stairs could not have been the making of the bandits; the craftsmanship and labor involved in such an undertaking would have taken years and years. Where the bandits' makeshift wooden structures still had green leaves sprouting from them, the stone of the staircase was bearded in bright green moss and worn in sections from heavy use. They looked like they'd been there for centuries. The absolute darkness into which the steps snaked intrigued Prue, and she almost then gave up the race to follow where they led.

Instead, she made sure the first kids to top the ladder saw that she'd gained the advantage, and then she was off, following a narrow band of rock that led back down into the depths of the chasm. The fifth flag could be seen waving just beyond a narrow gap in the rock. Prue couldn't believe it, but it seemed she was on track to take the race.

❧

"Elder Mystic!"

"Iphigenia!"

The voices were desperate, agitated. The old woman decided to find out what they were so concerned about. She opened her eyes and realized she was lying flat on her back, which was unusual. A crowd of Mystics, ten to be exact, hovered over her.

"You were straight out!"

"I've never seen you do that before."

Iphigenia's back was very cold, being pressed against snowy ground. However, the snow was rapidly melting and turning to water, which was making her back wet *and* cold. She reached her hands up imploringly; her fellow Mystics helped her to her feet.

"What happened?" asked one, a doe named Mabyn.

Iphigenia held her fingers to her temples. She had a terrible headache. The group of Yearlings who'd been playing in the field had stopped at the commotion; she could see them standing nearby, watching the Mystics. In her heart, a sudden concern erupted.

"I saw," she said, "I saw what must be done."

The collected Mystics all looked at one another, confused.

Iphigenia sighed heavily. "Though in my heart I fear it is a near-impossible task. One for which we are not well equipped." She wiped the dirt and snow from her sackcloth robe and looked at the Council Tree. Her eyes then moved to the line of trees at the edge of the clearing. A darkness was filling the spaces between. "And one I may not survive to witness."

"What can we do?" asked a slender gray-white coyote.

Iphigenia turned to the other Mystics with a renewed purpose.

"The children; we must get them to safety. Mabyn, Dawn, Anatolia, Damianos: Collect the Yearlings. Make sure they're kept from sight. Nikanor, Hydrangea, and Erastus: Keep the civilians from the clearing. No matter what occurs, they must not enter here." The Mystics did as they were instructed; Iphigenia turned to the three who had remained.

"Bion," she said to the gray fox.

"Eutropia," she said to the caramel-skinned woman.

"Timon," she said to the lithe antelope. "Together we must stand against the assassins."

❧

It had been an optical illusion. While the fifth flag did flutter within Prue's keen vision, it was not in easy grasp. The split in the rock that separated her from the banner was easily twenty feet wide; certainly too wide to leap.

The flag stood on a small outcrop on the far side of the gap; Prue studied it breathlessly. Clearly, it must be possible to reach the outcrop, she reasoned—otherwise, how had it got there? She looked all around her; there was no sign of a bridge or zip line. It was as if someone had flown in and dropped it there—but that didn't seem to make sense. Eliciting the help of an Avian didn't seem remotely likely, considering that the bandits-in-training wouldn't be able to rely on flight themselves. While she puzzled this out, the rest of the pack caught up with her. There were only five remaining: the two mischievous boys who'd cut the rope bridge, Curtis, Aisling, and another girl. They were completely out of breath when they joined Prue at the edge of the cliff.

"There it is!" shouted one of the boys.

Curtis stared at Prue. "I thought you'd dropped out!" he said. "How did you—"

"The talents of a natural-born bandit, actually," said Prue.

Aisling crossed her arms at her chest and pouted at the banner. "There's no way we can get that. How did they even get it there? That's, like, against the rules. Or something."

"There are no rules," Curtis reminded her.

"Later, suckers!" shouted one of the boys as he followed the ledge downward and away from the place where the others stood, his partner close behind.

"Where are they going?" asked the younger girl.

"I don't know," said Aisling. "But I'm guessing they know what they're doing. See you on the other side!" And she ran off after the two boys. The younger girl gave Prue and Curtis a look before darting after her.

"Well?" said Prue.

"Well," said Curtis.

"Got any ideas?"

Curtis rubbed his chin. "Not really. I'm pretty sure that's not the way. I've been through this part of the Gap before, and I think that just leads down toward the mess hall." He put his hands on his hips and eyed the cliff wall. "No, they must've gone back and crossed at another spot. Shoot." He went to spit on the ground but did it fairly clumsily. The spit dripped in a lazy string from his lips.

"Nice," said Prue sarcastically.

Curtis blushed and wiped the wetness from his chin. "It's something I'm working on," he said.

"Do you hear that?" asked Prue suddenly.

Curtis froze. "What?"

"That . . . moaning," said Prue. She looked at Curtis; he shrugged.

"I don't hear anything," he said.

Prue, understanding, smiled widely. "Of course you can't!" she said, recognizing the sound of the voice. She searched the chasm for the source and in doing so discovered, on the other side of a large rock, a little lip that led along the cliff around a sharp corner. After crawling carefully over the boulder, she followed the lip, her back braced against the cliff face, until she arrived at a place where a juvenile big-leaf maple tree, jutting from the rock, made a kind of bridge over a narrow part of the defile. It was moaning sorrowfully.

"Someone must've pushed it over, the poor thing, to make a bridge," said Prue as she arrived at the tree. She put her hand on its bark consolingly.

Curtis came up behind her. "What? Did you . . . hear the tree?"

"It's something I can do. Ever since the Plinth. I can . . . well, I can hear plants talk."

Curtis slapped his forehead. "Really? Prue McKeel? You can talk to plants?"

"They don't say anything intelligible," corrected Prue, "but I can hear them. It's weird. I haven't told most people."

"Well, whatever!" exclaimed Curtis. "Next stop, the fifth waymark!" He paused, thinking, before clambering onto the tree. He turned to Prue and waved her forward. "After you," he said. "You did discover the way, after all."

"Very kind of you," she said, and delicately stepped onto the tree-bridge, silently thanking the tree as she crossed.

The afternoon sky grew ominously gray; Iphigenia saw to it that each of the Yearlings were safely ushered away by the other Mystics as she watched the sky darken. One of the them, a little boy, looked at Iphigenia searchingly as he followed her command. "Are they coming?" he asked, his face betraying no emotion.

The Elder Mystic was surprised at the question. She looked at the boy blankly.

"I hear them coming," said the boy. He put his hand on Iphigenia's arm. "Be strong."

She nodded to the boy and then watched as he was led away, hand in hand with one of the Mystics. They were headed for the safety of the acolytes' ward. She smiled despite the gravity of the circumstances. The Yearlings were proving to be very powerful, she assessed, and she had no doubt that the next generation of Mystics would be a formidable one indeed. Their promise was heartening to her. She watched as the children disappeared behind the line of trees, then turned and looked back at the sky.

They were here.

Following the tall trunks of the Douglas fir trees down from their sky-tall tips to the black shallows between them, she saw three figures emerging from the dark. They were humans: two men and a woman. It was clear they were not from North Wood; the two men wore what appeared to be suit jackets, while the woman, in the center, wore a patterned dashiki.

"Good afternoon," said Iphigenia. "You look as if you've traveled far. We've not much to offer, but there is a warm hearth and a modest meal to be had at the hall, if you'd be our guests."

"Quiet, Mystic," said the woman. "We've come for you."

Iphigenia nodded, resigned. "Yes, I know," she said. "I felt you coming." She looked at the woman squarely. "You must be Darla."

The woman sneered, revealing a pair of distinctly inhuman canine teeth. "You—you and your friends—harried me once. I don't expect to be delayed from my task this time." The two men on either side of the woman straightened their bright red ties and stretched their necks. The three approached, crossing the snowy clearing; Iphigenia beckoned to her three fellow Mystics to keep by her. They rounded the large trunk of the Council Tree and stood in front of it protectively. The wind trembled the yellow blades of grass, sending little flurries of snow into the air.

"You won't find them, the children," said the Elder Mystic. "They're well hidden. Beyond your reach."

"Don't underestimate us," said Darla.

"I wouldn't think to. I know your kind."

They edged closer; their movements were silent and studied. The Mystics did not move.

"Who's sent you?" asked Iphigenia, her hands gently urging the three other Mystics to keep their ground.

"None of your business, old woman." This came from one of the men. His shoulders were hunched and shuddering within his natty three-piece suit.

"It's just that when one faces one's assassin, one likes to know who's doing the bidding," explained Iphigenia. "I always thought it was a final consideration paid by your kind—a last favor granted a doomed soul."

One of the men laughed; Darla shot him a glare. "It's actually quite the opposite," she said. "A true assassin never gives up her sponsor."

"An honorable profession," said Iphigenia, a wry smile on her otherwise stoic face. "Though I do wonder how much honor is to be found in infanticide."

Darla ignored this comment. She bared her teeth and growled. "Your time is through, old lady. Make way for the new regime."

With a flick of her wrist, she signaled the men, and the three of them suddenly hunched low, as if stricken with a sudden pain. Their bodies trembled and shook and their clothing undulated strangely as a transformation began to take place. Iphigenia watched placidly, though she could tell the sight awed the other Mystics. Within a few seconds, the three figures had shed their clothing and emerged from their human chrysalises in the form of three jet-black foxes, their hackles along their backs raised in wiry spikes.

Iphigenia, for her part, lifted her hands into the air and prepared for her supplication to the living green of the Wood.

"Ready?"

"Yeah. You ready?"

"Uh-huh."

Their temporary truce was over. Nearly tripping over each other, Prue and Curtis sprinted back over the fallen maple, eliciting another groan from the tree, and inched along the narrow lip of the cliff face. They clambered down a set of stairs, jousting elbows, and ran along a walkway to arrive at an outcrop from where the final waymark could be seen, fluttering wildly atop the camp's West Tower. Prue assumed that the other bandit trainees had been waylaid somewhere in the recesses of the gap; it was now just the two of them left.

They gave each other a quick, fleeting glance and then they were off, tearing across a swinging rope bridge to arrive at the circular stairs that climbed the side of the wooden tower. Whatever civility had been guiding their behavior prior to this moment was gone; Prue had a firm handful of the fringe hanging from one of Curtis's epaulets, and he was desperately elbowing her in the neck at every opportunity. They made their way, ungracefully, to the top of the tower, where they both fell to the ground, pulling and shoving, crawling the final feet to the waving banner.

It was Prue who broke away, who managed to shove past her friend and come within a finger's length of the final waymark. But something occurred; something she could not, at that moment, understand or explain. She froze while a feeling of absolute terror and hopelessness poured through her entire body.

❧

The three black foxes, freed of their former clothing, prowled closer to the Mystics, who had all outstretched their arms as if reaching to catch the lazy snowflakes that drifted down from the slate-gray sky.

This behavior seemed odd to the assassins, who were used to their victims whining and groveling when their end was in sight. It was no matter; this way, the whole ordeal was bound to be much less messy. Darla gave a quick glance to the other two foxes: Now was the time.

And then the ground came alive.

Suddenly, the grass beneath their paws was a bed of quivering, slithering life, snaking its way between their toes and around their ankles. Once it had wormed its way around their legs it held fast, imprisoning them. The two males snapped and growled, angrily trying to wrestle themselves free. One of them had come close to a small shrub of wax myrtle, which was busy entangling its palmlike leaves into the hairs of the fox's coat. Darla, held tight by a few patches of writhing grass, snapped loudly at the Mystics.

Iphigenia raised her hands out to the wax myrtle and closed her eyes. There was an earthy tearing sound, and little white tendrils of root erupted from the soil, winding around the body of one of the foxes. His snarls turned to helpless yelps as the roots, having made a kind of trough in the earth, began pulling him down into the ground. Within moments, all that remained at the spot where he'd been standing were a few loose piles of dirt and a patch of black fur.

Darla and the other fox helplessly watched their compatriot be buried alive. With renewed vigor, they growled and flexed their haunches. Suddenly, the grass tore away at their paws and the two foxes broke free of their bonds, leaping, teeth gnashing,

A length of bright golden filigree connected each of these objects in the mandala, one to the other, a sign of the interconnectedness of the Wood.

for the throats of the Mystics.

"Run, Elder!" shouted Bion, the gray fox, as he dove in the way of the pouncing Kitsunes. The bodies crashed together in an explosion of teeth, fur, and flesh. Iphigenia, thrown from her meditations, fell backward, landing with an agonized yawp on the ground. Were it not for the fact that the very blades of grass at her feet rose up to cushion her fall, she might not have been able to regain her footing. The human woman Mystic, Eutropia, helped her to her feet and held her arm as the foxes behind them fought bitterly.

"To the trees!" said Iphigenia, with some difficulty. "Our only hope."

Dutifully, the two Mystics escorted the Elder toward the line of trees at the edge of the clearing. The sound of the three foxes' melee could be heard behind them. A scream came from Bion; he shouted to the retreating Mystics, "RUN!"

Iphigenia turned to look and saw that he had been struck down, his muzzle flattened against the muddy ground. Blood seeped from his nostrils. The two Kitsunes bared their teeth and gave pursuit. Eutropia let go of the Elder Mystic's arm and turned to face the assassins.

Darla saw this. "Watch the plants!" she hissed to her fellow.

Eutropia held out her hands, palms open, to the ground below her feet. The tawny blades of grass leapt alive at her command and began whipping at the arms and legs of the approaching Kitsunes. But the assassins had better judged their opponent; they stepped quickly through the thickets of grass and avoided the larger bushes; the quivering greenery could not hold their prey. Before the Mystic had a chance to engage, the foxes had leapt with fearsome agility and barreled the woman to the ground, teeth gnashing.

Iphigenia and the antelope Timon heard their fellow Mystic's screams as they fled for the safety of the tree line; they did not hazard a backward glance for fear of losing what little distance they'd put between themselves and their pursuers. "Quick, Elder," said Timon. "Climb on my back." Iphigenia did so, wrapping her arms around the antelope's slender neck. With a grunt, the Mystic kicked into a gallop, racing for the edge of the clearing. They could hear the foxes behind them, freed of the clutching grass, tearing after.

Iphigenia, astride the antelope, did what she could to hamper the assassins: The varied plant life of the meadow struck out wildly at the sprinting foxes. It wasn't until they'd made the line of trees, though, that she was able to create any significant obstacle. She looked to the high boughs of the trees—the fir, the maple, the hemlock—and she beseeched them to help in their flight.

Branches, whipping lightning-fast from the heavens, descended on the two black foxes as they reached the edge of the clearing, and they yelped in pain, the wood making bright red lacerations along their sides. Timon leapt the trunk of a bent hemlock that had tipped sideways into the ground, and Iphigenia grunted at the collision when the antelope made landfall on the other side.

Darla, neatly dodging an arcing cedar bough, bounded over the hemlock while the other Kitsune ducked low and scrambled beneath. Iphigenia saw this; she breathed deep and conjured. The male Kitsune made it only halfway under before the tree bore down in a quick, groaning motion and pinned the fox, hard, to the loamy ground. He yelped loudly, but his compatriot, Darla, did not stop to assist. She did not see him pushed farther down into the ground; she did not see the little fingers of plants' roots make a white web over his head and suck him deep into a furrow that closed over him like a lapping mouth.

Despite the tactical advantage of the woods, the trees and bushes all working in tandem to check the pursuit of the assassin, Darla was gaining on the two Mystics. Timon was unable to fully gallop carrying the weight of the Elder Mystic; he faltered by a stand of willows. Iphigenia slipped off and whispered in his ear, "Go. Go to the two half-breed children. Warn them." He gave her a quick worried look, and then, in a shot, disappeared into the knot of trees. Iphigenia turned to face her attacker. She calmed the quaking greenery. It trembled to a stop.

Untrusting, Darla slowed her pace to a deliberate, silent stalk. "This is it, crone," said Darla as she rounded the old woman.

"Yes, it is, isn't it?" said Iphigenia. With that, she sat down on the cushion of salal vines at her feet and deftly wrapped her legs in lotus position. Her eyes fell peaceably closed.

The fox leapt. The surrounding forest, under no command or request, convulsed mournfully as the assassin hit her mark.

❧

Prue collapsed on the wooden floor of the tower, suddenly overcome with the worst pain she'd ever experienced; it felt like all her blood had stopped flowing and her every nerve ending was set to flame. Her mouth was opened to scream, but no voice came. Everything green around her was shouting at her, hollering through the cavity of her skull, as if each and every piece of vegetation, from the smallest patch of moss to the tallest tree, had witnessed some horrible degradation. She put her hands on her ears to blot the sound, but it was no use.

Her eyes darted around her, trying to figure out how and why this was happening. She saw Curtis above her; his lips were moving, but she couldn't hear his voice. She felt him grab her shoulders and shake them. Her whole frame felt frozen and impotent. She found herself teetering on the edge of unconsciousness; and yet the screaming was so much more intense than it had been that day on the bluff. And then, as soon as it had begun, it all stopped.

She stared up at Curtis, wild-eyed, and grabbed his arm, her voice suddenly returned to her in this new vacuum of silence.

"It's Iphigenia, Curtis," she choked. "She's . . . she's . . ." But what, exactly, Prue couldn't know.

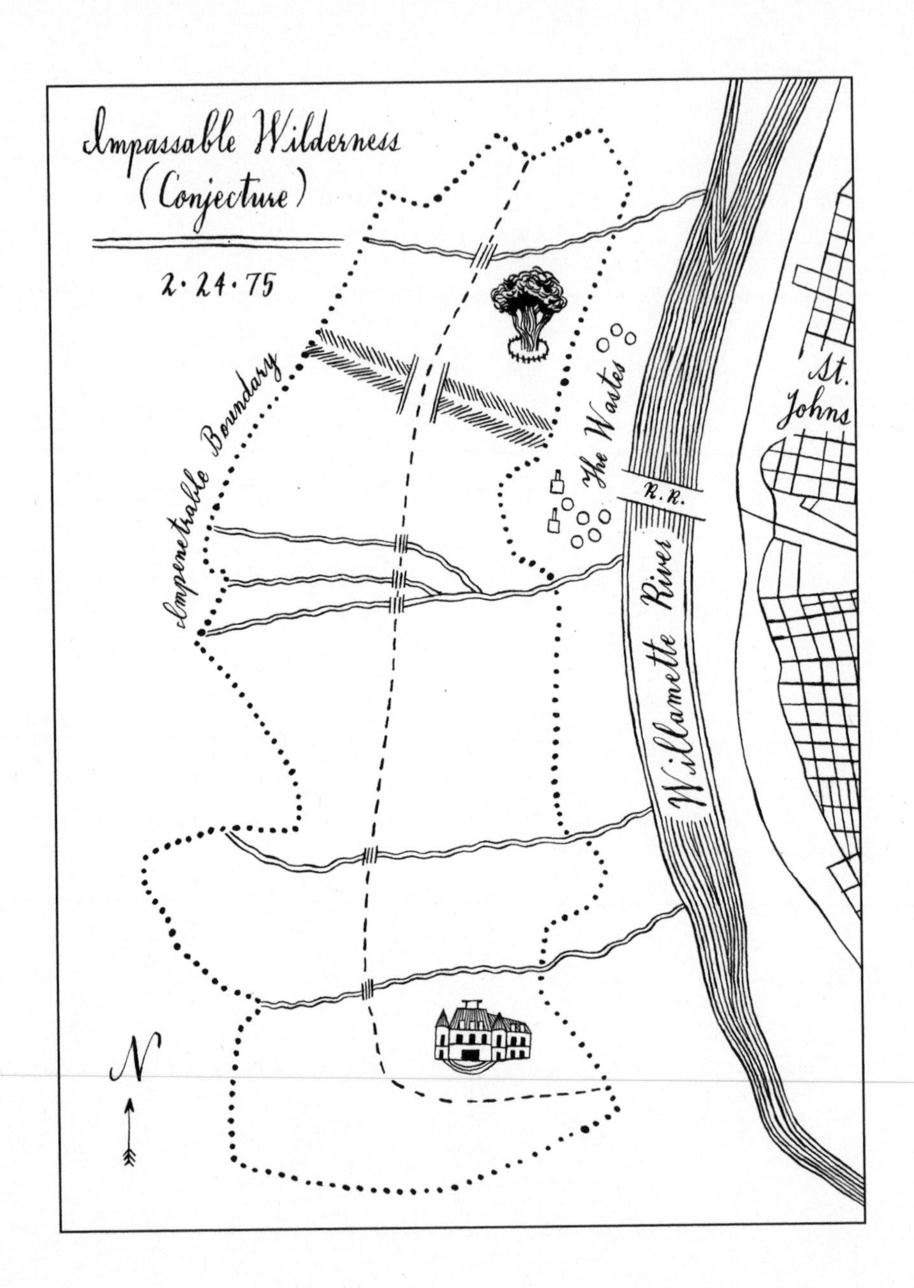
Impassable Wilderness
(Conjecture)
2·24·75
Impenetrable Boundary
The Wastes
R.R.
Willamette River
St. Johns
N

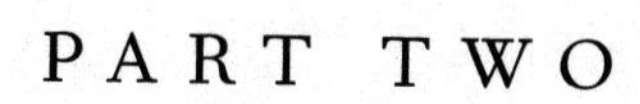

PART TWO

C H A P T E R 9

Unadoptable

They had all borne witness. Clearly, that had been the intention; that way the boy would serve as an example to them all. It had happened quickly and it was over quickly. After it happened, the other children in the machine shop returned, seemingly unmoved, to their duties, and the puffing and clanking of the room's machines continued unabated. They had seen it before, many times.

The boy's name was Carl. Elsie had spoken to him once in the cafeteria. He was a year older than her and was a heavyset child with red curly hair. He'd been nice to her—he'd noticed her Intrepid Tina doll and had said that he'd been a fan of the TV show, when he was still living with his birth parents, before they'd perished in a strange Jet Ski accident. And that was the sole interaction Elsie had had with the boy.

The incident began with a whimper, literally. A whimper that could be heard throughout the ringing shop. It came from Carl himself as he stood at his station, manning a machine that was easily one hundred times his size and mass. It was called a Bifurcated U-Bolt Bender, and it did what its name implied: it bent bifurcated U-bolts. He'd obviously been spacing out, as he'd pressed the purple button when he should've pressed the black. He let out his knowing whimper; at that point, the Bifurcated U-Bolt Bender had ceased bending bifurcated U-bolts and began bending itself. Two loud popping noises sounded from within the machine, and then it came to a rattling halt, smoke belching from its riveted seams.

Some sort of emergency power shutoff must've been triggered, because all the machines in the shop suddenly ground to a stop, and the pale fluorescent light that typically bathed the warehouse was replaced by a demonic, flashing red. Everybody began casting about, trying to figure out what had caused the stoppage; their eyes eventually landed on Carl, who was standing by the smoking Bifurcated U-Bolt Bender with a guilty look on his face. Martha, at the conveyor belt, had removed her goggles and blanched. "Oh no," she'd whispered.

"What?" hissed Elsie, standing back from her inoperative machine. The upside-down ice-cream-cone-shaped insignia was flashing angrily. It was the only time Elsie'd seen it actually do something.

"He's already got two," said Martha cryptically.

"Two what?" asked Elsie, but in the time it took to say those words, she understood. "Demerits?"

Martha nodded.

The room flooded with light, and the machines made a strange hum; footsteps pounded the stairs to the factory floor. It was Mr. Unthank, who had apparently restarted the power to the room. A glower clouded his goateed face, and it looked as if he'd been interrupted from his lunch: A narrow band of what appeared to be tomato soup made a kind of second mustache on his upper lip.

"What was *that?*" he demanded. No one answered. He stalked to the obvious culprit, Carl and his machine, and glared.

"What have you done, boy?" he asked.

"I'm really sorry, Mr. Unthank, sir. I didn't mean nothin'. I just . . ." Here, he swallowed so loud that Elsie heard the *gulp!* from across the room. "I just pressed the purple button when I shoulda pushed the black one."

"Purple," repeated Unthank, as if needing to restate the words for comprehension. "Black."

"Uh-huh."

Unthank rubbed his small beard thoughtfully. His hand recoiled when his fingers met the tomato soup remnant, and he studied them before licking them clean and wiping them on his argyle sweater. "What's your name, little boy?"

"Carl, sir."

"Carl, do you know how much one of these machines costs? Hmm?"

"N-no sir."

"A LOT OF MONEY!" Unthank yelled abruptly. He took a deep breath and regained his composure. "Not only that, Carl, but it's going to take time to repair. Time this machine could spend bending bifurcated bolts." The words seemed to trip from his lips effortlessly.

"Right, sir," said the boy.

"I'm afraid I've got no choice but to hand down a demerit for this mistake, Carl."

The boy began to cry. Little tears fell from his eyes and cascaded down his cheek. Unthank guessed at his dismay. "Miss Mudrak?" he called out.

The loudspeaker popped with static. "Yes, Joffrey?" came Desdemona's voice.

"Will you look and see how many demerits are on record for Carl . . ." He paused and motioned to the boy. "Carl . . . ?"

"Carl Rehnquist, sir."

Unthank nodded, attempting empathy. Then, to the loudspeaker: "Carl Rehnquist."

There was a moment of absolute silence, broken only by the sound of the machines slowly rebooting.

"Two demerits, this boy has," came the answer from the loudspeaker.

Carl began to sob unabatedly. Unthank frowned. "It would seem, Carl, that you've managed to rack up a third demerit. You know what that means?"

The boy tried to respond between fits of crying. "Mm-hmm," he finally managed.

"What does it mean? Help me here, Carl."

"Unadoptable," said Carl quietly.

"Why don't you say it so the rest of the room can hear you."

"Unadoptable," said Carl, a little louder.

"Right," said Unthank as

he surveyed the room. "Listen up, kiddos. You break my machines, you pay with your freedom. Is that clear?"

The room murmured understanding.

"Now, if you wouldn't mind, Carl," said Unthank, putting his hand on the boy's shoulder and leading him away from the factory floor, "I'd appreciate it if you went upstairs and got cleaned up. Miss Mudrak will then escort you to my office. Yes?"

"Yes, sir."

Unthank turned to the rest of the children in the room. "Back to work, kids," he said. "And let this be a lesson to you all." And that was how Carl Rehnquist, machinist, orphan, Intrepid Tina fan, was led out of the machine shop and out of the lives of his fellow internees at the Unthank Home for Wayward Youth.

That night, Rachel steamed over the incident. She sat in her bed, her knees pulled tight against her chest, and glared into the half-light. The other girls were chatting with one another, enjoying what little free time they had after the long work day.

"I can't believe it," she said. "He's just gone? Like that? I mean, what did they do to him?"

Elsie shrugged. She was combing Intrepid Tina's hair; it had become somewhat of a pre-bedtime routine for her. She found it calmed her when she was most anxious, and that seemed to be just about every day. Her nerves felt particularly jangled this evening, and that was why she was combing Tina's hair in an almost frenetic, distracted way. The Mehlberg sisters were nearly a week into their internment at the factory and Elsie wasn't in the mood to ask too many questions.

"I mean, don't you wonder?" asked Rachel.

"Yeah, I s'pose so." She paused in her combing and looked at her sister. "Don't you think they just let him go somewhere else? Like, he'd just go to another orphanage or foster home or something? Sounds like a pretty good deal to me."

"Maybe, though I don't know," chimed in Martha from the other side of Elsie's bed. She was lying on her mattress with her arms behind her head. "They all get taken to Mr. Unthank's office. And then—who knows? But I never saw any Unadoptable be, like, escorted from the building or anything."

"That's the thing, huh, Goggles," said Rachel, spinning sideways on her bed and dropping her feet to the floor. She looked at Elsie and Martha conspiratorially. "They don't come back out. And you know why, I think?" Here she slid her finger across her throat. "Chop 'em up into little bits. Feed 'em to the stray cats in the neighborhood."

Martha made a face. Elsie blanched. *Really?* she mouthed to her sister.

"Your sister's weird," said Martha.

"You guys are kidding yourselves if you don't think that's what happens," said Rachel. "You think there's, like, a magic chute in Mr. Unthank's office and he just throws them down it and—poof!—they're back in the outside world?"

"Well," said Elsie, "whatever happens, we've only got another week here, huh, Rachel? So we should just try not to get any demerits."

Rachel swiveled back on to her bed. "I've already got one. It's like I'm marked. I could end up like that kid Carl at any moment." She shivered visibly, her voice having grown low and serious.

"C'mon, Rach," said Elsie, "cheer up. We really don't have much time left."

"Yeah," said Martha. "Count yourself lucky."

The three girls fell silent. Finally, Rachel said, "I'm going in there."

"What?" said Elsie and Martha in unison.

"Into Mr. Unthank's office," said Rachel. "I'm going to find that boy Carl—or what remains of him—and I'm going to expose this whole insane place for what it really is."

"Rachel!" This was Elsie, her voice a quavering whisper. "You'll—you'll get a demerit!"

"Or two. Or five," said Martha. Then, almost to herself: "I wonder what happens to you when you get more demerits than you need to be Unadoptable."

Rachel ignored them. She popped off her bed and kneeled down by Elsie's. She waved Martha in close. "I'm sneaking in there. While you guys have been dead asleep, I've been watching; two nights ago,

I had to pee and on my way back I noticed there wasn't anyone at the door. Turns out Miss Talbot does a shift change at midnight and it takes, like, fifteen minutes for the replacement to come. I made it all the way to Mr. Unthank's office door before I got too spooked and came back."

"But doesn't he keep it locked?" asked Elsie.

Rachel smiled knowingly and reached behind her, pulling from beneath her pillow a little brass key on a yellow ribbon. She dangled it playfully in front of the two girls.

Martha gasped. "Where'd you get that?"

"Janitor's closet," said Rachel. "A pit stop on the way back to the dorm. Couldn't help myself: Miss Talbot had left it open. It had spare keys for all the rooms. This one was labeled 'J. U. Office.'"

"Whoa," said Martha.

Elsie was not so impressed. "You stole that, Rachel," she said, feeling perturbed. "You shouldn't steal stuff."

"I'm just borrowing it."

"Still."

"When you gonna go?" asked Martha.

"Tonight," said Rachel, flipping the key back into her palm and tightly closing her fist around it. She gave a quick look at the loudspeaker above the doors. "After lights-out," she whispered. "When Miss Talbot does her shift change."

Martha, by this point, had climbed out of her bed and was kneeling on Elsie's, her body leaning forward to better hear Rachel's plans. "I wanna go," she said.

Elsie stared at her. "You guys. This is crazy. You'll get demerits! Rachel, you'll get a second demerit!"

Rachel cocked an eyebrow at Martha.

"I'm a clean slate," Martha responded. "No demerits. I've been here, what, five years? And always the good girl. I'm sick of it, actually. I'm ready to make some mischief."

Rachel reached her hand out; Martha shook it firmly.

"Tonight it is," said Rachel.

"Oh no," said Elsie.

❧

Martha Song's first march into the dormitory of the Unthank Home for Wayward Youth, some five years prior, came back to her in a sudden, lucid flash as she and Rachel Mehlberg crept into the darkened hallway and made their way toward the proprietor's locked office. It was strange; she'd walked the hallway many times since and had never experienced such a flash of remembrance. But now she could feel her father's calloused hand in hers, the citrus blossom of her mother's perfume. They were being sent back to Korea, they'd explained. They'd come back for her in time.

Maybe this sudden memory-recall was why she didn't see that Rachel had stopped suddenly and Martha bumped into her, hard. Or maybe it was because she was wearing her goggles.

"Hey," whispered Rachel angrily. "Watch it."

"Sorry," said Martha.

"Why do you have your goggles on?"

"For good luck."

"Are they still good luck if you wear them on your forehead, off your eyes?"

"Maybe."

"Give it a shot."

"Okay." They continued down the empty staircase. In a short time, they arrived at the office door. Martha kept an eye on the long hallway while Rachel pulled the key from her coverall pocket and fit it into the keyhole. The door unlocked with a low click. Martha heard

the sound and watched as Rachel slowly opened the door; it gave a wheezy creak. A dim glow shone from within and illuminated the checkerboard tile of the hallway with a long, thin column of light. Rachel looked inside the room and sucked in her breath.

"What?" asked Martha, craning her head over Rachel's shoulder to try and see past the crack in the doorway.

"What are all those things?" rasped Rachel, despite herself.

"What? I can't see!" whispered Martha.

Rachel cracked the door open wider; Martha peered in. The sight was astounding. It was a large room, large enough to easily accommodate a huge wooden desk and, facing it, a set of leather chairs. The desk was cluttered with sheaves of paper and what looked to be glass vials. What was remarkable about the room, though, was the fact that the walls were lined with tall shelves, shelves that held a dizzying array of jars, bottles, and crocks. The setup reminded Martha of some wizard's apothecary or an ancient Chinese pharmacy. There was, however, one section of shelving that was empty of these bottles and vials but instead stored about three dozen white metal boxes. A small red light on each of the boxes blinked intermittently, out of time from its neighbors, so as to resemble a Christmas decoration gone haywire.

In the center of the room, just in front of the shelf with the metal boxes, sat what appeared to be a dentist's chair from some forgotten century. The imposing chair was built of a series of stiff-looking white cushions, all held together by a twisting black metal framework. On either armrest, an iron cuff lay ominously open; likewise, two similar clasps extended from the chair's footrest. It would seem that whatever dentist had used this chair in the past, he had had to confine his patients to it by force. Martha, as if out of fear, pulled her goggles back over her eyes.

"Oh . . . my . . . God," she said.

Rachel was silent. It was tacitly understood between the two girls: However much frightening *stuff* had been crammed into Joffrey Unthank's office, there was one thing that was conspicuously absent: Carl Rehnquist.

Rachel waved the all clear. The two girls crept into the office and quietly shut the door behind them. The only light in the room came from a dim desk lamp. Martha wandered over to three windows in the wall behind the desk: The view beyond looked down onto the dormant factory floor. Rachel looked at her watch. "We've got ten minutes," she said.

The desk brought that of a school principal's to mind: It was industrial green and made of polished metal. Martha idly picked her way through the glass vials on the desktop, peering into their mouths; they were all empty. Her attention then fell on a stack of paper in the center of the desk, what looked to be a collection of maps. She leafed through the stack. The maps seemed to be from a variety of eras: Some were ancient-looking, their paper long turned tawny from age and their edges foxed with mildew. Others looked like contemporary topographical maps, with contours written in spidery lines. Martha didn't recognize any of the places they served to illustrate; one looked to be a wide continent—almost European-looking—with a mountain range surrounding a central peak to the southeast. Another was of a long peninsula, its northern border marked by a rocky defile; a train track cutting through the canyon wall seemed to be the only thing connecting this strange country with its neighbors. One map caught Martha's eye, its corner jutting out conspicuously from the bottom of the pile. Pulling it out, she saw that it was an older map (it was dated 02.24.75) and was titled "Impassable Wilderness (Conjecture)." Martha recognized a careful drawing of St. Johns's grid of streets on the side of the page, the lazy sway of the Willamette River next to it, the little smokestacks and chemical tanks of the Industrial Wastes. But most of the page was dedicated to the Impassable Wilderness, set off from the world by a dotted border labeled "Impenetrable Boundary." Martha had seen the I.W. labeled on maps before, but it always existed as a nameless, featureless oblong green rectangle. In this map, someone had included actual points of interest. A canyonlike gorge cut through the wilderness; a curious turreted house was drawn in the middle of the southerly section. To the north, the cartographer had drawn a gnarled tree and had scribbled little figures standing around it in a circle. A road, somewhat arbitrarily drawn, connected this northern part to its southern border. The map seemed to Martha the work of someone suffering from a fantastic bout of dementia.

Stepping away from the desk, Martha milled around the dentist's chair, studying its lockable clasps with a knot in her throat, before she wandered over to the bookshelves and began browsing the many jars and canisters. She murmured the names, all neatly labeled in a fine cursive hand, as she went: "Bovine Adrenal, Myrrh Resin, Belladonna, Nux Vomica—bleagh. What *is* this stuff?" She grabbed one of the jars off the shelf and twisted open the lid. She took a quick whiff and her nose was filled with a smell not unlike a dog show's worth of wet canines in an underarm deodorant factory. She quickly screwed the lid tightly closed. "Sorry," she said.

Rachel was crouched down, studying the little metal boxes and their flashing red lights. Martha knelt down beside her. Each box had a kind of meter on the face of it, protected behind glass. It reminded Martha of a car's gas gauge, but on each of the boxes, the needle was firmly buried in what would be the EMPTY position. A small black line made an arc across the gauge, and it was dotted with numbers: 1, 1.5, 3, 5, 10. Occasionally, a needle on one of the gauges would give a little flutter, and the red light below it would flicker dimly. Above the meter window on each of the boxes was a little square of white tape with two letters inscribed on it. H.K., one read. G.W., read another.

"I could not be more confused," said Martha. Rachel was silent; she was tapping her finger against her upper lip in thought. Suddenly, her eyes lit up and she pointed at one of the boxes.

"Look at this!" she said. The box was labeled C.R. The writing was significantly less faded than that on the other boxes. It seemed to be freshly scrawled.

"What?" asked Martha, trying to puzzle it out.

"What do you think that stands for? C.R.?"

Martha puzzled. "Cranky Robot?"

Rachel rolled her eyes. "These are initials." She tapped her finger against the tape. "That must stand for Carl Rehnquist!"

A chilly gloom fell over Martha. She began looking at the other boxes, their needles quivering and their red lights quietly winking; she started deciphering the names. "Harold Klein," she intoned, "Leslie Brumm. J . . . Josh? Josh Tennyson. Greg Wheeler. Cynthia . . . Smith? No: Schmidt. Cynthia Schmidt." She remembered them all, all their names. "Oh my God, Rachel. These are all the Unadoptables. As long as I've been around, anyway. Probably a bunch from before I came."

Just then, there was a noise from the hallway. Martha and Rachel made quick eye contact as they heard the doorknob turning. They dove for the desk on the other side of the room; the noise of the door opening must have cloaked their scrambling, because they arrived at the shelter of the desk's underside undetected. Huddled there, they listened as footsteps sounded into the center of the room and stopped. "Hello?" came the voice. It was old Mr. Grimble, the night watchman. "Mr. Unthank?"

Martha and Rachel refused to breathe.

Mr. Grimble grumbled (it was a hallmark of his—the Grimble Grumble, as the kids called it—and it sounded like the grunt of a hibernating bear with sleep apnea) as he surveyed the room. Satisfied, he turned and left, shutting the door noisily behind him. The two girls waited until the sound of his footsteps faded away before they let out their breaths.

"Let's get out of here," said Martha.

Rachel nodded. "I'll meet you in the hall."

Martha crept to the door and slowly opened it, keeping her eyes intently on the space outside the room. When she saw there was no one there, that the hallway extended into quiet darkness, she pushed the door open and began tiptoeing out onto the checkerboard parquet of the hallway floor. It was a few moments before she noticed Rachel was not behind her.

"Rachel!" she whispered. "Are you coming?"

The girl appeared from around the office door; she silently closed it and threw the bolt with the key. She then turned to Martha and nodded. "Let's go," she said. Together they padded back to the dormitory, and Martha whispered a sigh of thanks to the heavens once she'd stowed herself underneath her blanket. In the rush, she hadn't noticed that Rachel had left the office with something small and square tucked under her arm.

❧

Elsie had just delicately removed a nut from the mouth of the RBO—an action that was almost involuntary now that she'd been in the machine shop for over a week—when Unthank came storming down the stairwell with a strange white box in his hand. Desdemona Mudrak, in tall heels, stepped gingerly after. Elsie hadn't initially thought anything of it, but her mind quickly put two and two together. Both Martha and Rachel had been very quiet that morning over their hasty breakfast in the cafeteria; they hadn't divulged anything from their late-night recon mission. They promised they would fill Elsie in that night, when there were "fewer prying eyes around," as Martha had described it.

"Girls and boys!" shouted Desdemona. "Please to listen closely."

Unthank strode to the middle of the factory floor and raised the box high so that everyone could see it. Its black power cord dangled from it like a tail. Desdemona, standing at his side, held a wooden clipboard.

Elsie looked over at Martha, who'd removed her goggles and was looking fixedly at Rachel, who was, in turn, staring down at the ground.

"Does this look *familiar* to anyone?" asked Unthank. He had to raise his voice to beat the racket of the machines and it echoed in the cavernous space.

No one spoke. Unthank shook the metal thing in his hand. It made a kind of rattle.

"I'm willing to make an offer to whoever took this," he said. "If you come forward and fess up, I'll be happy to not punish everyone on this factory floor with three extra work hours a day. And even though this infraction is so great as to merit instant Unadoptable status, I will be merciful and give only two demerits for your honesty. Now: Who took this?" He surveyed the attentive children, who had emitted a collective groan at the suggestion of an even longer workday.

Elsie looked at Rachel and Martha; Martha was staring at her sister with wide, accusing eyes.

But no one spoke. Aside from the groan, the room remained silent.

In this vacuum of sound, Martha Song stepped forward.

"It was me," she said. "I snuck into your office. I took that thing off the shelf. I'm really sorry, Mr. Unthank, sir."

Elsie's jaw dropped. She noticed that Rachel was shooting Martha a shocked look.

Unthank gave a smile. The beard and mustache portions of his goatee parted at his lips like a pair of stretching meerkats. "Very noble of you, Song," he said. "And I'll be pleased to hand you down two demerits for volunteering this information. Your first two, if memory serves."

Martha nodded, putting on a despondent face.

Unthank had paused in his speaking as he scanned the room. He then said more loudly, "However, I happen to know that you are not, in fact, the culprit." This observation elicited a few gasps from the crowd; Rachel was still looking at her shoes. Elsie felt her heart leap. "I have to say it disappoints me greatly to know that the real criminal, the trespasser, will not reveal themselves," he continued. "Or herself, I should say. This piece of expensive equipment"—here he shook the metal box again—"was found in the footlocker of bed twenty-three. And bed twenty-three belongs to . . ."

"Rachel Mehlverg," finished Desdemona icily.

Elsie let out a quick, high moan. She looked over at Rachel, whose shoulders could be seen shaking slightly. Her face was downcast.

"Miss Mehlberg, for reasons unknown to me, decided to deceive the staff of the Home for Wayward Youth—and, by extension, the entire workforce—by sneaking into my office and *stealing* this piece of valuable equipment. I ask you, children, what family would want to adopt a girl who would do such a thing?"

"I'm not *up* for adoption," countered Rachel suddenly. She'd raised her head.

"Well, you certainly aren't now," said Unthank. "In fact, I'd go so far as to say that you're quite . . . Unadoptable." He laughed a little at his own joke; Desdemona cracked a thin smile.

Rachel's hair fell back over her face; her shoulders sagged.

"NO!" shouted Elsie, the tears springing to her eyes.

Joffrey ignored the outburst, instead rounding on Martha, who was still standing stock-still. "As for you, Miss Song, your dishonesty is most distressing. I will have to award you an extra demerit for lying. That makes three demerits in as many minutes." He then proclaimed flatly, "Unadoptable," while Miss Mudrak made some scribbles on her notepad.

Elsie stared at Martha, whose face had grown sheet-pale, creating a stark contrast to the black smudges of grease on her cheek. A boy standing next to Martha whispered angrily, "He tricked you!" Desdemona shot the boy a glare.

Unthank gestured to Rachel and Martha to come to the center of the floor. They marched sullenly over to his and Desdemona's side. He put his arms on the shoulders of the two girls and looked out at the rest of the children.

"At Unthank Machine Parts," he said loudly, "we believe in worker solidarity, solidarity in making the best machine parts we can possibly make. When that fundamental value is undermined by wrongdoers, liars, and thieves, it is imperative that justice is served for the good of the company."

The two girls at his either side carried themselves in two distinctly different ways: Martha's head was held high, and a terrified look graced her brow; Rachel's hair hung like curtains, shielding her eyes.

"I have absolute faith," continued Unthank, "that this unhappy event will only make our productivity greater. The more demerits handed out, the more Unadoptables we create, the greater our discipline will grow. Good day."

And with that, he began leading Martha and Rachel from the factory floor.

Elsie turned to her machine and pulled the lever on its side; a metal nut was spit out in its mouth. Immediately, she pulled the lever again and the machine's teeth came down, crunching the newly created nut with a loud *CLANK!*

Unthank stopped at the stairs and turned. "What was that?" he asked, searching the room. His eyes landed on Elsie. "What did you do?"

"Oops," said Elsie. She pulled the lever again. A new nut was spit out. Again she destroyed it by bringing the machine's teeth down on it.

Unthank's face turned beet red. He stepped away from Martha and Rachel and walked toward Elsie. "That's two demerits, little girl," he said.

Elsie's hand went back to the lever. Rachel looked up through her strands of hair. "Elsie!" she said. "Don't do this!"

"Sorry, sis," Elsie said. "I can't let you go alone." She pulled the lever, twice. A High-Alloy Rhomboid Oscillated Bolt Nut was created and destroyed in the passing of a few seconds.

"THREE DEMERITS!" shouted Unthank, spittle flying from his mouth. "UNADOPTABLE!" He strode briskly to where Elsie stood and grabbed her, hard, by the shoulder. He then walked her to the stairwell and shoved her in line with Martha and Rachel. He looked back out over the machine shop. "Anyone else? Anyone want to try me?"

The room was silent.

Unthank smoothed the front of his argyle sweater, which had become very rumpled from the activity. He pushed a few strands of hair back from his brow. "Right," he said, his earlier composure lost. "Back to work."

The goateed man had been pushed to the end of his patience; he did not instruct Martha, Rachel, and Elsie to go to the dormitory, clean up, and collect their personal effects. Instead, he shoved them rudely up the stairs, away from the shop floor, and marched them directly down the checkerboard hallway to the door of his office.

CHAPTER 10

The Foundering Antelope; A Long Journey

If anything, the woman elicited sympathy from the passing travelers along the Road. She passed easily as a wayward vagabond, her flower-printed dashiki flecked with mud and torn at the shoulder. A gypsy caravan driver even stopped and gave her a knitted shawl, which she accepted with mumbled thanks. Certainly, the few passersby who saw her decided she must have suffered some sort of great misfortune that she should be out traveling the Long Road in this cold, wintry weather in such wretched clothing. One pilgrim sought to give her a few coins as he passed but recoiled when he saw her lacerated, bloodied face. He dropped the silver to the ground and continued on his way. She did not stop to pick them up.

The snow blew wildly at the top of the pass, and the woman held the shawl she'd been given tight at her throat. The terrain was steep and inhospitable here, and the snow collected on the ground in heaping drifts. The visibility grew dim, and the woman gritted her teeth in determination. Finally, she arrived at the faded wooden sign that marked the border between North Wood and Wildwood, at which point she took a small trail that led off the road and into the trees. Before long, she came to a cave in the mountainside. A warm fire crackled within and she entered, greeting the inhabitants curtly.

"It's done, Darla?" asked one of the fireside-sitters. He was a dark-haired man, dressed in a black three-piece suit.

She nodded as she sat by the fire. She reached her hands out to warm them. Her fingers were blotched with dark red stains.

"Good," said a woman on the other side of the fire pit. She had her hair cropped close to her skull and wore a sort of terrycloth tracksuit.

Darla exhaled a sigh of relief as the warmth of the cave settled around her. She shook a few errant flakes of snow from her long black hair before she looked at the fourth occupant of the cave: a wolf wearing an eye patch.

"Now, Corporal," said Darla, "if you would kindly tell us exactly where this bandit enclave is, we can issue you your reward."

The wolf huffed agreement and took a long draw off a flagon of beer.

❧

"I don't know if this is such a good idea, Prue," said Curtis, watching his friend frantically pack a knapsack with a few days' worth of supplies. They were standing in the bandits' kitchen; Prue was pulling items from a makeshift larder while the kitchen staff looked on. "I mean, we're supposed to keep you safe. Hidden."

"Hold this," said Prue, putting the half-filled pack in his arms. She stuck an apple in her mouth, clasping it with her teeth, while she searched through a basket of tarnished silver utensils. Finding an oak-handled buck knife, she opened it and tested the blade. Satisfied, she turned and threw it into the knapsack in Curtis's hands.

She took the apple out of her mouth to speak. "I have to. I have to see her. I have to see what happened. I have to see the tree."

"What tree?"

"The Council Tree," Prue said as she began rummaging about in the knapsack, taking stock. "After I came to, after the screaming stopped, I felt this weird pull. It felt a little like homesickness. But it wasn't, 'cause I wasn't sick for *my* home. It's like if I don't do this, I can't see the way forward. Besides, maybe I can help." She grabbed the bag from Curtis and slung it over her back.

"But what about Brendan?" Curtis said, his voice low so as not to attract too much attention. The bandits of the kitchen staff returned to their work, skinning potatoes and dropping bowlfuls

of carrots into a steaming pot on a crackling fire. "What about our instructions? To keep you safe? You know, it was Iphigenia herself who gave them to us."

"Bye," said Prue.

Curtis chased after as Prue walked out of the cave and onto a swaying rope bridge. "Now hold on here," he said.

"I can't explain it, Curtis," said Prue, moving briskly.

"So you just heard all this screaming. . . ."

"Yes."

"And you nearly passed out."

"Yes."

"And now you have to come out of hiding—even though your life is threatened by a shape-changing assassin—to walk however many miles in a snowstorm to go talk to a tree."

"Yup."

"I'm coming with you," said Curtis.

Together, they threaded the various walkways and bridges of the bandit encampment. Soon, they arrived at the bottom of the cliff wall they'd climbed to enter. Two cables hung down from the precipice above, their ends pooled in a coil. Curtis and Prue helped each other lock into the climbing harnesses; arriving at the top, they were greeted by a familiar voice.

"What's up, kids?" asked Septimus the rat, standing at eye level on a low branch. He was picking his teeth with a twig.

"Did you just now get back from the North?" asked Curtis, a little out of breath from the climb.

The rat nodded. "Flying's not natural for a guy of my species. Besides, it was a nice walk. Took a little detour on the way, helped out some folks, did some good deeds; I go where I'm most needed." He puffed up his chest a little. He then eyed Prue's knapsack. "Where are you guys headed?"

"Back to North Wood," said Curtis.

"Back?" The rat groaned. "Aren't you supposed to be in hiding?" He was pointing his twig at Prue.

"I'll take my chances," she said.

"Does Brendan know?" asked the rat.

"No," said Curtis. "And we'd like to keep it that way."

Septimus stuck the twig in his mouth and chewed on it thoughtfully. "Well," he said, "I'm no good at keeping secrets. Guess I'll have to come with you guys. Besides, I don't want to be in the room when he finds out; the man's got a temper." He hopped nimbly from the tree branch and landed squarely on Curtis's shoulder. "Onward!" he said, pointing the twig northward like a saber.

The trio made their way through the tunnel in the salal bushes. Their feet quietly crunched through the light layer of snow on the groundcover. It was cold enough that they could see their breaths, but once they'd gotten moving, their bodies warmed to the weather. They walked in silence; Prue was busy trying to untangle the strange resonances she'd received at that moment when the trees started screaming and the world seemed to give way beneath her. The pull to return to North Wood had been so great; regardless of the possibility that she was putting her life—and her friends' lives—in danger by doing this. She could only trust her intuition. Occasionally as she walked she listened in on the noises of the Wood—the chatter of the flora—and was dismayed to hear only, still, the voiceless noise of their seemingly unknowable language.

Finally, a voice she understood broke through. "So why, exactly, are we going to North Wood?" It was Septimus. Frankly, it was amazing he'd been able to keep quiet as long as he had.

"A calling," said Prue cryptically. In truth, it was the best explanation she could muster.

"Oh," said Septimus. "Like, a phone calling?"

Prue considered this before replying: "Sort of. But, like, in my soul."

"Neat," said the rat. "A soul phone."

The sky had darkened; as they began climbing up a steep hillside, the snow began to fall. It appeared in Prue's vision like sparks of pure white, sailing down from the tops of the trees. She could feel the little flakes alight on her cheek and burn away to nothing. She wore a dark-green knitted hat, given her by a bandit on her arrival, and she pulled it low over her brow. Reaching a level area of ground, she paused. "The way I figure it," she said, "we should keep to the woods. We're more likely to be detected on the Road, right?" She eyed the terrain warily. "But where to from here?"

"Hold on," said Curtis. "Let a native handle this." He proudly strode past Prue and skidded down a steep slope on the other side of the flat area. She followed. Before long, Curtis had peeled away a thick blanket of briar to reveal a game trail leading through the bracken. "I got an 'exceptional' in Wildwood Geography last quarter," he said, smiling.

They followed the trail quietly, the two kids winding the snaking path by foot while Septimus stayed in the canopy of the trees, scouting the way as they traveled. They'd been walking for several hours when Prue and Curtis heard a hissing from the boughs above their heads.

"Guys!" It was Septimus. "Get hidden! Something's coming!"

Without speaking, Prue and Curtis dove into the brush alongside the winding trail, hiding themselves in the prehistoric stands of sword fern that lined the way. Ahead, the trail gave onto an open, grassy meadow; this was where the two kids trained their eyes. A little bit of snow fell down the back of Prue's coat when she disrupted the fern fronds, and she winced at the sudden chill.

A crackle could be heard in the underbrush ahead, in the stand of trees that lined the far edge of the meadow. It sounded to Prue like something coming on four feet. She lowered her head farther to the ground; she imagined a black fox emerging, its teeth bared, and her chest sputtered with pinpricks of fright.

But no: It was an antelope. And a very tired-looking one at that. It stopped on the edge of the clearing and sniffed at the frozen ground. As it turned its head, Prue noticed that it was wearing the sackcloth robe of the North Wood Mystics; as if compelled, Prue burst out of hiding, startling the antelope badly.

"Hello!" she called. "It's me, Prue!"

The antelope spooked; its legs articulated toward the earth, ready to spring away at lightning speed. When it saw Prue, a look of surprise fell over its face.

"The half-breed girl!" said the antelope. "How glad I am to see you!"

Prue waved Curtis from his place in the stand of ferns. "What are you doing in Wildwood?" she asked.

"I thought I'd never find you!" continued the antelope. "In all of Wildwood, and I was prepared to search high and low."

"You came for *us*?" asked Curtis, standing and wiping snow from his pants.

"Yes," said the antelope. The astonishment drifted from his face and was replaced by a despondent frown. "My name's Timon. The Elder Mystic, she sent me to find you. To warn you."

Prue froze, a quiet realization coming over her. The Mystic needn't have even spoken; she understood what he had come to say. It was what she had expected, what she had intuited from the trees.

"Iphigenia," said Prue.

The antelope nodded ruefully. His knees buckled, and he sat down on the ground. He began shaking his head. "Oh my, oh my," he chanted.

"Is she okay?"

"Oh, Prue," said the Mystic, lost in his own sorrow. "Oh, dear Prue."

She shared a glance with Curtis before approaching the antelope. She knelt down by his side and began petting the brushlike fur of his neck. "Calm down," she said, attempting to sound consoling. She tried to channel her parents, the way they warmly rubbed her back as she lamented some lost pet or forgotten toy. "It's okay," she said. "It's all right."

The antelope brought his hoof to his eye and wiped a tear from his cheek. "I just don't know what to say; I hadn't allowed myself to even think until now. I was so intent on finding you, on doing the Elder Mystic's bidding. And it all seemed so hopeless, but at least I had something to keep my mind off that terrible, terrible scene."

"What scene?" asked Prue. Curtis had arrived at their side. He gave Prue a long, searching look. "Iphigenia—is she okay?"

"I don't know," said the Mystic. "I left her while she was still being pursued. She bid me find you. That's the last thing she said to me. 'Find the half-breed children. Warn them.' But I hadn't traveled far before I felt a grave foreboding from the trees. I fear she may be

gone." He collapsed into swelling sobs.

Curtis stubbed his boot angrily in the ground. "It was that fox, huh? That woman-turned-fox."

Timon, gaining control again, nodded. "She's a formidable foe," he said. "We knocked out her partners, but she herself was too strong and fleet of foot."

"How many were there?" asked Prue.

"Three: Two men, one woman."

"Darla," said Prue. "Darla Thennis."

"You've met?" asked Timon.

"Yeah, she was my science teacher."

Timon looked at her, perplexed.

"But she survived?" asked Curtis.

"Yes," said Timon. "And there may be more. Kitsunes never engage in packs larger than three. Their training revolves around the concept of the strategic triangle. So while she might be deprived of her two partners, no doubt she has more somewhere."

"Well, that settles it," Curtis said, sounding almost relieved to hear this foreboding news. "Guess we should head back to the camp."

Prue ignored him. Instead, she spoke to the antelope. "How are you, strength-wise? Can you make it back to North Wood safely?"

The Mystic huffed a little breath of steam from his nostrils and pushed himself onto his hooves. "Yes, fine," he said. "Plenty strong."

"Do you think you could carry two kids on your back?"

"Wait a second, Prue," interrupted Curtis. "Did you hear a thing he just said? The Kitsunes are in North Wood. They're looking for *us*. You just want to go announce yourself to them?"

"I told you: I don't have a choice," said Prue. "I've got to go, science teacher or no. Stay if you want." Then, to the antelope: "Will you take me?"

The antelope hemmed uncertainly and pawed at the ground. "If that is your wish, Prue," he said. "Though you may be putting yourself in serious danger."

"It is."

"Very well," the antelope said, and he crouched low so that she could climb astride his slim back. Curtis stood, fidgeting in his boots.

"Are you coming or not?" Prue asked.

He pointed an accusing finger at his friend. "You!" he said. "You are *infuriating*!" Having given his accusation, Curtis promptly capitulated and climbed onto the back of the antelope. Curling his arms around Prue's belly, he braced himself as the animal broke into a trot and began heading north. The rat in the tree boughs overhead leapt nimbly from branch to branch, preceding the party as they went.

❧

The closer Prue moved to the tree, the more certain she felt in her decision to make the journey. Like a kind of thirst that grows stronger once you're holding the glass of water in your hand, when she'd crossed over the boundary between Wildwood and North Wood, the desire to be at the tree was nearly unendurable. The going had been tough; the coming storm blanketed the tall hills and peaks of the Cathedral Mountains, and they were forced to stop on several occasions to wait out the flurry of a particularly bad squall. The antelope was strong and sure-footed; he made careful but steady time over the little notches in the mountainside they were forced to cross.

They were given fresh water and food by a badger who lived in a cabin in the hills; a wandering swan, white as the snow on the ground, gave them clear directions once they'd come down into the valleys of the North Wood and were uncertain of their way. Both animals had seen the antelope's robe and had made every effort to help them. The going was arduous; anytime they found themselves coming closer to any well-trod road, they instinctively moved away from it, preferring instead to remain in the safe concealment of the dense forest. Occasionally, the two kids would opt to walk alongside the antelope, giving him a break from carrying them.

They'd only just remounted the back of the antelope when they arrived at the great clearing in the woods. The tug of the tree at that point was so distracting and powerful in its strength that Prue could barely stay steady in her seat. Curtis had to hold her tight against his chest; she'd nearly fallen from the Mystic's back twice. They broke through a line of trees where they could see brimming daylight and found themselves on the edge of the great meadow that surrounded the Council Tree.

The mysterious pull that Prue had been feeling since the day before suddenly dissipated, like a wisp of smoke. She had arrived at the source.

Curtis, who hadn't set eyes on the great tree before, caught his breath in his throat when he saw it. The sun was setting, and a gray pallor was cast over the wide clearing; the gnarled and ancient tree loomed tall over the disappearing light in the meadow, its branches bereft of leaves. At the base of its trunk, a pallet had been constructed of moss and stone. Seeing this, the antelope issued a sorrowful moan. Prue and Curtis slid from his back and watched as the Mystic stumbled toward the tree. They numbly followed. Prue guessed at the reason for the simple construction; she mouthed a *no* as she hurried after the antelope.

The pallet was tucked into one of the tree's large exposed roots like a baby cradled in the arm of a protective parent. The surface was made of a thick blanket of moss and was strewn with the simple hues of winter flora: the soft white globes of the snowberry bush, the bright-red-berried holly, and the pale green of the thistle. All this lovely detritus served to make a kind of bed. Arriving there, Prue looked to Timon and rasped a desperate, "Is it?"

Timon, his eyes choked with tears, nodded.

Just then, a flickering motion from the edge of the clearing caught their eyes. A procession was approaching: A group of robed figures carrying torches issued from the tree line. As they poured into the meadow, they gathered in a line and made their way toward the mossy bed. In the middle of the procession, several of the figures walked under the weight of a stiff stretcher, bearing what looked to be the shrouded body of a woman. Prue and Curtis were frozen in place as they watched the solemn parade. When the first of the figures arrived at the pallet, they moved outward, creating a semicircle around the structure. They walked in silence, their eyes downcast.

The stretcher was placed on the pallet's bed of moss; the body was covered in a simple quilt, which one of the Mystics pulled back to reveal the face of Iphigenia.

The Elder Mystic's eyes were peacefully closed. Her face, pale and still, was set in a look of quiet grace. She looked as if she'd just had a pleasant meal and was enjoying the afterglow. Tears immediately sprang to Prue's eyes as she watched the ceremony proceed.

Once the body had been laid on the pallet and the torch-bearing Mystics had fanned out to surround it, a new group of mourners appeared from the edge of the clearing: the acolytes. They came from the surrounding woods bearing objects in their arms: blankets and robes, papers and plants. Prue guessed the objects to be the possessions of the Elder Mystic, carried from her home. They were each placed carefully around Iphigenia's still body. Many of the bearers touched the hem of her shroud lovingly before stepping back to join the crowd.

"I can't believe this," whispered Curtis as they stood among the gathered Mystics and acolytes. "I just saw her. She was so . . . alive."

Prue wiped tears from her eyes with the sleeve of her jacket. "I wish I'd had the chance to see her again," she said. "I wish I'd had the chance just to talk with her."

Curtis put his arm around Prue's shoulder. They both let the tears fall freely.

One of the Mystics, an older man with long, braided hair and a white-flecked beard, stepped forward. He walked to the pallet and placed his hand softly on Iphigenia's body before turning to the crowd and speaking.

"Tonight, we return the vessel of Iphigenia to the Wood, her spirit having already been absorbed by the fabric of the cosmos. And with her, we return the trappings of her earthly life to the ground." His voice was calm, benevolent.

He then nodded to the surrounding Mystics, and they began to make a semicircle around Iphigenia's body. A young boy, an acolyte, held the center of the arc as each one, in turn, sat down and arranged their legs into lotus position. They began to meditate. Prue instinctively held her hand to her lips, her eyes full of tears.

There then came a sound from the base of the pallet, a kind of earthy tearing noise, as the grass and bracken surrounding the bed began to undulate alive. Prue felt a kind of electricity surging through the ground at her feet; she could now hear the collective vegetation of the clearing begin its sorrowful keening.

AAAAAAAAAA.

It issued from every blade of grass, every branch and bramble. The mossy bed shook; the ground beneath began to tremble. Little tendrils of root shot up the side of the pallet and made a kind of webby cocoon before the earth below yawned open and the body of Iphigenia, Elder Mystic of North Wood, was consumed by the earth.

The world was silent.

The acolytes and Mystics awoke from their meditation. Prue remained as if paralyzed, staring at the virgin ground where the bed of moss had stood. Curtis grabbed her arm. "Whoa," he said.

The boy who'd been the center of the meditators' arc was standing farther off, just beyond the ring of light emanating from the torchbearers on the crowd's fringe. Prue couldn't help but notice that he seemed to be watching her.

After a time, the collected Mystics and acolytes began to move away from the circle and started mingling among the crowd. Prue noticed that many of the local townspeople and farmers had arrived, standing at a polite distance from the ceremony. They now joined the crowd, and an air of conviviality overtook the previously somber proceedings. Smiles started appearing on faces. Hands were shaken genially, people shared warm embraces. Prue turned and saw that Timon was not far off, speaking with a few of the younger acolytes. She brushed her hand against his side.

"Ah, Prue," he said, smiling to see her. "I am speechless; however broken my heart, I am happy we made it in time for this. Regardless of the circumstances."

"Yes," said Prue. "Thank you for carrying us so far." She paused, at a loss for words. Then: "I'm so confused! I'd come all this way, following some weird pull, some *calling*. I was sure she was the thing, the—whatever—that was pulling me. I can't believe she's gone and I'm here. I mean, what do I do now?"

"It will be revealed," said Timon. "It will be revealed. I have no doubt."

Curtis appeared at Prue's side. "Where do we go from here?" he asked.

"A potluck is to be held at the Great Hall," said Timon. "Even in times of rationing, a wake requires a gathering. Do you suppose it will be safe for you to attend?"

Septimus, who'd been on Curtis's shoulder, spoke up. "My guess is this is the last place they'd think to look for you. No one in their right mind would've done what you've done. I mean, you'd have to have a serious nut loose to come to the scene of your own assassin's crime."

"Thanks," said Prue.

"Just telling it like it is."

"Or it's a trap," said Curtis. "They might've guessed we would make the journey. But it's true: It doesn't totally make sense. They couldn't know *why* we came."

"Exactly," said Prue. "And that's something I'm still working out." She looked past the milling figures in the meadow to the tree. The glow from the torches sent little flickers of pale yellow light along its knobby trunk.

Why have you called me here?

The meadow was emptying of mourners. Those bearing torches were leading the way toward the eastern edge of the clearing. "You guys go on ahead," said Prue. "I'll be along in a bit. I'll find my way."

The three of them, Septimus, Timon, and Curtis, followed the potluck goers away from the funeral site. Prue watched them leave. A heaviness had lodged itself in the cavity of her chest. She walked around the far side of the tree, away from the burial site, to a little nook made by a particularly large limb of the tree's exposed roots. Here, she placed both hands on the cold, silent wood and closed her eyes.

What is it? Why am I here?

There was no response; if the tree was now communicating with her, she was unable to register its thoughts.

What do you want me to do?

"You've come a long way."

Prue opened her eyes. The voice was not coming from inside her mind; rather, she heard it behind her. She turned to see a young boy, maybe seven years old, standing there, holding a short lit candle. He wore the brown, hempen robe of the Mystics.

"And you put yourself in tremendous danger," he said. Prue recognized him to be the boy who'd been at the center of the meditations; clearly, his station must've been high to be given that responsibility. As he walked closer, she noticed that he tended to look off to one side of her, as if he were watching something just beyond her shoulder.

"Are you a Mystic?" asked Prue. When the boy nodded, she said, "You're so young!"

"I'm a Yearling," said the boy, still looking away. "They call us that. The younger acolytes."

"What's your name?"

"I'm Alister. And you are Prue."

Prue nodded, somewhat unnerved by the Yearling's bearing. He seemed unconcerned with easing into an introduction.

"You knew the Elder Mystic?" he asked.

"I did, yeah," said Prue. "She was, well, I suppose she was a friend. I didn't know her that well, or for that long. But she was really important to me."

"Me too, but now she is dead," said the boy. His face betrayed no emotion at this abrupt declaration. His eyes strayed farther afield to look at the tree. He stood for a moment, silent, as he studied the lines in the wood. "It wants to tell you something."

Prue was shocked. "What? Who?"

"The tree," Alister said. "It's called you here, you know."

"How can you—how can you *hear* it?"

The boy shrugged. "Just something I've always been able to do. I don't know why. I haven't told my teachers, the older Mystics. They say I'm not supposed to be able to. I guess I just haven't thought to correct them."

Prue moved closer to the boy. "What's it saying?"

The boy didn't respond. Prue wasn't sure whether he'd heard her. She repeated the question, but the boy still didn't answer.

Finally, his attention now turned to Prue's feet, he spoke. "It says that you can bring the severed three together."

"I don't know what that means," said Prue, blinking rapidly.

"The Three Trees of the Wood," explained Alister. "You can unite them. But . . ." He paused, his eyes looking skyward. The look on his face suggested that he was in the process of *receiving*. After the look faded, he nodded in quiet understanding. "But that is far off." He smiled warmly at the vacant space just next to Prue's left cheek. "You will rise to great prominence. A sovereign, perhaps."

Prue was dumbfounded.

The child spoke again. "But first, the true heir must be . . . be . . ." Now Alister's brow was furrowed in deep concentration. Whatever was being communicated to him was difficult to unpack. He reminded Prue of someone slowly translating a difficult language, like the few kids at her school for whom English was their second language. They were brimming with ideas; they just had a hard time getting them out in the language they were expected to use. His eyes then suggested that he'd arrived at a satisfactory translation. "Reanimated," he said. "Yes, that's it. Reanimated. The true heir must be reanimated." However sure he was of the word, he seemed be to as flummoxed by it as Prue. "Do you know what that means?" he asked.

"Reanimated. Like, brought back to life? From the dead?"

"No, not quite," said Alister. "Like a machine. Repair. I don't know if there's a human word for it."

"Reanimate the true heir. Like a machine." Prue puzzled over the words. "Who's the true heir?"

The boy shrugged.

Somewhere, on the periphery of her thinking, something swirled, batting at her consciousness like a moth at a lightbulb. The answer was there, somewhere.

The Yearling continued his channeling haltingly. "This is the thing—the only thing—that will bring peace. And save you—you and your friends' lives. But you're—you're not the only one. They know. The others know. They will be trying as well. And if they succeed, all is lost." And then: "Reanimate the true heir. The twice-died boy."

Prue had scarcely heard this last flow of information; she was too busy searching her brain for clues that might shed some light on this mysterious phrase. *Reanimate the true heir. Like a machine. The twice-died boy.* What did that even mean? And then it struck her. "Alexei!" she said aloud. "The boy prince!"

"The tree does not recognize cultural signifiers," Alister said, and Prue cocked an eyebrow at him.

"*Anyway*," she said, "it must mean Alexei, Alexandra's—the Dowager Governess's—son! When he died, she brought him back to life as a mechanical—thing! Then . . ." Something weird and gross involving teeth, she remembered. It had been so long ago, her meeting with Owl Rex. That night when she'd slipped away from the Mansion and arrived at his South Wood residence. They'd sat in front of the blazing fire, sipping tea. He'd told her many incredible things, stories of the Dowager Governess and her husband, the late Grigor Svik. And of their young son, Alexei, who'd died in a—what?—hunting accident? She couldn't quite remember the details. But yes: Alexandra, in her grief, had brought him back to life as a—what had been Owl's word for it? An automaton. That was it. She'd had a mechanical replica built of her son, and she'd brought him back to life by sticking his full set of teeth, which she'd saved, into the machine's mouth. The mother and son were reunited. But, the story went, sometime later Alexei discovered the mystery of his existence and he, in his despair, removed something, some vital bit from his metal body, and destroyed it. He perished, this time for good; he was irreparable. *The twice-died boy.* The people of South Wood rose up against Alexandra, and she was exiled to Wildwood. And now the tree wanted someone to bring Alexei back? All these thoughts raced through Prue's mind while the boy Yearling looked on.

"Yes," was all he said. "That's right."

"Wait," said Prue. "Did you just read my mind?"

"I didn't. The tree did."

She looked up at the tall, twisted boughs of the Council Tree. *Periwinkle sousaphone,* she thought.

"That's silly," said the boy.

"Just testing."

"Oh."

"But how are we supposed to do . . . ," she began, before transitioning to thought: *How do we reanimate him?*

The boy answered, "Find the makers. The makers must remake. Reanimate the true heir, the twice-died. This will bring peace. But know this: Your path will be uncommon. Sometimes it is necessary to go under to get above." The boy's face, after issuing the decree, went blank. He was silent for a time and his eyes gravitated toward the trunk of the tree, as if searching for something lost. "And that's it. That's all it can say."

"That's all? Nothing about how to do it?" Prue was becoming frantic in her questioning. "Or who these makers are? And how to find them?"

The boy only shook his head.

"That's maddening," said Prue. And then, for good measure, she turned to the tree and thought, *That's maddening.* The wind whipped through the meadow; now the only light came from a few torches on the far side of the tree. They cast the trunk in a ghostly silhouette. The boy began wandering away, his eyes fixated on something in the distance.

"Wait!" called Prue, carefully stepping after him.

"Find the makers," said the boy, as if to himself. "Reanimate the true heir."

"I don't know what this means!" shouted Prue. The boy had moved beyond the illuminated halo of the torches; he had disappeared into the bordering dark.

"Find the makers," Prue heard the boy's voice sound. "Reanimate the true heir."

And then she was alone.

CHAPTER 11

Across the Boundary

Unthank led the three girls into the office and shut the door behind them. To Elsie, the sound of the door latching cracked like a lightning strike, and she cringed to hear it. What's more, she hadn't even been allowed to go to the dormitory to get her Intrepid Tina doll, and her hands felt very empty without her. No one had spoken since they'd left the factory floor; the silence had been oppressive, ominous. Only their footsteps, echoing noisily on the hallway floor, broke the quiet. Inside the office, Elsie was greeted with a very strange array of sights: a weird, metallic chair in the center of the room, bookshelves stacked with little glass jars and vials, the blinking lights of a bunch of little white boxes—the same kind that Unthank had carried with him when he made his accusations to the kids in the machine shop.

He'd been positively apoplectic then; now he seemed to be almost giddy. Once he'd shepherded the girls into the office and closed the door, he lined Elsie, Rachel, and Martha up in front of his desk and began rubbing his hands together excitedly.

"Three of you," he said. "Three live specimens. It's not often that such an opportunity presents itself."

Miss Mudrak stood to the side of the line of three, looking down with a disinterested scowl on her face.

"What have you done with Carl?" Rachel asked Unthank, her voice imbued with a rare kind of bravery.

"And all the others?" added Martha.

Unthank responded, "Shush, girls. Think of it this way: You're making an enormous contribution to science. Not only to science, actually, but the progress of humankind. You will be remembered and lauded. When people talk about space flight, it's the ones who took the risks who are most remembered. We don't know much about those Russian scientists, but we sure know who the first into space was, don't we?" He didn't wait for an answer. "Laika!"

"That was a dog," said Martha.

"Doesn't matter. A very famous dog."

"And didn't she die?" she pressed.

Unthank only glared at her.

"What are you getting at?" asked Rachel. "What are you going to do with us?"

Unthank paused, as if collecting his thoughts. He knelt down in front of the three girls like a proud parent, sizing up his brood after a successful holiday recital. "Girls," he said. "Girls."

Elsie was suspicious of this turn of events; his earlier frustration and anger seemed to have vanished completely.

He continued, "I have a dream. I have a great ambition. And with your help, I'm going to achieve it." He looked off to his right, where a set of high windows let in the gray light of the winter day. A few trees could be seen distantly through the foggy panes. He stood and walked to those windows, peering out of them. "Out there," he said, pointing to the trees, "out there is a vast swath of untouched, untrammeled *resources*. Trees. Minerals. *Land.* Thousands upon thousands of acres of it. This so-called Impassable Wilderness, this wild area, which so far no man or woman has had the guts and the guile to conquer—I intend to be the one, when the history is written, to have finally overcome the challenges of the place to call it my own." The color in his face was rising; he was getting very excited. He jogged over to his desk, piled high with papers. Pulling a few maps from the surface, he waved them at the three girls.

"Look at this," he said. "I mean: There are no deeds, no tax records, no Bureau of Land Management surveys. This place would seem to not even exist! And yet it's right there, on the cusp of our city, taunting us. Toying with us. As if the whole place were just wagging its great green tongue at us."

The girls just stared at the man.

"Well, I'm this close—this close!" He was holding his thumb and index finger a few inches apart. "I've had a few ideas the past week—a few, in the parlance of us scientists, 'eureka moments.' I thought I'd have to wait and parse out those ideas over weeks and weeks, as more kids became Unadoptable. But now I have three. Three pitch-perfect Unadoptable children on which to try the spoils of my research."

Elsie couldn't keep silent any longer. "Sir, Mr. Unthank," she said, pleadingly. "Me and my sister's parents are coming for us in less than a week. Please, sir, let us go. They're expecting us to be safe here."

"Parents," he said, pausing as if trying to remember the meaning of the word. "Coming for you?" He looked at Desdemona.

"This is true," said Miss Mudrak icily.

Rachel interceded. "Yeah, they were only boarding us here. They went to Turkey to look for my brother. They'll be back really soon. Plus, my dad's really big and knows how to knife-fight."

"He knows how to knife-fight?" asked Elsie, unable to stop herself. Rachel just shot her a glare.

"Well," said Unthank, "that sounds scary. How about you? Should we be worried about your parents?" He had rounded on Martha.

Desdemona answered for her: "The Chinese is orphan."

"My name's Martha," corrected the girl angrily, "and I'm Korean." Her voice pitched down a somber octave as she said, "My parents aren't coming back for me."

"Well, that's convenient, at least," said Unthank. He looked back at the Mehlbergs. "As for you two, I'm sorry to say that your parents were well aware of the agreed terms and conditions associated with boarding children at the Unthank Home. I'll show you." He walked back to the desk and, rifling through an overcrowded file cabinet, returned with a piece of paper. It was an application of some sort. Elsie and Rachel's names had been written—in her mother's hand—at the top of the page. Both her mother and father had signed the document. Unthank traced his finger along a paragraph of text below the signature line, text printed so small as to be almost illegible.

"You'll see here, at the bottom of the page, where it says (and I quote): 'The Proprietors reserve the right to mete punishment at their discretion if the child is deemed a hazard to themselves or the greater population. Three such infractions will render the child Unadoptable, at which point the Proprietors reserve the right to remove such a child from the adoptive population of the Home.'" He looked up from the page. "Pretty clear, really. Wouldn't you say, Miss Mudrak?"

"Clear as windshield," said Desdemona.

"And you'll see that it's been initialed, right there at the bottom, by a certain . . ." Unthank screwed up his face to decipher the writing. "D. M. Your father, I presume?"

"David," said Elsie flatly. "Yeah. But I don't really know what that all means. How could he know?"

"And besides, they were in a big hurry—they had to catch a plane," said Rachel. "There's no way they would agree to this. You'll see."

"Hmm," hemmed Unthank. "We will see, won't we? For example, we'll see how much traction that line of argument gets in a court of law." He shook the document in their faces briefly before returning it to the filing cabinet. Back in front of the line of girls, he clapped his hands.

"Now," he said, "let's get started. I'll need a volunteer."

The girls remained silent. Unthank was standing at the dentist chair, wiping imagined dust from the seat cushion. "Anyone?" he asked. "Very well." His finger pointed at the girls, he began counting off: "Eeny, meeny, miney, mo."

The last word landed on Martha. She steeled herself and said: "I'm ready."

"Very brave," said Unthank. "Very brave indeed. Now, if you wouldn't mind climbing into this seat, we can begin."

Desdemona stood guard over Rachel and Elsie as Martha did as the man instructed. Once she'd been settled into the chair, a worried look draped across her face, Unthank threw the clasps at her hands and feet. He smiled apologetically. "Just a precaution," he explained. "Once bitten, twice shy, as they say. Can't afford a runner." His specimen confined to the chair, Unthank walked to the rows of bookshelves and began browsing the contents, murmuring to himself. He held a dog-eared black notebook in his hand and flipped the pages eagerly, his fingers dragging over the book's words. Glancing back to the shelf, he grabbed a handful of bottles and returned to the desk, where he proceeded to combine the bottles' contents with a mortar and pestle.

"What is he doing?" Elsie whispered, as if to herself. She was promptly shushed by Miss Mudrak.

Having made some sort of shiny green paste (he had lifted the pestle and studied the resulting mixture; he seemed satisfied with having made, to Elsie's best approximation, toothpaste the color of snot), he stepped back to Martha in the chair. "Now," he said, "I'm going to put this in your ear."

Martha flinched, her eyes wild. She shuddered in her binds. "What is that stuff?"

"Relax," said Unthank. "It's just a mixture of thimbleberry, tannis root, and squirrel bile. With a little peanut butter to keep it binding."

Elsie heard Rachel gag a little.

"Harmless," Unthank said. "Perfectly harmless. I have a

suspicion, though, that this impenetrable boundary that keeps swallowing my specimens is, at its root, a biological function. Applied to the ear canal, so as to be in contact with the tympanic membrane—which, as no doubt you know, is a center of balance and equilibrium and thus dictates navigation and direction—this salve *should* grant you the ability to pass beyond the boundary." He spoke while he was applying the stuff to Martha's ear; she wore a quiet grimace.

"What boundary?" asked Rachel. No sooner had the words left her mouth than Desdemona went to shush her; Unthank raised a hand to Miss Mudrak and responded.

"A very good question," he said, scraping more of the paste from the bowl, "and one that has been my chief concern for these past many years. I think we've all, since time immemorial, assumed that the Impassable Wilderness was just that: an overgrown stretch of woods that no one would care to explore, let alone try to develop. We were all complicit in our ignorance. And those over-curious enough to make the journey were rewarded with being lost forever, or else journeying through a seemingly endless repetition of the same landscape for days and days before finally breaking through and finding themselves just where they'd started." He added a final dollop to Martha's other ear before standing back to study his work. "I'd heard the tales, I'd even interviewed some of the survivors. Yes, they are still around, a few of them. Takes a little bit of persuasion to get them to sing, but I have my ways." Evidently satisfied with the amount of salve he'd applied to Martha's ear, he returned to the desk and retrieved what Elsie saw to be a kind of shiny metal gun. "Now," he said to Martha, "hold very still."

Martha's eyes widened. Unthank held the gun up to her earlobe and pressed the trigger. A little *snap* sounded, and Martha gave a shrill yelp. Unthank pulled his hand away and there, freshly affixed to Martha's ear, was a small yellow tag attached to a silver stud.

"Next!" said Unthank.

The clasps were thrown open and Martha stumbled out of the chair. Back in line with Elsie and Rachel, she felt at the piercing she'd just been given. "What is it?" she asked.

"Looks like a price tag," said Elsie.

"Careful," said Desdemona. "It may infect. Don't be touching."

Unthank gestured Elsie to the chair. "*Mademoiselle?*" he said, affecting a gracious tone.

Rachel pushed Elsie aside. "I'll go."

"Good girl," said Unthank. He helped Rachel to the chair. As he concocted a new salve, he continued his monologue. "Turns out, every survivor of the Impassable Wilderness has the same tale to tell: No matter how far they walked in the woods, they got the strange impression that they were not, in fact, *going anywhere*. Bizarre, huh?"

This question was directed to Rachel, who was confined to the chair. Unthank had come back from the desk with a bowl of brown mush, and he hovered the applicator above Rachel's face as he spoke. "The olfactory sense. Very important." He took a deep, dramatic inhalation through his nostrils. "Something we might take for granted. In all fairness, it tends to pale in comparison with the other human senses. However, I happen to have done extensive research on the importance of the olfactory, and I'm given to understand that the nasal cavity is a *direct* conduit to the brain. Ninety-three percent of our total perception relies on the way things smell. Did you know that? I sure didn't. But armed thus, I've got a good sense that were we to somehow treat that conduit with natural elements, harvested from the Impassable Wilderness itself, the *perception* of confinement would be dramatically altered, and, hopefully, allow the specimen to cross over, beyond what I've termed the Impenetrable Boundary."

With that declaration, he promptly scooped up a bunch of the brown slime and shoved it, rudely, up Rachel's nose. She sputtered helplessly.

"Mwat ith that stunff?" she said, talking around her slime-plugged nose.

"All natural. One hundred percent organic," replied Unthank. "Pureed oyster mushroom, slug residue, and bark dust."

Rachel had a horrified look on her face. "Slung wesidue?"

"Now," said Unthank, taking up the piercing gun, "I have firsthand accounts—based on somewhat hazy conjecture, mind you—that there is a world existing beyond this boundary. An entire, vibrant, living world. One that we could see if only we were able to open our eyes to it. I don't know what's going on, or who's running things in this forgotten country, but I have every intention of introducing them to the modern miracle that is free market capitalism. There will unlikely be any dissenters; if there's one thing I've learned as a Titan of Industry, it's that people *love* capitalism." Without warning, he stuck the gun to Rachel's ear and—*snap*—pierced her lobe with a yellow-tagged silver stud, identical to the one he'd given Martha. Rachel winced. "Provided they're given the right incentives," he qualified. He then undid the restraints on the dentist chair, and Rachel was returned to Martha and Elsie's side, her nostrils brimful of a brown, brackish paste and a yellow tag hanging from her right ear. She looked miserable.

Then, like a barber preparing his stall for another customer, Unthank swiveled the chair to face Elsie. She felt a little push at her shoulder; it was Desdemona. Dutifully, Elsie climbed up onto the seat. Unthank's back was now to her; he was studying the jars on the shelf. He selected a small blue vial and brought it over to where Elsie sat. After twisting the cap open, he shook a tiny white ball, the size of a cake sprinkle, into the palm of his hand and held it at eye level.

"I've taken a single mote of dust that once graced the barbule of a feather retrieved from the Impassable Wilderness and diluted its essence one thousand times over with sterilized water; a single drop of that water has been placed on this tiny sugar pill, endowing it with the very memory of the place from whence the mote came. It is as sound as science gets; should my other experiments fail me, I have every confidence that this will give you the power to walk beyond the boundary and into the heart of this Wilderness." He held the pill to Elsie's mouth. "Open up, dear," he said.

Elsie did so; Unthank dropped the pill into her mouth. It dissolved in a matter of seconds, leaving the fleeting taste of something sweet on her tongue. She, too, was given a piercing on her right ear—the sting felt like a sharp pinch—and returned to stand in a line with Martha and Rachel.

"Desdemona, if you would," said Unthank as he wiped his hands clean on a nearby rag.

Miss Mudrak walked to the shelf and grabbed three of the unlabeled

white boxes. She brought them over to Unthank, who proceeded to fiddle with the small black knobs on their faces. Then, taking a roll of white gaff tape, he placed a little square of the tape on each of the boxes and scrawled a few letters on them with a black marker. He set them each, carefully, on the desk next to the girls.

"I know what those are," said Rachel. "Those are initials you just wrote." With the brown paste stuffed into her nose, she sounded like she had a particularly bad head cold.

"Very intuitive," said Unthank.

"Where's Carl Rehnquist?" asked Martha.

"Carl Rehnquist?" Unthank paused in thought.

"Yeah, you know: C.R."

"Right. Carl. That was last week, wasn't it?" He stared at the shelf of white boxes, as if using them to jog his memory. "Copper," he said finally. "A kind of copper wire crown. He wore it on his head. Sadly, didn't work." He took up his black notebook, and flipping to the back pages, he began to read: "Cynthia Schmidt: pine resin inhalant. Promising, that. Let's see: William Hatfield. Oh yes: This was a good one. Underwear made of grape leaves. Went a little bit out on a limb there. Jenny Tummel, weighted shoes. Awfully sure of that one. Went to a lot of trouble building those shoes. Didn't work." He snapped the book closed and placed it back on his desk. "Every misstep, though, has led me closer to the true answer."

"Tremendously brave, darling," said Desdemona.

Unthank registered the compliment with a wan smile. He then surveyed the three girls like a sergeant sizing up his platoon. "You girls," he said proudly, "are the front line of science and exploration. I salute you." He abruptly held his hand to his forehead, his back rigid. "And now, unto the breach!"

❧

They marched in single file, with Unthank leading and Desdemona taking up the rear. The three girls walked between the two adults, sullenly shuffling their feet through the gravel of the road that led from the Unthank Home. Rows of chemical tanks, with weird twisted plumbing extending from them like spiders' legs, lined the way. Occasionally, some exhaust pipe in the distance would emit a giant fireball into the air, and the girls would spook at the noise. The air was thick with the smell of melted plastic; a chemical haze hung in the air and surrounded them like a heavy blanket. Elsie found herself coughing every dozen steps or so; the smog was so dense it felt like her lungs had been lined with Saran Wrap.

Finally, they reached a tall chain-link fence topped with Slinky-like coils of concertina wire. A gate barred their exit. Unthank undid a padlock and swung the gate open, letting the procession through before shutting it behind them. The distinctly man-made features of the Industrial Wastes stopped abruptly here at the fence line; beyond it was a wall of absolute green. They were on the border of the Impassable Wilderness.

The trees seemed to blot out the sky; Elsie couldn't imagine any living thing could grow so tall. The in-between spaces were filled with a botanical garden's worth of leafy things, of every imaginable hue of green, all dipped in bright white snow and growing into everything, as if the whole forest was caught in some kind of wild, familial embrace.

Unthank walked up the side of a culvert, just before the first row of trees. He peered into the woods, his hands on his hips. Elsie thought maybe he was looking for his other lost specimens, the children he'd sacrificed to the forest and its so-called impenetrable boundary. Instead, he looked down at the bracken at his feet and revealed a wooden stake that had been hammered into the frozen ground. Pulling a ball of twine from his pocket, he began spooling it out, measuring the length by his forearm. He made three such pieces of twine this way, attaching one end of each to the stake. Returning to Desdemona's side, he grabbed the first of the three white boxes and began to adjust the dials. "R.M.—Rachel Mehlberg," he said, "please step forward."

She did so, her arms shivering beneath the army-issue trench coat each of the girls had been given for the event.

"This experiment requires one thing of its specimens. That you walk fifty yards into the woods and attempt to return to the very place you entered. You'll have this piece of twine to measure the distance as well as to guide you back. I will be tracking you via the transponders. Should you attempt a very inadvisable escape, I will track you down, using your transponder, and you will be very sorry for your transgression. You no longer exist to the outside world; you are lost children. Your admission data has been erased and your records interred. Escape is not a judicious choice. However: If you return to me after walking the requisite fifty yards using the twine, I will be happy to grant you your freedom."

Rachel and Elsie exchanged a look. Martha breathed deeply.

"Yes, you will be freed from the shackles of your internment at the Unthank Home, no longer forced to clean, scrape, and assemble minuscule yet inordinately expensive machine parts. Join another orphanage! Find your long-lost auntie Myra! Do what you please; on top of this, whatever money I manage to gross in the harnessing of this vast swath of natural resources, I will cut you in fifteen percent. In a trust fund, under your name. Accessible only by you. Your reward for having helped in such an enormous scientific and cultural breakthrough. How's all that sound?"

The girls gave no answer. They were all looking straight ahead into the wild of the tree line.

"I'll take your silence as consent," he said, holding up one of the white boxes. "Now, Rachel Mehlberg, please take hold of one of the coils of twine and begin walking. Good luck and Godspeed."

Rachel gave a final look to her sister before she began to walk.

between the shoulder blades that she was able to shake the feeling.

"Hey," he said, "welcome to the party. Now *this* is the way to celebrate an incredible life." He raised his own tankard in a toast.

Several partygoers were clearing away tables from one end of the hall for a dance floor; a boy was scattering sawdust on the worn floorboards as the younger members of the party gathered around excitedly. Prue smiled and took a sip from her cup; the warm liquid seemed to pour itself through her every vein, bringing much-needed heat to her cold and tired limbs. Suddenly, she heard her name being called. She turned to see Sterling Fox standing before her, an unhappy look on his face.

"Prue McKeel," he said. "What are you *doing* here?" He then shot a glance at Curtis. "And you! Bandit Curtis! You're supposed to be keeping her out of sight in your little camp."

Curtis was speechless; he turned to Prue for support.

"It's nice to see you, too, Sterling," said Prue.

The fox glared.

"It's okay," she consoled. "We're safe. We're fine. We had to come see Iphigenia, to see the tree."

Sterling, at the mention of the Elder Mystic's name, looked down sorrowfully into the pewter mug he held in his paw. "Gods rest her soul," he said. "I know she wouldn't go in fer that claptrap, the gods and all, but I say it anyways. Gods rest her, she was a lovely woman."

"Yes, she was," said Curtis, hoping that the fox's dour mood would distract him.

Sterling's stern tone was renewed. "But that don't change things a bit," he said. He gave a worried look over his shoulder before whispering, "That was her instructions. Keep the kid at the camp. Simple and plain."

Prue interjected, "It's not Curtis's fault. It's me. I couldn't stay put. I can't explain it, but I *felt* Iphigenia's, you know, passing. I *felt* it. And then I felt the intense pull to come to North Wood, to see the tree."

"Well, did you do it?" asked the fox. "Did you see the tree?"

"I did, yes."

"Then get back to that bandit camp. On the double. We can find you horses to ride if need be."

"We will," said Curtis. "We promise. Let us just get our bearings and rest a bit before we start back."

The fox looked at the two children out of the corner of his eye. Finally, he relented. "All right, then," he said. "Just tonight. Then I want you out of here come morning."

"Got it!" said Prue. Curtis waved to the fox and dragged his friend away toward the warmth of the fire.

"Come on," he said. "You seem exhausted."

"I just need to sit down for a second," said Prue.

A bonfire blazed in the stone hearth, and Prue took a seat at one of the benches surrounding it. Curtis plopped down by her side. The joyous revelry of the party was broken here and there by groups of people consoling one another in hushed, warm tones and smiling through their tears. A drawing of the Elder Mystic, rendered lovingly in pencil, had been set on the banquet table on the far side of the room. Garlands of green and white bulbs, the first of the season, were laid around it. On the other side of the fire pit, Septimus was in the process of regaling some lady rat with his version of the Battle for the Plinth. She was smiling shyly. Prue and Curtis stared into the yellow flames.

"What's up?" asked Curtis.

Prue rubbed her eyes. "I don't know. I just had a sort of weird interaction. Trying to figure it all out."

"What happened?"

"I spoke with the tree. Or, it spoke to me. Sort of. It spoke to me through a kid."

"Really? What did it say?"

"To raise the true heir. Sorry: reanimate the true heir."

"Okay," Curtis said before taking a sip from his mug. "Weird."

"Do you know what that means?"

He looked off for a moment, as if running the words through his head. "Nothing's coming to me," he said finally.

"Alexei," said Prue. "We need to bring Alexei back."

"Oh," said Curtis, and then: "OH! You mean, Alexandra's son? The one who died?"

"Yes."

"But why? What's that going to do?"

"I don't know. Something about bringing peace. Uniting the Three Trees."

"There are three trees? Like the Council Tree?"

"Apparently," said Prue, staring into the copper-colored liquid in her cup. "It also said that it would save my life and my friends' lives."

"Well, that's something I can get behind," said Curtis.

"Me too," Prue said, trying a smile.

The band had switched to a mid-tempo waltz, and a fiddle had taken up its soaring melody. The sound of feet sweeping across the sawdust-covered floor gave a kind of solemn rhythm to the song.

During the interval of quiet between the two kids, Curtis had a moment to think. "Okay. I mean, if that's what it told you, then I guess it has to be done, right? How's it supposed to go down?"

"'Bring back the makers,'" said Prue. "That's what the tree said. Someone needs to find them so they can fix the mechanical boy prince."

Curtis wiped his hand across his face in perplexed frustration. "That's a pretty bossy tree there," he said. And then: "Where's Alexei now? The body, I mean."

"Probably in some crypt somewhere, I suppose."

"Bleagh," said Curtis, making a disgusted face before correcting himself: "Oh well, at least he's a machine. He wouldn't be, like, a rotting corpse or anything. So we just head to South Wood and tell the folks in charge that that's what needs to happen, and our work here is done, right?"

Prue shook her head. "I don't think so. The tree also said that other people would be attempting to do it; that if they were to succeed, it would spell failure for us, for the tree. From what you've told me about the situation in South Wood, I'm guessing it wouldn't be a good idea just to go down there and advertise what we're doing. I think there are probably quite a few people who would try to stand in our way."

"But it's you!" said Curtis, holding his hand patriotically at his heart. "The Bicycle Maiden! Come to set things to right! Surely folks'd be bending over backward to do your bidding."

Prue slapped his hand down, embarrassed. "I'm not so sure. I mean, with some folks, maybe. But I bet I've got a lot of enemies down there now."

Curtis gave a little huff of agreement. "Jeez," he said. "Grown-ups. They've got the run of a magical kingdom and they still manage to always mess things up."

"Plus, there's the whole thing about the shape-shifting assassins coming after us," said Prue.

Together they took resigned swigs of their spiced ciders. The lady rat Septimus had been entertaining was in a fit of laughter over something he'd just said. The jug band in the corner announced a square dance, and couples were lining up for the opportunity. Curtis looked to his friend. "Wanna?" he asked.

"What?"

"Sometimes, when the world is falling apart around you, all that's left to do is dance, right?" Curtis stood, bowed, and proffered his hand.

Prue smiled shyly. She rose from the bench and curtsied, though she didn't think she'd ever curtsied before in her life. "I'd be happy to," she said, and the both of them made their way, hand in hand, to the dance floor.

The young man with the fiddle stepped forward as the floor began to fill with eager dancers. He carried his instrument under his right arm, the bow dangling from the hook of his finger. "Ladies and gentlemen," he said in a sonorous voice, "animals, all. The next number will be a jig to the tune of 'Colton's Fancy.' Please take your partners." He hefted the violin to his neck and began sawing out a quick and vibrant tune, which was soon picked up by the ensemble behind him. The bear slapped mightily at the single string of his washtub bass, his claws giving the instrument's low tones a fine edge; the girl with the banjo, a teenager in blond braids, focused in on her whirling fingers as she plucked out a staccato roll. The rhythm was held down by an acoustic guitar, wildly beaten by a mustachioed young man in overalls sitting on an upturned apple crate. The music soared over the crowd and wove its way between the rafters of the hall like a murmuration of sprites. From the first note, the crowd came alive, and Prue and Curtis were swept up into a whirlwind dance, all led by the band as the fiddle player occasionally pulled his instrument from his chin and called out instructions.

"Promenade!"

"Do-si-do!"

"And swing your partner, round and round!"

The two of them had spent enough time running square dances in gym class to keep up with the more basic moves; when they fell out of step, there were always plenty of revelers around to catch them up. By the time the song wound to a halt, their faces were flushed and strands of Prue's bangs clung to her forehead, wet with sweat. They barely had time to catch their breaths before the fiddle player stepped

forward to announce another number.

That was when the commotion sounded from the back of the hall.

A tussle of some sort had broken out near the door. The band tried gamely to play over the ruckus, but after a time, everyone's attention was so diverted that they had to grind to a stop. The chill wind of the outside had been let into the hall; a shower of fine snowflakes blew frantic cyclones in the air, like unwanted revelers rushing into the room. Prue and Curtis looked over to see a grizzled old wolf with an eye patch scrapping in the open doorway with two members of the local constabulary. One of them was a hare wearing a colander on his head.

"Hands off, vipers!" the wolf was shouting. "Get yer mitts off me!"

Sterling, who'd been planted by the banquet table most of the evening, sprang into action. "What's this?" he demanded of the constables. "Why's this wolf being handled this way? Samuel?"

The hare stepped forward and, adjusting the rake of his colander, presented himself. "Chief Constable, we found this one in a ditch off the Long Road, babbling to himself in a very loud and disruptive manner. By my figuring, he was not comporting himself in an appropriate way in public. Reeks of drink, this one. He's raving. Keeps talking the craziest things. I'd say he's taken one too many flagons of poppy beer; he's got the hallucinations. Anyways, I thought it was prudent to check in with ye before we haul him down to the drunk tank so's he can sleep it off."

The wolf had slumped down to his knees, and the two constables struggled to keep his arms secured. He now began to weep. His sobs came in sloppy waves, and huge tears welled and fell from his one unpatched eye.

Sterling, suddenly recognizing the drunkard, strove to contain his anger. Grabbing the wolf by the front of his worn military jacket, he hefted him to eye level. "Corporal Donalbain," he hissed, "what do you have to say for yourself?"

The wolf's weeping suddenly turned to fits of strange laughter as he was confronted by the chief constable. "Ha!" he said loudly. "Do yer worst, friend. Do yer worst." His words were badly slurred, and flecks of spittle flew from his mouth as he spoke. "I ain't afeard of you shape-shiftin' fffff-oxes." He shoved free of Sterling and staggered a couple steps back, pulling his paws up as if he intended to challenge the fox to fisticuffs.

"What on *earth* are you talking about?" asked Sterling. "You're clearly off your rocker."

"Wait a second!" This was Prue, who had raced from the dance floor to watch the commotion. "Shape-shifting foxes. The Kitsunes! What does he know about them?"

Curtis had followed her. He eyed the corporal with pity. "This is the wolf who warned us about the assassin. The real question is: What's he even doing here?"

"Answer, wolf," demanded Sterling. "Why are you out of hiding?"

But the corporal seemed oblivious to the fox's demands. He was suddenly staring at Prue and Curtis, a horrified look on his face. He stumbled momentarily and reached for a nearby table, upsetting a platter of silver mugs in the process. "You!" he shouted. "You—children!"

"What's the matter?" asked Curtis, inching forward.

"NO!" shouted the wolf shrilly. "NO! You—you're supposed to be—to be *dead!*"

Prue and Curtis shared a worried look. "What are you talking about?" asked Prue.

"Away!" shrieked Donalbain. "Away, foul spirits! Back to the netherworld from whence ye came!" He had grabbed a slotted spoon from the table and began brandishing it wildly, like a sword. Those guests within swing range leapt to a safe distance. Sterling had drawn a pair of pruning shears, his weapon of choice, from his belt; Samuel pulled out a small gardening spade.

"Take it easy," said Sterling. "Relax there, old man."

Donalbain did not take his one eye off Prue and Curtis; it was wide and bloodshot and darted crazily in the cavity of his skull. His lips were pulled back in a snarl, and his yellow teeth were bared inside the matted gray of his muzzle. And then something changed in him, as a look of realization suddenly poured over his face and his mouth contorted into a severe pout. Tears sprang to his eye as he again collapsed into a heap on the floorboards.

"Oh, I'm so sorry," he blathered. "So, so sorry."

Despite Sterling's sputtered objections, Prue ran to the wolf's side. She put her arm on his shoulder. "What's the matter?" she asked.

The wolf looked up at her tearfully. "Blast it all. Blast me. I've sold you away for the price of a pint of poppy beer."

"What do you mean, sold me away?"

"You and the boy. And the old woman. All of 'em. Sold 'em down the river. And I'm ever so sorry." His words were lost in a new torrent of sobs.

"Pull it together, man!" shouted Sterling. Prue waved him away angrily.

The wolf spoke again. "That demon liquid. That ambrosia, sweet and vile. It's all I've got. It's all I've got. Can you blame me? They came to me, those black foxes, in my hour of deepest need, and it seemed like such a small thing, then. Just to talk, that's all they wanted. Words. And so I gave 'em their words, the ones they wanted, as it was such a small thing between me and more heavenly bliss. I told 'em: The boy and the girl's done gone to the camp, the camp what's snuck away in the Gap, and they're hidden there, and the King too."

Prue listened in shocked silence.

"What have you done?" whispered Curtis.

"And that was it!" moaned the wolf; his voice had devolved into a kind of mad singsong. "That was all I needed to do, and it seemed like such a small thing, then. But the dram's dry and here be I, a wretched, wretched thing. No poppy beer to whet my thirst, but plenty of blood on my paws." He held them out, his paws, and

stared at them ruefully. "Look!" he shouted. "Blood! Reddest blood! The blood of children!" But all that was there was his gray fur, flecked with dirt.

They wasted no time in getting ready for the trip. Sterling managed to arrange for two saddled horses from a nearby farm's stable, though he let fly an endless string of objections at the two children in the process. "This is crazy," came one. "You're going straight into the jaws of the enemy," came another. "You're riding a runaway train into a tunnel that leads into a station where there's a welcome-home party from all your worst nightmares," came a longer one.

"I agree with you there, that last one," said Septimus, dutifully adhered to Curtis's shoulder.

It was Curtis, mostly, who deflected these objections. He was intent on making it back to the bandit camp as quickly as possible. As he said, Brendan and the bandits had to be warned. He had defied his King's orders and in doing so had not only risked the location of the hard-won camp but also put the entire bandit family in danger. The rat, for his part, agreed, though he'd not been a full-sworn bandit. In truth, there was no telling what these shape-shifting foxes would do to get to their quarry. And no bandit worth their salt would give up the secret of Prue's location; they would rather die. This was a chief concern as well.

He spoke very little to Prue as they readied themselves for their flight. She could see the percolating resentment in his eyes but knew that he was fighting the urge to lash out at her. It was, after all, her fault that they'd come out of hiding. But it didn't change the fact that Donalbain would've likely revealed their location anyway; and what then? No, she figured, Curtis was angry about his not being there, at the camp, at the hour of its greatest need. It was unbandit-like to abandon your family. And the bandits were his family now.

Above the distant peaks of the Cathedral Mountains, a storm could be seen brewing. Dark clouds hung and obscured the mountains' tops as they climbed astride the horses and bid a quick farewell to the milling crowds outside the Long Hall. They wore heavy woolen stoles around their shoulders, given them by one of the farmers. It was approaching midnight; a sliver of moon peeked from behind a trough of clouds like a pale white eye. They kicked at the horses' flanks and galloped off toward the Long Road.

They traveled fleetly over the snow-swept highway, which was all but empty of its daytime traffic. Prue took up the rear, as each time she tried to ride abreast of her friend, he would spur his horse forward and take the lead. They didn't speak during their travels, stopping once to water the horses and eat the dried rations they'd packed in Prue's knapsack. They'd stood awkwardly in silence, Curtis with his eyes downcast the whole time.

"Curtis," Prue had ventured, "it's okay. We'll get there in time."

He didn't respond but abruptly chucked his half-eaten apple into the surrounding woods and climbed back onto his chestnut mare. "Come on, Septimus," he said. The rat made brief eye contact with Prue, shrugged, and hopped onto the back of Curtis's horse. Saddened by her friend's silence, Prue dumbly followed.

The storm that had settled over the spine of mountains separating North Wood and Wildwood hampered their travel significantly. The visibility had been reduced to nearly zero as the way before them became engulfed in a dense white cloud. They wrapped their stoles around their faces to protect them from the driving snow. A warming hut had been built on the side of the road, where a tall stone cairn stood, and a light poured from the windows. As they passed, a man entreated them to come inside, out of the cold. However, when Prue called to Curtis and suggested they take up the man's offer, the look he shot her was enough to let her know what he thought of the idea. She thanked the man, then pressed the wool of the stole to her cheeks, and they continued on their way.

They traveled all night; Prue was dozing off in her saddle when Septimus, scouting ahead, called from the overhanging branches; he'd located one of the bandits' secondary supply trails. Silently, they broke away from the road and began to follow it through the trees. The dark was dissipating now, giving way to an eerie film of light that saturated the snow-draped world around them. At this early hour, there was a renewed urgency in the way Curtis was traveling, watching the surrounding forest; he drove his horse on, kicking at her flanks, though it was clear that the animal desperately needed a rest.

"What is it?" Prue called, through the fog of her tiredness. Curtis didn't answer. They followed the game trail for a while before they came to the wall of salal bushes and blackberry vines that concealed the entrance to the bandit encampment. Septimus was standing there, waiting for them.

"Take a look at this," he said.

Someone—or something—had torn a massive hole in the clutch of green leaves and brown stalks, and Curtis leapt from his horse at the sight. The sharp, ashy smell of smoke was in the air. The understanding was mutual and wordless between the three riders; they'd come too late.

Just past the wall of bushes, where the green, mossy ground gave way to the abrupt cliff face, black, acrid clouds of smoke were issuing from the chasm. They wasted no time in rappelling down to the lower platform, where the rope walkway bridged the wide gap. There was no lamp glowing on the far side.

"What's happened?" Prue rasped. "Where is everyone?"

They ran across the bridge and found that the lantern that had previously been used to announce visitors was thrown to the ground in a scattering of bent metal and broken glass. Prue ran her fingers along a scratch in the wood of the platform's guardrail: white splinters scarred the worn surface. Some blood had been spilled. No sound came from the camp, farther along the walkways.

"No, no, no, no," Curtis was repeating incessantly.

They stepped along the walkway, unsure of who might be awaiting them, but could get no farther than the top of the East Tower before they were stopped by a downed rope bridge; there was no place to cross. The night's fall of snow had nearly obscured an army of footprints in the white blanket that covered every surface along the ravine. From their vantage, black clouds of smoke could be seen hurtling up from the caves in the rock face. Flames licked at a distant wooden structure; a staircase, collapsed in a black heap, smoldered in the cold air. A snap sounded, and Prue looked in time to see one of the ravine's many zip lines break and fall with a resounding clatter. A fire gutted the last brace of its anchor and it, too, fell into the void.

"Brendan!" Curtis shouted, his hands cupped to his mouth. There was no answer. "Aisling! Anyone!" Still, silence.

Septimus dashed down a hempen cable to a lower structure on the cliff face; his voice echoed up shortly after: "All gone! Not a soul!" It was the first time that Prue had heard the rat sound genuinely concerned about anything.

"Maybe they got out, before the foxes arrived," she suggested. Curtis continued to ignore her. "Listen, Curtis," she said. "You've got to think that they're smarter than those Kitsunes. They must've seen them coming. Maybe this is just a decoy."

"A decoy?" asked Curtis, turning on her. "Are you kidding me? Do you know how long it took to build this camp? Months and months of nonstop work. This is not a decoy. This is the wreckage of a battle. A battle that destroyed a home. My home." He slumped against the balustrade and folded his arms across his chest, burrowing his chin into his stole as if he was trying to climb into it to hide. Prue instinctively kept her distance.

"I'm sorry," she said. "So sorry."

"It's my fault," said Curtis. "I should've been here. I should've been at their side."

"I shouldn't have made you leave. I should've stayed here, where Iphigenia wanted me."

Curtis's face became flushed with anger. "Yes! You should've! It *is* all your fault. I told you to stay. I explained to you what we were supposed to do. But you had to go, didn't you?"

"You could've stayed behind," responded Prue, suddenly rising to the boy's provocation. "I didn't, like, force you to come or anything."

"But you didn't give me much choice, did you?" He had pushed himself up from his leaning position and was standing squarely in front of her. "You. Everything's always about you, isn't it, Prue? Big Prue McKeel: always knows what's up. Always in charge. You never give much a thought to what other people might think, do you?"

"That's not true and you know it."

"Pah!" laughed Curtis. "I've been living in your shadow ever since we walked into this place. You just go steamrolling through, ruining everything in your path."

Tears leapt to Prue's eyes at the accusation. Curtis did not relent. "And we're all expected to bend over backward for you, just like that. Well, I had a family here, Prue. Friends. And now they're gone. I abandoned them." He was viciously slapping himself in the chest as he spoke. "Like you'd know what that meant. Where are your friends, Prue, huh? Do you have any anymore? Am I your only friend, Prue? Huh?" When she did not respond, he said, "No wonder."

Stung, Prue looked up at Curtis through tear-wet eyes. "Like you should talk. The bandit band isn't the first family you've abandoned," she said, though she immediately regretted it.

Curtis stared at her, silent.

She realized she'd reached the point of no return. Speaking loudly: "What about your *real* family? Huh? Your sisters? Your mother and father? Ever think about them? Talk about only looking out for yourself." Prue wiped her eyes free of tears as she spoke.

Curtis's lower lip jutted out from his face. "You take that back," he said, jabbing a finger at Prue. "You take that back!"

"Easy!" Septimus's snout appeared from over the balustrade. "Isn't there some rule about fighting with your own friends? Something in the bandit code?"

"Like you'd know, rat," said a huffy Curtis, crossing his arms.

"There you go. Lashing out. I can take it."

Curtis seemed chastened; he stood quietly. Prue watched him, her eyes ripe with the threat of more tears. The rat stood on a crenellation and stared dolefully out at the smoking remnants of the camp. He tapped at his teeth with an idle finger. "Awful," he said. "No way fifteen Kitsunes could do this, let alone three."

Prue looked to Curtis. "We have to move on."

He remained silent. Septimus studied him. Prue repeated herself. "We have to find the makers, Curtis. The tree—"

"Oh, quiet about the tree," Curtis flung. "My place is here. With the bandits."

"The bandits are gone, Curtis." She stepped forward to place her hand on his arm; the boy flinched.

"Just leave me alone," he said.

That was when the voice came from across the gap. It was a woman's voice.

"Children," it said. "Don't tussle."

Prue and Curtis looked over to see a black fox, her fur wind-whipped and stained with blood, appear from the mouth of a cave. A second fox trailed after her, baring its yellow teeth.

Prue stumbled backward; Curtis reached for the sling at his belt.

"I couldn't help but overhear, and I have to say there's really no sense in bickering over trivial things." The voice issuing from the muzzle of the fox was familiar to Prue—she remembered that same feminine timbre detailing the anatomy of a flower stamen. "Don't waste your last breaths on who did what and who abandoned who." A narrow gap separated Prue and Curtis from the two foxes, once traversed by a short rope bridge. The animals leapt it handily, landing at the base of the circular stairs that climbed the outside of the tower. Curtis notched a stone into his sling and began swinging it.

"Back off," he said. "Don't you dare come closer." Septimus was at his shoulder, gripping the fabric of his epaulet.

Darla sneered. "Oh? What are you going to do? Throw a pebble at me?"

As the foxes rounded the first set of stairs, Curtis found a clear shot and let the stone fly; it hit the second fox in the side with a resounding *thump*. The animal leapt and whimpered, nearly losing his footing on the stairs.

"Nice one," prompted Septimus.

"Don't do that again, *boy*," said Darla. Curtis pulled another stone from a pouch at his belt and slipped it into the sling's cradle. He stepped forward to meet their attackers.

"Plenty more where that came from," he said defiantly. "You've got one more bandit to deal with before you're done."

Prue grabbed at Curtis's coat sleeve and pulled him toward the walkway behind them. It led down the side of the tower wall toward the platform where they'd found the shattered lantern. They still had time to escape, she reasoned. She couldn't imagine what had happened to the entire hale band of bandits, but she didn't want to see what kind of work the two assassin foxes would make of a couple of preteen humans.

The foxes made neat paw prints in the snow that covered the tower stairs. Curtis let another stone fly. Darla dodged it, her hackles raised.

"I said," she growled, "don't do that *again*!"

With that demand, she crouched and leapt the last few stairs. She stalked her two victims, approaching them in a slow, methodical way. Prue was backing down the icy walkway, trying to drag Curtis with her. Curtis, for his part, was trying to load another stone into his sling. His fingers were cold; he slipped, and the stone fell with a *thunk* to the wood floor of the tower top.

"Come on, Curtis!" hissed Prue.

"Don't bother running, children," said Darla, clearly enjoying the final phase of her hunt. "You've really got nowhere to go. One way or another, you're going to end up under our claws. We've been through a lot to find you; I would appreciate it if you didn't make this last moment *too* labor intensive."

Curtis was cursing under his breath, searching in the bag for another stone; Prue let out a scream as she slipped on the walkway's boards and slid several feet to where it leveled out. Hearing that, Curtis turned and, holding on to the banisters, shot down to where Prue had fallen. He helped her to her feet, and the two of them continued backing away from the approaching foxes.

"What happened to all the bandits? What have you done?" Curtis had abandoned the idea of fighting with the sling; it had shown no appreciable effect on the foxes' advance.

"Oh, some died," answered Darla casually. "Some ran off. They're a scrappy bunch, I'll give them that. But in the end, it really is brains over brawn. I'm sorry to say, Curtis, that they gave the both of you up rather quickly. So much for familial loyalty, eh?"

"You're lying," responded Curtis. They had arrived at the wooden platform; all that remained between them and the other side of the ravine where the coiled ropes lay was a rope bridge; they picked up their pace as they moved onto its rickety slats. The wind buffeted through the gap, and the bridge swayed and creaked. Septimus leapt down from Curtis's shoulder and began capering along one of the anchor ropes. He'd nearly made it to the far side when he let out a shout: A woman dressed in a green tracksuit had just scaled down the side of the cliff wall where the ropes were and was approaching them from the other side of the bridge.

"Ah, Callista," said Darla, seeing the woman. "So glad you could join us."

"Don't move!" whispered Septimus, returning to the two kids' side. "We're surrounded."

The three assassins slowed their approach, two on one side of the bridge, one on the other. They stepped silently, deliberately. In the center of the bridge, Curtis and Prue were pinned together, back to back, staring at their oncoming assailants.

"This is it, Prue," said Curtis.

"Uh-huh," said Prue.

"I'm sorry I said those things back there."

"Me too. I don't think you're selfish. I think you're actually a really great person."

"Really? You think that?" asked Curtis.

"Uh-huh."

The Kitsunes came closer.

"Well, I think you're pretty great too," said Curtis.

"Thanks."

The Kitsunes were now within leaping distance. Prue, in a moment of desperation, made a fleeting survey of her surroundings. There was no way they could escape past the oncoming assassins. The only way out was down.

She looked over the edge of the bridge into the darkness of the ravine. The implacable stone of the cliff wall disappeared into a veil of absolute black. In her searching, she chanced to see that the cable support by her hand was frayed down to the quick; a few single strands of fiber kept it intact. Swinging her knapsack over her shoulder, she retrieved the buck knife she'd stowed there. She flipped open the blade and flourished it dramatically over the cable.

"Come any closer," she yelled, "and I'll cut the bridge."

"What?" said Curtis.

"What?" said Septimus.

The tracksuited Kitsune, Callista, paused in her slow creep. She looked at Prue skeptically. "You wouldn't," she said.

"Yeah," agreed Curtis, his voice shaking. "You wouldn't, right?"

"Try me," said Prue. She craned her head over to see Darla, who'd stopped on the fourth plank of the bridge.

"You're bluffing," said Darla.

"No, I'm not," said Prue.

"Are you sure you're not bluffing?" asked Septimus.

Prue held the blade of the knife to the frayed rope. Darla watched her intently. She nodded to Callista, and the woman began to back away.

"Put down the knife, dear," said Darla. "This is all very foolish. How about this: You submit to us and we'll consider letting you live."

Prue scoffed, "That's the biggest load of junk I've ever heard. You killed Iphigenia. You evil, evil woman. Fox. Whatever. What's going to stop you from killing us?"

"Alas, then we are at an impasse, yes?" sighed the fox. She set a single paw forward, closer to the children. Prue could see her haunches begin to quiver. It became clear she was about to pounce.

"Hold on, guys," said Prue as she took a deep breath and cut the rope.

Someone screamed. Prue, in the flash of the moment, couldn't tell who it was. It sounded like a woman, though she'd heard Curtis scream like that before. In any case, the world pinwheeled beneath her feet as the bridge gave way on one side and the wooden slats tipped sideways in a quick, violent motion. She heard someone else yell "NO!" as if they were mourning the loss of a dear loved one, as if they were witnessing one of the great traumatic experiences of their lifetime. In that flicker of time, she came to realize it was Darla, and she experienced a flush of sympathy for the woman-turned-fox. Prue's hand, as if under the control of someone other than herself, shot out and grabbed one of the rope struts of the bridge, which was in the process of losing its bridgeness, like a puppet snipped of its strings. Her body swung around, at the mercy of the crazed motion of the rope, and she saw Callista pitch, screaming, into the blank emptiness below them.

The strap of Prue's knapsack made a hard jerk and was suddenly pulling heavily at her neck; she saw that it was Curtis, Septimus doggedly affixed to his shoulder, who'd managed to grab hold of the bag and was dangling above the ravine by a single buckle. The boy and the rat screamed in unison, at which point Prue realized it was, in fact, Septimus who'd made that very ladylike shriek just moments before. Her fingers steadily turned from bright, ruby red to bloodless white in the fraction of a second as the weight of both her and Curtis bore down on the thin rope in her hand.

"Curtis!" she shouted hoarsely. "I can't!"

But at that moment she looked over to see Darla, having shape-shifted back into human form, swinging hand over hand toward her. Her floral dashiki was torn at the cuffs and stained with mud and blood. A look of absolute rage was in the process of distorting her face. She seemed to straddle the world between human and animal, as if in the violence of the instant, she was frozen in transformation. She reached out to Prue, and Prue could see the little filigree of black hair on her wrists and the claws of her fingernails. The world slowed to a crawl.

That was when the last support of the bridge broke and the entire apparatus split in two, with Prue and Curtis swinging one way and Darla swinging the other. Septimus clung to a single strand of fringe on Curtis's epaulet, his feminine howl having turned into a steady stream of pronouncements: "Oh oh, oh, oh, oh, oh, oh." Prue watched Darla hit, hard, against the opposing cliff face, though she barely had a chance to revel in this turn of events when she, too, slammed against the rock. Her fingers, having valiantly obeyed the commands of their master for so long, simply went slack, and the three of them, Prue, Curtis, and Septimus, went spiraling downward, down into the blackness.

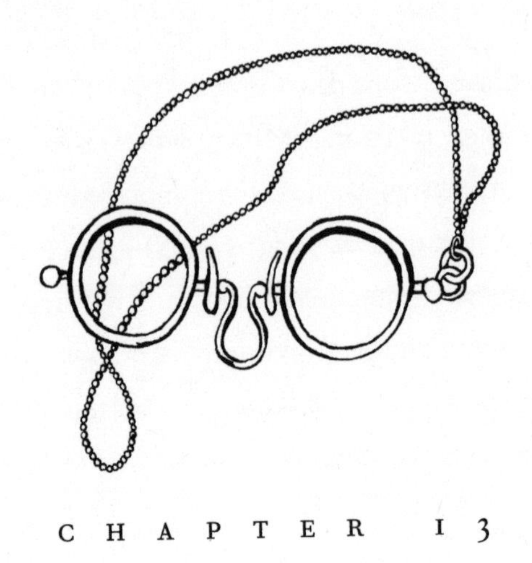

CHAPTER 13

A Promising Commission

The door shut heavily behind Unthank and he paused by the jamb, staring at the clutter of his office in quiet despair. He leaned backward against the hard wood of the door, which made the fedora on the crown of his head tip forward and fall to the ground. Swiping it up in a quick, agitated motion, he walked to his desk and threw himself into his chair, which gave up a squeaky moan. He tried to Frisbee the fedora onto the hat rack by the wardrobe, but he missed, pitifully. It tumbled into a nearby wastebasket. Unthank sat frozen for a time before he let his head fall into his palms on the surface of his desk.

A knock came at the door. "Joffrey, dear?" It was Desdemona.

"One moment, honey," he called. He sat up straight and wiped his eyes free of the few tears that were beginning to show. "Come in."

The door wheezed open. Miss Mudrak, in her sparkling gown, entered carrying a briefcase. "Are you okay?" she asked.

"Yes, yes," said Joffrey. "Just taking a moment, that's all."

"I have here the equipment."

"Oh, right. Go ahead."

Desdemona brought the briefcase across the room and, undoing the buckles, began placing the three white boxes on the shelf with their nearly identical counterparts. The little strips of tape on them read R.M., E.M., and M.S. She gave them an almost motherly look before she turned and faced Unthank.

"They will show, I think," she said.

Unthank laughed under his breath. "Yes, maybe they will."

"It seemed to me that the Chinese stayed longer on the screen. Her blip did not so disappear quickly."

"You think?"

"I do think this."

"Well, darling, sweetheart," said Unthank, "apple of my eye, you'd be wrong." He slammed his hand on the desktop. "All three of them. All three of their blips. Disappeared. *Blip. Blip. Blip.* Just like that. Once they'd gone twenty yards, easy. Gone."

Desdemona was startled by his sudden explosion. "Do not be hard upon yourself," she said. "Perhaps next time it will not be so."

"Next time?" asked Unthank, exasperated. "What about the last time? Huh? What's his name . . . Carl. Carl Rehnquist. The chubby kid. I worked for *weeks*, literally, on that copper . . . crown-thing. I studied volumes and volumes of research on the properties of copper and its effect on magnetic domains, saturation, and ferromagnetics. All that work—for nothing!"

"Calm yourself, darling," soothed Desdemona.

"And why," he said, standing up from his chair and walking toward the shelf of white boxes. "Why haven't literally *any* of them shown up again? I mean, even if that particular salve or ointment or prosthetic didn't work, you'd think that maybe one of them would find their way. What about those old men, those survivors? The ones who managed to get out? The ones I painstakingly interviewed? Were they all . . . lying to me?"

"It's best not to get so upset," said Desdemona.

Unthank lifted his finger. "That's it. This is all an elaborate joke. All those men in those dive bars that I visited; the ones in mental institutions, the ones raving about bands of coyotes dressed in nineteenth-century military uniform. They were just having me on. And guess what? I fell for it. I *flipping* fell for it, didn't I?" He stalked over to the desk and began rudely tousling the sheaves of paper on its surface. "Ha-ha. Joke's on Unthank. The kid who everyone said wouldn't amount to anything. And guess what? I did. I became a Titan. Machine parts. Showed them, didn't I? But the other guys always get the last laugh, huh? Like the guy who made this." Here, he began searching through the paper stack for something in particular, and, not finding it, he stopped in his ramblings and thrust his hands into his pockets. His eyes scanned the room. "Where is it?"

"What, dear?"

"The map. The *flipping* map, Desdemona. The one that the old man gave me."

Desdemona, sensing Joffrey's rising anger, began stepping toward the door. "I am not knowing what you talk about, map."

Unthank, rifling back through the papers, was shouting now: "The map! The map! The one with the . . . the *things* on it. The one that was given to the old man, who gave it me. With the big tree and the mansion!"

"Is not there?"

"No, it's not there." Suddenly, a thought occurred to him. "Those kids. The ones who took the transponder unit. One of them must've . . ." His voice trailed off.

"Must've . . . ?" prompted Desdemona.

Unthank thrust a finger at Miss Mudrak. "Go search through those girls' footlockers. They've got to have it. They must've stolen it."

"Okay, darling. I will do this. But you must be calmed. You are much too божевіл'ний." She huffed loudly and turned to go. But before she did so, she exclaimed, "And do not yell. It is ungentleman." And with that, Joffrey Unthank found that he was once more alone in the office.

He collapsed his weight into the chair and placed his head on the cool of the desk's surface. His remaining hair, in the tirade, had been upset and now jutted from his pate like the feathers of a peacock. A bit of snot dripped to the tip of his nose, and he wiped it away on the hem of his sleeve. He sat this way for a considerable time, torturing himself with the memories of his many years of experimentation. He was so tortured by these specters, in fact, that he briefly considered standing up, rushing to the bookshelf, and destroying every glass vial and philter and bringing a crashing end to his life's endeavor of finding a way into the Impassable Wilderness in a single, ear-shattering moment.

That is to say: He would've done this if a knock, at that moment, hadn't sounded at the door.

"What?" asked Unthank, exasperated.

"Sir," came a voice. It was Miss Talbot. "Someone to see you, sir."

He wiped his nose again and flattened the rumpled front of his sweater. "I'm not taking visitors right now, thanks very much, Miss Talbot."

"It's a man. He says it's very important."

Unthank glared at the door. "I *said*, Miss Talbot, that I am *not* receiving visitors."

There was a long pause, after which Miss Talbot's voice sounded again through the wood of the door. "The gentleman really won't take no for an answer, sir."

"Is he an attorney?" asked Unthank, groaning. He'd had his share of ambulance-chasing lawyers attempting legal sieges on his unscrupulous and somewhat negligent business practices before, though it was never anything a written check and a call to a state senator couldn't fix.

"I don't know, sir," said Miss Talbot.

"You don't know?"

Another pause. "He's . . . well, there's something fairly strange about him, sir. Something I can't rightly put my finger on."

Unthank stared at his hands as he tented them on his desk surface. What was it those Mehlberg girls had said? That their parents were returning shortly? There had been, on rare occasions, parents returning for their children, and it was often a fairly sticky wicket to navigate. He'd found, though, that with the correct tone, even a guilt-ridden parent coming back for a child they'd knowingly orphaned could be easy to placate. He sat back in his chair and tried to assume a calm demeanor. "Very well," he said. "Show him in."

A few minutes passed. Then the door creaked open and Miss Talbot shuffled into the room. Behind her walked a tall, thin man in an elegant suit, which struck Joffrey as being out of style by an easy century. His hair was neatly pomaded back from his forehead, and he wore a close-shorn beard. Perched on his nose was something resembling glasses.

"Is that . . . ," started Joffrey, searching for the word, "a pince-nez?"

The man ignored him as he strode confidently into the room. He carried a worn leather briefcase under his arm, and he seemed to be surrounded by an aura that Joffrey could only later describe as being somewhat otherworldly, as if every time you glanced in his direction it was like you'd just woken from a very strange and wonderful dream. Joffrey remained frozen for a time, marveling at the man, before he remembered his objective.

"Dear sir," said Unthank, before the thin man had an opportunity to speak, "I realize that you might be unhappy with your decision to—how should I put this?—*part ways* with your child or children, but I can assure you that—"

The thin man interrupted him. "Are you Joffrey Unthank, machine parts manufacturer?"

"I am," said Joffrey, after first sharing a questioning look with Miss Talbot. She'd evidently decided her job was done, as she promptly turned about and left the room, closing the door behind her. The thin man waited until she'd gone before he continued.

"I'd like to commission an object," said the man.

"A . . . what?" asked Unthank, confused.

"An object. A machine part. I'm given to understand that is your specialty?"

"Well, yes. But wait a second. Who are you? What's your name?"

"My name is incidental," said the thin man.

Unthank cracked a wry smile. "It might be to you, but I like to know with whom I'm doing business." He leaned back in his chair, waiting for the man to respond.

"Very well," said the thin man after a moment of hesitation. "If you insist. My name is Roger. Roger Swindon. And I wish to have a machine part made."

"Nice to meet you, Roger," said Unthank.

"May I sit?" asked Roger.

"Sure, Mr. Swindon. Have a seat." Joffrey waved at one of the leather chairs in front of the desk.

Setting the briefcase down at his feet, Roger first fanned out the twin tails of his black suit jacket before setting himself on the edge of the leather chair. He then picked up the briefcase and set it on his lap. Unthank was still staring at his suit.

"That's a fancy getup you've got there," Joffrey said. "You going to a costume party?"

This comment was ignored. "A very great deal depends on the manufacture of this object, and I would prefer if it could be done with the speediest diligence." He began unfastening the buckles on the leather briefcase as he spoke. "I have procured the design, no small feat, which should make the entire process fairly simple. I am told, by trustworthy sources, that you are the best." He paused and peered up at Unthank over his pince-nez.

Unthank smiled warily. "I like your sources," he said. "Can I ask who they are?"

"That is of scant importance." The man continued opening the briefcase. There seemed to be an inordinate number of buckles on the thing. "It would behoove me to point out at this juncture, though, that I expect you to work in absolute secrecy. No one must know that you are crafting this object. You are to speak only to me."

"Listen, buddy," said Unthank, growing weary of the man's attitude. "You come in here, insisting on seeing me. You interrupt me from my work. You won't tell me who referred you. And then you just assume that I'm going to bend over backward to—what—make some kind of *object* for you? It doesn't work that way. I have contracts with major appliance manufacturers, relationships I've fostered over years and years of hard work. I've got my hands full as it is. I can't rightly drop everything I'm doing in order to make this object for you—I owe it to my clients to make sure their work comes first. And also: I don't like secrets. I don't like working in secret. Secrecy means illegality, and that's the last thing I need right now." Unthank pulled open the center drawer of the desk and began rummaging through its contents. "I can give you the names and numbers of a few smaller-quantity manufacturers; they don't quite get the quality I do, but they'll suffice for whatever dryer manifold or replacement blender blade you're looking for."

The man listened to Unthank's monologue quietly. When Joffrey had finished and was offering Swindon a small, gold-foil business card, the man spoke again. "You'll be rewarded for your services, Mr. Unthank. I think it is in your interest to take this commission."

Unthank waved the business card impatiently. "I'm doing just fine, thanks very much. Here, take this card. This guy's pretty good."

"I can offer a very, very appealing exchange, Mr. Unthank."

"I don't work in exchanges. Maybe this guy will." He was still wagging the business card when the thin man said something that made him stop.

"Access, Mr. Unthank. I can offer access."

Joffrey raised his right eyebrow. "What kind of access?" he asked.

"The kind of access you've been looking for, Mr. Unthank."

The way the man kept saying his name was unnerving. "What are you talking about?"

"We've been watching you. We've been witness to your work. We can help you, Mr. Unthank. We can get you into the Impassable Wilderness."

Joffrey let the business card fall to the desk. He suddenly felt unable to move, as if his muscles had simply ceased functioning. He stared intently at the man, at the little black hairs of his beard, at the gold of his pince-nez. Finally, he found his voice. "You can?" he croaked.

Roger nodded. "Now, can we continue?"

"Wait a second," said Joffrey. "How?"

"That, too, is unimportant right now."

"I think it's pretty important, actually. How do you get in? How will you get me in? I need to have some sort of assurance before I agree to anything."

The thin man sighed resignedly. "Suffice it to say that I, and anyone who travels with me, am unaffected by the Periphery Bind. I am of Woods Magic."

"You're *what*?"

"Really, Mr. Unthank, I don't think nattering over trivial details is the best use of our time."

"The Periphery Bind—is that the boundary?"

The man nodded.

Joffrey fell back in his chair, his eyes wide. He thrust his hands into his hair and pushed it back compulsively, flattening the greasy strands against his scalp. "Oh man," he said. Then he said it again: "Oh man."

Roger, having finally managed to undo all the clasps of the briefcase, produced a yellowing piece of paper, folded into quadrants, and began to flatten it out on his lap. When it had been unfolded, he set it gently on Joffrey's desk. "Take a look at the schematic," he said. "Tell me how soon you can produce it."

Shaking himself from his shocked delirium, Joffrey blinked

rapidly to clear his eyes and squinted at the piece of paper. The shape of something came into view, and he knitted his brow to try to make sense of it. When he did, finally, his mouth nearly fell open in shock.

You see, Joffrey Unthank knew machine-part schematics. It was in his blood. His great-grandfather, Linus Mortimer Unthank, had started Unthank Machine Parts in 1914, right at the start of the Great War. The old man's portrait hung in the main hall of the building. Joffrey had met him only once, though it could be said that he'd only had half a meeting with the man. It had been at his great-grandfather's deathbed, and Unthank, all of five years old, had been shepherded to the bedside of the dying patriarch to say hello and good-bye. Joffrey remembered the exchange vividly. The smell of the room was close and stifling; the ashy, pale skin of his great-grandfather was almost indistinguishable from the starched white sheets. "Mr. Unthank?" said his father, who'd always referred to his grandfather that way, "I'd like you to meet your great-grandson, Joffrey." The old man had twisted his head slightly, with apparent difficulty, and spied him out of the corner of his eye. His mouth contorted to speak. "Don't," he began. "Don't. Don't let it die." And then, quite coincidentally, he died. No one was ever entirely sure what he meant by *it* (his prided pot of gardenias was in desperate need of watering just then), but Joffrey always felt, in his heart of hearts, that he meant the shop. Don't let the machine shop, Unthank Machine Parts, die. And so, as soon as he was able, Unthank threw himself into the business with the enthusiasm of a true entrepreneur. He slashed budgets, he discarded languishing accounts, he fired inefficient employees and hired efficient ones. And to top it all off, he incorporated the nearby orphanage into his business and began using the children for cheap (read: free) labor. He spent every leisure hour studying the history of the trade like an archaeologist, poring over detailed part schematics until his eyes went blurry from the strain. He learned every new machine that came into the shop and studied its inner workings meticulously. His entire life revolved around the shop; even when he was elected to the Quintet, the hierarchy of Industrial Titans, he skipped out on his award ceremony early because he'd only recently bought a collection of early-twentieth-century manifold schematics and was eager to get back to his office and study them. There was not a single blueprint, spec sheet, or circuit diagram with which he was not intimately acquainted.

Until now.

"What is this?" Unthank asked breathlessly.

"A Möbius Cog. Have you never seen one?"

Unthank, despite himself, said, "No."

Roger frowned.

"What does it—?" Unthank stuttered, his attention thoroughly captured by what he saw. "How does it—?" His fingers drifted over the page, feeling the smoothness of the paper. Drawn there in blue-gray ink was the most precise and careful rendering of a machine part that Unthank had ever seen. Every single curve had been painstakingly measured and labeled; every angle drafted with footnoted graphs. As a man who'd studied nearly every schematic to leave a draftsman's pen, one would assume that Unthank would be able to easily make sense of the cog's design; but no: It was baffling to him.

Consisting of three toothed rings, the cog was more like a series of gears, revolving around an orblike core. The three rings themselves were toothed like spur gears, but they were each twisted in a way that defied logic, as if each outside surface was also the gear's inside surface. Somehow, in all their twisting, the teeth of the three gears made contact with one another at just the right spots to create, the schematic presumed, a smooth motion between the separate pieces. Unthank traced the circumference of the entwined cogs and mumbled to himself. Finally, he looked at his visitor with a look of abject surrender.

"It's not possible," he said.

The thin man would not be denied. "Surely, that is not so."

"I mean, it just defies logic. I can't even imagine the amount of work that was involved in drawing up this blueprint; to actually build it? Impossible. This design, pretty though it is, is pure conjecture! A thing of beauty, no doubt, but so are unicorns, my friend."

"It is not conjecture."

Unthank seemed to not hear him. He was back admiring the schematic. "I have to admit, it's awfully impressive. I'd even go so far as to say genius. Gotta hand it to a guy to have such a fertile imagination to make up something like this." He clucked his tongue and shook his head.

"Mr. Unthank, I assure you it is not imaginary. It has been made before."

"By whom?"

"Two very gifted machinists. It is presumed that they worked together in solitude in a rudimentary workshop, with nothing more than a few hammers and chisels at their disposal. I would assume, since you are in control of an entire machine shop, the creation of the cog should come easily to you."

Unthank laughed, once, very loudly. He set down the schematic and looked Roger squarely in the eye. "This . . . thing is one of the most incredibly designed machine parts I've ever seen. Even with my entire shop devoted to the creation of this thing . . ." His eyes traveled over the words on the schematic, carefully unpacking their meaning. He murmured to himself as he read. After a moment, he looked back up at Roger. "These machinists—they did this with hammer and chisel? I've got to think that your Woodsy Magic had something to do with it."

"Woods Magic," the thin man corrected.

"Right." Unthank paused. "What is that, exactly?"

"It's the essence of the Wood, and it flows in the blood of anyone born to it. It is believed we are descended of the trees themselves.

You Outsiders are shamefully ignorant of what happens beyond the Periphery, in these woods you so colloquially call the Impassable Wilderness. It is a vibrant and vital place. And I am offering you exclusive access, something that, to my knowledge, no Woodian has offered an Outsider in the history of our parallel existences."

"Yeah, you mentioned that," said Unthank. "What exactly does that entail, this access?"

"Absolute, unfettered access. A chaperone at your disposal to walk you in and out of the Periphery until such time that the Bind can be dismantled. The opportunity to market your wares to an entirely new world of buyers. Complete control over the resources of a country teeming with ancient forests. Trees, thousands of years old. Perhaps, once our dominion is cemented, you will be included in the administration. Machine Part Manufacturer to the Dauphin. How does that sound?"

"Intriguing," said Unthank. He looked back at the schematic. "I mean, I suppose it could be . . . well, I don't want to speak too hastily, but I've attempted these kinds of experimental projects in the past. Lord knows I have the shop for it. If this has been built before—if it has existed in the world—I've got to assume that if anyone's got the stuff to make it again, it's me. But it's no small feat, I tell you." He paused for a moment. "Did you say something about a dolphin?"

The man fixed Unthank with a perplexed look. "No," he said. "The Dauphin. The young king."

"And I would be, like, his main guy?"

"If that is what you wish."

"Who is he, this Dauphin? And why doesn't he just order this thing made?"

"Because he is currently indisposed. But this is unimportant information. I ask you: Will you make this cog, Mr. Unthank?"

Joffrey, his elbows resting on the arms of his chair, wove his fingers together in front of his lips. He looked down at the schematic of the Möbius Cog and back at Roger. Finally, he spoke. "How much time do I have?"

"Five days."

"Five?" Unthank's hands dropped to the desktop. "You've got to be kidding me. I mean, it'll take that long just to let the metal cure. I need a week, at least."

"A week is not an option. There are others, Mr. Unthank, who would seek to make this piece as well; if they should succeed, all is lost. I have seen your work; I've been apprised of your abilities. I do not think five days is beyond your capability."

"I mean, if I worked through the night—if I shut down all other operations . . ."

"If that is what needs be done, then it should be so."

"But I'll accrue costs—it's going to cost a fortune to turn everything over to this. And what about my clients? I've got fifteen hundred dishwasher intake valves to make by Tuesday."

Roger cleared his throat politely. "You will be more than compensated, Mr. Unthank, for whatever costs you accrue. I cannot stress enough how much this is worth your while. I'm promising you a world at your disposal, Mr. Unthank. Please consider that."

Unthank lifted his hands to his face and tapped his lips with the tips of his fingers. "And what about these others—your competitors? The ones who want to make it too. What happens if they manage to create it before I do? What then?"

"That is not an option. Besides, I've taken steps to—how shall I say—hamper their progress, if not stop them altogether. But that is none of your concern, Mr. Unthank. Yours is simply the manufacture of this piece. That is all."

Joffrey's gaze wandered from the strange man in the leather chair to the line of windows above the shelf of blinking transponders. The wall of trees, the sight that greeted him every day as he walked into his office, was still there, standing vigilant in the gray light. A bird wheeled about one the tallest conifers. Somewhere, Unthank surmised, in that knot of forest, were the three girls he'd wantonly sent into its strange world, along with the dozens of others who'd suffered a similar fate. He imagined them frozen in place, like statues, victims to the terrible enchantments of that alien place. Or worse: being slowly digested by the very trees. And to what end? It had been a long, arduous voyage for Joffrey Unthank, but he felt as if he'd finally arrived at his just reward, though in a way he'd never, in his wildest dreams, anticipated.

He looked back at Roger. "It's a deal," he said.

❧

"Rachel!"

The forest gave up nothing.

"RACHEL!"

Still, not a sound. A tremendous panic was welling up in the pit of Elsie's stomach. She'd never been so terrified in her life. The tall trees seemed to bow around her like a concave mirror, and she grew flushed and light-headed as she ran. She didn't know where she was running. She didn't know where she'd end up. She only knew what she'd promised: that she would find her sister. She thrashed through the heavy underbrush as fast as her little legs could muster, having to contend with the thick wool of the several-sizes-too-large trench coat she'd been given. She'd had dreams like this before; tired, confused, and running through an endless wilderness while her legs moved like molasses. The thought occurred to her, briefly: Maybe this *was* a dream. All it took was a particularly angry thorn scratch to her left hand, as real as pain can get, to remind her that she was, in fact, quite awake.

She tried again, this time stopping to catch her breath before cupping her hands around her mouth. "Rachel!" She listened in the quiet that followed.

The whisper of a breeze. A branch swaying in the slight wind and rubbing against a neighboring tree.

Elsie took stock. She was standing in the middle of a deep, dense wood, one that had been known to swallow its explorers whole. A quick survey of her body, however, taught her that she was still very much intact. Her feet were cold and her nose felt chapped. Otherwise everything seemed to check out. She looked at her hands. They were red and glistening with melted snow. She blew on them, which seemed to bring some warm feeling back to the tips of her fingers. She didn't know how long ago she'd dropped the twine, the length of brown string Unthank had instructed her to carry—it seemed like a bit of a blur in her memory. She now questioned whether she'd willfully dropped the twine or if it had simply fallen away from her hand. However, her intent remained clear: She had to find her sister.

"RACHEL!" she hollered again. Still, no answer. She squinted into the distance; a break in the trees allowed a clear view. She walked toward the break and saw, on the other side, a wide meadow amid the woods. In the middle of the clearing was a small white rabbit.

The rabbit paused in its activity—it seemed to be munching on some kind of foraged root—and looked directly at Elsie. She'd seen rabbits at pet stores before, and her friend Karma had a small hutch in her backyard, but there was something about this particular rabbit that struck Elsie as being strange. There was a kind of bright intelligence in its eyes she hadn't seen before in other animals. It twitched its nose a few times, shook its ears, and hopped away from the girl,

toward the edge of the meadow. Before it left Elsie's view, however, it stopped and looked back at her, as if willing her to follow. Elsie complied.

She wandered after the rabbit in a trance. It seemed her best option at present. She'd already become hopelessly turned around in this labyrinth of trees—therefore, she reasoned, it didn't really matter what direction she went in. Also, she found it unsettling that the rabbit seemed to keep waiting for her: Anytime she fell too far behind and thought she'd lost its trail, she'd see the rabbit standing by a clutch of ferns, wiggling its nose and looking at her. Once she'd drawn closer,

the rabbit would continue moving.

They hadn't traveled very far before a noise came from the surrounding woods; Elsie held her breath, trying to silence the sound of the blood beating in her ears. The white rabbit had stopped too; its ears perked to listen. The sound came again. It was, distinctly, someone yelling Elsie's name. The rabbit startled and dove into the underbrush, disappearing from Elsie's sight.

"Don't go!" called Elsie. She'd felt strangely compelled to follow the rabbit. She'd intuited that it wanted to show her something.

The voice came again, this time clearer. It was her sister. Elsie stood there for a moment, knee deep in the bracken of the woods, torn between the two aims: the anchor of her sister's voice, or the strange call of the rabbit's trail.

"Elsie!" the cry came again.

"Rachel!" yelled Elsie. She turned and ran in the direction of her sister's voice.

Breaking through a screen of young pines, the two sisters were reunited in a crash of arms and green trench coats. They hugged each other for a long time before finally pulling apart.

"Are you okay?" asked Rachel.

"Yeah," said Elsie, "I think so."

Rachel searched her sister's face. She saw the welts on her cheek, the little pinpricks of blood on her hands. "You're all scraped up," she said.

"I was running. I was so scared. I was looking for you." Elsie found she was trembling wildly.

"It's okay, sis," consoled Rachel, straightening Elsie's hair. It had become wild and tousled in her scramble. Little twigs jutted out here and there like antennae, and Rachel tenderly removed them. "Listen: You've got to help me find Goggles."

"Where is she?"

"I don't know. She was right behind me. We managed to meet up just after she made it in. We had a plan: We were getting ready to look for you. I thought I heard you yelling earlier, so I went walking in that direction, and the next thing I knew Martha was gone. Just disappeared."

Elsie looked up at her sister. "You've got something in your . . ."

Rachel guessed at what her sister saw. "Ugh," she said. "That gunk in my nose. I thought I got it all out." She turned and, holding a finger to one nostril, executed what Elsie's dad had always called a "farmer blow." Little bits of brown paste spackled the fronds of a nearby fern.

"C'mon," Rachel said. "Let's go find her."

They stayed close by each other as they searched for their friend, their twin voices echoing each other's as they hollered the girl's name to the surrounding trees. They moved slowly, methodically, not wanting to miss a single sound. What if she'd fallen and hurt herself? Elsie imagined Martha lying on the ground, her leg pinned beneath a fallen tree. It gave her the shudders.

"Hey!" came a voice from a nearby stand of dogwoods.

"Martha?" called Rachel.

To Elsie and Rachel's great relief, the leafless red sticks of the dogwood parted and Martha appeared, goggles perched on her forehead and a green goo dripping down her cheek. "What happened to you guys?" she asked. As she spoke, she absently wormed her finger in her ear canal, trying to clear it of Unthank's concoction.

"You were right behind me!" exclaimed Rachel. "What happened to you?"

"I thought you'd ditched me," said Martha. "I kept yelling your name, but you were just gone into the woods. I got totally turned around."

"Are you okay?" asked Elsie, the image of Martha caught beneath the fallen tree still fresh in her mind.

"Yeah, fine." She wiped her hands on her trench coat. "Now that we're all accounted for, we'll just need to follow one of you guys' strings back to where Mr. Unthank is. Freedom is in our reach, ladies." As if to underscore what she'd said, she pushed her goggles over her eyes and flashed a smile. Rachel looked at Elsie.

"Where's your string?" Rachel asked.

"I was going to ask you the same," responded Elsie.

Martha, goggled, stared at them both. "You don't have your twine?"

"Well, I don't see you have yours either," said Rachel.

"I dropped it somewhere," said Martha defensively. "Or something."

"Then don't, like, get in my face about it," said Rachel.

"I wasn't getting in your face about it," shot back Martha. "I just thought at least one of you would've had the sense to hold on to your string."

"You guys," said Elsie softly.

Rachel took up the bait. "How about this good sense: I'd like to knock you in the nose right about now."

"I'd like to see you try," said Martha. She was brushing off her hands.

"You guys!" Elsie said, louder. "Are you crazy? Don't do this." She stepped between the two girls, her arms raised. When they'd settled back, she spoke again. "This is *exactly* the sort of thing that Intrepid Tina warns against, you know. You know what she'd say? She'd say something like . . ." Here she tried to mine the collected bons mots of her doll for the appropriate comment. She was drawing a blank. "She'd say, 'Friends should stay together and be friends.'" It wasn't an actual Intrepid Tina quote, but she figured it was a sentiment Tina could probably get behind.

"She never says that," said Rachel.

"It's true, though," said Martha. "We shouldn't get all freaked out here. We need level heads."

"Right," said Elsie. "Level heads."

"So what do we do?" asked Rachel.

"Well, I figure we just try to find our way back out of here," said Martha, "back to Unthank. Demand our reward. We just need to decide which way to go."

The three girls paused as they stood, their eyes casting over the knot of green, all dusted with white snow, for a suggestion of which direction might be the way out. Just then, Elsie remembered the rabbit.

"Hey," she said. "This is going to sound crazy, but over there a little ways, when I was still on my own, I saw a rabbit. A white rabbit. But he didn't run when he saw me. Instead, he kinda waited for me, like he was leading the way."

Rachel looked at her sister askance. "You *did* get too wrapped up in that book we were reading over the summer."

"This is not a joke. I'm serious. I feel like he was wanting me to follow. Maybe he was going to show the way out."

Martha shrugged. "It's as good an option as any. Show the way."

It was fairly easy for Elsie to retrace her steps to the meadow where she first had seen the rabbit; she could even find, here and there, the little indentations that her boots had made in the fine, light snow. Once she'd found the place where she'd heard Rachel calling for her, she began tracing the rabbit's little paw prints through the bushes. She'd never done something as careful as tracking wild animals, and it required all her concentration. After she'd walked this way for a while, she heard her sister speak up behind her.

"Hold up," Rachel said. "Where's Martha?"

Elsie turned to look at her sister. There seemed to be a kind of notable absence in the space next to where Rachel stood. The two Mehlbergs blinked and stared at the spot.

"She was just here," said Rachel. "Just a second ago."

Without saying another word, they both turned and began retracing their steps, all the while yelling Martha's name. They followed their own footmarks in the snow; conspicuously, there were only two pairs of them. Martha's seemed to have dropped away long before they'd come to the meadow. After a time, they arrived back where they'd started, where the flurry of their combined footprints made a wide crater in the snow.

"Goggles!" shouted Rachel.

There, sitting on a felled cottonwood tree, sat Martha. She was picking mud from her boots. "You guys," she said when they arrived. "You can't ditch me like that."

"We didn't ditch you," said Elsie. "We thought you were right behind us."

"I was until you just disappeared. I called your name. Didn't you hear me?"

Rachel and Elsie exchanged a glance. "No," they said in unison.

"Did you see the meadow?" asked Rachel. "Did you make it that far?"

"Huh-uh," Martha responded in the negative. "You guys just took off, right outside this bunch of trees."

"Let's try again," said Rachel. There was an uneasy hitch in her voice.

"Just don't run off," warned Martha as she pushed herself up from her seat.

They hadn't traveled very far, though, before Martha had again vanished from the group. Determined to keep her in sight, Rachel had been looking back every couple of seconds. After they'd lost her, Rachel explained that it was like Martha had stepped briefly behind a tree and then did not appear on the other side. The sisters returned to find the missing girl standing, bemused, in the middle of the little clearing by the fallen cottonwood.

"You did it again," she accused.

"What is *happening*?" Rachel said, clearly at her wit's end. She was massaging her temples with her fingers.

Just then, a dog ran past them.

They all froze.

The dog, perhaps following the specter of a woodland creature, tore through their clearing with the speed and obliviousness that only a canine could muster. It leapt over the fallen cottonwood without giving a second glance at the three girls and disappeared into the bushes.

"Did you see that?" asked Martha.

"Yeah," said Rachel. "That was a dog. I think it was a retriever." She paused before adding, "I don't really like dogs."

"Oh," said Martha. "Still, that was strange."

The girls barely had a chance to wonder where the dog had come from and where it was running off to in such a hurry before another dog, this one a large malamute with light gray fur, came tearing across the clearing. It, too, leapt the cottonwood and vanished on the trail of the first dog. In a matter of seconds a third and fourth dog, each different from the ones before, appeared from the one side of the clearing and ran after the other two. When a fifth appeared, Elsie tried to step in its way.

"Hey, boy," she called. "Here, boy."

The dog, a collie, merely dashed around Elsie; it was gone in a flash.

Then came the deluge.

It was like a buffalo stampede. This was the first thing that sprang to Elsie's mind as she saw what could only be described as a clamoring herd of dogs crashing through the edge of the clearing and running toward them. There were easily thirty dogs, of every breed imaginable, and they were sprinting after their forerunners with gleeful, slobbering abandon.

Martha let out a scream and nearly fell from her perch on the tree; Rachel, exhibiting a show of athletic prowess Elsie'd never before seen, hurdled the cottonwood in a single bound and began sprinting away from the charging tide of dogs. Elsie, for her part, stood stock-still. The furry wave crested and spilled around her; it was clear that the three girls were the least of the dogs' concerns. They were too busy chasing after the disembodied thing that had so enticed the preceding five dogs. One of them, a black pug who was taking up the rear on account of his stubby legs, even stopped and slobbered a little on Elsie's boot; she petted him, and he yipped appreciatively before continuing on his way.

"Rachel!" she hollered, having recovered from her shock. "Martha!" Elsie vaulted the fallen tree and found Martha in a clump on the forest floor, trying to wipe mud from her goggles.

"What was *that?*" she asked.

"I don't know," said Elsie. "But we need to go after my sister. She's kind of scared of dogs."

The two girls took up the chase. It was fairly easy to stay on the dogs' trail; their wake in the snow resembled the path of a frenzied pack of football fans looking for a fast-food joint. The dogs' paws, in their plurality, laid flat every plant in their path. Not far along, they heard a quiet whimpering; they found Rachel, petrified with fear, clinging to the lower branches of a maple tree.

"You okay, Rach?" called Elsie.

"I think they're gone now," suggested Martha.

"Oh my God," said Rachel, lowering herself from her branch. "Tell me what just happened."

"We got stampeded by dogs," answered Elsie.

"Seriously," added Martha.

Rachel, now on the ground, brushed some moss from her coat. Her face was streaked with dirt, and the hem of her jacket was dappled in mud. She held her nose to the air. "Is that smoke?" she asked.

Sure enough, Elsie caught a whiff of it too. It smelled like the tailings of a wood fire, like the smell of a late fall day in a country neighborhood. It seemed to be coming from the direction that the dogs had traveled. Without speaking, the three girls began following the smell; it led them along the wide swath in the vegetation blazed by the pack of dogs. As they came closer to the source of the smoke, they could see evidence of habitation. Trees had been felled and sawed; a stack of freshly chopped wood lay in a pile by a large chopping block. They also began to hear voices: children's voices. The three girls, silent in their approach, crested a small hillock and found themselves looking down into the trough of a narrow vale, where lay nestled a quaint wooden cottage. A thin stream of white smoke drifted from its chimney.

A group of perhaps fifteen children, of all ages, milled about several large garden plots in front of the cottage. They seemed to range in age from eight to eighteen and were intent on a variety of different activities: some were playing games, while others seemed to be engaged in more domestic chores like hanging clothing on a drying line and chopping wood. Several tended to the garden beds, weeding and pruning the winter greens. There was one thing, however, that Elsie, Martha, and Rachel noticed was the same about all the children: They each had little yellow tags hanging from the lobes of their ears.

CHAPTER 14

Icy Water, Water Everywhere

It would seem that fortune smiled on Prue McKeel and Curtis Mehlberg that day, the day that they both plummeted from the broken rope bridge into the fathomless depths of the Long Gap. Not only smiled, but also moved in to plant a wet, lazy kiss on their respective foreheads.

The cliff wall on the side of the chasm they fell toward when the bridge was rent in two was not entirely vertical; rather, it sloped away from the cliff's edge at a slight diagonal, which became more pronounced as it descended. This meant that the two children didn't necessarily plummet or fall but rather slid at a very fast pace down this sloping slab of rock.

Callista, the Kitsune who'd fallen on the same side of the Gap as they had, did not fare so well. In falling nearer the center of the ravine, by the time she made contact with the slope of the cliff wall, it was too late. The evidence of her demise was laid bare to Curtis, who, upon waking from a brief bout of unconsciousness, saw her still body lying lifeless some ten feet from where he'd landed. In the throes of death, she'd shape-shifted back to her original form. It was a dead black fox he saw when he woke.

As for Septimus the rat, it was too soon to tell. For all Curtis knew, he was the only faller to have survived. He gave his cheeks a quick pat to make sure this was the case; his hands felt chalky and badly scraped, but they made a satisfying contact with his face. He felt nothing if not alive.

"Prue?" he rasped. The darkness of the ravine was all-consuming. The smallest sliver of light could be seen above, like a plane's vapor trail, but the distance to the surface seemed unimaginable. The ride to where he lay, while not being deadly, had not been smooth in the slightest. The slope of the rock had acted like a very fast slide, one that went perfectly vertical at certain stages, making for several moments during the fall where Curtis was certain that he would die a very painful, bone-crushing death. The last of these drops had deposited him, bones intact (as far as he knew), on this little shelf of dirt and rock, some ways down the shaft of the ravine.

"Prue! Septimus!" he called, louder. He heard a pained grunting coming from some distance away. Not bothering to lift himself to his feet (he still wasn't sure if he hadn't somehow broken every bone in his body), he crawled along the narrow floor of the shelf, away from the fox's bent frame, toward the noise. He arrived at the edge and said again, "Prue! Is that you?"

"Yeah," replied his friend. "It's me."

It was too dark to see where she was. "Are you okay?"

"I think I messed up my ankle. Again. Same one from last time." By last time, she meant the fall she'd taken, some months ago, when the coyote soldiers had shot down the eagle she'd been riding. Curtis grimaced.

"How bad?" he asked.

There came a pause as Curtis imagined Prue applying weight to the sore spot. "I think it's okay," she said. "Is Septimus with you?"

He looked about him; the darkness was pervasive. "No," he said, before shouting, "SEPTIMUS!" No answer. Curtis cursed under his breath. The rat was small and lithe, he told himself. Maybe he was still clinging to the rope above them. Maybe he'd made it to safety.

"Are you all right?" called Prue.

"I think so. That other fox is dead. She didn't survive the fall."

"What about Darla?"

"I don't know. I didn't really see what happened." He paused. "No Septimus, though."

"But you're okay?"

Curtis, girding himself, began testing his individual muscles and joints, surveying the damage wrought by the fall. Miraculously, aside from a few bruises, he seemed to have avoided any major injury. "I think I'm all right," he said.

A scraping noise, inscrutable in the deep dark, sounded. Cloth against cloth. Another grunt. A buckle undone. Then the distinct sound of a match head scraping against the striking surface; a small yellow light sparked. Curtis looked over the edge of the rock shelf and saw Prue, kneeling, hold the match to a camping lantern—she must've packed a small one in her knapsack. She waited for it to take; she waved the flame of the match out and flicked it away. A globe of light extended from the source, illuminating their surroundings.

"Where are we?" said Curtis. The lantern light barely made a scratch on the surrounding blackness, but it was enough for them to see that a pair of boulders, the size of small houses, had created the rock shelves that had saved their lives. He saw that he was separated from Prue by only a drop of ten feet or so. The chasm narrowed substantially here, and the twin walls of the ravine were barely five feet apart. It occurred to Curtis that they'd slid into some remote crevice of the gap; there was no telling how far down they were. One thing was clear: There was no going up. He cupped his hands to his mouth and yelled again, "SEPTIMUS!"

Prue was silent as she stood and, gingerly putting weight on her bad ankle, began to hobble around her small perch and take in their surroundings. It didn't take long; she'd barely the space of a department-store changing room to explore. "Curtis," she said, craning her neck to look upward at the faraway glint of daylight, a thin string of white in their dark heaven, "I don't know about this."

"Hold on," said Curtis. He eased himself over the lip of the shelf and dropped the several feet to where Prue stood. He smacked some white dust off her jacket's shoulder. "Let me see your ankle," he said.

Together, they eased her boot from her foot. It was red and swollen, though Prue said it didn't hurt enough to be sprained. "You can walk on it okay?" he asked.

Prue nodded. There was a look of resigned quiet on her face. A mounting sadness.

"We're going to get out of here," he said. "We are."

"How?" asked Prue.

Curtis eyed the rock wall. "I suppose we climb." Even he knew this was hopeless. It was as if he'd said it in order to give it to the air, this idea. As if by saying it, he'd whispered a necessary incantation, one that dissipated into smoke as soon as it was breathed alive.

Prue just shook her head.

They both hunkered down on the rocky floor of the shelf. "Nothing over there?" she asked, nodding to the place where Curtis had landed; where the dead fox lay.

"No," he said. "Just a drop on the other side."

"This is ridiculous," said Prue. "I mean, we survive the fall just to die slowly at the bottom of this shaft?"

"Someone's got a cruel sense of humor, that's for sure," said Curtis. "You know, God or whatever."

There came a quiet between the two of them; Prue began to cry. "Oh, I screwed all of this up," she said.

"What are you talking about?" consoled Curtis. He placed his hand between her shoulder blades.

"This," said Prue. "The whole plan. What about what the tree said? That we need to reanimate the true heir, before the others do. Whoever the others are. But how are we going to do that stuck in this . . . this . . . hole? I bet 'the others' are halfway to rebuilding him by now."

"So? Maybe that's for the best. Maybe that's what the tree wanted. Just *someone* to build him. Maybe Alexei's a great person deep down, even if he is a kind of robot. Maybe he'll still restore peace, whoever reanimates him."

"I'm not so sure," said Prue. "Why else would the tree have said that? No, it was supposed to be us. And we screwed it up." She grew silent, her hand to her mouth, and remained deep in thought.

"Don't beat yourself up. Maybe there are some bandits who'll come back; maybe if we scream loud enough, they'll hear us." Curtis glared up at the little daylight they could see; it seemed improbable.

"Not likely," said Prue.

"No, I guess not."

Curtis puffed up his cheeks and blew out a breath through his puckered lips. "Well, I said, 'This is it,' up there." He pointed to the crack of light above. "But I guess I was wrong. I suppose *this* is it. Kind of funny, in a way. Not often a guy gets to think 'this is it' twice in the span of a few minutes. Or maybe that always happens. Maybe death is just a series of 'this is it' thoughts until you finally—"

"HELP!" came a voice, interrupting Curtis from his macabre musings. It issued from the dark space beneath the shelf, just beyond the lip of the rock. "I've been blinded! Struck blind!"

It was undeniably the voice of Septimus the rat, pitched high with fear. Curtis rolled onto his belly and inched to the very edge of the shelf. He gestured to Prue, who handed him the lantern. Waving it into the darkness, he saw movement some thirty feet below them, on yet another boulder lodged in this narrowing of the twin cliffs.

"Oh," said Septimus, blinking up at the swinging lantern in Curtis's hand. "Never mind. I can see. That was an overreaction. On my part."

out? On top of all that, Darla might be up there, just waiting for us to make a move. She might have more of those . . . those *things* with her."

"I don't know, Prue. I mean, we have no idea what's down there. Right?" He soon realized that his objections were still doggedly anchored to the belief that the bandits were still alive; that they hadn't been completely routed by the assassins.

Without answering, Prue swooped up the lantern and undid the cord attached to the handle. She threw one end of the rope to Curtis and tied the other end to her midsection. "Hold tight," she instructed before slowly lowering her body over the edge of the rock. Curtis strained under the weight, gritting his teeth and wedging his feet inside the recess between the boulder and the cliff wall. Finally, the weight abated, and Prue gave the rope a few tugs. He found he had no more energy to fight. Breathing a quiet oath, he looped the rope around a tooth of rock on the far side of the shelf. He then lowered himself down with Prue anchoring from below.

"Welcome," announced Septimus when they'd both arrived.

They continued on that way, slowly moving themselves downward from rock to rock. Each time they tested the depth of the darkness below them by dropping stones and judging the time that passed before they heard the noise of its landing, like a boat sounding the depths. With each passable drop, they marveled at their good fortune. They wondered, inwardly, when that fortune would run its course.

Finally, after perhaps ten such descents, they found themselves on a small niche of rock where the two sides of the ravine wall came together in a V shape. In front of them was a jumble of stones that had fallen and become lodged in the V. Prue inspected the pile and, finding a loose stone, began to pry it away. Curtis helped. When the stone had been cleared of remnant rock, they were both able to peel it back from the pile to reveal a small, angular hole. He wasn't sure whether it was his imagination, but Curtis thought he felt the whiff of a breeze emerge from the hole when they'd removed the rock.

They stared into the blankness of the opening.

"What do you suppose is down there?" said Curtis.

"I don't know," said Prue. Then: "What did Brendan say about this place? Something about people living down here? A long time ago?"

"Cliff people, yeah," said Curtis. "Sign of it. I guess they found, like, paintings and things. But that was a lot farther up. As far as I know, no one's been down this deep."

Prue's eyes moved from Curtis's face to the rat that was sitting on his shoulder. "Septimus," she said, "this is where you could really come in handy."

"Let me guess. You want me. To go in there." He smoothed back his whiskers nervously.

"Please," she said.

"Come on, Septimus," said Curtis. "We need you."

Prue held up the lantern; its illumination cast a glow into the hole.

Septimus grumbled. He then hopped from Curtis's shoulder to his elbow and from there to the hard floor of the chasm's bottom. He paused for a moment at the opening, sniffing at the ground suspiciously.

"It's what a true bandit would do," prompted Curtis.

"I'm no sworn bandit," said the rat. "I'm a free agent. And I choose to go in there on my own terms." With that, he disappeared into the hole.

Prue and Curtis waited patiently. The minutes ticked away. The chill of the cavern's air needled at Curtis's skin below his torn and dirtied officer's coat. Finally, there came the unmistakable noise of Septimus's claws against stone. The rat reappeared at the mouth of the hole, now coated in a fresh layer of gray dust. He held his paw out in front of him, his face puckered and flinching.

"What did you see?" asked Curtis, alarmed.

The rat continued to hold out his hand. He waved it frantically; his eyes were tightly closed, and he shook his snout back and forth as if he were trying to cast something from his mind.

"Septimus!" yelled Prue.

And then he stopped. Opening his mouth wide, he batted at his nose with his thin fingers. "Sorry," he said. "Thought I was going to sneeze there."

Prue and Curtis, together, released a breath of relief.

Once the rat had recovered, he continued, "There's a tunnel in there. And I think it's big enough for all of us."

❧

They traveled downward.

They'd only needed to chip away a few armloads of stone before the opening was big enough for the larger members of their party. The passageway beyond was not so much a tunnel as it was an emptied vein in the rock made of fallen slabs of stone, pinioned together. Several times, the going became so tight that Prue and Curtis were forced to slide on their bellies to arrive at the other side of a particularly small fissure. Occasionally, Curtis would discern that the tunnel was beginning to climb, and he felt a thrilled leap in his stomach. But invariably, the ascent would be minor, and then the tunnel would slope down and they would lose, to Curtis's best estimation, whatever altitude they'd gained. The longer they spent down here, the further they got away from the true goal of this journey: to get topside, to find out what had happened to the bandits. He worried that Prue did not share the same thinking.

The tunnel continued down.

Curtis remembered a trip he'd taken several years ago, with his school, to some nearby caverns. The caverns, he was told, were discovered by spelunkers who'd happened on a small crack in a cliff face and decided to explore; one of their number had died after he'd followed an artery of the cavern and, not reading the geography correctly, had gotten stuck. They didn't find his body for three weeks. Despite Curtis's best efforts to dispel this thought from his mind, it continued to haunt him. At one point, he grabbed Prue's boot and shook it.

"Hey," he called.

She stopped. "Yeah?"

"So when do we finally decide this is crazy?"

A pause. "I've kinda already decided that."

"Really?"

"But as long as there's an opening here, I think we should continue."

"I was just thinking—"

Prue interrupted him. "About that spelunker who got stuck in that cavern, the one that we visited on the class trip a few years ago?"

"How'd you know?"

"I'm thinking the same thing."

"Let's not do that, okay?"

"Okay."

Septimus's voice came echoing down the shaft; he moved more swiftly than his humanoid compatriots, using the extra time to check out the upcoming terrain. "It gets bigger," he hollered. "Just ahead."

To their relief, the rat spoke true: The tunnel gradually began to widen until it was big enough for them to sit up in. They stopped and opened Prue's knapsack, rifling through it for the last of the remaining victuals she'd packed. The tally was three pieces of jerky in parchment, two apples, and a few heels of bread. They split one piece of the dried meat and shaved a few slices off an apple with Prue's hunting knife, which had miraculously survived the fall from the rope bridge, landing within inches of her head. Curtis, who was starting to feel a pang of thirst, sucked at his apple slice, drawing every bit of liquid from it before popping the desiccated thing into his mouth. Prue pulled off her boot and they inspected her ankle; the swelling seemed mild.

"At least I don't have to walk on it," Prue said with a half smile.

They continued on. Curtis took the lead with the lantern, and Prue scraped along behind him. The tunnel was not yet tall enough to stand in; they remained on all fours, though their knees and palms were beginning to smart. Curtis could see Septimus in the barely visible distance, hopping along through the small tunnel as if it were a second home to him.

After traveling this way for a time, Curtis saw the rat come up abruptly at a sharp turn in the passage. He cocked his head and looked at the two children. "Listen," he said. "Do you hear that?"

Prue concentrated. "No," she said. "What is it?"

"It's like a . . . I don't know . . . slushing sound," Septimus said cryptically. Shrugging, the rat continued on into the darkness.

Curtis crawled a few more feet forward, and the ground below his knees promptly gave way.

He fell.

It would be a stretch to say that Prue saw it happen; more like: She saw him there, in front of her, and then he was simply not there anymore. It was like he'd vanished.

"CURTIS!" screamed Prue. She was petrified, too scared to move.

A loud splash.

"That's what I heard," said Septimus, peering over the break in the tunnel. "Water."

Prue ignored the rat. She yelled Curtis's name again, mustering all the volume she could manage. The tunnel rang with the sound.

A surprised yelp met her cry. "WATER!" Curtis shouted back, shrilly, from below. "*COLD* WATER!"

Luckily, the lantern had not fallen with him; it remained, tipped sideways, in the narrow tunnel. Prue grabbed it and swung it in front of her, trying to get her bearings. There was a gaping hole in the rock directly in front of her; it was roughly Curtis-sized. Oddly, the edges of the hole seemed to be angular, though the reason behind this did not immediately occur to Prue. She was too focused on the well-being of her friend.

"Are you all right?" she called to Curtis.

"Y-yeah!" he sputtered. His voice reverberated eerily; it occurred to Prue that it was the voice of someone occupying a very large space.

"What happened?"

"I fell into this—this pool!" he called. There was some more frantic splashing. "It's really cold!"

"Hold up," Prue called. "I'm going to try something." She cocked an eyebrow at Septimus. Her tongue fixed between her lips, she quickly unspooled the rope from her bag. Once she had it in hand, she waved the rat toward her.

"Hold on to this," she said, handing him the lantern.

He did as she instructed, though he eyed her warily as she tied the end of the rope around his belly and pushed him toward the hole in the floor.

"I got it," he reassured. "I got it."

Light began to flood the lower chamber once the rat had been dangled into the orifice. Septimus squirmed uncomfortably against the rope at his waist but continued to hold tight to the lantern.

"Over here, Septimus! Keep it c-coming!" Curtis shivered. "I can start to see . . . There!" There came more splashing; Prue peered over the edge of the hole and saw her friend swimming, frantically, in the middle of a vast pool of jet-black water. The light, cast backward toward the hole he'd fallen through, illuminated in silhouette the distinct pattern of brickwork, like a collapsed wall on some old abandoned house.

Curtis let out a loud gasp of relief. "God, that's cold," he yelled. He'd reached dry land.

"You guys," shouted Septimus. "Look at this."

Prue peered her head over the edge of the hole and found the rat's swaying shape. The lantern light was dim, but she could see it illuminating the space as the rat swung it about his head. "It's a chamber of some sort. Man-made!" She felt at the break in the tunnel floor—felt the cool, damp roughness of the bricks. She must've gotten overzealous in her inspection, as the mortar crumbled again and Prue went crashing, rat, rope, knapsack, lantern and all, into the giant pool.

The water was positively freezing; Curtis's shrieks had even undersold it. She felt a lightninglike bolt fly through her body, from her feet to her head, as she plunged into the cavern pool. The lantern was immediately extinguished; it was like someone had thrown a black shroud over the world. For a second, she floated in the black fluid, feeling the frigid water find its way into every fold of her clothing. She felt suspended there, like some ancient insect hovering in amber. And then she exploded to the surface, gasping for air.

"PRUE!" she could hear Curtis shout.

She was having a hard time getting air into her lungs. Her whole body was searing with sharp, cold pain. She hiccuped; she gasped.

"Over here!" yelled Curtis. She desperately swam for the source of the sound.

"I can't see anything!"

"Here! Follow my voice!"

Paddling with abandon, one of her swim strokes made contact

with hard rock. She felt Curtis's hand grasping hers, and she was hauled to the bank of the pool. Water poured from her hair; her skin was a million pinpricks of icy cold. She was racked with shivers.

"Septimus!" hollered Curtis, once he'd gotten the girl to safety. A series of frantic splashing noises was sounding from the middle of the chamber.

"Help!" shouted the rat. "The lantern!"

Curtis dove back into the pool. He reemerged, sputtering, minutes later. Septimus was clinging to his back, badly coughing water. The rope was still tied to his belly and the lantern still gripped in his paws, though it was now quite extinguished.

The three of them, prey to the cold subterranean air, succumbed to violent shivers, and they began to push their bodies closer together in order to kindle whatever heat they could create. With fumbling fingers, Curtis opened the lantern door and felt at the soaked wick. Prue grabbed the waxed cotton pouch that housed the matches; she was amazed to find that the cloth had kept the box of matches dry. She handed Curtis the box and he, with some difficulty, managed to get one of the matches alight. The wick of the lantern, however, was soaked beyond hope.

"Here," said Prue, "let me try." She grabbed the lantern and, pulling a small tin of kerosene from the knapsack, emptied the lantern of the water that had collected in the tank. Refilling it with the kerosene, she soaked the wick and set a lit match to the fabric. To her relief, it caught flame; a warm pulse of light came from within the glass.

In these brief, flickering cadences of light, the cavern in which they sat was revealed to them: the walls, brick and stone covered in ages-old layers of lichen, rose up from the dark pool to an arched apex, where a sizable hole—the one they'd fallen through—had been broken. One thing was imminently clear: the chamber had been built by human—or animal—hands. The three of them followed the glow of the lantern as it revealed more of the room; it illuminated, in slow mosaic, the brickwork of a forgotten century, from the hands of forgotten masons, before falling on an arched doorway, just yards from where they sat.

CHAPTER 15

A Place of Salvation and Solace

The record player was dug up from its tomb in the hallway closet; the speakers, rescued from their tenure in purgatory as end tables, were wheeled to face the room. A favorite LP, *Betty Wells's All-Time Favorite Two-Steps*, was unearthed from the cabinet and placed, spinning, on the platter. The lonesome tones of a sole pedal steel guitar moaned, and Joffrey Unthank took Desdemona Mudrak by the hand and danced her, amorously, to the middle of the office.

"What is this?" asked a surprised Desdemona, who'd just returned from the girls' dormitory to report that the map Unthank had been looking for was not, in fact, in number twenty-three's footlocker. She'd expected unmitigated rage; she got country music.

"Baby," Unthank cooed, "just follow my lead. Step. Step. And step back. Step. Step . . ."

"Yes, I know this two-step," said Desdemona. She'd played Annie Oakley in a Ukrainian biopic, shot in Odessa; the cast had been taught the dance by an American expat. "But my question is why."

Her boyfriend of thirteen years looked her directly in the eye and said, "I did it."

Desdemona's eyes went wide. She nearly stepped on his toe as they shuffled about the room. "Have girls returned?" she asked.

"No, no, no," he said. "All that—that's gone now. Done with. That's the past."

"And so what is future?" she asked, eyeing him warily.

"This." Never losing a beat, he ushered their marching dance steps to the desk, where the schematic for the Möbius Cog lay. Desdemona barely had a chance to look at the thing, with its hieroglyphic-like scrawls and enigmatic diagrams, before Unthank led her in a pretzel-like swing that left her on the other side of the room.

"What is that?" she asked, catching her breath.

"I don't know," Unthank said gleefully. "But I'm gonna make it."

"Darling," chided Desdemona, "I'm very confused."

"No worries, baby," said Unthank. "In fact, when we're living off the fat of the land, there won't be a single worry to your name. I should clarify: living off the fat of the Impassable Wilderness, that is."

"What is this? What has happened?"

He spun her around so that they were both facing forward; they did a promenade around the dentist's chair in the middle of the room. "Let's just say I received a visit from the ghost of Christmas future. And we're gonna have a full stocking next year."

"Still, I am not understanding."

"Baby, come this time two months down the road, we'll be living high on the hog. Old Wigman's gonna be begging me for favors when all the cards have been dealt."

"Stop with metaphors!" shouted Desdemona.

Unthank smiled. "This guy, this guy who wants me to build that cog there is gonna get me into the Impassable Wilderness. Not only get me in there, but he's gonna give me the run of the place. As far as I can tell. And then: no more sad machine shop, no more whining kids, no more complaining parents. It's going to be wine and roses, champagne on tap. Good times, metaphorically speaking."

Desdemona tried a smile. "And film studio? What of film studio?"

"Pah! Dessie, baby, you're going to be queen of this place. You won't need to make those silly movies anymore. Condescending directors, overprivileged producers. Who needs 'em? And dirty old Los Angeles? That's not good enough for you, baby. In the Impassable

Wilderness, you're going to be too busy eating caviar from a palm leaf. Or something like that."

The music was still going; Desdemona ground their dance steps to a halt. "Silly movies? Condescending directors? Dirty Los Angeles? Joffrey, this is lifeblood to me."

"Listen, I—"

"No, you listen here of me. I could care less of Impassable Wilderness. It is nothing. It is just dirt. And trees. I have, for these years, listened to your shoutings about getting into this place because I think it is your hobby, and every man should have hobby. Boris Nudnink, great Ukraine actor, he had hobby: building replica of Soviet-era memorial statues with Legos. It is silly, yes? But who are we to judge? It does him some good. This is how I see your Impassable Wilderness. Sputnik statue in Lego. But I go along and I carry transponder units and I make sure girls and boys do not run away. This is what I do for your hobby."

Unthank had fallen silent; he listened to the barrage with the obedience of a lapdog. The music carried on in the background.

Desdemona continued, "All in the hope that one day you will be good on promise, promise you made thirteen years ago when first I meet you. Desdemona, you say, one day I'll leave this machine-part making behind, and we will live to Los Angeles. I will make movie studio there, and together we will make great movies, great American movies. Like Scorsese and Tarantino and Bay. I will produce and you will star, you say. In Los Angeles. Not Portland. Not this Industrial Waste. And *not* Impassable Wilderness. This is the promise you make."

"I know, honey, but I just think—"

"No, that is your problem. You do not think. Only for yourself."

And with that, she pivoted on her heels and strode from the room, leaving a drifting wake of lavender perfume behind her.

Betty Wells was singing longingly about a west Texas gaucho when Joffrey Unthank, pulling the needle from the platter, cut her off midsentence. The speakers issued a little *skrick*. Stuffing his hands in his chinos pockets, he strolled over to his desk and, standing before it, began looking down at the Cog's schematic. Like a composer tapping out the music of his written notation without touching an instrument, Joffrey allowed the schematic to come to life in his mind: The little gears rotated around the axis in a fluid, silent motion, setting the blue-gray writing into a flurry around the rotating cog. He'd already forgotten what Desdemona had said to him; his mind was deeply in the world of parts mechanics, where no trivial distraction could hope to divert him from his task.

❧

When Elsie, Rachel, and Martha descended from the trees and approached the milling crowd of children in the house's yard, a kind of quiet fell over the kids. It was a quiet of resignation, of surrender. They saw the yellow tags on the three girls' ears; there was no need for explanation as to why they were there. For Martha, the faces of the children were like a flood of old memories: There was plump Carl Rehnquist, shaking dust from a rug. And Cynthia Schmidt, red-haired and pimply; she was carrying wood from a pile and stacking it neatly near the house. Dale Turner, always quiet as a mouse, was reading a book on the porch while two little girls, Louise Embersol and Sattie Keenan, looked over his shoulder. The children all murmured hello to the newcomers as they walked, trancelike, into the yard before turning back to their tasks.

The house itself seemed to be as old as the hills themselves; it was mostly made of rough-hewn logs, lain one on top of the other, sitting on top of a foundation of river stones. The wood had been deeply stained by time and weather. The sloped roof, cedar shingles under a layer of bright snow, crested at a high gable that boasted a copper rooster weather vane, its ancient patina a beaten green. A wide porch gave shelter to a few benches and a washtub.

As if mute, the three girls said nothing as they approached the house. Finally, Martha broke the silence: She saw a boy walk out of the front door of the cottage, carrying a bucket of what looked to be kitchen scraps. "Michael!" she shouted. The boy, dark skinned and sporting a red bandanna around his neck, smiled broadly to see her.

"Martha!" he replied. He set down the bucket. Martha ran to meet him; they gave each other an enormous hug before pulling apart.

"How did you—" sputtered Martha. "What did you—"

The three girls crested a small hillock and found themselves looking down into the trough of a narrow vale, where lay nestled a quaint wooden cottage.

The boy was about to answer when the dale was suddenly alive with the barking of dogs; the stampeding herd, which had so eluded the three girls, came galloping down the slope and into the yard. As soon as it came in contact with the laboring children, the pack splintered as the children were forced to drop the instruments of their chores to meet the demands of the happily barking and slobbering canines. The pug who Elsie had briefly pet came running up to her leg; she knelt down and started scratching the underside of his neck, and he let his tongue loll from the side of his mouth with pleasure. Rachel cringed and held her hands defensively to her chest.

"What's going on here?" Martha asked the boy, Michael. A golden retriever was in the process of lying on his side near them, and Michael had dutifully taken up petting his tawny fur.

"This is where we live now, Martha," said the boy.

"What? This whole time?"

"This whole time," confirmed Michael.

"But you were made Unadoptable, like, three years ago!"

"Has it been so long?" asked the boy, musingly, as he patted the retriever's belly.

"Do you live here, in this cottage?"

"We all do, Martha. We all live here. This is our home."

Martha remained mystified. "Did you, like, build it?"

"No, we found it," said Michael. He looked at Elsie and Rachel warmly. "Just like you have. And I see you've brought some friends with you."

"Oh yeah," Martha said. "This is Elsie and Rachel Mehlberg. They were there for only a week before they were made Unadoptable."

The kids all murmured hellos to one another. Michael returned his warm gaze to Martha. "Martha Song," he said, "I was wondering when you'd make it in here. I mean, not to be cruel—I know it's a little hard at first—but I was sort of hoping that you'd be made Unadoptable sooner. I kinda missed you."

Martha smiled. "Yeah, I missed you too, Michael." She turned to Elsie and Rachel. "Michael and I ended up at the Unthank Home around the same time; we'd been really close since we were kids." Looking back at the boy: "It broke my heart when you left. I cried for, like, three days straight."

"I know, Martha," he said. "It's so good to see you again."

Martha studied the boy for a moment before saying, "You don't look any different. I mean, not a lick different."

Michael only smiled. Turning to Elsie and Rachel, he said, "You'll have to meet Carol."

"Who's Carol?" asked Martha.

"He's kind of our father here. The patriarch of our big brood." Michael stood up, and, opening the screen door to the cottage, he yelled the man's name. "We've got a few more family members to welcome to the dale!"

While they waited for the man to come, Martha peppered Michael with questions. She, like Elsie and Rachel, was feeling deeply baffled by the afternoon's events.

"When I came here," the boy was telling, "I was as scared as you guys are. Believe me. All of us, it's all the same. Unthank had me drink this weird pink cordial. It made me so sick. As soon as I crossed into the woods I was, like, puking my guts out. But once I'd gotten my bearings, I started wandering. I was intent on getting my freedom—I knew some kids in town who'd be willing to take me in, and needless to say, I was really excited to be freed of that terrible machine shop. But I found—like everyone else—that somewhere along the way I'd lost the twine that Unthank had given me. And no matter how much I wandered, I always seemed to end up in the same place. I started getting really scared; it was clear that I was caught up in some kind of weird maze. So instead of trying to get *out*, I just sort of focused my mind and started walking *in*. That's the only way I can describe it. And eventually I came here, to this house. There were maybe a few other kids here—Unthank had only started the whole Unadoptable thing a few months before—and a whole lot of dogs."

"Yeah—what's up with the dogs?" asked Rachel, her hands still defensively folded at her chest. A black Lab was trying to lick her elbow.

"They're neighborhood dogs, run away. This place is, like, the receptacle for lost dogs and cats who've wandered from their homes and into the Impassable Wilderness. We get a new one every few months or so."

"Whoa," murmured Elsie. She looked at her sister. "I wonder if Fortinbras is in here." That had been the name of their tabby cat; he'd disappeared the summer before.

"You're free to look. No promises. Anyway," Michael continued, "Carol had been here all along. He'd come years before, and he'd found this house and kept it up. He took us in, all of us lost orphans, and made us a real home here. A better home than I ever had in the Outside, that's for sure."

A voice, warm and crackly, came from within the house. "Who's tellin tales about me, eh?"

Michael, hearing the voice, beamed. "Here he is."

The screen door swung open; a graying old man appeared at the doorway. A young girl stood at his arm and helped him walk onto the porch.

"Who's here, Michael?" called out the old man. "Who's come to join our family?"

The man's face was pale and freckled with liver spots; deep wrinkles crisscrossed his brow and cheeks and made troughlike pockets below his eyes. It was his eyes, in fact, that caught Elsie's attention. They seemed to be looking just beyond the girls' heads, though his body was facing in their direction. On closer inspection, his eyes seemed to be painted on and lifeless, like the rolling eyes of a baby doll. She saw the girl at his elbow guide him to the middle of the porch until his feet were planted firmly on the wood planks. His hand pawed at the air, uncertain, until it found Michael's shoulder, where it came to rest.

"He's blind!" said Elsie, despite herself.

In any other circumstance, Rachel would've shushed her sister for being rude, but she, too, was captivated by the old man's appearance.

The man laughed at the observation. "Eh, but who needs eyes when you've got thirty-five pair at yer disposal, eh? These"—here he waved his arm to gesture to the children in the yard—"these are my eyes."

The two eyes currently resting in his sockets moved a little as he spoke, looking cockeyed across the heads of the three girls. Elsie realized they were made of wood; two blue irises had been painted, somewhat crudely, on their polished surfaces.

"But I've not introduced myself," said the man. "Name's Carol. Carol Grod. And I welcome you, castoffs and castaways, to our little family." He swiveled to face Michael. "How many we got here?"

"Three, Carol," said Michael. "Three girls. One of 'em I know pretty well. We were friends, back in the Outside. Her name's Martha. And this is Elsie and Rachel."

"Aha!" exclaimed the man. "Three! That's quite the bumper crop.

Ol' Unthank must've had his hands full with you bunch." Two dogs, a collie and a German shepherd, had run up to the old man and yipped at him playfully. Dropping his hand from Michael's shoulder, he gave them each an affectionate pat. An orange-striped cat on the banister of the porch slunk away from the collected dogs. "Come closer, you three," he said. "Let me see you."

Obeying his command, Elsie, Rachel, and Martha stepped closer; the old man lifted his hand from petting the dog and touched each of their faces in sequence. When he arrived at Elsie's face, he paused. A slight frown played across his face. "Who's this one?" he asked.

"I'm Elsie," she said.

His eyebrows lifted as he continued to rest his palm on her cheek. "Elsie, eh? What a beautiful name. And which is your sister?"

"She's right here, next to me," said Elsie. He shifted from Elsie and let his hand gently rest on Rachel's cheek. His brow seemed to buckle a little under some deeper assessment. "Elsie and Rachel," he said, his voice a low purr.

"Is something the matter, Carol?" asked Michael.

The old man's demeanor abruptly changed. "No, no," he said, his hand lifting from Rachel's face. "Nothing at all." He patted Rachel affectionately on the shoulder. "It's good to meet you three. And welcome to our happy family. Whatever misfortunes have befallen us in our past are forgotten here; this is a place of salvation and solace. You can be happy here. Come," he said, gesturing to the open door of the cottage. "Come in and we'll show you around the place. Sandra's made some lentil stew; you must be very hungry."

And to be honest, they were that, very much.

❧

Once they'd finished eating the hearty vegetable stew (Elsie hadn't let up until every last morsel had been removed from the bowl, with the aid of a spongy piece of sourdough bread), the three girls sat back in their chairs, reveling in the glow of their satiated hunger. Carol had sat with them, merrily laughing at the sounds of their eating. "Nice to hear appreciative eaters," he said. The table cleared, Carol called for his pipe, which was dutifully brought by a young boy who'd been collecting vegetable scraps for the compost. As he packed it, he spoke in the direction of the three new arrivals.

"So, I suppose we'll be needin to find you a job among us," he said. "But don't worry: We won't be workin you like you're used to. Everybody here works to their own ability. We're not slave drivers. As long as the house is properly functioning, everybody's happy."

Michael, who sat next to Martha, intruded on the conversation with pride. "It really works," he said. "Nobody has incentive to be lazy. We each contribute what we're best at, whatever that may be."

"Sandra makes a fine stew," said Carol. "It's a real passion of hers. She's got a gift fer it. Likewise, Cynthia is a marvelous painter, that one. So she gets put to work providin the artwork you see around the house."

Elsie, licking her lips of the last drops of the delicious stew, surveyed the walls of the house; each was veritably covered with oil landscapes, on canvas, set in makeshift tree-branch frames.

"Michael, Peter, and Cynthia are handy with a snare, so they're out evenings and early mornings tracking game for the dinner table. And young Miles is a marvelous storyteller; he gets the young ones into bed early." Carol puffed at his pipe, letting curlicues of smoke drift into the rafters of the cottage.

"It all fits very nicely; we're a working family," said Michael, tearing off a hunk of bread. Two younger girls were washing dishes in the basin; they sang as they worked, and their high, lilting voices rang through the house. "We're content here," he said. He then reached into his pocket and retrieved a little white clay pipe, and, borrowing some brown tobacco from Carol's pouch, he packed it full and began to smoke it. This was met by looks of shock from the new arrivals. Michael checked their reactions with pride.

Martha was the first to comment. "What are you doing?"

Michael only shrugged. "We can do what we want here. No parents to bug us about what we should or shouldn't do. It's a dream!" He puffed at his pipe, shooting little circles of smoke into the air.

Rachel, who'd lapsed into silence after eating her fill, finally spoke up. "But what is this place?" she asked. "Why are you all here? Why are we all here?"

Swiveling his body to face Rachel, Carol leaned back in his chair.

It let out an aching creak. "This is the Periphery, dear," he said. "An ancient magic, woven into the trees by the old Mystics. It was built to keep folks like you and me *out*. And you might as well get used to it, 'cause we're stuck here."

Martha had let her spoon clatter from her fingers to the tabletop. She apologized for the noise before saying, "You said what? Magic?"

Carol tugged again at his pipe a few times before speaking. "Indeed. I can only tell you what I know. And I know this: When it was decided, some centuries ago, that the Wood and the Outside could no longer live in peaceful harmony, a Binding spell was placed on the ribbon of trees surrounding the Wood; so that every Outsider, when attempting to cross over, would be lost in a veritable maze of trees. Every turn would resemble the last, each square of land doubling itself into infinity. What's more, time itself remains at a standstill, and while the sun sets and the moon rises and does so in its own patterns, the days never shift into the next."

Michael smiled at Martha when this last thing was said. "Get it?" he said. "We never get old."

The three girls were speechless as they tried to wrap their heads around the implication.

"That's insane," said Rachel.

"Indeed," added Carol. "It's as if we are all simply suspended in time here. Never feeling the ravages of the seasons' turns."

"How long have you been here?" asked Martha.

"Oh, years, I suppose. Though when the effects of time have no sway, one stops paying quite so much attention to its passage."

"But how do you know so much about the . . . what did you call it . . . Periphery? And the Impassable Wilderness?" Rachel ventured.

"I had my moment," said Carol. "I walked among them. The people of South Wood. And then I was discarded."

"South Wood?" asked Elsie. "What's that?"

"And why were you discarded?" This was from Rachel.

Carol laughed a craggy, wheezing laugh before taking a few puffs from his pipe and continuing. "Girls, so many questions. First, South Wood is the populous place, where the Mansion and the seat of government is. There's a whole world there. And the entire place is bloomin with strange and magical things. Things that'd make your eyes pop out your skull. Anyhow: I was called up. From the Outside. And when they were done with me, they sent me away."

"Sent you away?" This came from Rachel. She'd pushed her hair back from her face and was staring at the old man intently.

Carol grumbled and chewed at the tip of his pipe. "Yup. Sent me away. Won't go into it; but somes in South Wood feel like this—the Periphery, mind—is as good a place as any to discard the old, used-up rubbish. Not bein of the Wood, mind, all's it took was to throw me in here, and I was good as dead to them."

Michael, his brow fretted, gave Elsie and Rachel a look that clearly discouraged them from delving any deeper.

"So's anyway," continued Carol. "Here I am. In my new home. In my purgatory. But least I got company. Must be two years now, when the first one came over. Little Edmund Carter. I was just sitting on the porch, talkin to the dogs—which were my only source of companionship and conversation at the time—when up he comes over the ridge. Been wanderin for days, I suppose. Some kids find us sooner than others. Took him in; gave him some food. We been growin as a family ever since."

"But . . . ," began Elsie. "There has to be a way out. We can't all be stuck here, forever?"

"Yeah," said Rachel. "What about the people who've made it out—Unthank said something about them. Survivors of the Impassable Wilderness, he called them."

"Well," Carol said, shifting in his chair, "I ain't never heard of that. Could be myth. Legend. Could be true, though, I s'pose. Though we spent a lot of time lookin for a way out, and we're all here as witness to that not necessarily workin out, if you get my figure."

Michael interjected, "And we're happy here. You'll come to see it that way, too. No rules. Do what you like. Sleep all day, if it's what you want. Stay up late. Tell dirty jokes!" As if to punctuate the idea, Michael let loose a curse word, apropos of nothing, that made Elsie blush a deep violet.

Carol laughed. "Yes, I don't cotton much to the idea of movin at this point. We've got a good thing here. In the Outside, I was a loner. In the Wood, among those strange peoples, I was ostracized. Here, I am a father to an ever-growin batch of good kids, all of 'em needin a place to live and some folks to call a family."

Elsie, out of the corner of her eye, saw Martha slowly nod in agreement. Rachel had seen it too; she spoke up. "You mean, you're all just going to stay here? Just like that?"

Michael shrugged. "As if we have a choice." His pipe was making lazy strings of smoke curl into the air.

Rachel stanched a laugh. "You guys are crazy," she said. Elsie glared at her. "And what about this magical world? All in here, in the I.W.?"

"It's true," said Michael.

"I think it's a load of crap," said Rachel.

"Why do you think you're stuck here?" This was Carol, who was looking at Rachel in a way that might be described as "intently," if it was possible for a blind man to do so. His wooden eyes lolled in his head as he turned.

"I don't know," said Rachel. "I've only been in here for a little bit. There has to be a way out."

"There's no way out," said Michael. "*We* know."

"Yeah," Martha interjected. "I'd be inclined to believe them." She then reached into her back pocket and pulled out a large piece of paper that'd been folded into little squares. Carefully, she began to flatten it out, revealing a large hand-drawn map. The first corner to be revealed had handwriting on it that read: "Impassable Wilderness, conjecture."

"That's the map from Unthank's office!" exclaimed Rachel.

"Uh-huh," said Martha. "I stole it." She looked at everyone present in a proud way.

"Michael," said Carol, "what is this? What has the girl brought?"

"It's a map," Michael said as more of Martha's bounty was revealed. "It's . . . the Wood, all right. It's got the mansion, just like you said.

And there's a big tree drawn on the north part."

"See?" said Elsie to her sister. "He does know what he's talking about." She reached her hand across the table and touched one of Carol's ancient knuckles. She felt an ingrained suspicion, long harbored, welling up in her stomach, like something she'd always known to be true was finally being confirmed to her. What's more, she knew there was a clue to her brother's disappearance, packed deep into Carol's story. "Tell us more about this place."

Carol smiled. He tapped out the remnant ash of his pipe into his hand, scattered it onto the knobby boards of the floor, and spoke. He told the girls about the Wood, about Wildwood and the North and South Wood. About the animals and the humans living among one another. About the Mystics. He told them what he knew, which was limited, but nonetheless was enough to upset the collected worldviews of the three girls in such a way that they would never see the world in the same light again.

CHAPTER 16

Under Wildwood

To Curtis, it looked like a coiled snake. Prue disagreed; she said it seemed aboriginal. Curtis had asked what "aboriginal" meant, and Prue said it had something to do with Australia. The native people there. Curtis replied curtly that he *knew* what aboriginal *meant* but he just wondered what on earth something aboriginal would be doing in the middle of the Pacific Northwest, to which Prue responded that there were a lot stranger things happening around them—a *lot* stranger—and that she'd given up trying to piece together how and why things occurred in this place. Curtis

didn't have a response to this observation. One thing was certain: The design that had been engraved on the keystone of the tunnel's tall archway had undoubtedly been made by *somebody*.

"I'm getting a real 'snakes ahead' vibe from it," suggested Septimus, shivering.

The design was a simple coil, carved into the rock. Below the archway, a tunnel, perhaps the height of two very tall men, extended beyond sight into darkness.

"I'm not sure," answered Prue. "Seems to me like these sorts of things mean, like, the circle of life. Stuff like that."

"Wonder who made it," mused Curtis.

"Probably can keep wondering. Looks like it's been here a long time, whoever carved it," said Prue.

"At least we know somebody got down here. There must be a way to the surface." Curtis, by the light of the lantern, had taken his socks off and was busy wringing the icy cold water from them.

"Sure," said Prue. "But given the choice, is that where we want to be right now?"

Curtis regarded his friend coolly. "You may be right."

"Even if Darla didn't survive the fall, who knows if there are more of them, these foxes, out there. Not quite sure how we're going to find the makers and get Alexei reanimated, down here."

"That's still the goal, huh?"

"Of course it's still the goal," said Prue.

Curtis shared a glance with Septimus before saying, "What about the bandits? We need to find out what happened to them." Little rivulets of water were pouring from the fabric of his socks; his bare feet were the color and texture of one of the jarred pig fetuses that had lined the shelves of their Life Science lab room.

"Also," added Septimus, "we did almost die. Twice. Sometimes that can, you know, rejigger priorities."

"Twice?" asked Curtis.

"I'm counting the fox-woman attack as one. Then the fall."

"Got it," said Curtis, before adding, "Though I tend to think the whole episode was one big death-avoidance thing."

Prue, annoyed, rounded on them both. "Well, it hasn't. Rejiggered priorities," she said.

"The whole camp was wiped out, Prue," said Curtis. "It's sort of a miracle that we survived the fall. I mean, for all I know, Septimus and I are the last remaining Wildwood Bandits. We owe it to the rest of the band to find out what happened."

Prue seemed like she was prepared for Curtis's objection. "I have a really good hunch that the tree knew about this all along. I'm thinking that, somehow, reanimating Alexei will go a long way to helping everyone. Including the bandits. I mean, think about it. We fall into the Long Gap—that certainly wasn't part of our plan—and we wind up finding this tunnel—that boy had said to me, 'You have to go under to get above.' I swear. I'm totally quoting him there."

"So you said."

"And the tree—or the boy—also said that we needed to reanimate the true heir to save our lives and our friends' lives. However that works, I think the meaning's pretty clear. This is what we *have* to do."

"You're the oracle here. You're the one with the voices in her head."

Prue ignored this little slight. She was dragging her fingers through her hair, squeezing water from the damp strands, and thinking. "It's just that it's not entirely clear how we go about it, being underground. I mean, clearly it's going to be hard to do what the tree wants us to do in our, you know, present circumstances. South Wood's a far way away. And who knows how many of those assassins are out there. One thing is certain: We're safest down here, out of sight, in the underground."

"Or aboveground," said Curtis. A light had come over his face. "Hear me out: If things are really as they are in South Wood, everyone thrown into a patriotic tizzy over this and that, and we know that *somebody* with a horse in that race is wanting us killed—don't you suppose that being out in the open might be safer than hanging out in some anonymous hole where we could be dispatched without anyone knowing it? I mean, I know I've joked about it, but you're the Bicycle Maiden. You're, like, the mascot of the revolution. I mean, who knows, right? You show up and everybody might be bending over backward to please you and make sure you're—and hopefully, me too—safe."

"And that's how we get to Alexei, and start looking for the makers," said Prue.

"We've got to tell them what's happened to us, to the bandits," Curtis added. "Someone's got to help."

Septimus interjected, "Don't we still have an emissary there? Brendan sent Angus not too long ago. He's got to still be there."

Prue nodded. "Maybe that is the best course." She paused and stared at the lichen-covered walls of the chamber, their greenness an almost neon in the lantern's light. The void beyond the archway was chilling to her. "Assuming we can even get out of here. It's just as likely this tunnel will just lead to a dead end somewhere. Though—I do remember . . ." Here, she began chewing on a nagging fingernail, trying to conjure a memory from the previous autumn. "Penny, the housemaid at the Mansion. When she snuck me out of there, when I went to meet Owl Rex, she took me through these crazy tunnels. I think she said something about them being there before the Mansion had even been built. Maybe they extend all over the Wood!"

"Maybe so." Curtis, having wrung as much water from his wool socks as he could manage, cringed as he rolled them back onto his feet. When he was done, he slipped his boots back on and stood gingerly. He made little sloshing noises as he shifted from one foot to the other.

"Close enough," he said. "You guys good to go?"

Prue tested her bad ankle with a few steps. "I think so," she said.

"You two first," said the rat. "You can soak up all the snakes." Curtis waved the way for Prue; together they crossed through the archway and into the tunnel.

The dampness seemed to engulf them. Even if their clothes weren't already drenched to the skin, they would've felt the air, thick with moisture, closing in around them. Thankfully, it had grown warmer as they traveled farther into the tunnel, which went a long way toward making their slow progress at least somewhat comfortable. Prue had to walk carefully, her ankle still smarting from the fall. The walls of the tunnel climbed high above their heads to arrive at its arched spine, aloft at the height of a basketball backboard. The stones that made up the wall looked as if they'd been meticulously chiseled into usable form by hand, with the aid of some archaic tool. Prue wondered what sort of hands would've done this work: The amount of time it would've taken to do even a small section of the tunnel seemed unfathomable to her. She imagined the creatures, animal and human, working together over centuries to craft this single artery, so deep in the underground, the chamber echoing with the sounds of their work, with the sounds of their songs.

Curtis, meanwhile, took up the rear with Septimus, looking behind him every now and then to make sure the inevitable serpent the rat kept going on about wasn't mounting a rear attack. James Earl Jones horribly transforming into a giant, toothy snake in the original *Conan* movie was branded on his brain, ever since he'd watched it with his dad when he was younger. He wondered if he'd be that creeped out, though, if whatever specter he imagined arriving was, in fact, James Earl Jones, who came crawling up behind them and transformed himself into a poisonous reptile; Curtis thought that that might be cool. Especially if he talked, because then you could hear James Earl Jones's voice in real life. And before he knew it, Curtis was mumbling something aloud in his best James Earl Jones voice.

"You have failed me for the last time, Admiral," he said.

"What?" asked Prue, stopping in her tracks.

"Did I say that? Sorry." He realized his mind had been wandering, though the natural reverb of the tunnel did lend a kind of authenticity to his impression.

"Come on, I think I see something ahead," said Prue.

The tunnel hit a T intersection, some thirty feet from where they stood. A little stream of water dribbled from a hole in the masonry. Another stone had been set into the endless repetition of gray rock: the now familiar coiled circle. Below it, the designers of the tunnel had set two decorated stones, faded with time, next to each other. A circle was carved into one; a triangle in the other. Prue and Curtis studied these stones for a time, each alternately stepping forward and wiping the accumulated mud from the stones' engravings.

"I'm thinking triangle," said Curtis. "Though circle is awfully tempting as well."

Prue was silent. She held the lantern out and studied both of the options; each direction from the junction looked identical.

"Don't suppose the circle means bathroom, do you?" asked Curtis. "I should've gone in that pool, but it was just too cold."

"You're in an abandoned tunnel system," said Septimus, having caught up. "I think it's safe to say the world is your commode."

Without speaking, Prue turned left and began following the "circle" artery. Curtis followed, Septimus astride his epaulet.

"What'd you do there?" asked Curtis.

"Just following a hunch," replied Prue.

They came to several more such intersections; and with each one, it became increasingly arbitrary which direction they chose. A few times they found themselves dead-ended in a chamber similar to the one into which they'd fallen; in such cases, they simply turned around and chose the other direction. Since they didn't really have a viable entryway—they'd fallen through a makeshift tunnel that itself had led from the bottom of an unscalable shaft—Prue had reasoned that it didn't really matter which direction they went or that they kept track of their steps. She'd said this much to Curtis and Septimus while they were sitting at an intersection, sharing another piece of jerky.

The unspoken subtext there, Curtis decided, was that they were basically marching until they ran out of food and starved to death or found an exit to the surface—whichever came first. It was enough to send shivers up his spine.

They continued on; finally, after several hours of wandering the maze, they saw that the walls of the tunnel seemed to fall away, and a cool, empty breeze suddenly passed over them. Holding out the lantern, they saw that they had entered a massive chamber, for which there was no visible ceiling or floor, and the stone path they were walking on was, in fact, a bridge to the other side. To their dismay, the light of the lantern revealed a dizzying crisscross of identical bridges, spanning the chasm directly below them; the scene repeated above them as well. It reminded Curtis of the videos he'd seen at the local science museum: the vast linking tendrils of tissue that made up the human brain.

"Oh man," Curtis heard Septimus say at his shoulder.

"Just . . . ," began Prue. She was sounding desperate, afraid. "Let's just keep going."

As if to underscore the seriousness of their situation, Curtis's stomach let out a little hungry grumble. "Ignore that," he said.

They crossed the bridge. In time, they came to another split in the tunnel; both sides led to short flights of stairs. They took the one to the left. It split twice more before they found themselves again crossing a massive chasm, spanned by a multitude of other bridges above and below them. It was impossible to know where they were in relation to their previous position—or, really, whether this was the same chasm they'd traversed just a short time before. Prue's limping was becoming more pronounced. "Let's stop," suggested Curtis. "You look like you're in pain."

Prue ignored him and kept moving, blindly following the myriad pathways of the tunnel system. "There has to be a way," he heard her whisper.

They climbed stairways that seemed to get more and more vertical as they went, until they found themselves scaling the footholds of the stone wall the staircase had inexplicably become; they followed bridges that narrowed, at points, to barely the width of a single step. They wandered tunnels that seemed to curve, looping, impossibly in on themselves; tunnels that were fashioned for the easy passage of mutant-tall giants but then would end abruptly in a short doorway, leading on to passageways that they would have to follow on their hands and knees. A great, spiraling stairway led them down the wall of a massive cylinder-shaped chamber, at the bottom of which was a broken ladder, leading farther into blackness below them. At one point, at the crown of an arched bridge, they stopped and ate. Curtis, while munching on the last of his apple slices, saw Prue nod off into slumber. Pushing himself against her, he too fell into a deep sleep. Septimus prodded them both awake some time later, though it was impossible to know how long they'd been out; in this dark underworld, the passage of time seemed irrelevant.

They checked their remaining rations; they had perhaps another day's worth of sustenance. Curtis massaged his temples with his fingers. The idea that they would perish in this underground labyrinth was steadily becoming more of a likely outcome. How had he been drawn so far astray from his bandit cohorts? He was sure there was something in the oath, the one he'd taken that night at the strange altar in the woods, that insisted on you sticking with your fellow bandits. Not leaving their side—or something to that effect. He'd only been a bandit for a few months and already he'd failed them. Brendan, Aisling—all of them. His family.

He stopped there. What family? That wasn't his family; Prue had been right. His real family, he'd already left. What was his father doing now? His mother? He imagined his two sisters, going through their daily routine without a thought to the dire circumstances he presently found himself in. He scarcely had time to recollect the never-ending chirping of his younger sister's Intrepid Tina doll before he saw Prue's hand waving in his face. She was standing in front of him. Her face was flat, unemotional.

"Come on," she said. "Let's keep moving."

They hadn't traveled far—perhaps an hour or two—before Prue stopped abruptly. Curtis nearly ran into her back.

"What's up?" he asked.

"Shhh. Listen."

Curtis held his breath; the omnipresent *drip, drip* from the lichen was the only thing he heard.

"I don't hear any—"

"Shhh—there it goes again!" Prue had her finger to her mouth and was holding the lantern high.

Curtis again screwed up all his listening prowess; this time, he heard something, something other than dripping. "What is that?" It sounded like metal dragging over stone—but something small, like a key being slid along a brick wall. In the cavity of the tunnels, the sound took on a terrifyingly ominous aspect.

Prue didn't answer; she was too busy staring at the space in front of them. They'd just turned at a Y intersection, taking the left passageway, and were in the middle of one of the longer stretches of tunnels they'd been through. The sound seemed to be coming from the darkness ahead of them.

The lantern cast a dim light on the ground ahead; Curtis envisioned some eldritch creature, all tentacles and glistening eyeballs, carrying a—what?—an ax, maybe. Dragging on the ground. He shivered at the image. There was a nagging tug at his ear; Septimus had winnowed his claws into Curtis's earlobe and was holding on to it like a child squeezing a teddy bear. "Snake," he whispered. "I'd know that sound anywhere."

"Hello?" called Prue.

The sound stopped.

Prue thrust the lantern out farther, edging forward down the tunnel as she did.

A voice came from the deep black. "WHO GOES THERE?" it said. It didn't sound like any voice Curtis had ever heard; it sounded as if it'd been buried underground for centuries, deprived of the warming rays of the sun—if a voice could sound like such a thing. It was dark and pitched low; menacing.

The voice sounded again, echoing off the walls of the tunnel. "TRESPASSERS OF THE UNDERWOOD, STATE YOUR NAME AND BUSINESS. IF YOU BE AGENTS OF DENNIS, I WILL BE FORCED TO DECAPITATE YOU."

Septimus gave a terrified yelp before jumping from Curtis's coat and scurrying away down the passageway in the direction they'd just come. Curtis grabbed hold of Prue's shoulder, hard; to his mind, this was far worse than snake-transformed James Earl Jones appearing from the dark—at least that would be a known quantity. Rather, this *thing* seemed to be coming from the very core of the earth itself, its being having been forged in the crucible of the molten depths.

The metallic noise sounded again, this time as if it were right at their feet. Prue swung the lantern about them, trying to gauge where the sound was coming from. "Where is it?" she whispered.

"I don't know!" Curtis whispered back, shaking.

The voice gave an audible gasp. It sounded like it was coming from their feet. Prue let the lantern drop a little, lighting the floor.

There, standing directly in front of them, was a small, furry mole.

Curtis's face fell. "Did *you* say that stuff?" he asked.

The mole, all of three inches tall, was aiming his snout in their direction. He wore, strangely enough, a kind of suit of armor that looked to be fashioned out of old bottle caps. A sword hung at a belt around his diminutive waist. Except it was not so much a sword as it was a standard Walgreens-issue darning needle. "HEAVENLY CONFUSION!" he cried in his weird, plaintive voice. "OVER-DWELLERS!"

Curtis and Prue exchanged a confused glance.

The mole, with not a little panache, pulled the needle from his belt and planted its point on the stone of the tunnel floor. He then took a knee, like a football player in pregame meditation, and said, "GREAT, HOLY OVERDWELLERS, HAVE OUR LABORS BEEN BLESSED BY THE PANTHEON OF THE OVER-WORLD? HAVE YOU COME TO AID US IN OUR STRUGGLE TO PREVAIL AGAINST DENNIS THE USURPER AND RETAKE THE FORTRESS OF FANGGG? HAVE OUR SUP-PLICATIONS TO THE OVERDWELLER MOTHER BEEN ANSWERED?"

Curtis stood for a moment, shocked by the barrage of information, by the intense devotion of the small animal. He reached for Prue's hand in the expectation that they would then share a quiet moment of consultation—it seemed to him that the gibberish the strange

mole was babbling held some grave importance and that their answer should be carefully deliberated before they went about engaging with him. But he didn't get a chance.

Prue, without a moment's hesitation, said, "Yes."

And that was that.

In the misted distance, the roof gables of the pagoda were the first things to come into view. They were draped in heavy pillows of snow that followed the roof's sloped contour. The dragon heads that decorated the eaves were dusted with the white stuff, giving them the illusion of being bearded and white, wise to the ages. Seeing the building, the woman inwardly breathed a sigh of relief. The snow covered the sand gardens that surrounded it, obscuring the meticulous patterns raked into the fine gravel by the younger monks. A gosling, clearing snow from the stone path to the pagoda, stopped to greet her as she approached. The horrified look on the bird's face was enough to let the woman know that she probably looked terrible; she felt as much, her arm hanging like dead weight at her side, held straight by a cobbled-together splint she'd made from tree branches. Her left leg smarted—a bright bruise that had shifted, chameleon-like, through every color in the spectrum graffitied the skin of her thigh. Her dashiki was rent considerably, and she knew that her face was marred with dried blood, all black and chalky.

The old man was there at the top of the steps, waiting for her. His ancient face betrayed no emotion as she approached; he looked at her disinterestedly, as one would seeing the postman approach or a stranger on the street. When she reached the midpoint of the pagoda stairs, she fell to her knee.

"It's done," said the old man.

Darla found it hard to meet his eyes. "The old Mystic, yes. The half-breed children . . . are likely dead."

"The employer has signaled satisfaction."

Darla looked up at the man. "Satisfaction?" She paused, searching for the words. "I can't, in good conscience, confirm the kill."

"What happened?"

"They fell. Into the Long Gap. I couldn't follow."

"Come in, Darla," the old man said. "You must rest."

Inside, a brazier emitted a glow of heat from its red coals. The central chamber of the pagoda was decorated in an ascetic fashion: A few benches lined the wall; a series of woven mats covered the floor. The old man, in a simple burgundy wrap walked to the end of the mats and, flourishing the hem of his robe, sat down. Darla followed suit, lowering herself, with some difficulty, to her knees in front of him.

"How does the employer know?" Darla asked.

"It would appear that the Intuits, the ones that listen to the woods, no longer hear their presence."

"Are we discharged then?"

The old man massaged the knuckles of his fingers before speaking. "Yes," he said. "Until next I need you."

Darla, with some difficulty, managed to clap her hands together in front of her chest. She grimaced at the pain in her arm. "Thank you, daimyo," she said. She got up to leave the pagoda. Before she'd reached the door, however, she heard his voice again.

"Darla."

"Yes, daimyo."

"How certain are you?"

Their eyes met. Darla remained silent. The man nodded.

"Very well," he said. "Let us not take the employer's satisfaction as a signal of the end of the assignment. We shall remain vigilant."

"Yes, daimyo." She turned and left the room.

❧

The slate was cleared. All existing orders were shelved, current clients mollified with the explanation that the shop was getting a major overhaul—updating to the latest and greatest in machine-part manufacture. Production was ceased on every machine that, to Unthank's best estimation, wouldn't be absolutely necessary to anything but the task at hand. Molds were pulled from their cradles and stored; every nook and cranny was scoured of any contaminant that might compromise the manufacturing process. All the orphans were pulled from their normal assigned spots and put on call; he couldn't afford to delegate any responsibility to these urchins. Absolute perfection, at every step, was required to create something so meticulous and demanding as the Möbius Cog. If he managed it—and he was still leery that it was even possible—it would undoubtedly be the crowning achievement of his career.

Desdemona watched the proceedings silently. She helped him when she could, though it was clear that this was a mission that he himself would have to achieve. She brought him refilled jugs of water on the shop floor; she carried away his half-eaten sandwiches from his desk; she woke him at three in the morning when he'd fallen asleep on the pile of notes he'd amassed. She didn't bother bringing up his betrayal of her dream—of the dream she'd thought they shared—and stewed on it, wordlessly.

The machine shop was a ghost of its former self, removed of the hubbub of the working children. Now it was only Unthank on the shop floor, surrounded by a few orphans who served merely to do such menial tasks as carry the sheaves of paperwork he'd created in his research. Working into the early hours of the morning, he crafted the wax molds that would eventually be burned away to give birth to the three twisted gears, the orbiting rings of the Cog's magnetic core. A vat of molten brass bubbled and smoked at the far end of the shop, awaiting its moment when it would be carefully poured into the prepared ceramic die. From the outside, the windows of the Unthank Home glowed bright orange; inside, the heat and light could bring to mind some religious zealot's image of the Underworld, where eternal punishment is meted out to the unholy. Hephaestus himself would not seem out of place in this cauldron of fire, among the clanging of iron and the churn of hydraulic machinery. As the days wore on and the nights melted away like so much molten ore, Unthank began to see himself in an almost godlike light. He was the creator, the maker. He was breathing life, sacred life, into the coldness of these raw materials.

The God of Judeo-Christian belief had created the universe himself; Unthank saw multitudes contained in every tooth, sweep, and angle of the Cog's mechanic. God had seven days to make the universe; Unthank had been given five.

And he was determined to beat the spread.

THE
UNDERWOOD
TO WILDWOOD
THE CAVERN POOL
FORTRESS OF FANGGG
(LATER PRURTIMUS)
MOLE ARMY ENCAMPMENT
THE GREAT POOL
TO THE OUTSIDE

PART THREE

CHAPTER 17

Return of the Overdwellers

The floor of the chamber was alive.

At least, that was how it seemed. It undulated with the activity of a multitude of living things, all set on different activities and preparations. It was an army of mole knights, all similarly equipped with darning needle swords and bottle-cap armor, and they numbered in, perhaps, the high thousands. Prue had gasped when she'd turned the corner, following the lead of the mole knight, whose name they learned was Sir Henry Mole. Or, rather, "SIR HENRY MOLE" as he'd said in his inimitable voice when he'd finally ceased his prostrations and introduced himself.

("My name's Prue," she'd said in response. "This is Curtis."

"And this is Septimus," said Curtis, aware of the rat's familiar feet returned to his shoulder.

"PRUE, CURTIS, AND SEPTIMUS: BLESSED BE THY NAMES. THE BELLS OF THE OVERGROUND RING WITH HEAVENLY MUSIC AT THE UTTERING. I GENUFLECT TO THEE."

"Please don't," said Curtis. "I mean, you don't really need to."

"I think you've genuflected enough," added Prue.

"That's a mole," observed Septimus, who'd by now realized that they'd not been in danger of being overtaken by rat-eating snakes.

"MY AMAZEMENT AT YOUR SUBLIME PRESENCES INHIBITS ME FROM DOING OTHERWISE, O GREAT OVERDWELLERS." However, taking the two children's instruction as scripture, he'd stopped with his bowing and groveling. "WILL YOU ACCOMPANY THIS HUMBLE KNIGHT TO THE FRONT, FOR AN AUDIENCE WITH HIGH MASTER COMMANDER TIMOTHY, ESTEEMED LEADER OF THE KNIGHTS UNDERWOOD?"

"Sure," said Prue. Curtis was staying out of it; he assumed Prue had some sort of plan. While they were following the little mole through the twists and turns of the passageways, however, she admitted to her real motivation. "Seems like a good idea," she'd said.

"Besides, he's just a mole. What can go wrong?")

But nothing had prepared them for the sight of the entire army, the mass of little furry black bodies stretching on to the boundary of their vision in the dark chamber. When the moles had detected the presence of the two humans and the rat, the entire mob turned their snouts in their direction. The three of them were greeted by a multitude of gasps and "HUZZAHS" and general pronouncements of amazement at the arrived deities—though they were all clearly blind: The fur on their small, pointed faces was unbroken by the presence of what could be considered eyes.

Sir Henry had leapt up onto a piece of scaffolding, some five inches tall, and addressed the crowd. "COMPATRIOTS, BROTHERS-IN-ARMS, OUR SUPPLICATIONS HAVE BEEN ANSWERED. THE DEITY HAS BESTOWED ON US THREE DEMIGODS FROM THE OVERWORLD. OVERDWELLERS PRUE, CURTIS, AND SEPTIMUS. WITH THEIR AID, WE SHALL BE VICTORIOUS!"

More "HUZZAHS!" erupted from the crowd; Curtis noticed they all shared the same strange dialect and timbre as Sir Henry.

"Hello," said Curtis.

"Howdy," said Septimus.

"Hi," said Prue. They all waved timidly.

The mole army, silent, stood before them. Prue imagined that they might be expecting something more, some holy declaration. "Nice to meet you!" was all she could manage.

"I don't suppose you've got any food, like, for overdwellers," said Septimus.

Prue shot him a look; Curtis poked him in the ribs with his finger. It didn't seem like a very deity-like thing to say.

"THE OVERDWELLERS CALL FOR MANNA! QUICK, THE GRANOLA BARS!" came a call from the rear of the crowd.

"See?" said Septimus, vindicated.

Twin waves of moles, their bottle caps clanking, folded away to create a clear avenue down the center of the army. A group of the animals broke away from the whole and sprinted off to some unknown destination; they returned moments later, hauling a brown and mildewed cardboard box. They laid it at Prue's and Curtis's feet, prostrating themselves as they approached.

"OVERDWELLER AMBROSIA," explained Sir Henry. "FOOD OF THE GODS. SEVERAL BOXES OF IT WERE DEPOSITED IN A CHAMBER BY ONE OF YOUR KIND, MANY, MANY POOL EMPTYINGS PAST."

Prue picked up the box. It was a package of Nature's Friend granola bars, though the printing on the box had nearly faded away completely with age. She flipped it over and inspected the expiration date: 10/23/81.

"Uh," she said. "This expired in 1981."

There was no response from the mole army.

"Let me see it," said Curtis, grabbing the box from his friend. He tore open one of the green foil packets; he scarcely had time to examine the granola bar within when it was ripped from its packaging by the rat at his shoulder. "Meems okay to me," Septimus mumbled through the crumbs. "Mpretty mgood!"

The army erupted once more into shouts of praise and adulation. Curtis offered Prue one of the bars from the box; she took it, eyeing the bar skeptically.

Another tumult sounded from the rear of the army. The path was once again cleared, and a retinue of mole knights traveled up the center; a few of them were riding what appeared to be salamanders, each draped in a kind of livery made of repurposed cardboard squares. The mole in the lead, astride one such amphibian, wore a bottle-cap suit of armor that seemed, somehow, more impressive than the rest of the army's array. A thimble was perched on his head, held there by a thin, pink rubber band.

When he'd arrived at Prue's and Curtis's feet, he vaulted from his salamander with a dashing leap, like Errol Flynn launching from his steed to greet a maiden in distress, and dropped to one knee on the stone of the chamber floor. His armor clicked and clanked dramatically as he moved. "OVERDWELLERS! I AM SIR TIMOTHY, HIGH MASTER COMMANDER OF THE KNIGHTS UNDERWOOD. I SUBMIT MYSELF TO YOU. GRACIOUS OVERDWELLERS, WE GIVE THANKS FOR YOUR BLESSED REVELATION."

Curtis, having sated his hunger somewhat by the Reagan-era granola bar, took the bait; he'd been leery at first to dive into the strange endeavors of the mole army, but he was now taking to it with a real flair. "We are well pleased with your devotion, Sir Knight," he said. "And the Overdweller Mother has deemed you worthy of . . . intercession."

"Hold up," said Prue, ever the prudent one. The attention of the room swiveled in her direction. "We're not *really*, you know, gods. We're just . . ."

The room was silent as she searched for a description. Curtis was fixing her with an astonished glare. She swallowed loudly. It occurred to her, then, the implications of being imposters to such a devout race of animals. She envisioned the three of them being swarmed, Lilliput-like, by these armed insectivores. Those darning needles, while being somewhat harmless on their own, seemed frightening if employed en masse. Curtis intuited her change of heart.

"Demigods, more like," he finished for her. "You know, pretty much the same."

The room seemed to relax at this announcement.

Prue decided then that she would continue to let Curtis do the talking; he seemed to have the lingo down. He continued, "And we've been tasked to aid you in your struggle. However, the Overdweller Mother has demanded one condition to be met after your victory has been won."

"NAME THIS CONDITION, O GREAT ONES," said Sir Timothy.

"That we, in a, um, show of your faith, are brought in regal procession through the tunnels of the Underwood to the South—to the city of the Overdwellers in the South part of the Overworld."

Sir Timothy paused, his knee still firmly planted on the stone. He was working over what Curtis had just said. "THING IS, O GREAT ONE," he said after a moment, his voice trembling with fear of reprisal, "WE'VE NEVER BEEN TO THE CITY OF THE OVERDWELLERS OF THE SOUTH. THE WAY IS A MYSTERY TO US."

A voice came from behind him. "THERE IS A WAY!" The voice, while still carrying the strange resonances of the moles' speech, sounded old and decrepit. Sir Timothy turned to watch a mole, dressed in a robe and walking with the aid of a twiggy cane, approach from his throng of attendants. Oddly enough, the old mole sported a long white beard, which Curtis didn't recall being something that moles typically did.

"THERE IS A WAY," said the old mole again.

The chamber, the collected thousands of mole knights, all quieted to listen.

"THERE IS A WAY," he repeated. "THERE IS *A*—"

Sir Timothy finally interceded. "WHAT IS THE WAY, O ELDER KNIGHT?"

The senior mole chewed on his lip for a moment and stroked at his beard with his paw. "THE SIBYL, THE GOOD HIGH MASTER COMMANDER'S SISTER AND PROPHETESS TO DENNIS THE USURPER, KNOWS THE WAY TO THE LAND OF THE SOUTHERN OVERDWELLERS. SHE HAS THE KNOWLEDGE FROM HER VISIONS."

"INDEED!" exclaimed Sir Timothy. "MY DEAR SISTER, GWENDOLYN, IN THRALL TO THE USURPER. WHY DIDN'T I THINK OF THAT?"

The old mole shuffled in his robe, in shrugging humility. "'TIS NOTHING, HIGH MASTER COMMANDER," he said.

"Hold up," said Prue, stepping forward. She heard a scream issue from the ground at her feet; she'd stepped on one of the moles, a squire to the High Master.

"I'VE BEEN SMOTE!" shouted the squire. Prue quickly jumped back, removing the heel of her boot from his back.

"Sorry," she said, her hand at her mouth. "Is he okay?"

A few moles had rushed to the squire's side; with their help, he seemed to be recovering well.

"I'M OKAY!" he said.

"I didn't *mean* to, uh, smite him," said Prue.

She smiled apologetically. "What I wanted to ask was, who's this Dennis?"

"YOU DID NOT HEAR IN OUR SUPPLICATIONS? OUR OFFERINGS AT THE OVERDWELLER ALTAR?"

"Maybe we missed that part," interjected Septimus.

The moles, thankfully, did not fault them for their gap in omniscience. The old mole, his paws cradled at his belly in a kind of thoughtful pose, began speaking in a quavering tenor. "THREE EMPTYINGS OF THE GREAT POOL AGO, THREE EMPTYINGS PAST, WHEN THE OVERDWELLER ARCHITECT CEASED HIS VISITATION AND THE CITY OF MOLES HAD BEEN COMPLETED TO THE SATISFACTION OF THE OVERDWELLER ARCHITECT, WHO CAME NO MORE, DID THEN DENNIS WHO FORMERLY WENT AS THE CONSUL TO THE HIGH MOLE KING COME FORWARD AND, UPON THE DYING BREATH OF THE HIGH MOLE KING, SAY UNTO THE GATHERED CITIZENRY THAT HE HIMSELF HAD THUS BEEN BEQUEATHED THE KINGSHIP. UPON THE CORONATION, THUS DID DENNIS WAGE WAR UPON HIS FELLOW MOLES, CASTING OUT THE ENEMIES OF HIS CREST AND WILLFULLY IMPRISONING THOSE WHO DARED SPEAK OUT AGAINST HIS WANTON RULE. HOCHMEISTER SIR TIMOTHY, GREAT AND POWERFUL, WAS THE FIRST TO GATHER IN THE

WASTELANDS OF THE UNDERWOOD, BEYOND THE CRESTED BRIDGE, AND MUSTER AN ARMY TO CHALLENGE THE RULE OF DENNIS, DENNIS THE USURPER OF THE KINGSHIP, AND RECLAIM THE THRONE OF THE CITY OF MOLES FOR THE RIGHTFUL HEIRS, THE UNITED MOLES OF THE UNDERWOOD."

When the small, aged animal had finished his recitation, which sounded to Curtis like someone saying aloud some ancient scripture, a silence followed as the three Overdwellers attempted to digest the information they'd just been given.

"Okay," said Septimus. "That's Dennis."

The mole continued, "IT IS AUSPICIOUS, THE OVERDWELLERS' ARRIVAL AT OUR PLACE OF MUSTER. OUR PRAYERS HAVE BEEN ANSWERED BY THE OVERDWELLER MOTHER. THE SIEGE OF THE FORTRESS OF FANGGG MUST COMMENCE. WE SHALL BE VICTORIOUS WITH THE HOLY ASSISTANCE OF THE GREAT OVERDWELLER DEMIGODS CURTIS, PRUE, AND SEPTIMUS."

The chamber exploded with sound. Every last mole raised their voice in a warlike yowl, and the collected roar echoed endlessly through the stone tunnel; the floor was a prickly carpet of raised darning needles, brandished wildly in the air.

"One second," said Curtis, waving his hands out to the cheering mass. "I've got a few questions. So—we're going to help you defeat this guy, this Dennis the usurper? In his Fortress of Fang?"

"FANGGG," corrected one of the attendant moles.

"Fanggg," said Curtis.

"SUCH WAS THE NATURE OF OUR SUPPLICATIONS," said High Master Commander Sir Timothy.

"Okay," replied Curtis. "And if we do that, you'll, um, give us a procession to the Southern Overdweller land?"

"WHEN WE'VE FREED THE SIBYL, SHE WILL GUIDE THE PROCESSION."

"Right," said Curtis. "The Sibyl. She's got the directions." He paused and looked at Prue, then back at the moles. "Guess that's all my questions."

Prue spoke up. "You said something about another Overdweller. The architect? Who's that?"

Again, it was the decrepit mole who answered. "THE OVERDWELLER ARCHITECT CAME FROM THE OVERWORLD IN OUR TIME OF NEED, WHEN THE KINGSHIP WAS IN RUIN IN THE AFTERMATH OF THE SEVEN POOL EMPTYINGS WAR. THIS WAS MANY POOL EMPTYINGS AND REFILLINGS BEFORE THE RISE OF DENNIS THE USURPER. THE CITY OF MOLES LAY IN WASTE, ITS BRIDGES TORN ASUNDER AND ITS CITIZENRY CAST TO THE WIND. IT WAS A TIME OF GREAT STRIFE IN THE UNDERWOOD. THE ARCHITECT, SENT BY THE

OVERDWELLER MOTHER IN ANSWER TO THE SUPPLICATIONS OF THE MULTITUDE, DID ENDEAVOR TO REBUILD THE CITY OF MOLES AND CONSTRUCT THE FORTRESS OF FANGGG FROM THE BLESSED MATERIALS HE GATHERED IN HIS SOJOURNS TO THE OVERWORLD. ONCE HIS LABORS WERE FINISHED AND HE LOOKED ON THE CITY OF MOLES AND THE FORTRESS OF FANGGG WITH SATISFACTION, HE DID BID US GOODBYE AND THUS RETURNED TO THE BOSOM OF THE OVERDWELLER MOTHER. THUS SAYETH THE HISTORIES, AS WRITTEN BY SEER BARTHOLOMEW MOLE." The old man paused for a second before adding, "THAT'S ME."

"Huh," said Prue thoughtfully. Curtis tried to catch her eye to see what was transpiring in her mind, but she seemed too engrossed. Besides, the High Master Commander, Sir Timothy Mole, had raised his sewing pin to the crowd and said, as loudly as his little voice could manage, "WE MARCH FOR THE HONOR OF THE OVERDWELLER ARCHITECT, WE MARCH FOR THE HONOR OF THE CITIZENRY OF THE CITY OF MOLES, WE MARCH FOR THE INALIENABLE RIGHTS OF THE MOLES, AS CONVEYED BY THE GRACE OF THE OVERDWELLERS. KNIGHTS UNDERWOOD: WE MARCH NOW ON THE FORTRESS OF FANGGG!"

Another eruption of cheers sounded, and the entire mole army began preparing themselves for their great march. Prue and Curtis froze in place; the frantic activity below their feet was such that any wrong step could result in another inadvertent smiting. They watched breathlessly as siege towers, no taller than coffee tables, were carefully erected by teams of laboring moles; battering rams, made of what appeared to be pencils rubber-banded together, were shifted into position; while trebuchets and catapults, the size of children's toys, followed in the rear. The mole knights seemed well trained for this massive military action; they easily broke into their assigned phalanxes, with the halberd moles taking up the secondary position (wielding what looked like chopsticks with pieces of tin can attached to the tips), directly behind a veritable sea of needle-and-pin-armed infantry moles; the salamander-mounted cavalry moved noisily behind these two blocks of soldiers, their steeds snorting and bucking in a very horselike fashion. Once the thousands-strong army had arrived at its marching pattern, the entire chamber fell into a hushed quiet.

High Master Commander Sir Timothy Mole, his salamander a blazing black-dappled red, rode proudly up the side of the phalanx of soldiers. The only sound came from a single drum (an empty container of chewing tobacco) and the drummer, who beat a solemn, intermittent *prrap-a-tap-tap-tap* on its tin head. Each mole, regardless of their rank or station, stood rigidly still, their little black snouts held at a lofty angle. Sir Timothy, though blind, seemed to appraise his troops with a proud steeliness, the bottle caps of his armor (one read: LEMONY ZIP!) glinting in the Overdwellers' lantern light.

"This is so cool," whispered Curtis, enraptured by the proceedings.

"Uh-huh," was all Prue could manage.

Sir Timothy reined his salamander in at the front of the mole host. "KNIGHTS UNDERWOOD," he shouted. "WE MARCH!"

The drummers laid into their makeshift drums; a line of bagpipers took up a martialing tune. The thrum of a million tiny footsteps created a mighty din in the chamber as the mole army began their advance on the City of Moles.

❧

Desdemona was sitting on the sofa. She was staring distractedly at the variety of magazines that lay on the side table and finding herself not tempted to pick up a single one. *The 1% Journal*? What did that even mean? She didn't understand the industrialist sensibility; she never had. She'd fallen in with the crowd because she'd been attracted to the money—that was what her cousin Dmitri had advised in his email to her from New York. "If you're going to try to make it here, Dessie," he'd written, "you have to follow the money." And so she did. And the money had led her to Joffrey Unthank and the Quintet of industrialists. She felt that cousin Dmitri's advice had been sensible, though she understood now that there was more to success and satisfaction than just blindly following money. What that *more* was, she wasn't sure. But she was determined to find out.

The girl at the reception desk had been eyeing her ever since she'd stepped into the lobby of the Titan Tower, level thirty. She looked very young, this receptionist; she reminded Desdemona of herself when she'd been in her twenties—full of ambition and grace. She'd arrived in Portland in the possession of a film acting résumé that included *Odessa Drifters* and *The Godfather: Part Two*. The latter had been an unlicensed Ukrainian remake—but still: It looked great on a CV. The dream was still alive in her. However, there was something in the receptionist's occasional glare that made Desdemona think she was looking down on her; a decidedly there-but-for-the-grace-of-God-go-I kind of sneer. But could she blame her? Sure, Desdemona, at the receptionist's age, and seeing some poor woman in a second-hand gown and a plaster-cast of makeup to cover the encroaching menaces of age—wouldn't she have shot the same withering glance?

She thankfully did not have time to consider this thought before the phone rang at the receptionist's desk; the girl answered and, between smacks of her gum, said into the receiver, "Yeah, she's here, Mr. Wigman. Should I show her in?"

Apparently the voice on the other end answered in the affirmative, because the young receptionist stood up from her desk, smoothed the fabric of her skirt, and walked toward Desdemona. "He'll see you now, Miss . . ."

"Miss Mudrak," she answered.

"Riiiight. Mr. Wigman will see you now. This way, please."

Just you wait, little girl, Desdemona inwardly fumed. *Life will beat you down eventually.*

Together they walked to the large brass double doors at the other end of the lobby. The girl had some difficulty getting them open, but once she did, she gestured Desdemona inside. She was greeted by a booming and familiar voice.

"Dessie!" said Mr. Wigman. "Honey! Where you been all my life?"

"Hello, Mr. Wigman," answered Desdemona, affecting a purr. It was one of her go-to acting tools—the charming purr.

"Please, call me Brad. Let's drop the formalities here." He was standing at the head of a massive ovoid conference table; his immense frame was backlit by windows that overlooked the expanse of the Industrial Wastes.

"Yes, Brad. Of course. Between old friends."

Brad Wigman, Titan of Industry, laughed a resounding belly laugh, and the noise went rippling through the air of the conference room. The laugh was, in point of fact, the envy of the entire industrialist community. He'd actually been written up for it in the September issue of *Tax Bracket*. The cover line had read: "Brad Wigman's Laugh—A Bellwether for Prosperity? Tips on How to Make Your Own." It always made Desdemona cringe.

"Old friends," said Wigman, once the echoes of the laugh had subsided. "IN-deed. What can I do ya for, Dessie?"

"Well, Mr. Wigman—Brad—it is Joffrey. There is—something the matter."

Wigman's expression morphed into a deep frown. "Oh?" he asked.

"And you know how you say, every time we see, that if ever, ever I needing something—if I needing money or favor or just need some nice words, I come to you. Yes?"

"I do recall saying this, Dessie. And I meant it." He walked over to where she stood and put an arm on her shoulder. "You're a good girl. A fine girl. So: What's up with your man, there?"

"It is still . . . It is Impassable Wilderness."

Brad rolled his eyes and scoffed, "He won't give it up, will he?"

Desdemona shook her head, her eyes dramatically downcast.

"Bammer, Jimmy," Wigman called, snapping his fingers just over Desdemona's shoulder; two stevedores in matching red beanies came lumbering up. "Get this lovely lady a spritzer." To Desdemona: "How does that sound? A spritzer?"

"A spritzer would be very nice."

"A spritzer for the lady. And an espresso for me. In one of those, you know, small cups." As if to illustrate, he held his hands out, holding an invisible cup and saucer.

"Yes, Mr. Wigman," said the two stevedores in unison.

Wigman looked back at Desdemona, his gaze steely and intent. "So what's going on now?"

"It's just that . . . well, it is all he thinks of. All he talks of. It is never out of conversation with him, this Wilderness."

"It's an issue," said Brad Wigman, letting out a sigh. "We've been trying to curtail it."

"Yes, and I think he was good for a time. He focused on work, on the machine parts. But then . . ."

"Then?"

"Then, he's had a visitor."

Wigman raised his left eyebrow. "A visitor?" he asked.

"Yes, a man of mystery. He dresses like old times. He has—what do you call it—pince-nez."

"What, like on his nose?"

"Mm-hmm."

"For glasses?"

"Mm-hmm."

In truth, Wigman had been considering how to incorporate a pince-nez into his outfit; he'd ruled it out, deciding that it was pushing things just too far. And yet this gentleman had managed it; it gave him new hope. "Is he a Titan? An industrialist?"

Desdemona shook her head. "I'm not thinking so. He has strange thing about him—a thing I cannot explain. A якість."

"A yuckies?" That was how it had sounded.

"Yes," said Desdemona, assuming he'd understood the Ukrainian word. "Like special mist or shadow. I cannot explain."

"Go on," prompted Wigman.

"And ever since this meeting with this man, all operations stop. Everything. All clients, *poof!* Everything now is thing he must make."

"Wait a second." Brad's face had sobered considerably. "What are you talking about, *all operations stop*?"

"Exactly what I say! All machines, once making bolts and . . . bolts and things, now making this thing, this one machine part. Children are stopped working; they sit in bed all day, playing the poker." She mimed the dealing of cards with her long fingers.

Wigman waved his hands impatiently in the air. "Hold up, hold up," he said. "What is this thing?"

"It is thing he is told to make, from gentleman. It is some machine part. A cog." Desdemona was content that she'd got the Titan's full attention.

"A cog."

"Mm-hmm."

"And he's stopped all production to make this cog?"

"Yes, indeed." She was really getting somewhere; she was seeing the color rise in Wigman's cheeks.

The two stevedores, Bammer and Jimmy, returned with a small espresso cup and a glass of clear, bubbly liquid. Wigman took the espresso, slammed it back with a jerk of his head, and handed it, empty, to the stevedore. Desdemona politely took the glass of spritzer; she sipped at the contents.

Between sips, she continued to talk. "And it is all for Impassable Wilderness, Mr. Wigman. The gentleman says he will let Joffrey into I.W. if he makes this piece of machine for him."

"Is that so? Just . . . let him in? Like that?"

"It is true. But how is this possible? It is not possible. Mr. Wigman—Brad—I come to you like old friend. You and Betsy"—Betsy was Mrs. Wigman, a triathlete mother of five and member of the school board; she'd always rubbed Desdemona the wrong way—"have always been so kind. Ever since I come to United States. I ask you, please. Please to make Joffrey stop this madness with Impassable Wilderness. It is hurting business. It is hurting Quintet. It is hurting *me*." She glanced at him out of the corner of her eye to see that her story was hitting its intended mark.

Wigman looked distracted; he was chewing on his lower lip. He seemed to startle when he realized she was finished with her plea. "Oh," he said. "Oh, yeah. Well, that's clear." He straightened his tie, tightening the knot at his throat. "You know, I told that guy: Get your head out of the Impassable Wilderness junk. Told him plenty of times. But it doesn't sound like he's listening much. Tell you what, Dessie. If I popped over to the shop and had a little chitchat with your man there, would that smooth things over? Try to get his head back in the game?"

Desdemona smiled broadly, revealing her one gold tooth. "Yes, it would very much so."

"Good, good," he said. "I'm gonna go get that on the books straight away. 'Tween you and me, Dessie, we're going to get all this straightened out. Your man'll be back to normal in the time it'd take you to say 'environmental regulation loophole.'"

"Environmental regulation loophole," said Desdemona playfully.

Wigman smiled. "There you go. That's the spirit. C'mon, I'll walk you out."

Together they sauntered out of the conference room and through the tall brass double doors to the lobby. Wigman had his hand on Desdemona's shoulder as they walked. When they'd arrived at the secretary's desk, Wigman said, "Hey, doll—why don't you put me down for a little onsite visit to the Machine Parts Titan's place, as soon as you can swing it." He winked at Desdemona.

"Sure, Mr. Wigman," said the receptionist. She began stabbing a pink-nailed finger at the computer mouse, clicking her way through her boss's calendar. In the meantime, Wigman gave Desdemona a little pat on the back.

"Now, Dessie," he said. "I want you to head on back to that li'l orphanage of yours and take it easy; don't let this nonsense get to your head. We'll have it all sorted out in no time."

"Brad," said Desdemona, sneaking a look at the receptionist to see if she'd registered the first-name familiarity that the two of them had. "Bradley. This is so kind. So kind of you. You are old, true friend. If anything can get his mind back to important things, to machine parts, it is you."

"And that's just what we're going to do." He gave her another pat. "Now run along, Dessie. We'll be seeing you soon enough."

Desdemona smiled sheepishly, breathed another word of thanks, and headed toward the elevator doors at the other end of the room. Wigman watched her go. Once she'd disappeared beyond the closing doors, he put his hand to his chiseled chin and rubbed absently at the freshly shaved skin. He glanced at the ceiling-tall windows that made up the western wall of the lobby and stared at the wall of trees beyond the glass in a way that he hadn't remembered doing before—it was something that hadn't necessarily ever occurred to him. But now the wall of green seemed to take on a new—what had she said?—*yuckies*. It was distracting him; distracting him in a way that it hadn't before.

"You can do Wednesday, Mr. Wigman," said the receptionist, jarring him from his meditations.

"Wednesday," he said. "Great. Put me down." He spun about and walked back through the resplendent brass doors.

❦

What Wigman didn't know: On the hem of the forest's leafy fabric, all flocked with snow, there was a curious ribbon through which no one of Outside descent could travel. It was there that Elsie and Rachel Mehlberg had found themselves, quite trapped, among thirty-six children, several dozen stray dogs and cats, and an old blind man with wooden eyes. Two days had passed since they'd crossed over into the netherland, the Periphery, and while the rest of the children who called the place home seemed to enjoy their lives there, Elsie and Rachel were strangely discontented. For one thing, it would be a matter of days before their parents would return from their trip to Istanbul, hopefully with their brother in tow; they couldn't imagine their grief on arriving stateside only to discover that in the process of finding one child, they'd managed to lose the other two. It was paramount that Elsie and Rachel be there for them—their parents would undoubtedly die of heartbreak if they weren't.

However, it didn't seem like they had much of a choice. The magic of the Periphery was clearly very strong—why else would all these children and dogs and cats be stuck here? Besides, Elsie was very much under the sudden impression that her brother was not, in fact, in Istanbul at all. It was a feeling she'd had before, when she'd seen her brother's school friend at the pumpkin patch in the fall, though she now was suddenly able to correlate it with this place, the Wood and its enchanted boundary. And so the two sisters fell in line with the other children and chose tasks for themselves that they might better contribute to the community into which they'd been thrown.

Rachel, while initially resistant, found that the hewing and stacking of firewood appealed to a patch of her brain that longed for structure. The chopping part somehow ameliorated whatever frustrations she was having, and the loading and stacking felt like an elaborate game of Tetris. Elsie, too young for heavy physical work, had taken to mending clothes. She also endeavored to replace her Intrepid Tina doll with a facsimile that she'd made out of a few sticks and a handful of moss. Once she'd completed it, the doll became the envy of the other younger girls (and a few boys), and so she became busy satisfying the orders of a steady line of customers for the woody toy.

At night, the children would gather on the floor of the cottage's living room, where a fire burned merrily in the hearth. Carol would take his place in the rickety rocking chair, and the children would splay around him, wherever they could manage to fit. Puffing at his ever-present pipe, Carol could be induced to tell stories of his time inside the Impassable Wilderness—"The Wood," as he called it—and the children would thrill to the fascinating tales of talking animals, nature-attuned Mystics, and the comings and goings of kings and bird princes and Governors-Regent. In all his stories, however, he would always deflect the question of exactly *how* he came to be in the Periphery and what thing he'd done that had so angered the people of the Wood, enough to exile him to this strange purgatory.

Once the younger ones were tired, the children would shuffle off to their makeshift beds. The house managed to sleep all of them fairly comfortably, though they'd been forced to fill every available space with little fur cots. Once the few bedrooms had been filled, the attic then took the overflow; it wasn't long before that large room had reached capacity, and ever since, they'd been sticking little beds wherever they could manage in order to meet the demands of a slowly growing pool of children. Growing in number only, however. It was one of the advantages of the time-stoppage that occurred in the Periphery—the fact that the littlest ones, whose beds could fit easily in the cavity of a kitchen cabinet, would never outgrow their sleeping arrangements.

And so the days folded one into another, and thus would they continue to pass; or so Elsie and Rachel figured. That was, until they discovered something very strange, something that they wouldn't, in the immediate moment, be quite able to figure out or explain.

It happened one afternoon; the firewood had been stacked and the cleaning had been done. Most of the children were opting for an afternoon free of chores and were busy blocking out a hopscotch court in the snow of the yard. Elsie and Rachel were sitting on the porch of the cottage, watching the proceedings, when they saw Michael and Cynthia prepare themselves for an outing in the surrounding trees, setting snares for wild game. Rachel had asked what they were doing. Michael had responded with an invitation to come along.

"Sure," said Rachel. She then looked at her sister. "Wanna?"

"Yeah, okay," said Elsie, though she was a little leery. She kept flashing back to that rabbit she'd seen, their first day in the Periphery. It broke her heart, the idea of it snagged in a wire snare. "I'll go along just to keep company."

They followed the two older kids—Cynthia was a year Michael's senior, at eighteen—into the trees beyond the vale. Cynthia carried a few loops of wire at her belt; Michael had built several traps out of salvaged metal and wood which he held at his side as he walked. They stuck to familiar paths, worn into the forest floor by their own steps; after they'd been walking for a time, they stopped and studied the surrounding woods.

"It ends right about there," said Michael, pointing to a stand of trees in the distance, where the ground began to slope upward. "We've never been able to go beyond. We just keep ending up back here."

"That's weird," said Rachel.

"It is—and it's a little disorienting. I wouldn't advise it." This was Cynthia. She wore her auburn hair back in a knotted bandanna.

"Makes me a little, like, seasick every time," said Michael, miming rubbing his stomach. "It's gross. And then you're back where you were before. Easy to get lost that way."

Cynthia nodded before saying, "Since there's four of us, let's split up and see if we can't find any game trails. More eyes. Just stay clear of that line of trees. If you do happen to step over the Periphery Bind, just let out a holler. We should be able to find you."

"Got it," said Rachel.

Elsie said a quick good-bye to her sister; she didn't want to seem overly clingy, but the idea of getting lost again in the Periphery was a little frightening. What's more, it brought back memories of their initial march into the woods; she'd thought she would never see her sister again. It was strange to be reenacting the same scene, days later. However, she was determined to help out; she liked the idea of being a provider for their new family.

She walked toward the sloping hill but then skirted left, minding the warning of the older kids. The snow had let up the night before, and the temperature had warmed slightly; the snow was falling away from the trees in little clumps, revealing the deep green of their boughs. The floor was wet with the snowmelt, and little rivers of water could be seen, cutting their way through the shallow draws in the sloping wood. Little mushrooms sprouted from the carcasses of the fallen trees; a bird sounded in the boughs ahead. Elsie found that a tremendous peace had fallen over her; the first she'd felt in quite a while, since her parents had announced their decision to leave the country. It was refreshing, if such a word could describe the feeling.

Suddenly, a flash of white caught her eye. She looked over and saw, standing atop the broken stump of a cedar tree, a white rabbit. It was staring at her. Elsie immediately recognized it as the same one that had greeted her when she'd first ventured into the woods, those long days ago. Something in the way it twitched its ears when she approached; it seemed to recognize her as well.

"Hello, little rabbit," said Elsie.

She could swear that the rabbit opened its mouth to speak in response—though nothing came out. It was as if it had forgotten what it was about to say. Instead, the rabbit merely wiggled its nose. Seeming happy that it had gotten Elsie's attention, the rabbit bounded off the stump and began hopping its way up the hill. It hadn't gotten far, however, before it stopped and turned to look at Elsie again, beckoning her on.

"Okay," said Elsie, determined. "Where to?"

She marched through the hip-high bracken after the rabbit, which was thankfully mindful of her slow progress: It kept stopping and waiting as she managed the difficult terrain. She wasn't sure where they were going; she'd long lost any sense of where the edge of the Periphery was, as per Michael and Cynthia's warnings. Her curiosity was too great to be frightened off the rabbit's trail.

They crossed a hillock and continued down into a little rift, where a creek bubbled with muddy water; they wound along a snaking ridge and across a wide meadow, sparking with the green shoots of grass newly freed of its snowy blanket. All along, Elsie kept wondering how she could ever hunt or trap such a beautiful creature, so full of brightness and intelligence. She figured she wouldn't mention the appearance of the rabbit to Michael or Cynthia; she couldn't risk the possibility that they might be less humane than she.

And then the rabbit was gone. It had ducked behind a web of young trees and disappeared. Elsie called out, "Rabbit! Where did you go?" She was surprised at herself; what, was the rabbit supposed to holler back, "Right here!"? While distracted by her searching for the rabbit, she took an uncertain step farther, caught her shoe on a sticky bunch of ivy, and fell headlong onto a gravel road.

Elsie looked up; it was, in fact, a road. A very long road. One that cut an easy, snaking swath through the dense forest. She also saw a kind of waymark, a stone cairn, on the far side of the road; it looked like it had sat there for centuries. She looked around her, deeply confused. Why hadn't the others ever found this? And what was a road doing in the no-man's-land of the Periphery? And then it occurred to her: This was *not* a part of the Periphery. She'd somehow managed to break through the Bind and was now in the arms of the Impassable Wilderness. Or, as Carol called the area, Wildwood.

CHAPTER 18

The Great Siege; Elsie and the Road

They'd been instructed to wait in the corridor; the seer, Bartholomew Mole, counseled that it would be a better use of the element of surprise. The High Master Commander agreed, though he was sparking to begin the siege. Again, the seer advised that they make camp there, in the elbow of the tunnel, as the mole army had been marching for nearly two days.

They'd followed endless stretches of tunnel, watched the stonework change from smooth granite to rough slate and back to granite. They'd crossed more bridges than Curtis thought he'd ever seen in his life, spanning depths that seemed to reach into the very bowels of the earth itself. They camped on rocky outcrops and listened to the patient dripping of water from the lichen while the little campfires of the mole knights cast weird shadows on the walls. When the two days had passed—which, it was explained to the three deities, was about a week in Overdweller travel time—Sir Timothy stood at the head of the army and made a proud declaration.

"THE MARCH ON THE FORTRESS OF FANGGG WILL BE CELEBRATED IN THE ANNALS OF HISTORY. IT IS THE LONGEST ADVANCE EVER UNDERTAKEN BY A MOLE HOST," explained Sir Timothy.

The morning must've arrived; some three hours later, the mole camp, all small white canvas tents and campfires, was a-bustle with activity. The moment had finally come; the generals gathered to review the events of the day. The army would march to the gates of the city, instructing the citizenry to either take up arms with the Knights Underwood or risk falling to their sword. Then, Sir Timothy would confront Dennis the Usurper from afar (they had a goat's horn, attached to a wheeled cart, for such communications); assuming he would refuse to capitulate, Prue and Curtis would be signaled from their hiding place, at which point the battle would begin and the mole army, in its entirety, would fall on the City of Moles and the Fortress of Fanggg. It was suggested that the two large Overdwellers enter with as much ferocity as possible and perhaps, even though the blind moles would not actually see this taking place, wave their hands and gnash their teeth. This latter suggestion came from the mole squire whom Prue had nearly crushed earlier. The other moles roundly agreed: Yes, gnashing teeth would be very effective. Prue tried it out; she nearly bit her tongue. Curtis seemed to be an old hand at it, though.

"No, like this," he instructed, his eyes bugged out and his teeth noisily chomping together.

"You're weird," said Prue.

Septimus, for his part, had taken an interest in the gathering military formations, and since he was scarcely bigger than the largest of the mole knights, it was decided that he should lead a squadron of his own. The top brass had all agreed: A vanguard of soldiers marshaled by an Overdweller would go a long way to striking fear into the hearts of the fortress's defenders. As Septimus, Curtis, and Prue were conferring in a dark alcove, a retinue of knights approached, presenting to the rat a custom-built suit of armor made of pull tabs and interlinked sections of bicycle chain. Septimus, at Curtis's nudging, accepted with all the grace he could muster, and a trio of squires set about dressing him in the unwieldy outfit. By the time they were done, he looked like an animated pile of discarded parts one might find at the bottom of their junk drawer.

"It's really handsome," offered Prue.

Septimus's voice issued, echoing, from the inside of a halved tin can: "Well, at least if I *slay* anybody, I'll be spared having to actually see them." He moved his arms, with some apparent difficulty. "I could always just sit on the enemy, I suppose." It took a crew of fifteen mole squires to get him strapped onto his mount, a yellow salamander he promptly dubbed Sally.

Traveling along the damp passageway, the great army of Knights Underwood began their advance, following a sloping floor as the tunnel descended deeper into the ground. From the sound of their marching feet in the cavern, it was clear they were approaching some vast cavity in the stone. At this point, Prue and Curtis were advised to wait; Sir Timothy, having donned his formal attire, a bent washer crown with a red hummingbird feather attached, climbed astride his salamander and followed the wheeled goat's horn and its attendants around the corner and out of sight.

A short moment later, Timothy's voice could be heard, amplified through the horn and pouring into what sounded like a very large chamber.

"MOLES OF THE CITY OF MOLES," came Sir Timothy's voice. "THE KNIGHTS UNDERWOOD HAVE AMASSED OUTSIDE YOUR GATES. WE INTEND TO BRING EMANCIPATION TO ALL WHO DWELL IN THE UNDERWOOD. WE WILL LIBERATE YOU FROM THE TYRANNY OF DENNIS, THE USURPER OF THE THRONE. TURN AGAINST YOUR CAPTORS AND ALLY WITH US OR RISK PERISHING BY

FLAME AND SWORD."

A pause; there came the sound of a multitude of voices crying out: some in confusion, some in opposition, many in celebration.

Sir Timothy's voice sounded again: "DENNIS MOLE, YOUR DAY OF RECKONING IS AT HAND. COMPEL YOUR FORCES TO STAND DOWN."

There came another pause, after which a voice, distant but clear, rang out in the cavern, apparently amplified by a similar technology. "GO STICK IT!" it called. Curtis assumed this to be the voice of Dennis the Usurper. He didn't sound like a particularly considerate mole.

"VERY WELL, DESPOT!" At a full-throated call from Sir Timothy, the Knights Underwood at Prue's and Curtis's feet exploded into action and descended upon the gates of the City of Moles. And thus, the great siege began.

Prue and Curtis listened to the clamorous noises of war from their spot behind the wall of the tunnel. They'd been told their signal would be three short bursts from the goat's horn, and they attuned their ears the best they could for the sound—though it was certainly difficult to distinguish anything from amid the deafening din the siege had already managed to create. Curtis was about to sneak a peek behind the wall when the unmistakable *blat-blat-blat* of their signal to attack was sounded. Curtis held out his fist to Prue—she reluctantly bumped it with hers—and the Overdwellers emerged from their hiding place, doing their best to act like the ferocious, wrathful demigods they were expected to be.

As they rounded the corner, Prue was feeling sheepish about her performance; holding the lit lantern with one hand, she was brandishing the other arm dramatically, her fingers poised like claws, though the teeth gnashing continued to be elusive. Curtis, on the other hand, was relishing the opportunity and was taking to the part with gusto: Not only was he waving his arms and gnashing his teeth, but he was accompanying his every step with shouts like, "Overdweller ANGRY!" and "I will spit fire and brimstone upon thee!"

However, as soon as they'd come out of hiding and had traveled the few feet down the sloping floor of the tunnel, both of them were struck dumb by what they saw.

The chamber they'd walked into was so massive as to make the ceiling indistinguishable from a dome of sky. Much to Prue and Curtis's surprise, the lantern they were carrying was superfluous here; little electric lamps affixed to the wall of the chamber flooded it with light. It was the first full light they'd seen in days; their eyes took a moment to adjust. How they'd not noticed this before, even from the reach of their hiding place, was befuddling to them; perhaps the light from the lantern had obscured it.

The most incredible thing about the chamber, though, was the presence of the City of Moles itself. They'd never seen anything like it before in their lives. Given the opportunity to describe it, as Curtis and Prue were both pressed to do when, far into the future, they were asked, they'd each been at a loss for words. They'd fumble for explanation, the poverty of language laid plain to them.

It was as if someone, some intelligent being with a razor-sharp eye for mechanics and engineering, had taken a great crane with a gigantic vacuum cleaner attachment connected to it, and hovered it slowly over an entire city, sucking up every imaginable piece of scrap, fragment, or particle of unwanted, indeterminate junk—be it metal, plastic, or wood; this someone then deposited all of this mass of man-made detritus here on the floor of the chamber and endeavored to find a way in which every piece fit, one into another, to create a structure that used each particle as if it had been designed to be used in that very precise way.

A massive wall, made of aluminum and stone, surrounded a lattice of strange, oblong structures; a tangled series of tracks and chutes wove between them—some of them clearly fashioned from the remnants of toy train sets and race-car courses. A portcullis, made of what appeared to be a flattened colander, barred the gateway of the outer wall. Beyond it, the immediate interior of the city was a grid of boxy buildings, piled next to one another almost haphazardly (Curtis recognized an entire suburb made of cigar tins). Farther along, nearer the center of the city, the maze of structures grew even more dense and tightly knit as the city itself spiraled upward in an almost conical pattern to reach a plateaulike apex, a rise broken here and there by the presence of smaller walls that effectively turned the city into a succession of climbing tiers. At the apex, perhaps six feet tall, a cylindrical tower rose above the clutter, attached to the rest of the city by a series of bridges; the shaft of the tower looked to be a plain aluminum duct, but as it climbed it blossomed little auxiliary towers and turrets from its rounded side. The tower was topped with an onion-domed cupola; there, a flag with the initial *D* stenciled on it fluttered in the chamber's very slight breeze.

"Whoa," said Prue, forgetting herself.

Curtis hadn't dropped his act so easily; even in his shock at the sight of the City of Moles, he managed to continue acting wrathful. "Prue," he said through his gnashing teeth, "keep up the angry-god thing."

"Right," said Prue, and she set down her lantern, employing both of her arms as she approached this miraculous underground city.

As soon as they'd been spotted, a series of terrified screams came from within the mole compound. The defenders of the city, soldiers clad in what appeared to be suits made of aluminum foil, sensed the two Overdwellers' approach and shuddered, visibly, in their armor.

"Sally-ho!" came a shout at their feet. It was Septimus, astride his salamander, waving a darning needle wildly over his tin-can-covered head. A tide of foot soldiers, under his command, came tearing after him. They exploded onto the defending moles like the crest of a wave, sweeping away everything in their path. Septimus, rearing his salamander, towered over his enemies like a giant in the fray, and the city's defenders approached him quaking in their bottle caps.

"Have at thee!" he shouted, applying a healthy dose of old-world accent to his words as he fought. "Stay your blade, cretin!" was also used liberally, as was "To the Overworld with you, scamp!" Prue couldn't see his face through his helmet, but she could imagine him smiling from pink furry ear to pink furry ear.

While the enemy was thus engaged, the siege towers of the Knights Underwood had quickly made it through the first phalanx of defending soldiers and were now up against the outer wall, emitting a steady stream of knights into the first tier of the city. The multiple-pencil battering ram was pounding against the flattened colander portcullis as a multitude of knights waited impatiently behind it to pour through the gate. It held fast; one of the soldiers on salamander-back turned to Curtis and hollered, "OVER-DWELLER!"

It took a moment for Curtis to find the voice among the thousands-strong throng of battling moles. "Yes?" he asked when he'd finally found the source.

"WILT THOU USE THY DIVINE STRENGTH TO THROW THE PORTCULLIS?"

"Oh, yeah," said Curtis. "No problem."

Arriving at the wall, which came up no higher than his knee, he reached around the back and, finding the edge of the gate, pulled away the flattened piece of metal. The Knights Underwood yelled a cry of victory and went rushing through the opened gate, knocking down all who stood in their way. Curtis felt a pinch on his finger as he retracted his hand from the scene; it was a red-balled sewing pin, lodged in the fleshy webbing between his thumb and forefinger.

"Ouch," he said. He looked down; a mole from the opposing side was standing there, needle-less, pointing his snout in Curtis's general direction. He appeared to be sniveling with fear. For a moment, Curtis briefly considered picking him up and throwing him against the wall, but the tactic seemed too brutal, too inhumane. The idea frankly disturbed him. Instead, he plucked the stuck pin from his hand and tossed it across the chamber. "Watch it," he said to the mole, who scurried off into the fray.

The Knights Underwood, however, were not so merciful to their foes. Sir Timothy's warning, that the denizens of the city turn against the forces of Dennis the Usurper or die by the Knights' swords, was carried out with a marked consistency. Curtis blanched as he watched the moles pile into their enemies, tearing them apart with every weapon or instrument at their disposal. Blood ran freely in the gutters of the city's narrow streets; screams of anguished pain curdled the air. A baby mole, separated from its parents, sat on a side street and howled in fear; a mole in a blood-spattered dress stood in the doorway of a burning building and wept loudly over the body of a fallen soldier. Curtis looked over at Prue, who had stopped acting wrathful completely and was instead watching the proceedings with a look of disgust and pity.

"Ugh," she said. "This is terrible."

Curtis walked back to where she stood at the edge of the chamber and joined her in her witness of the events. The moles had broken through the second wall of the city; thin streams of smoke were now curling up from several houses and churches. The cacophony of the battle, the clashing of pins and bottle caps, echoed in the air.

"Can we stop it?" ventured Prue.

Curtis looked around; the streets of the city were swarming with frenzied warrior moles. "I don't know," he said. "I think we just have to let it run its course."

The third wall had been breached. The lifeless bodies of fallen moles curled limply over the ramparts.

"We have to," said Prue. Bent on the task, she approached the City of Moles, carefully watching each footfall so as to avoid adding any undue bloodshed to the chaos. She stepped easily over the first wall; the streets at this level were nearly deserted, save for a few moaning wounded; the thrust of the battle had forced most of the defenders up to the apex of the city. She crossed the second wall, then arrived at the third; the city here was too dense to allow the foot traffic of a human. Instead, she stopped and addressed the warring moles. "STOP!" she yelled. They weren't listening.

Gathering a deep breath, she summoned as much volume as she could muster: "STOP!"

Again, no response. The moles, lost in a stupor of violence and bloodlust, could not hear her. A group of defending moles were launching flaming arrows down onto the approaching army; a detachment of reinforcements were making their way down the spiraling streets to join their brothers-in-arms at the fray. Prue looked up to the very top of the tower in the center of the city and saw a single mole, dressed in what looked to be pajamas, taking in the goings-on indifferently.

"You!" she yelled. Even accounting for the diminutive footprint of the mole city, she was still easily fifteen feet away from the tower's top.

The mole seemed to have heard her. He flinched a little and pointed his eyeless snout in her direction.

"You make this stop!" she called. She could only guess at the mole's authority; the fact that he was neither fighting nor particularly disturbed by the untold number of deaths occurring at his feet led her to believe that he was someone of importance.

The mole, hearing her words, only shrugged. The war continued to wage.

"NOW!" she cried. She could feel her face contort as an unmitigated rage overtook her. The mole in the tower, evidently sensing her anger, gave a little squeak; he turned and ran for the cover of the tower's inner chamber.

"No you don't," hissed Prue, and she began climbing the pyramid of the mole city.

As her feet came down on the framework of the structures, she could feel them start to give way; it was clear that the city had not been built to withstand the weight of humans. Nonetheless, with every building, hovel, and home that was destroyed beneath her boot, she decided that it was all for the good of peace. The battle below her fell into a lull as each mole, regardless of their alliance, stopped to witness the massive Overdweller step across their heads and approach the Fortress of Fanggg. Arriving at the base of the tower, she braced herself against the aluminum shaft and stood, her eyes arriving at the level of the cupola.

Inside the dome she saw what appeared to be an ornate bedroom. Resplendent tapestries lined the walls. A miniature four-poster bed stood in the center of the room. It was there that Prue saw the pajamaed mole; or rather, she saw him under the bedsheets, creating a kind of mole-sized lump on the bed, a lump that was quivering with fear.

"Out of there, you," said Prue. "I can see you perfectly."

"NO THANKS," said the mole. "I'LL JUST STAY HERE."

"No you won't," said Prue, and she reached her arm into the bedroom and flicked the covers aside, revealing the cowering mole.

Before he was able to scurry away, she'd picked him up by the hem of his pajama pants and pulled him, screaming, from the protection of the cupola. She held him that way, dangling from her fingers, and brought him close to her face so she could better inspect him.

"Are you Dennis the Usurper?" she asked.

"NO, I'M NOT," said the mole. His voice was struck through with fear.

"YES, HE IS," came a voice from Prue's feet. She looked down; it was one of the knights. The fighting had stopped as both sides looked on at Prue's interrogation of the mole. "THAT'S HIM, ALL

RIGHT. I'D KNOW THAT VOICE ANYWHERE."

Dennis Mole seemed to curse his luck; he kicked impotently in Prue's grasp.

"I want you to stop this," said Prue, trying to look the mole in the eyes, despite the fact that he didn't really have them. "I want you to tell your soldiers to lay off."

"REALLY? I MEAN, NOW?"

Prue swung her arm around in a quick, fluid motion; she dangled him high above the clutter of the city streets. The soldiers below gasped; Dennis shrieked. A little wet spot developed in the crotch of his pajamas.

"I'll do it," said Prue. "I'm not above sacrificing one mole for the good of the entire city."

"OKAY, OKAY," sputtered Dennis. He waved his little arms above the gathered crowd below. "I GIVE IN! YOU CAN HAVE YOUR STUPID FORTRESS OF FANGGG BACK."

The cheer that met this proclamation, even issuing from such small creatures as the moles, was overwhelming. Whatever noise the battling armies had created during the siege was dwarfed by this one unified shout of pure joy. The Knights Underwood hefted their swords and halberds; the army of Dennis the Usurper threw down their weapons in a shower of tiny metal instruments. The two sides rushed together at the declaration of peace; long-separated family members were reunited; friends rent asunder by the division were once more trading hugs and handshakes. The scene was so moving to Prue that she nearly forgot she still had Dennis suspended in the air by her fingers.

"SO CAN YOU LET ME DOWN NOW?" he asked.

"Oh, sure." She paused, eyeing the former despot warily. "Though I think I should probably hand you over to the authorities. Where's Sir Timothy?"

A cry came from the crowd at her feet. "MAKE WAY! MAKE WAY!"

The tone of the celebrations suddenly grew somber; Prue turned to see the gathered armies part to allow passage to a group of stalwart knights bearing a makeshift stretcher on their shoulders; on the stretcher was none other than the still body of High Master Commander Sir Timothy. Septimus walked at the head of the procession, his patchwork armor stained in the blood of the fallen. As the moles recognized the nature of the procession, they each in turn fell to their knees in mournful silence. Prue put her hand to her mouth.

"Is he okay?" she asked.

Septimus removed his helmet and threw it to the ground. His brow was drenched with sweat. He shook his head sadly in response to the question.

"HE'S GRAVELY WOUNDED," responded the Seer Bartholomew, who stood by the rat.

The sound of weeping could be heard welling up from the crowd;

a few shouted, "NOT SIR TIMOTHY!"

"We were side by side at the end there," recounted Septimus. "Fought like a true hero."

The stretcher was placed in the middle of a city square, just beyond the third wall. The surviving knights gathered around it. Prue, holding Dennis Mole's pajama bottoms tightly in her fingers, knelt down. Sir Timothy was struggling to speak.

"ARE WE," he said, his voice brittle and quiet, "ARE WE VICTORIOUS?"

A knight at his side choked back his tears and said, "YES, SIR TIMOTHY. THE DAY IS OURS."

A faint smile played across the lips of the wounded mole. "IS THE OVERDWELLER WARRIOR STILL BY MY SIDE?"

Septimus stepped forward and took his hand. "Yes, Sir Timothy."

The knight smiled warmly at his battle companion. "WHAT OF YOUR FELLOW DEITIES? HAVE THEY SURVIVED?"

Prue looked over at Curtis, who'd been hovering just beyond the outer wall. She gestured with her head; he should hear this. Curtis nodded and gingerly stepped into the mole city, trying to avoid further disturbance to the ravaged streets of the metropolis. He joined Prue, though there was little room for them both to kneel down.

Another furor was taking place; shouts sounded from within the Fortress of Fanggg. Within moments, a troop of Knights Underwood appeared from one of the lower portals, leading a mole in a white robe. The crowd surrounding Sir Timothy's stretcher hushed; someone said, "THE SIBYL!" As soon as she saw the wounded knight, the robed mole overtook her liberators and ran to his side.

"GWENDOLYN!" said Sir Timothy, after feeling her paws touch the bloodied metal of his armor.

"BROTHER, IT IS I." The mole was fighting tears.

"GOOD SISTER," said Sir Timothy, "YOU ARE FREED. IT IS THE THING I MOST DESIRED. I GO NOW, SISTER, TO THE OVERWORLD, TO THE BOSOM OF THE OVERDWELLERS."

"SWEET TIMOTHY," said Gwendolyn, "SWEET, BRAVE TIMOTHY. YOU HAVE NOT GIVEN YOUR LIFE IN VAIN. YOU HAVE FREED YOUR PEOPLE FROM THE THUMB OF THEIR OPPRESSOR. YOU HAVE FREED ME FROM MY SERVITUDE. YOU HAVE LIVED A VALIANT LIFE; YOU GO TO THE OVERWORLD IN GLORY."

Sir Timothy attempted a smile, though his face fell as the racking of a cough overcame him. Little flecks of blood speckled his worn armor. "OVERDWELLERS," he said, beckoning to Prue and Curtis. "COME CLOSE."

The two children did as they were told. Septimus kneeled at the dying knight's side.

"YOUR DIVINE PRESENCE WON US THIS DAY. WHILE IN MY HEART OF HEARTS I NEVER DOUBTED THE

JUSTICE OF OUR STRUGGLE, YOUR APPEARANCE, YOUR REVELATION, CONFIRMED MY GREATEST HOPES. PERHAPS WE FOUR WILL BE REUNITED WHEN I WALK AMONG THE GODS IN THE OVERWORLD."

Prue found that she was fighting tears. "Sure, Sir Timothy," she said. "We'll do that." It seemed like an inappropriate time to lay bare the real nature of the so-called Overworld. There was no sense in disturbing the brave knight's solace.

Holding his sister's paw tightly, their long, fleshy fingers intertwined, the knight turned his face to the sky. As if compelled, the velvety fur of his face contracted and he seemed to be endeavoring to open his eyes. Two tiny black dots appeared on the fur of his face as his brow contracted. "I SEE," he rasped, in delirium. "I . . . SEE!"

And then he spoke no more.

❧

It was, no doubt about it, a road. Rachel stood in the middle of it with her arms akimbo. She kicked at the dirt, as if testing its realness. Then she turned to her sister.

"Yep," she said. "It's a road, all right."

"What do we do now?" Elsie was sitting on the remains of a tree stump, taking a bite out of a crisp apple.

"Wonder where it goes?" asked Rachel, having ignored her sister's question.

Elsie supplied her own answer. "We should find Michael and Cynthia," she said.

"Right," said Rachel, snapping from her trance. "We should."

It had taken a while for Elsie to find her sister in that maze of woods, but once she did, she was able to lead her back to the road with some ease—she'd marked the way by tying little strands of ivy to the tree trunks that lined the rabbit's path. Having confirmed the existence of the road, the two sisters dove back into the veil of woods and began following the waymarks back to the interior of the Periphery. They hollered the names of their hunting companions as they went. Before long, they found the two teenagers setting a little wire trap beneath a tussock of branches.

"What's up?" asked Michael when they'd arrived, all breathless and flushed.

"A road!" Elsie blurted.

"Elsie found it," added Rachel. "It's not far."

Cynthia shot Michael a glance. "That's not possible," she said.

"I swear," said Elsie. "It's really there."

"We've been over every square inch of this godforsaken place. We ain't never seen a road." Michael was coiling some wire at his hip as he spoke; he hadn't actually used the word *godforsaken* but rather another word that Elsie had only heard aloud once before. Her father had dropped the lid of a Dutch oven on his foot; the word had resounded throughout the house.

"What, are you calling my sister a liar?" asked Rachel, suddenly annoyed by the older kids' attitudes.

"Don't get all worked up," said Michael, laughing. "I'm just saying, if there was a road here, we'd have found it by now."

"Maybe it's a trick of the light or something," suggested Cynthia. "Sometimes the forest can look kind of funny at certain times of the day."

"It wasn't," said Rachel. "I saw it. With my own eyes."

"Come on," Elsie said. "Just come see it. It's really not that far off."

Michael looked at the two sisters calmly, measuring them up. Finally, he shook his head and continued coiling the wire. "Listen," he said. "It's getting late. We should really be back at the cottage. Carol'll be expecting us. It's getting on dinnertime."

"Really?" asked Rachel in disbelief. "You're not going to just come and see it?"

"We'll set out tomorrow, promise. First thing. Then we'll all get a good look at this road of yours." He threw his arm over Elsie's shoulder and gave her a little rub on her hair with his knuckles. "Plus, you got a line of kids waiting for those dolls you make; you got some work to do."

Elsie smiled briefly, then said, "But we'll go see the road tomorrow?"

"Promise," said Michael.

"A road? What, like a paved road?"

Carol had paused in mid-puff and was staring in the direction of the two girls' voices, his pipe poised only inches from his lips. It seemed to be frozen there, as if it too was suspended in the same gel as the movement of time in the Periphery.

Elsie looked at her sister hesitantly; she sipped at her mint tea. She and Rachel, with the two teenaged hunters, had cornered Carol after they'd bused the dirty plates from the house's five dinner tables and stacked them on the counter by the sink. Two boys laughed quietly over some shared joke as they ran the dishes through the soapy water. The younger children had been sent to their beds; the older children were scattered about the house, enjoying the last few moments of the evening.

"Not paved, so much," said Rachel. "More like a gravel road. Or maybe there were some stones there. It looked like it'd been there for a long time."

The two wooden eyes shifted in Carol's head; still, in the half-light of the candles, they showed two bright blue irises. Elsie could even see the brush marks.

"And there was a pillarlike thing, like a mile marker or something. On the other side." This was Elsie.

Michael had remained silent for most of the conversation; he, too, was packing his pipe with tobacco. The boy finally spoke up. "What did it say? Did it have anything on it?"

Rachel nodded; she'd seen it up close. When Elsie had brought her to the site of the road, she'd mentally jotted down the carved insignia in her explorations. "An arrow, with a picture of a bird," she said.

Carol blew out a breath. It sounded like "HOOO!"

The children all looked to him.

"That'd be about right," he said. He finally brought the lip of the pipe to his mouth and took a long, ponderous drag. "Direction marker. You were pointed toward the Avian Principality, if memory serves."

Michael stared at the old man intently; Cynthia dropped the spoon she'd been using to stir the cream into her tea.

"Seems like you guys found a way through the Bind," said Carol. "Some kinda break or something. You remember passing through anythin out of the ordinary? Something that might've looked like a passageway or somethin? I 'member folks talkin about such things; rifts and such. But I never knew any to exist."

"Not really," said Elsie. "I mean, I think I would've remembered something like that. I don't think I followed the exact same way when I went back. I tied ivy stalks to the trees, but I didn't, like, use my exact footsteps on the way when I showed it to Rachel."

Rachel nodded in affirmation; she was absently batting her yellow tag earring with her finger.

"Well," said Carol after a significant pause, "I suppose we'll have to go look at this road of yours."

Michael looked shocked. "It seems like it might be a long way, Carol. Sure you can manage?"

Carol batted a friendly hand toward the boy's voice. "I'll be fine. I could use a little walk around the place, anyway. Been settin on these bones a little too long." He pulled on his pipe again. The clinking of dishes in the washing sink had ceased; the children had all moved to their tucked-away beds. The candlelight reflected from the painted-on pupils of Carol's eyes. "Dark now," he said. "Best to head out first light. Let's not let the little ones in on this; don't want them to get their hopes up about nothin. Could be it's just a trick of the light; a well-used game trail through the Periphery. No offense to the girls here; it's easy to get confused in these woods. They got a lot of tricks." He thumped his pipe against his dungarees, the smoking ash falling to the floor. "Could be, though, it's our ticket out."

Michael eyed the two sisters as he smoked. Cynthia stirred her tea. Carol ground his boot heel into the scatter of ash he'd made. "Could be," he repeated.

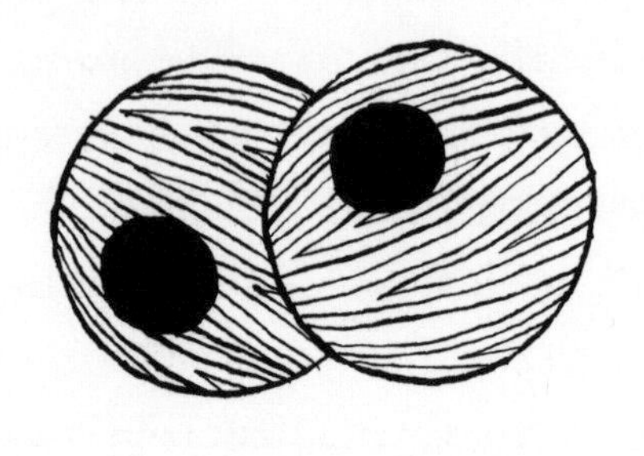

CHAPTER 19

Sir Timothy's Conveyance to the Beyond

The moles spared no expense or extravagance for the funeral of the High Master Commander Sir Timothy Mole. He was borne from the fortress in the ceremonial armor of his grandfather, on a pallet covered in the greenest lichen. The townsfolk lined the labyrinthine city streets to watch the procession pass by. The air was filled with the mournful cries of the citizenry, so great was their appreciation to Sir Timothy and his valiant cohort of Knights Underwood for saving them from the domination of Dennis the Usurper, who was now serving a life sentence in the deepest cell of the Fortress of Fanggg's dungeon. A petite brass band led the way; they played a loping fanfare that sounded to Curtis's ears as being both joyous and heartbreaking at the same time. The two Overdwellers watched on from the open plaza beyond the outer wall of the city.

The parade followed a well-worn path to a part of the chamber Curtis had not seen before. About thirty feet from the walls of the city was a massive pool, fed by a steady drip from the unseen ceiling. It occurred to Curtis that this must be the pool that was being referenced when the moles spoke of the passage of time: "this many emptyings and refillings of the pool." Moles, young and old, lined the path from the front gate to the water's banks. When the parade had arrived there, a few words were spoken by the deceased knight's sister, the Sibyl Gwendolyn, before the pallet was pushed into the water. An eddying current took the body away from the mourners into the farthest dark of the chamber. The knight's soul, so said the Sibyl, had gone on to join its brethren in the world of the Overdwellers.

As the congregation returned to the city to host a banquet at the recently liberated Fortress of Fanggg (for which the reconvened Mole Council had proposed a name change to the Fortress of Prurtimus—in honor of the three Overdwellers who had been so instrumental in Dennis's defeat), the Sibyl tarried at the feet of Prue and Curtis, nodding up to them as she approached. Septimus, finally freed of his armor, bowed low to see her.

"It was a beautiful ceremony," said Prue, breaking the silence.

The mole nodded solemnly.

"Sorry for your loss," added Curtis.

"He's in the Overworld now, at peace." This was Prue; she was sensing the deep sadness in the Sibyl's comportment. She'd spent the entire service searching for the appropriate thing to say.

She was surprised to see Gwendolyn make a dismissive wave. "PISH," she said. "IT'S ALL HOGWASH. I DON'T KNOW WHERE HE'S GOING, BUT I DON'T SEE MUCH EVIDENCE OF HIS SOUL TAKING FLIGHT TO THE VERY CORPOREAL ABOVE-GROUND. THAT'S JUST SUPERSTITION, AS FAR AS I CAN TELL. YOU DON'T HAVE TO KEEP UP THE MASQUERADE WITH ME."

Curtis was taken aback. "Aren't you, like, the religious leader?"

"I'M A PROPHETESS," said the Sibyl. "KIND OF THE SAME, KIND OF DIFFERENT. AS FAR AS I CAN TELL, MY JOB IS TO SEEK THE TRUTH, BY WHICH I CAN BETTER

COUNSEL MY LEADERS. AND IN MY SEARCHINGS, I'VE NOT HAD A WHOLE LOT OF EVIDENCE THAT SUCH A THING AS THE OVERWORLD EXISTS. AT LEAST NOT IN THE WAY THAT WE UNDERWOOD MOLES SEE IT."

"So why did you . . . ," began Prue.

Curtis finished for her: "Say all those things back there, about his afterlife?"

"TRADITION," said the Sibyl. "FAITH. IT'S AN AWFULLY BEAUTIFUL IDEA, ISN'T IT? I'M FOND OF THE POETRY OF IT. AS LONG AS IT'S NOT DOING ANYONE ANY HARM, I DON'T SEE THE REASON FOR PULLING THE VEIL AWAY. BESIDES, I'VE NEVER BEEN TO THIS OVERWORLD OF YOURS. DON'T THINK I'D BE ABLE TO SAY ANYTHING DEFINITIVELY UNTIL I HAD EVIDENCE." The Mole marked the two children's confusion. "IT'S COMPLICATED," she said. "SOMETHING I'M WORKING ON. HOWEVER: I CAN SAY FOR CERTAIN THAT IT'S NICE TO BE BREATHING CLEAN CAVERN AIR AGAIN. I'VE BEEN LOCKED UP IN THAT DUNGEON SO LONG, AT THE BECK AND CALL OF THAT IDIOT, DENNIS MOLE."

"Right," said Curtis. "At least . . . that."

"WALK WITH ME," suggested the Sibyl. "I'M NOT SURE OUR MOLE FOOD WILL SATIATE YOUR OVERDWELLER APPETITES, BUT THERE IS A BANQUET TO BE HAD.

AND I'M SURE YOU'LL BE EXPECTED THERE; YOU ARE GREAT HEROES IN THIS STORY."

They did so, though walking with the mole was more akin to walking in slow motion as they allowed the Sibyl to keep pace with their gargantuan steps. Septimus strode proudly at her side, the darning needle still hanging at his waist. It was the only remnant of his battle attire.

"I SUSPECT YOU'LL BE WANTING DIRECTIONS TO THE REALM OF THE SOUTHERN OVERDWELLERS, CORRECT?" asked Gwendolyn as they walked. "BARTHOLOMEW HAS TOLD ME AS MUCH. THAT WAS THE DEAL?"

"Yes," said Curtis. "Thanks for remembering."

"We have friends—Overdwellers—who have gone missing," said Septimus. "Long story; but we have to find them. Somehow."

"And you know the way?" asked Prue.

"I DO. AS I SAID: IN MY SEARCHINGS, MY TRAVELS, I'VE DISCOVERED MANY SECRETS HIDDEN IN THIS PLACE WE CALL THE UNDERWOOD. IT WAS I, IN FACT, WHO FIRST FOUND THE ARCHITECT AND BROUGHT HIM TO THE RUINED CITY OF MOLES. THIS WAS BEFORE I WAS MADE SIBYL, WHEN I WAS JUST A WANDERER, CURIOUS ABOUT THE WORLD THAT SURROUNDED ME."

"Who was he, this architect?" asked Prue. It was a question that

She approached the City of Moles, carefully watching each footfall so as to avoid adding any undue bloodshed to the chaos.

had been swirling in her brain, ever since she'd clapped eyes on the City of Moles, with its incredible array of man-made junk repurposed as buildings, monuments, and thoroughfares.

"HE WAS AN OVERDWELLER, LIKE YOURSELF. I FOUND HIM IN ONE OF THE DEEPEST RECESSES OF THE UNDERWOOD. FINDING LIFE IN THAT DARK ABYSS WAS THE LAST THING I EXPECTED, I CAN TELL YOU. I'D NEVER GONE SO DEEP IN MY EXPLORATIONS. YOU CAN IMAGINE MY SURPRISE. HE WAS IN TERRIBLE SHAPE; HE'D BEEN CAST OUT BY HIS PEOPLE. WHAT'S MORE, WHOEVER HAD DECIDED HIS FATE HAD ALSO TAKEN THE VERY ODIOUS EXTRA MEASURE OF SEVERING HIS HANDS FROM HIS ARMS."

"Eugh," said Prue, reflexively.

"I NOURISHED HIM TO HEALTH, USING THOSE VERY SAME BRICKS OF OVERDWELLER RATION AS I UNDERSTAND YOU WERE GIVEN."

Septimus's stomach grumbled at the mention. "Sorry," he said.

Gwendolyn continued, "ONCE HE WAS HEALTHY ENOUGH TO TRAVEL, I BROUGHT HIM BEFORE THE MOLE COUNCIL. HE WAS TREMENDOUSLY THANKFUL FOR WHAT I'D DONE. I SUPPOSE I'D SAVED HIS LIFE. HE PROMISED TO REPAY THE MOLES IN KIND BY REBUILDING THE CITY, WHICH HAD BEEN REDUCED

TO ALMOST COMPLETE RUBBLE BY THE SEVEN POOL EMPTYINGS WAR. HE SAID THAT HE'D DONE SIMILAR WORK IN THE OVERWORLD, THAT HE'D BUILT THINGS WITH HIS HANDS. AMAZING, BEAUTIFUL THINGS. AND WHILE HE'D BEEN DEPRIVED OF THE TWO TOOLS ON WHICH HE MOST DEPENDED, HIS VERY HANDS, HE THOUGHT HE COULD STILL MANAGE WITH THE AID OF THE MOLES. IT WAS TRUE: WHILE HE HAD NO HANDS, WE HAD NO EYES. TOGETHER, WE WORKED SYMBIOTICALLY.

"IN MY EXPLORATIONS, I'D FOUND A PASSAGE THAT, AFTER MANY WEEKS OF MOLE-TRAVEL, LED TO WHAT THE OVERDWELLERS CALL 'SUNLIGHT.' INDEED, TO THE OVERWORLD ITSELF—THOUGH FAR OFF TO THE EAST. I TOLD HIM OF THIS PASSAGE, AND HE BEGAN TO USE IT TO FORAGE FOR CASTOFF OVERDWELLER ITEMS. HE RAN LONG STRANDS OF ELECTRIC CABLE FROM THE OVERWORLD TO GIVE POWER TO THE LIGHTS THAT TODAY ILLUMINATE THE CHAMBER—THOUGH CERTAINLY OF NO USE TO THE MOLES. AND HE SET ABOUT REBUILDING OUR GREAT CITY. IT TOOK HIM MANY WEEKS. WE WORKED TIRELESSLY WITH HIM, BEING HIS HANDS. AND, IN A SINGLE EMPTYING AND REFILLING OF THE POOL, WE'D MANAGED TO

NOT ONLY REBUILD THE CITY, BUT IMPROVE IT FAR MORE THAN ANYONE COULD'VE IMAGINED.

"IN OUR THANKS, THOUGH THE ARCHITECT INSISTED WE OWED HIM NONE, OUR BEST MOLE SMITHS CRAFTED TWO GOLDEN HOOKS THAT HE MIGHT USE IN PLACE OF HIS MISSING HANDS. NEEDLESS TO SAY, I COULD HEAR THE TEARS FALLING FROM HIS EYES WHEN HE BID US ADIEU. AND THEN HE WAS GONE. HE FOLLOWED THOSE POWER LINES THAT HE HAD LAID OUT INTO THE SUNLIGHT OF THE OVERWORLD, AND WE HAVEN'T HEARD FROM HIM SINCE."

"Wow," said Curtis. "What a story." They'd arrived at the front gates of the City of Moles; Curtis was able to look at it in a completely different light. He started seeing the entirety of the amazing structure for what it was: a million little salvaged pieces, all meticulously crafted together to create a fluid, working whole.

Prue was chewing on her lower lip, which almost always meant that there was some bigger thought brewing in her mind. Curtis eyed her suspiciously. She then knelt down so as to be closer to the Sibyl when she asked, "Did he ever tell you what he had done to be exiled? From the Overworld?"

"HE DID, YES."

"And what was it?"

"A STRANGE CASE, TO SAY THE LEAST. THERE'S NO

ACCOUNTING FOR OVERDWELLER FANCIES. AN OVERDWELLER QUEEN, GONE MAD, HAD COMMISSIONED HIM TO BUILD A MECHANICAL REPLICA OF HER DEAD SON."

Septimus hiccuped, loudly. Prue nearly fell over.

"WHEN HE'D FINISHED, THE OVERDWELLER QUEEN HAD HIM EXILED SO HE WOULD NEVER REVEAL THE SECRET OF THE BOY'S EXISTENCE TO THE OVERWORLD. AND, SO THAT HE COULD NEVER CRAFT ANOTHER PIECE TO RIVAL IT, SHE HAD THE ARCHITECT'S HANDS CHOPPED OFF."

"Oh my God," said Prue, a look of sudden realization lighting her face. Septimus was still hiccuping. Curtis, absorbed in the Sibyl's words, told her to continue.

"THAT'S NOT THE WORST OF IT," said the Sibyl, shaking her head at the folly of the Overdwellers. "THERE WAS A SECOND MAKER; HE AND THE ARCHITECT WORKED TOGETHER TO CRAFT THE BOY. THIS ONE WAS EXILED AS WELL. BUT THIS ONE, THE QUEEN FIRST HAD HIM BLINDED. BOTH EYES. POPPED OUT."

The noise of the banquet could be heard within the city walls. Someone was singing a high, lonesome tune, to which the gathered revelers were hollering along. The Sibyl was still shaking her head. "BLIND," she said, "AS A MOLE."

❧

Carol's eyes were on the kitchen table. Elsie was staring at them, strangely mystified. She poked at one with a nearby butter knife; it wobbled a little on the wooden surface. For some reason, they continued to gross her out. Not because they were a prosthetic for the old man's missing eyes—she'd been around enough people with synthetic limbs—but because they seemed so puppetlike. And she always felt like they were looking at her, suspiciously.

Morning had come; the sun had again risen on the in-between world, though by Elsie's reckoning it must still be the same as the day before. Her head spun as it tried to grapple with the idea that, while the days and nights tumbled one into another, the hours never actually shifted forward in time. It didn't seem to have an effect on her body yet, though there was this strange twinge in her mind, a quiet shake, that told her things were not as they should be. And the eyes were still staring at her.

"Good morning!" came a voice behind her. It was Carol.

"Hi, Carol," said Elsie. "You left these here. On the table."

She grabbed his arm and led his hand to the pair of eyes. "Ah," he said. "Thanks. Was wonderin what I'd did with those." He gamely popped them back into the twin cavities on either side of his red, ruddy nose. They swiveled there a moment before settling, and the old man smiled. "There we go. Ready for the day."

"Can you, like, see better?" Elsie kicked herself as soon as the words came out. Of course he couldn't see better. He was blind.

Thankfully, the old man took her question in stride. "Not that I can tell," he said, laughing. "Maybe I just feel a little more—I don't know—complete with 'em in. How'd you sleep, hon?"

Elsie felt at a sore shoulder. "Okay, I guess," she said. The bed assigned her was one of the drawers of a wardrobe in the dining room. She wasn't the only one in the wardrobe—she had upstairs and downstairs neighbors in the other drawers. As a consequence, they all had to sleep with their drawers pushed in, which gave the arrangement a fairly coffinlike feel. "How about you?"

"Can't complain," said Carol. Rachel appeared at the top of the stairs. She was in the process of flattening the rat's nest that was her hair; she was using a brush made out of pine needles, and it didn't seem to be doing a particularly good job.

"You guys ready?" she asked as she arrived in the kitchen.

"As we'll ever be," proclaimed Carol. "And I'd be awfully appreciative if I could count on the steady arms of two such lovely girls as you." He proffered his elbows. Elsie and Rachel each took one. "All right then," he said. "Let's go see the great Mehlberg Road."

On the porch, Michael and Cynthia were waiting, leaning up against the opposing posts on either side of the steps. Martha was there too, her goggles gamely set on her forehead.

"What are you up to?" asked Rachel as she and her sister eased the blind man out onto the planks of the porch. It was still very early; only the first shimmers of dawn were making their way through the trees.

"Coming along. I want to see this road," said Martha.

Michael and Cynthia exchanged glances; Elsie spoke up. "I thought no one was supposed to know about this. What about the little ones . . . ?"

"Oh, come on," said Martha. "I'm as old as you are. Besides, everyone's talking. All the kids know. You found a road. One that's probably outside the Periphery."

Carol frowned. "They should be counseled to keep their expectations low. This 'road' sighting has not been confirmed."

"Well, you ought to do that soon," said Martha. "Everyone's awake and waiting to hear the news."

"Cynthia, would you mind staying behind and speaking to the rest of the children? Explain the situation to them." Carol shifted in his worn shoes; Elsie gripped his elbow as he eased down the steps to the grass of the yard. He sensed Cynthia's disappointment; she looked at Michael and gave a kind of huffy sigh. "Cynthia, do this thing. The young ones look up to you."

"Okay, Carol," she said finally.

"Martha, you'll round out our reconnaissance party. Quickly, let's be on the move. I don't walk as fleetly as I used to, and we don't want this road disappearing before we can get to it, do we?" Carol winked one of his wooden eyes at Elsie.

And so, they set out.

They soon arrived in the cottonwood clearing, the small meadow where Rachel, Elsie, and Martha had first spotted the pack of dogs. From there, Elsie took up the lead, winding through the soaring conifers and the bare, twiggy fingers of the drooping maples. They moved slowly, hampered by Carol's careful movements, and Elsie, in her enthusiasm, would find herself getting too far ahead of the rest of the party. Finally, she decided it would be best if she just stayed at Carol's side. She took Rachel's spot at his elbow; Martha had taken his other. Michael, his pipe firmly clenched in his teeth, followed behind.

There was no rabbit to lead their way now, and though Elsie had found the road twice without the animal's aid, it was still tricky to find the spot where her vine-tied tree trunks began. At one point, at the edge of a shallow culvert, Elsie had to stop and reflect. "This wasn't part of it," she said. "I don't remember this part."

A resigned puff of air sounded from the back of the group. It was Michael. "At what point," he said, somewhat caustically, "do we call this off? Or are we going to be wandering the Periphery all day? To be honest, following the girl's lead, I'm a little concerned we're going to stumble into some undiscovered bit and be stuck there forever."

"She knows where she's going," Rachel struck back. "I saw it. With my own eyes." She then turned to her sister. "C'mon, Els, think. Which way?"

"Patience, children," chided Carol. "No sense in bickering over it. There is no shame in having fallen prey to an illusion. This forest offers up many tricks."

"It *wasn't* an illusion," said Elsie, before grabbing Carol's elbow and drawing him away from the edge of the culvert. "This way. I'm sure of it."

When the first fir sapling came into view, its midsection neatly knotted with a green ivy stalk, Elsie didn't take a single look behind her. "There it is!" she shouted, and began urging Carol along. Even his mutterings of caution could not dissuade her from pulling him by the elbow quickly through the weave of trees. They now came in a steady succession, these waymarked trees; as soon as she thought she'd lost the way, another one would hove into view in the distance. After a time, a rise in the terrain appeared, and, reaching its crest, Carol let out a cry of surprise to find his feet resting firmly on the gravel surface of the road.

Elsie, nearly out of breath, smiled widely. "You see?" she said. "It's not an illusion!"

Carol let out a loud guffaw, despite himself. He patted Elsie fondly on the head, his face beaming. "You weren't kidding, were you?" He took a deep breath, as if inhaling the air for the first time. "How far does it go? Can you describe it?"

Summoning all her descriptive prowess, Elsie began breathlessly cataloging every detail of the road. "It's long. It's all snowy. It looks like it's been driven at some point; look, there are little wheel tracks underneath last night's fall of snow. And—I don't know what those are—hoof prints, maybe. Horses." She took in the scene behind her. "It kinda snakes along. It's like a ribbon, or something. Like a country road. It reminds me of . . . We rented a cabin one summer, my family. In the Sisters Wilderness. The road that led to the cabin looked like this. An awful lot like this. And there's the stone thing, across the road, with the picture on it. A picture of a bird and an arrow. Just like we told you."

Carol remained smiling through Elsie's long monologue. "Indeed," he said. "Indeed. This was no illusion. This was no trick of the light. You, Elsie, have a gift."

"Well, my second-grade teacher did say I described stuff well."

"No," corrected Carol. "Your gift is the ability to pass through the Periphery. You are not beholden to its laws. You, Elsie, are of *Woods Magic.*"

The wind whistled along Elsie's ribbon of road. The girl was at a loss for words. She heard a noise from the side of the road; looking over, she saw her sister break through the bracken, her jumpsuit streaked with mud. "Sorry," she said. "I kinda fell back there. Glad I found you." She paused, taking in the two figures' silent pose. "What's up? You found the road. That's good."

"Is it Rachel?" asked Carol. "It's your sister!"

"Yes," was all Elsie managed to say.

"She too!" said the ebullient old man. "I knew it! As soon as I saw—or felt—you both. I could just feel it. Couldn't quite put my finger on it, but now it's clear. Clear as crystal. Woods Magic, the both of you. It runs in your family—it must! But how . . ." Here he paused as the corners of his mouth folded into a ponderous frown. "How did you manage to . . ." His hand slipped to the fabric of his coat at the elbow, to the place where Elsie's hand had so recently been. "You—you—" he stammered. "You walked me in. You brought me with you. By touch. By touching." The smile returned to his lips. "That's it! That's been it all along!"

The old man, unanchored from his helpers, began stumbling in a little celebratory dance in the middle of the road. "How simple!" he called, his voice reverberating in the air. "So incredibly simple." His hands flew out, searching for a body with which to connect. "Elsie, Rachel," he called. "Come here! Come here!"

The two of them obeyed the old man's call; he grabbed their

shoulders and gave them an affectionate squeeze. "You've saved us!" he said. "Who knew? Who ever knows what they possess in the deepest depths of their being?"

Elsie stood with a smile plastered across her face. There were so many things streaming through her head, it was nearly impossible to get them all straight. What did it mean, this Woods Magic? And how could it run in their family? Immediately, her mind flashed to her brother, Curtis. Necessarily, he must be of Woods Magic as well. The idea unleashed a multitude of possibilities in her mind. Briefly she surveyed the scene. "Where's Martha? And Michael?" she asked. She wanted them to share in the celebration as well.

"I thought Martha was with you guys; she had Carol's other arm," said Rachel.

Carol put his finger to his nose in a knowing gesture. "They're back in the Periphery. Don't you see? It's simple. Perfectly simple."

"I don't get it," said Rachel.

"In those last moments, Elsie was the only one guidin me; Martha had fallen back. That must've occurred some time ago; before we crossed the Periphery Bind. If my guess is correct, and I'm of a good mind that it is, they'll be way behind us, stuck in that refractin, infinite expanse of sameness that we've all come to call home. Come on! Let's get them!" At this he began shuffling toward the end of the road, quite free of any helping hand—as if he'd momentarily forgotten his disability. He stopped and snapped his fingers. "Sorry. Gettin ahead of myself. I can't actually see the way." Rachel and Elsie, stunned to silence with this new information they'd been given, grabbed his elbows. Together, the three of them stepped back into the woods.

CHAPTER 20

Follow the Green Cable

"Will that be all, Mr. Unthank, sir?"

To Joffrey, the voice arrived as if it had issued from across some vast vacuum of space; like the faint sound of a radio turned on at its lowest volume and murmuring from the attic of a house in which you are sitting at the dining room table. It was undeniably there, yet so removed as to be almost imperceptible. But wait: It came again.

"I think I'll turn in for the evening, Mr. Unthank. If that'd be all right."

For the eternity of a moment, Joffrey Unthank pulled himself away from the thing he was holding in his hand and focused his attention on the present circumstances: He was in the machine shop. The mechanical burble of the various belching machines colored the air. The windows were dark. He had no idea what time it was or how long he'd been standing in this position. In fact, it was as if everything in his mind had been erased in this fraction of a second. Looking down, he saw that he was standing with his hands cupped closed at the level of his stomach, like a pontificating priest. And then it all came back to him.

"Sir?" sounded the voice again. It was, unmistakably, Mr. Grimble.

"Yes, Grimble," responded Joffrey.

"So I'll see you in the morning, then, sir."

"Yes, Grimble."

"Bright and early."

"Bright and early, Grimble." It all flooded in; he glanced at his closed hands. Slowly opening them, he saw a thing in his hand. He saw that it was made of brass. And he saw that it was very nearly perfect. The most exacting and immaculate thing he'd ever produced in his history as a maker and crafter of machine parts. It, on its own, was enough to make the most hardened machinist break down weeping, so flawless was its diamond-cut teeth, its smooth parabolic curvature. To imagine its intended function, to fly seamlessly with its sibling gears in a dance of liquid, flowing motion was to see the deity itself.

And yet, it was only nearly perfect. It was not perfect enough.

He turned and chucked it into a nearby garbage canister, where its landing was broken by a pile of similarly nearly perfect but similarly discarded gears. It made a little sorrowful *clink!*

"Better luck tomorrow, eh, Mr. Unthank, sir?"

"Yes, Grimble," Joffrey began before adding, "What day is tomorrow?"

"Why, it's Wednesday, sir."

"Wednesday." He repeated it softly, as if the word were some magic sigil. It held a particular resonance: It was the final day of his labors. The strange man with the pince-nez would return, expecting his finished piece. Unthank had never let a client down before; he'd always outmatched his competitors in quality and speed. It was unnerving to him the amount of trial and error involved in the creation of this single piece. The thoughts swam in schools around his skull: Why had he even agreed? It was ludicrous, the deadline. To create such an exacting piece in such a short amount of time. Even with every state-of-the-art machine at his disposal, he'd gotten so very close, and yet not quite close enough. He was a practical and industrious man; what had driven him to agree to such a ridiculous proposal?

In one word: monomania. It was a word that he remembered being taught in school, when the teacher had written the words "MOBY

DICK" on the chalkboard in tall white letters. The captain of the ship in Melville's novel had been monomaniacal in his desire to catch the titular white whale. Every decision he made was in relation to this all-consuming obsession. In the end, it had been his undoing. The realization dawned on Unthank with cold precision; it was as if someone had suddenly set a bright, unfeeling spotlight on his face. His vanity was laid bare. He was the captain of this ship and the white whale was the Impassable Wilderness. It was too late to turn back; the harpoon had already been thrown. The line was pulling taut.

This is what happened next:

Septimus stood with his claws on his darning-needle hilt, shaking his head. Curtis stared at the mole in disbelief as Prue nearly swept down to grab the Sibyl and hoist her into the air for a celebratory shake. She thought twice, seeing the look of terror cross the mole's face when she sensed what was happening. Instead, she gave Gwendolyn a happy chuck on her shoulder with the tip of her finger.

"I can't believe it!" she said. "This is crazy!"

The Sibyl, still confused by the Overdwellers' sudden swelling of emotion, handled the barrage of questions that followed as willingly as she could.

"So he was a machinist, a maker?" asked Prue, somewhat rhetorically.

The mole nodded.

"And he made this . . . replica of a boy."

Curtis added, "For a crazy Governess. I mean, queen."

Again, the Sibyl responded in the affirmative.

"Gwendolyn, you wouldn't believe the coincidence in this. We have to find him, your architect." Prue was smiling ear to ear. Not only had the tree's advice proved true, but it seemed, in many ways, to be subtly pointing them in the direction they needed to go.

"What did he look like?" asked Curtis.

The Sibyl made a bemused gesture at her hidden eyes.

Curtis, chastened, blushed. She was blind. "Oh yeah. Sorry."

Prue took up the line, though. "But were there any distinguishing features—anything we could use to identify him?"

"WELL, THE TWO GOLDEN HOOKS IN THE PLACE OF HIS HANDS. THAT SHOULD BE A GOOD STARTING PLACE. BUT WHAT IS THIS ALL ABOUT? WHY MUST YOU FIND THE ARCHITECT?" The congregation had passed them by; Bartholomew the Seer, hobbling slowly on his knobby cane, stopped to see what the excitement was all about.

"Long story," said Curtis.

Prue ignored him. "There's . . . there's problems. In the Overworld. Lots of 'em. The tree—the Council Tree—told me—via a little boy, a strange little boy—that we needed to reanimate the true heir. The true heir, apparently, being Alexei. Who is the son of this crazy queen, who was actually known as the Dowager Governess."

Curtis made a kind of spinning motion at his temple with a finger to illustrate the description. The moles didn't see it, being blind, and he again blushed at his own forgetfulness.

"WAS?" asked the Sibyl.

"She got swallowed by ivy," Curtis explained before turning to Prue. "Keep going."

"The tree said to find the makers. The makers of the boy, the replica. And it sounds like we know who at least one of them was."

The interrogation continued for some time; both Gwendolyn and Bartholomew offered as much assistance as they could. The architect, they said, had been a quiet individual. He had kept to himself, choosing to sleep in one of the more isolated redoubts of the tunnel system. He had worked tirelessly, though, to rebuild the city. His eyes were very powerful, even if he had lost the use of his hands. And then one morning he was gone, explained the moles, leaving without so much as a forwarding address. He'd simply followed the green electrical cable he'd run to give light to his workspace; it was the direction he'd gone every day in search of more building material. He'd left them a perfectly functioning modern city; for that, they were eternally grateful.

"HIS NAME WAS ESBEN CLAMPETT," said Gwendolyn. "HE WAS A VERY KIND SOUL."

Prue and Curtis agreed to stay for the Sibyl's coronation as the new queen of the City of Moles, to reside in the Fortress of Prurtimus; it was to happen that evening. The consent had been unanimous. She was the sister of the deceased victor, Sir Timothy; there were no other claimants to the throne. What's more, she was immensely popular, having spent her time while imprisoned feeding Dennis the Usurper far-fetched prophecies that stayed the executioner's ax for many an unjustly convicted mole. Once she'd been released, she was the toast of the city. When the idea of naming her queen was floated, there were no objections from the Mole Council, nor from any of the citizens.

It was a beautiful ceremony; but the three Overdwellers were itching to head out, though they differed in direction. For Prue, it was simple: They had a clear route to the surface—they needed only follow the fat green electrical cable—and an unimpeachable lead on one of Alexei's two makers. The tree had spoken true and had not misled them. One of the makers was out there, and they knew how to find him.

"You see?" said Prue, her understanding of the world having suffered another strange imbalance. They were preparing to leave, and she couldn't stop talking about the prescience of the Yearling's words. "It's as if the tree was leading us, all along. As if it knew our fates. 'You have to go under to get above.' It's all falling into place in the weirdest way."

Septimus was chewing on another of the granola bars; the stash was considerable. The moles had brought them to it. There had been other food items in the remote grotto that housed the Overdweller rations: cans of pork and beans, tomato soup, Hormel chili. They'd also found a yellowed pamphlet, much abused by the mildewing elements of the underground tunnels, which boasted the title: *So You've Survived the Nuclear Holocaust. What Next?* Whoever had made this place his fallout shelter had gone to great lengths to get away from the above-ground.

"Mm-hmm," said Septimus, his mouth full of an Oats 'n' Honey Trail Bar.

"What about the bandits?" Curtis asked Prue as she began packing her knapsack full of traveling supplies.

Prue bit her lip and responded as if she hadn't heard the boy's question. "Well, I still think you're right—I still think we'll be safer aboveground in South Wood. Once we've found the maker, we'll head to South Wood. I have a feeling there are a lot of folks there who would be happy to help us. Who knows, maybe someone in the Mansion will even know where the second maker is. Maybe there are records that will tell us where he was exiled."

Curtis frowned.

"Or where the bandits are," added Prue.

"Wildwood," said Curtis, after a moment of contemplation. "That's where we belong. Or where I belong."

"Back at the camp?"

Curtis nodded.

"And then what?" challenged Prue.

"And then . . . I don't know. Put together a search party. Find the survivors."

"You won't be safe there, Curtis. The Kitsunes could still be lurking. Darla could still be alive."

"It's a risk I'll have to take. I made a vow."

"I know you did," said Prue. "And I think you're keeping it by helping me. You're not doing anyone any good by getting yourself killed. Even Brendan would tell you that."

Curtis looked at her blankly.

"It's for the good of the Wood, I know it," she continued, her voice growing more urgent. "You have to trust me on this."

Curtis looked over at Septimus; the rat had made his way through one granola bar and was about to sink his teeth into a second. When he saw Curtis looking, he froze. His eyes darted back and forth between the two kids before he shrugged and kept eating. "Meither way," he said through his full mouth, "sounds mrisky."

"Okay," said Curtis. "One thing I did swear: I said I'd keep you safe. I intend to do that. But only till we find your maker. And then you're on your own. I'm going back to the camp."

"Fine," said Prue, relieved.

They picked through the stockpile for the least suspicious food items and the ones that wouldn't require a can opener; they fit what they could into Prue's knapsack. There was no telling how long they'd be traveling. The shadows of their complaining and empty stomachs from the days prior to discovering the moles still hovered in their minds.

A grand send-off was arranged; Prue, Curtis, and Septimus were each given the highest decoration the moles could offer: the Star of the Underwood. The medal itself was a tangle of rusted wire around a salvaged badge that had clearly found its way to the moles' possession from the Outside: Prue's read I'M A RAINBOW READER! above the crude drawing of an open book sprouting the identifying rainbow. Septimus's badge boasted the logo of some forgotten food co-op. Curtis's just had a picture of a middle-aged man giving the camera a thumbs-up. Below the face it simply read ZEKE in bold letters. They accepted the medals with a quiet dignity.

Leaving the city behind, the three travelers followed the thick green cable that had been stretched along the floor of the tunnel. It led them over long, thin bridges across wide wells. It led them up staircases and down raked floors. It led them down iron ladders and up wooden ones. So many were the twists and turns in the cable's path that they became amazed by the amount of attention and diligence the marking of the way must've demanded of the mole and her Overdweller friend. Prue, for one, could only imagine the potential wrong turns one could take in the maze of tunnels. It was best to just concentrate on the green cable, to follow it blindly.

The way was far. They were forced to stop many times in their travels.

The rough-hewn stone, after a time, gave way to rougher brick as the construction of the tunnel system seemed to transform into the product of a distinctly more modern era. It began to remind Prue of the passageways she'd traversed in South Wood, when she'd gone to see Owl Rex. It gave her hope that they were making progress. However, judging from the kind of cast-off junk that the architect had brought to build his mole city, it was clear that he was sourcing from the Outside—from beyond the Wood. If this was the case, then the two of them seemed to be walking a conduit between the Outside and the Impassable Wilderness—something she believed even many of the older citizens of the Wood that she'd met didn't know existed. Frankly, the implications seemed astonishing. She'd just about gotten around to considering whether the Periphery Bind extended into the underground when a loud *clank* disrupted her from her thinking.

"What was that?" she asked.

Curtis, in front of her, was bending down, inspecting something on the tunnel floor. He'd accidentally kicked it as he walked. "A bottle," he said.

"What? What kind of bottle?"

"A beer bottle," said Curtis. He handed it to Prue. She studied it in the glare of the lantern light.

"Pabst Blue Ribbon," Prue read from the torn label. That, to her best recollection, was *not* of Woodian brew.

Septimus, at Curtis's shoulder, began to wax somewhat pathetically about how he imagined a cool drink would taste right about now when suddenly they heard whistling coming from the darkness ahead. Prue lifted the lantern; the outer rings of its illumination revealed a crude open doorway. The whistling was persistent, growing closer. A click; light flooded in.

Prue's eyes had grown so accustomed to the faint glow of their lantern that this new light, harsh and fluorescent, felt as if they were looking directly into the sun. They cringed and squinted. A figure came into view; he was carrying a box.

They moved forward cautiously. The figure must've heard them, because his whistling abruptly ceased. As they approached, they were better able to make out the man's features. He was a young man, perhaps in his twenties, and he was wearing a bowler hat and a natty vest. He was clean shaven, save for a thick mustache which he'd pomaded into little curls on either side of his mouth. He looked like he'd emerged from another century—which made him a dead ringer for a citizen of South Wood.

"Hello?" called Prue.

The man had stopped and was peering down the passageway at the two of them; he seemed to be having trouble making sense of their presence.

"What are you doing down here?" he asked.

"We'd ask you the same," said Curtis.

"I'm just working," explained the man.

"Is this South Wood? How near are we to the Mansion?" Prue was tired from all the walking; her patience was stretched thin.

This question seemed to flummox the young man completely. "Huh?" was all he managed.

"South Wood. Are we below South Wood?" repeated Curtis, irritated by the man's stupor.

"I don't know what you're talking about. This is Old Town. Like, downtown Portland. I'm just stocking the reach-in."

Now it was Prue and Curtis's chance to be confused. "What?" they asked simultaneously.

"I'm getting beer. For the bar." When this didn't seem to satisfy his interrogators, he tried another angle. "Listen, I'm new. Started, like, a week ago. So if you guys are, like, messing with me . . ." Something seemed to occur to him; a bright recognition had descended over his face. "Oh, I see," he said. "Were you kids on one of those, like, Shanghai Tunnel tours? Did you guys get separated?"

Curtis was still aghast; Prue made quick sense of their predicament. "Yeah," she responded. "Sorry. Just a little confused. Did you see where the rest of the group went?" There was a tunnel system that ran under the oldest part of Portland; everyone called it the Shanghai Tunnels. Prue had gone on a tour of these tunnels with her parents last year; they'd taken the ghost-themed tour, and the guide, a curly-haired, mustachioed guy, had really laid it on thick about the spirits that haunted these subterranean passageways. Supposedly, the tunnels had been used to abduct drunken sailors, who would wake up from their drugged unconsciousness far out to sea on a clipper bound for the West Indies. That was the tale, anyway. In retrospect, that tour guide, with all his stories of trapdoors and revenge-seeking poltergeists, didn't know the half of it.

"Man, I don't know. I just got here. You can head up topside with me if you'd like. Though you're gonna be too young to be in the bar." Seeing Septimus, he added, "And we have a pretty strict no-pets rule."

"I'm not a pet," said Septimus.

The man blanched. "What?" he asked, very confused.

Curtis gave his shoulder a jerk in an attempt to admonish the rat. He then responded to the man's question, saying, "I said, I'll bet. As in: I'll bet we won't be let in."

The man seemed unsatisfied with the explanation, but he evidently preferred it to having witnessed a talking rat. "I think we could find you another way out, if you'd like," he said.

Prue glanced down at the architect's green electrical cable on the floor; it stretched out into the distance, through another tunnel opening just beyond where the young man stood. "Nah," she said. "We'll find them down here somewhere."

"Cool," said the man. He looked over at Curtis. "Nice jacket, by the way. Where'd you get it?"

Curtis looked down; covered in a solid layer of dust and dirt was his military uniform, all brocaded cuffs and gold epaulets. He couldn't really think of another answer: "From some bandits," he replied.

The young man didn't seem to bat an eyelash. "Oh," he said. "Cool." And then he was gone, his whistling resuming as he plodded his way up the rickety stairs to the above-ground.

"Septimus," said Curtis when they were alone again. "You can't do that."

"What?" asked the rat.

"Talk. While we're in the Outside. It's just too . . . complicated."

The rat harrumphed. "What am I supposed to say?"

Curtis thought about it for a second. "I don't know. Squeak or something."

"*Squeak?*" repeated the rat. "I'm not a squeaker."

Prue put in, "Then keep your mouth shut. Whatever. We can't be raising suspicions here."

"Got it," said the rat. "Squeak."

Curtis put his hand against one of the brick walls of the tunnel, feeling the chill of the rough surface. "So I'm guessing we're in Old Town, huh? Weird."

"I know," responded Prue. "Culture shock."

"And these tunnels that we've been following—they connect with the Shanghai Tunnels?"

"It would appear that way."

"I thought those tunnels were a hoax. Like, a touristy thing."

Prue shrugged. "I thought so too. Maybe they still are. Obviously, people don't know where they *really* lead. I guess folks just never thought to explore the tunnels farther."

"I wonder if the Periphery . . ."

"I was wondering the same thing. If it protects the tunnels, too."

"It'd be a shame if people figured it out."

"Yeah," said Prue. "Let's keep this one a secret, how about that?"

"Agreed." They shook hands.

They continued on; the tunnel ended abruptly at a brick wall. The green cable, however, soon pointed the way. It led to a small shaft just to the side of the wall, where an iron ladder gave access to the darkness below. They climbed down carefully; it deposited them in a cylindrical tunnel, easily twenty feet tall from floor to ceiling, that appeared to play host to a congregation of the city's electrical wiring. The green cable spooled innocuously down from the shaft and became intermixed in the thousands of other multihued cables that splayed along the tunnel floor. A metal maintenance walkway had been bolted to the wall of the cylinder, and it was this that Prue and Curtis followed, always keeping an eye on their little green cable.

The cylinder was as straight as an arrow. At one point, Curtis said he could hear the rushing of water above them—though it was hard to tell. One thing was clear: They were crossing under the Willamette River, heading farther east. Both Prue and Curtis were of North Portland stock. The Southeast side was an undiscovered country to them, though they'd both spent plenty of afternoons as younger children mooning over the IMAX at the Museum of Science and Industry. Beyond that, it was a no-man's-land as far as they were concerned.

They nearly missed it; thankfully Septimus had been scouting ahead, keeping a keen eye on the meandering cable. At a curve in the tunnel, it suddenly broke away from the mass of wiring and snaked up toward a ladder on the wall of the cylinder. Climbing this, they found themselves in another low tunnel that crawled along for what felt like several miles. Finally, a glimmer of light could be seen in the distance; it was the scant sunlight allowed between the cracks of a weathered old wooden door. Opening it, they found themselves bathed in daylight, breathing the clear, crisp air of the Outside.

Except that it wasn't quite so idyllic, their reunion with the aboveground; they found themselves in the middle of a junk heap that extended as far as the eye could see. Tall towers of discarded rubbish were piled high in every direction: rusted, emptied-out car chassis, refrigerators with their doors yawning open, hubcaps, and bottle caps. There were reams of abandoned *National Geographic* magazines papering the ground; there were half-chewed, one-eyed stuffed animals, orphaned from their owners. White plastic bags floated like jellyfish on the air, and the ground was pockmarked with potholes, filled to the brim with oil-iridescent water. There was barely any snow remaining; the little that did was black with soot.

"Lovely place, the Outside," said Septimus. "Nice to be home?" Prue glared at him, to which he replied, "Squeak."

Curtis gave them both an unenthused look. "Let's find this guy," he said. "And get out of here."

They all took the opportunity to take in their surroundings; it didn't seem like the sort of place anyone would want to hang out in for too long. The horizon was all but blotted out by the towers of debris. It was clear: This had been the source of the building materials for the City of Moles. The green cable, the thing that had been their lifeline for the entirety of their journey to the surface, ended here. A stump of a post jutted from the ground; bolted to it was a small gray power box. It was to this that the cable had been tethered.

"I guess he could be anywhere now, huh?" noted Prue.

THIS END UP
THANK YOU

"Yep. Any ideas where to start looking?" asked Curtis.

"I guess the immediate vicinity would be a good starting point," said Prue.

Curtis nodded. "Great idea."

And so they began searching for this elusive architect, the one with two golden hooks for hands, so that they might convince him to rebuild some integral part of a mechanical boy prince—all at the behest of a clairvoyant, sentient tree. Prue, since first being introduced to Wildwood, had learned to not consider the minutiae of things, but rather take each episode as it came. Otherwise, she figured, the ridiculousness might fry some essential lobe of her brain—the sensible part. Taken as a whole, their quest seemed fairly ridiculous, but there wasn't really anything strange about looking for someone in the midst of a waste dump. At least, she didn't think so.

"Mr. Architect!" called Curtis as he began to scale one of the mountains of junk. Septimus was winnowing in and out of towers of metallic bric-a-brac, squeaking with all the energy he could muster.

"Esben!" yelled Prue, getting into the search as well. She was peering into the windows of a disemboweled Ford Focus. "Esben Clampett!"

He was not in the stack of cars; nor was he in the tower of washing machines that seemed to balance impossibly one on top of the other. He wasn't in the claw-foot bathtub filled with thick, muddy water. And he wasn't beneath the A-frame of corrugated metal that made, to

Curtis's estimation, a pretty nifty fort—it did look like it had given someone shelter for a time; the black remnants of a campfire marked the ground beneath it.

An hour passed. Then two. Prue was pushing aside a broken screen door to get at a little cavity in a heap of jumbled, broken bicycles when she heard Septimus mewling loudly from afar.

She looked up. The rat was standing at the far end of the dump, in the trough between two building-tall piles of garbage. He was pointing at the far horizon and squeaking with all the determination of a rocking chair in need of a good oiling.

Wiping off her jeans, she jogged over to where a pile of old tube televisions made a kind of staircase, and there she began to climb to where Septimus stood. "What is it?"

Curtis, hearing the commotion, found his way to their side. Septimus continued to squeak, running in circles and flailing his small arms in the direction of the city.

The two kids were flummoxed. "I'm not sure what you're getting at, Septimus," said Curtis icily. "I think you're taking this whole squeaking thing too far."

Finally, the rat stopped his game of charades and looked at Prue and Curtis with his hands on his hips. "So I can talk now?" he asked.

Prue rolled her eyes. "Yes, Septimus. You can talk."

"I think we have our man," he said, pointing.

From the height at which they stood, they could see that the junk heap ended just a few hundred feet on; there, a railroad track created a boundary between the dump and what appeared to be an amusement park. Prue was amazed that they hadn't heard the noise before. Now it was clear: The singsong lilt of a pump organ colored the late afternoon air. The lights of the Ferris wheel were just winking on, and the sound of the park's whirring, churning machines could be heard amid the occasional shouts from the few attendants who milled like ants about the grounds. In the center of the amusement park was a giant circus tent, colored garishly blue and yellow; a sign in front of the entrance boldly advertised the evening's main event in a typeface so big as to be perfectly legible even from where the three of them stood. It read THE AMAZING, THE INCREDIBLE, THE ONE AND ONLY: ESBEN THE GREAT!

CHAPTER 21

Return to Childhood; A Cog in the Hand

The meeting was quickly convened at the cottage. Carol stood at the fireplace mantel, while the younger kids streamed down the wooden stairs from the attic; the older kids, those who'd been diligently setting about doing their afternoon chores, came in from the outside and stood, curious, in the large family room.

"Children," said Carol, "we have some fascinating news to impart. Yesterday, while joining Michael and Cynthia on their trapping rounds, our newest family member Elsie Mehlberg found something. It was something that exists beyond the Periphery."

A collective gasp met this revelation. Elsie, sitting on a bench by the fire, felt every eye in the room land on her.

"It's a road." Another gasp; the frenetic sound of excited children whispering to one another. Carol held up his hand. "Now, hold up. You should know that this road runs through the interior of this country. I'm not suggesting we follow it. However, it does make one thing perfectly clear: Elsie is not affected by the constraints of the Periphery Bind. It would appear that she—and her sister as well—are able to walk, quite freely, through it."

Now the room could barely contain its excitement. The girl sitting next to Elsie was staring at her, as if she'd inadvertently sat down next to some Hollywood starlet and was only just now realizing it. There were a few hoots from the older kids in the back—also a few "Way to go, Elsie and Rachel!" Then it appeared that the realization dawned on the celebrating crowd. One kid asked, "That's great for them. What about us?"

"That's just the thing, isn't it?" replied Carol. "I've asked myself the same question for a long time—how is it that those who are unaffected by the Bind are able to come and go so freely? When I first was brought here, I was deposited by a group of the Mansion guards. And yet once they'd left, it was as if they'd thrown the lock on my cell door. And yet no door existed."

Another voice took up the explanation. It was Michael. "What he's saying is they can walk us out. We just need to be making physical contact with them."

Everyone's head had swiveled to face the new speaker. He continued, "They found out because they were walking Carol through the woods—might not've discovered this little trick otherwise. When they went and found us, me and Cynthia, we lost them as soon as they'd gotten very far. But if we all held hands, we were all able to make it to this road. Simple as that."

Carol nodded. "Yep," he said. "Simple as that. So simple, in fact, that it's no wonder I hadn't been able to figure it out. So all's it took was someone of Woods Magic to come in here and we were free. Thing is, I don't think the Mansion ever thought there'd be a couple kids born with it just wanderin into the Periphery."

Now the girl sitting next to Elsie was looking at her as if she were a ghost; a look of surprise, intrigue, and not a little fear had fallen over her face.

"They're, like, from *there*?" asked a boy, sitting cross-legged in front of Carol.

"No, no," the old man replied. "But they were somehow born with it, this thing the Woods folk call Woods Magic. Other folks'd called it Woodblood. Whichever. My guess is, it runs in families. Somewhere in the Mehlberg family tree, there's a Woodian, just keepin things quiet in the Outside world."

Elsie and Rachel made brief eye contact from across the room. Rachel was sitting at the dining room table, idly drawing on the grain of the wood with her finger. She seemed uncomfortable with this new information. The room was awash with excited voices; everyone seemed to have a different opinion about what to do next.

"I want to go home!" a younger girl, Elsie's age, cried plaintively.

"What home?" shot back another girl.

"Maybe we should explore this road. See where it leads." This was Carl Rehnquist; he was knitting.

"No way," replied Cynthia Schmidt. "From what Carol tells us, that place is freaky."

"And dangerous," added Lizzie Collins.

"What about Unthank? What about the promise of all that money?"

"And our freedom!"

"Ha!" retorted Michael, sucking on his pipe. "That's a joke. He'll just put us right back to work."

"And make Elsie and Rachel take him into the woods."

Elsie shuddered at the idea. It was true: They undoubtedly would be Joffrey's key to getting past the Periphery Bind. The idea of being a shepherd for Unthank and what would likely be a constant stream of other industrialists seemed like a fate worse than death.

"This is our home. This is our place." Michael had spoken the words; the entire room had fallen into silence in their wake. "There's nothing out there for us. In the outside world, we were orphans. In here, we're a family. Right, Carol?"

The old man wore a thoughtful frown. He was rubbing the gray stubble of his cheek, his mouth slack. Finally, he spoke. "Well, as much as I have come to love the place, I can't say I wouldn't mind seein that outside world again. I s'pose my son'll be gettin on forty by now. We never did talk much after his mother died, but I guess it wouldn't do no harm to just drop in."

One of the children nodded in agreement. "I'd like to eat a Starburst again," said one, and a few other kids tittered with laughter at the suggestion.

"Or chocolate!" threw in another. This elicited a new round of enthusiasm.

"Caramel sundaes! Whipped cream!"

"Nickel video games at Wonderland!"

"The Burnside skateboard park!"

"Coffee! So much coffee!" The kids all wheeled to look at this one; it was Carl Rehnquist. Apparently, now that he'd tasted the fruits of the grown-up world, he was keen to explore more of it.

"That's the thing, ain't it," countered Michael. The passion was rising in his voice. "You go back out there, you're kids again. No drinking coffee. No swearing. No smoking. No staying up late. And you gotta go to school, every day. That's the rules."

The collective mood of the children was considerably tamped down by this very true observation. They began to grumble to one another, cataloging all the daily expectations thrust on them by the adult world. Here, in the Periphery, they made their own rules.

"Besides, where are we going to go?" This, again, was Michael, pressing his advantage. He paused to let the full implication of the words sink in. "We're not going back to Unthank's, that's for sure. But we don't have parents. We don't have families. There's nothing waiting for us beyond those trees."

The youngest of the children, a girl named Annalisa, began to cry.

Michael continued, "No, I say we stay. Let the magic Mehlbergs leave if they want to, but I, for one, am not going with." He looked over at his friend and hunting partner, Cynthia. "You with me?"

She hesitated. "I don't know, Michael," she said, after a time, her eyes downcast. "I just don't know."

Before Michael could upbraid his friend for not backing him up, Martha Song stepped forward. She'd been watching the proceedings quietly from the back of the room. She cleared her voice and spoke. "Why don't we just make *this*, out *there*?"

The room quieted to hear Martha's proposal.

"Who's to say we can't have this place, this family in the outside world? Things aren't that much different, right? I mean, you guys are freaked out about being forced to go to school, and yet you're fine with doing the chores that are assigned to you every day. I got a theory about that; it's because it wasn't given to you by an adult. Because we're all taken as equal to one another, and you realize that the, you know, well-being of the house depends on what every kid does—it just makes sense. So what if you can't smoke or drink or swear in the outside world? Big deal. I think we'll all have plenty of time to do that when we're grown up. And that's another thing: While this whole time-stop weirdness is pretty cool and magic and all, I'd actually like to make it past nine. I was kinda looking forward to being a teenager, actually."

A mumble of agreement came from the gathered children.

"I say we all leave. All of us. All together. And we find some nice, abandoned house on the outskirts of the city and we build *this*"—here she made a sweeping gesture with her arm—"again. But this time, we'll have Starbursts and chocolate and skateboards and the whole lot. What do you say?"

Carl Rehnquist jumped to his feet and began applauding madly, his knitting falling to the floor. When he noticed that no one else had been so enthusiastically moved by the girl's speech, he blushed and sat back down. "I think we should do that," he said meekly.

But the speech had been persuasive. The Unadoptables gathered in the cottage now looked at one another in a new light, with a new hope. This thing Martha was proposing—it did seem possible. And perfect.

Carol, his wooden eyes staring out over the heads of the gathered children, could almost read their thoughts, so palpable was the desire in the room to leave their in-between purgatory and pioneer a new home. He cleared his throat and spoke. "Very well. A show of hands. How many would like to leave this place, start afresh in the outside?"

Though he was bereft of sight, his vision having been painfully stolen on the callous whim of an evil woman, Carol could hear the sound of dozens of jumpsuits rustling as nearly every kid in the house raised their hands in near-unanimous consent. He could hear the sudden inbreaths from each child as they reckoned with their future, surprised at their own ability to create a powerful consensus. He could then hear laughter—celebratory laughter, laughter in disbelief—trickling up from the youngest kids until it infected everyone in the room. What Carol wouldn't have heard, though he guessed at it, was the newfound sadness that etched itself on the boy Michael's brow.

He'd been the only holdout. When the vote had been called, his arm had remained fixedly at his side. He was watching the jubilant kids as they slapped one another on the back and swapped high fives. He stayed silent amid the celebrations. Inwardly, he mourned.

❧

Unthank was holding the cog. It glowed mysteriously in his hand as its three gears moved smoothly around the shining core. It emitted a faint hum as it moved; an aura of turbulence surrounded it too, as his fingers felt the constant pull and contraction of the magnets at work. It truly was a thing of beauty. His eyes became wet with tears of relief and joy. He sniffled a little, smiling at the miraculous outcome of his hard work.

"Joffrey!" called his mother.

A look of confusion clouded his face. What was his mother doing here?

"Joffrey!" she called again. It was the unmistakable tone of Priscilla Unthank at her most petulant. "Come down for supper!"

Joffrey looked around him; he was in his childhood bedroom. Posters of comic book supervillains lined the walls. A calm blue fish swam in an aquarium on his desk. He'd gotten the fish when he was eleven. He'd desperately wanted to have a pet then, but his tremendous allergy to cat dander prevented him that simple childhood pleasure. He'd named the fish Harold, for reasons he could barely remember.

"Aren't you going to go down?" asked Harold, the fish. "She's made your favorite: Möbius Meat Loaf."

"Oh no," said Joffrey, a cold realization dawning on him. The beautiful cog still spun in his hands. "Please, no."

"Joffrey!" yelled his mother. "Why will not you come down?" Priscilla's voice had suddenly developed a distinctly Eastern European dialect, which Joffrey found odd, considering that she was originally from Salem, Oregon.

"Just a moment," said stunned Joffrey Unthank, trying to work out his surroundings. He wanted the illusion of the finished cog to remain just a little longer. The feeling of having achieved the impossible task was as true a bliss as he'd ever felt.

"Why will you not? You say we make movies. Hollywood movies. But you will not eat the meat loaf!" His mother's voice had now morphed completely into that of Desdemona's. The fish winked at him from behind the glass. It was clear what was happening.

"No!" Joffrey moaned to Harold. He looked down in his hands. The cog was gone; in its place was a giant, meaty heart. It beat calmly, spitting little fountains of blood onto his Star Wars bedsheets. Flecks of the warm, sticky liquid spattered on his face and his hands.

"Joffrey!" called Desdemona.

"Please, no!" he said again, increasingly desperate. The fish began laughing.

The voice of Desdemona was close now; she was knocking on his bedroom door and shouting, "Joffrey, what are you doing?"

And then he woke up.

The knocking persisted. He was in his office. The wetness on his cheek was, in fact, the surprising quantity of drool that had spilled from his mouth. It was pooling onto the stack of paper that had been his makeshift pillow; on top of the stack was the Möbius Cog schematic. In a sudden panic, he grabbed the end of his tie and wiped away the liquid, relieved that it hadn't blurred out some consequential phrase or equation.

The knock came again. "Joffrey! Door is locked. I know you are there." It was Desdemona, at his office door.

"I was just napping," said Joffrey, his voice hoarse. "What is it?"

"This man is to see you," said Desdemona. "Roger. You remember."

Unthank's eyes went wide. He looked at the calendar on his desk ("*A Prairie Home Companion* Joke-a-Day!") and saw that it cited the date as being Wednesday. The fifth day of his commission; the deadline for the production of the Cog.

"Uh," he muttered while he braced his hands on the desk, taking stock of his surroundings. "Yeah. Go ahead and send him in." He straightened his tie, still damp from its use as a sponge, and flattened the rumpled mess of his hair. He then pushed himself out from behind his desk and walked to the office door. He threw the latch, unlocking it.

Before long, the door swung open. Desdemona gave him a

searching look, briefly, before ushering the visitor into the room.

"Roger," said Joffrey, doing his best to feign attentiveness. The pall of the dream still hung over him; he was having a hard time fully transitioning back to his strange reality.

The man wore the same vintage suit; the pince-nez still remained affixed at the bridge of his nose. "Well?" said the man, after very little time had elapsed. "You've finished the Cog?"

Unthank gave a quick, toothy smile to Desdemona before he shooed her from the doorway and shut the door. "That's just the thing, Roger," he said. "I'm awfully close."

"Close?" The man had been about to sit in one of the office's chairs. Unthank's admission had stopped him dead. "What do you mean, close?"

"This is a gorgeous piece of work, I can tell you that. A real once-in-a-lifetime part. I think the guy who made this should win a Nobel Prize or something. I mean, it's that good." Even Unthank was aware of his own stalling.

"Listen, Mr. Unthank: You either have the Cog or you don't. Which is it?"

"I don't." The sudden confession felt strangely good.

"And why don't you?"

"I need more time."

"More time?" Roger's face had grown considerably redder. His manicured beard twitched at his chin. "We don't have *more time*."

"A piece of this complexity, sir—I can't imagine that your competitors are having any more luck."

"My competitors are dead," said Roger.

Unthank gulped, once, very loudly. "Okay," he managed.

"But I can't expect that there won't be others to rise in their place. This needs to happen now, Mr. Unthank. Or I shall have to find another machinist."

The implications of being fired by this odd and vindictive man seemed to be very serious indeed. "I don't think you'll need to do that. I—"

His stammered rebuttal was interrupted by a loud knock on the door. Unthank smiled sheepishly at Roger before calling, "What is it?"

"Joffrey, dear." It was Desdemona. "Mr. Wigman is here to see you."

Roger cocked an eyebrow. Joffrey felt rivulets of sweat appear at his brow. "Tell him . . . ," he began. An unannounced visit from the Chief Titan? It immediately spelled trouble to the beleaguered Unthank. "Tell him I'm busy."

Another knock came. This one was a good degree louder, as if coming from the fist of a much larger person than lithe Desdemona Mudrak. "Machine Parts!" came a man's thunderous voice. The two words sent shudders of dread through Unthank's body. It was Brad Wigman himself.

"Quick!" hissed Unthank. "Into the closet!" Roger gave him an affronted look.

"Why on earth . . . ," Roger began as Unthank started pushing him toward a door opposite the desk.

"Unthank, I can hear you in there," came Wigman's voice. "What's going on?" He tried the handle; Joffrey had locked it after he'd let Roger in. "Dammit, man. Let me in."

Unthank was busy trying to hush Roger's murmurs of objection as he guided him to the closet door. "Just trust me," he said. "It's better that he doesn't know about you." The man in the pince-nez finally conceded and allowed Joffrey to shutter him into the closet, surrounded as he was by ink cartridge boxes and cases of Lemony Zip.

Just then the door to the office flew open; Desdemona had, at Wigman's behest, fetched the key and undone the lock. Unthank turned from the closet and saw the doorway filled—very nearly to capacity—with the broad-shouldered frame of Brad Wigman, Chief Titan.

"Hi, Mr. Wigman," squeaked Unthank.

Brad's eyes searched the room suspiciously. "What's going on in here? Why'd it take you so long to get the door?"

"So sorry. That door tends to get stuck. Been meaning to fix it." Here Joffrey walked to the door and mimed a careful inspection of the handle. "Jeez," he said, appearing baffled. "They sure don't make 'em like they—"

But his cheap explanation was cut short. Wigman walked directly up to him, as he was often wont to do, and stood so close to Unthank's face that he could smell the Chief Titan's mouthwash of choice: Sprig O'Cinnamon. "Cut the crap, Machine Parts," said Wigman. "What are you up to?"

The two of them stood that way, face-to-face—though it was more akin to face-to-clavicle, as Unthank only came up to his boss's collarbone—for a time. The little droplets of sweat that had appeared on Joffrey's forehead only moments earlier turned into proper bulbs of perspiration and began dripping down the side of his face. Wigman's eyes followed one such drop as it traveled from the man's hairline to his chin. Unthank could only smile.

"Just, you know, working," was all that Joffrey could manage.

"What are you working on there, Machine Parts?"

"Just, you know, some stuff. Making, you know, machine parts."

"What *kind* of machine parts?"

"Bolts," replied Unthank. "Screws. Spigots. Alternator caps. Crank shaft housings—"

"Actually, I happen to know that you haven't been making *any* machine parts, Joffrey. I happen to have that information on good authority."

"Oh, really?" Unthank was desperately trying to unknot his vocal cords; it felt like a python had curled its way around his throat and was squeezing. He swallowed hard, though it didn't seem to have much effect.

"Yes, really," said Wigman. "I had my girl bring up some recent records. It appears that production is down seventy-five percent this week. I asked around; turns out some of your clients haven't heard from you since last Thursday; they say all their shipments are late."

Unthank squirmed under Wigman's glare. How did he know to look? Someone must've tipped him off. His mind searched for answers.

"So," said Wigman, "I guess I've come to do a little recon myself." With that, he stepped away from Joffrey's face, releasing him from the cloud of Sprig O'Cinnamon, and walked toward the bookshelf. His eyes wandered over the fanciful names on the bottles that lined the shelves. He knelt down and flicked a finger at one of the white transponder boxes. "You got some weird stuff in here, Joffrey," he said. "But I've never been one to hold a guy's obsessions against him." By this time, he'd made it over to Unthank's desk. Remembering the schematic, Joffrey dove to stand in the way between it and the Chief Titan.

"Listen," said Joffrey, his voice unknotting slightly, "why don't we take a walk? I'll show you the machine shop—it's been so long since you visited. Maybe go grab a bit of lunch at the Rusty Sprocket? I don't know about you, but I'm famished."

"What's that?" asked Wigman dryly.

"What's what?"

"Don't play dumb with me, Machine Parts," said Wigman. He jabbed a finger in the direction of the paper stack on the desk. "What's that blueprint thing?"

Unthank craned his neck to look in the direction of Wigman's pointing finger. "Oh, that? That's nothing, really. Just a little something I'm working on in my spare—"

Wigman pivoted and stepped around Joffrey. He grabbed the schematic from the desk and shook it flat. His left eyebrow risen to its most impressive height, Wigman studied the plan. When he'd finished scanning the page, he turned to Joffrey. "If you don't tell me what this is and what it's doing on your desk, I swear I'll—"

"That, sir, is a Möbius Cog." These words had not come from the quivering mouth of Joffrey Unthank. Instead, they seemed to be issuing from the closet on the far side of the room. Both Joffrey and Wigman turned to see the words' source.

Roger Swindon stood in the open door of the closet, straightening the lapel of his coat. An aghast silence from Unthank and Wigman had followed his abrupt entrance; Roger chose to fill it with an explanation: "I've commissioned your man there to make it for me. The fate of the Wood—your term for the place, I believe, is the Impassable Wilderness—hangs in the balance. The Möbius Cog must be made, Mr. Wigman. It is that simple."

The schematic drifted from Wigman's fingers to the carpeted floor as he stared at the man in the closet, trying to make sense of the very strange aura that exuded from him. It was, he reasoned, the pince-nez. The man really knew how to wear a pince-nez.

CHAPTER 22

Procession; Final Performance Tonight!

They held hands in a long line, all thirty-eight of them. The line stretched from the front porch of the cottage and extended up over the lip of the vale. Those who were able also held the leashes of as many dogs as they could manage to round up. It was agreed that Rachel should be first in the line. There was no telling the effect the Periphery could have on someone without Woods Magic emerging first. Elsie would take up the rear, so as best to distribute the current. These were the precautions that they'd all worked out, carefully, after the rousing meeting in the cottage dining room.

Rachel shouted from the front. "All connected?"

Each Unadoptable, Carol among them, sounded out along the line. "Yep!" "Uh-huh!" "I am!"

"Okay!" hollered Rachel. "We're moving."

And so the line began to snake away from their solitary home in the midst of the Periphery, the one that they'd shared for so many days and nights—days and nights that would've amounted to years and years in the outside world; but in here, in this purgatory, it had been like the same day replaying itself, over and over again. They each in turn gave a final glance to the sad little glade and the dilapidated cottage that sat nestled in it. A remnant wisp of smoke trailed from the chimney, like a waving hand bidding them adieu.

As they walked, Elsie wondered on all the things that had transpired over the previous few days. The revelation of her connection to the Impassable Wilderness, while being strange, had somehow not been as big of a surprise to her as she would have expected. It was as if she'd known all along that she'd harbored something bizarre and special. What's more, the feeling that this gift had some bearing on her brother's disappearance grew by the hour. Deep down, she'd felt some weird resonance in the circumstances around his leaving, and she could no longer brush it aside as a hallucination.

Rachel, on the other hand, had bristled at the mention of their incredible pedigree. She seemed to wear it like a shameful label. The night before they left, when preparations were being made, Rachel had shushed her sister anytime she'd wanted to bring it up. "It's nothing," she'd said. "We should be focusing on just getting out of here."

There was one thing, though, in all the children's planning, that they'd failed to consider. They'd forgotten about their identical earrings, the yellow tags hanging from the lobes of their ears. They'd become so accustomed to them, no one thought to imagine what they were for. By the time they'd headed away from the direction of the road and toward what they figured was the eastern edge of the Bind, it was too late.

"Who are you?" demanded Wigman, after he'd recovered from his shock. It was rare that Brad Wigman found himself in a room where he didn't know absolutely everyone of consequence—particularly

considering that the man who had emerged from the closet had a kind of dapper raiment that Wigman could only dream of pulling off.

"Name's Roger Swindon. I'm not of the Outside."

"What are you doing here?" Remembering where he was, Wigman turned to Unthank. "What's he doing here?"

"Well, it's a bit of a long story—" began Joffrey. He was cut off by Roger.

"As I said, I've commissioned him to build a cog. One that will, once it's finished, prove to have great influence on the affairs of my home country. I've offered him a stake in the winnings. He's failed in the attempt."

"Failed?"

"I gave him five days to build this cog, the one that you saw in the schematic. He has just told me that he is unable to make it." The strange man walked confidently between Unthank and Wigman and scooped the blueprint from the floor. He shook it out and began to

fold it by its worn creases. "Unfortunately, I'm now forced to bring my proposal to another manufacturer. I'd been told he was the best; I see now I was sadly mistaken."

Wigman glared over at Unthank, who was cowering slightly. "Is this true?"

Joffrey nodded.

"Why didn't you tell me about this, Machine Parts?" asked Wigman.

"Well, you were so, I don't know, unhappy about my . . . my interest in the Impassable Wilderness. I thought it best to just do it in secret. I was going to tell you eventually, promise." Unthank was lying to the Chief Titan. In a way, it felt good.

"Joffrey, Joffrey," chided Wigman. "You have to tell me about these things. I could help you, old man."

Joffrey began to protest, stammering something about how he *had* told the Chief Titan about it, and Wigman had only ever given him scorn and reprimands.

Wigman wasn't listening. "What were the terms?" he asked, speaking over Unthank as he turned to face Roger.

"Produce the Cog, have free and unfettered access to the Impassable Wilderness and all the resources you can plunder. Simple as that."

Unthank objected. "Well, it's not quite that simple. This piece, this Möbius Cog, is one of the most complex and intricate things I've—"

Wigman waved him aside. "Suppose I got involved. Redoubled

our attempt. Would you give us more time?"

Roger seemed to chew on the idea for a moment. Finally, he said, "I'm afraid my confidence in your man has been badly shaken. Redoubling efforts is the least that can be done—but may yet prove to be insufficient. No, I shall have to find another manufacturer, someone who can meet my demands."

Joffrey, despite himself, stifled a laugh. "Mr. Swindon, sir, with all due respect, there is no . . ." He paused, a thought coming over him. "Unless. Unless."

"Unless?" asked Wigman.

"Wait a second," said Unthank. "Hear me out for a second. I got really, really close to making this thing, to succeeding. So close that I could taste it. If I just had a little help, I'm sure I could build it." He reached his hand out to Roger, asking for the blueprint. It was given with some reluctance. He then waved the two men to the desk, where he flattened the schematic out on the surface. He pointed to two scrawled names on the bottom of the page. Unthank read them aloud; he'd spent many hours marveling over the two names—imagining what these men must've looked like. The skill that had been required to not only build the thing, but to design it, was simply staggering. "Esben Clampett. Carol Grod," he intoned. "I need them."

"Well, where are they?" asked an indignant Wigman.

"Exiled," said Roger.

"Why on earth were they exiled?"

"To prevent this precise thing from happening—so that no one could ever replicate the work they'd done. So that no one, not even the makers themselves, could somehow outdo or create a better version of the thing itself." Roger waved his hand dismissively in the air. "The woman who hired them—she was a madwoman. Raving." He said it as if it were an adequate explanation.

Wigman laughed under his breath. He'd had experiences like this before—not necessarily finding people in exile, but certainly gaining access to people who'd been sheltered from potential competitors. It was, in fact, one of Wigman's most prized qualities, his ability to convince engineers and chemists to leave competing companies. It was called poaching; it wasn't a very honest way of dealing, but honesty rarely got anyone anywhere in his line of work. "Nothing a few sawbucks couldn't fix," said Wigman. "And let's say we only found one. Wouldn't that do the trick?"

Unthank looked to Roger imploringly.

"You don't understand," said Roger. "This is not your everyday exile. These makers were put in places where they could not be reached without considerable effort. And you'd have to locate both. Their employer took very severe measures to make sure that they'd both be needed in order to recreate the thing."

"Severe measures?"

"One was blinded, one had his hands chopped off."

Unthank blanched. The Impassable Wilderness was suddenly

seeming a very vulgar and rough place. It was the first time that his monomania, his obsession with the I.W., was put into question.

Wigman, on the other hand, was not daunted. In fact, he was quite the opposite. "Impressive," he said. "I'll have to meet this woman. I like the way she works."

"Her essence was swallowed by living ivy," explained Roger. "So that won't be happening."

"Shame," said Wigman. Then: "Wait—what?"

Roger again waved his hand dismissively. "But this is all neither here nor there, gentlemen." He looked to Unthank. "If we find them, do you think you'll be successful?"

"Think?" Joffrey said, smiling. "I know I will be. With the two designers here, even without their, um, salient body parts, I have no doubt we can—"

But he didn't have a chance to finish his sentence. At that moment, every last white transponder unit on the bookshelves of Unthank's office let out a shrill, deafening staccato of BEEPS. They were a winking city of flashing red lights, these metal boxes, their needles flying wildly in the peaks of their gauges. The three men stared, immobilized, at the display.

The Unadoptables had returned.

Prue and Curtis were out of breath by the time they'd made it down the sloping hill of junk and had crossed the rusted rails of the train track. The carnival was in full swing, though its swing seemed to be of a fairly dismal arc. There were perhaps three families milling about the grounds, eyeing the yelping barkers and counting out change for the cotton candy machine. The blue-and-yellow big top tent held the center of the carnival's meandering layout like a great eye, and the two friends paused only briefly to catch their breath before jogging the final yards to what they guessed to be the backstage entrance. A grumpy-looking man stood guard.

"We have—" sputtered Prue, her breath coming in heaves. "We have to get back . . . we have to see Esben."

The man, chewing on a toothpick, looked at them askance. "Who says?"

"We say," insisted Curtis. He thought quickly. "We're relatives."

Prue caught on quick. "Yeah," she said. "That's our dad. We need to see him."

The man looked at them both, very carefully, before giving out a loud, braying laugh. "Thought I'd heard 'em all," he said. He squared up and pulled the toothpick from his mouth before adding, "The show's about to start, anyway. They ain't lettin' anybody back."

Prue's heart sank a little. Septimus said, "Squeak." Curtis didn't miss a beat.

"Where do we get tickets?" he asked.

Not far off, a sign above the ticket taker's booth read FINAL PERFORMANCE TONIGHT! CHILDREN TEN AND UNDER FREE! Arriving there, Prue tapped on the glass, startling the man sitting within. He'd been reading a tattered paperback, and he looked up at the two children at the window as if he'd just teleported from the astral plane.

"Two tickets, please," said Prue. She held her two fingers up.

The man looked down at them through his bifocals. "How old are you?"

"Ten," said Curtis.

"Twelve," corrected Prue, elbowing Curtis in the ribs.

He glowered at them. "Eighteen bucks."

Prue gaped dramatically at the man in the booth. The price seemed awfully expensive for an event at a near-abandoned carnival by a trash heap. She looked helplessly at Curtis. He gave her a shrug. She flipped her knapsack over and searched the contents for cash; none was forthcoming. Then she remembered something; a nagging memory, calling to her from what felt to be another century. In her jeans pocket were the crushed dollars that her mother had given her to buy naan bread, so many days previous. She heaved a sigh of relief as she extricated them from her pocket. She began flattening them out, one by one, on the booth counter. There were ten, all told. She smiled at the ticket taker.

"It's all we have," she said. She flashed then on her parents; they had sent her out to a neighborhood restaurant on a simple errand. What must they be thinking now? Would they ever have imagined—would she ever have imagined—what she would, in the end, be using these few crumpled dollars for?

"We really want to see this show," said Curtis.

The man arched an eyebrow. "Oh yeah?" He studied them both. "Well, you and about nobody else. Thank God they're movin' on tonight. The show stinks. I mean, besides Esben." He grumbled a little and started pulling on the roll of blue tickets by his side. He slid two of them through the hole in the window; depositing them there, he begrudgingly began sorting out the mass of crumpled dollar bills Prue had given him.

"Enjoy the show," he said before turning back to his book.

They found their seats in the audience of the big top tent; a gray-haired woman handed them a program. The room was nearly empty. Two teenagers were giggling in the back row of the bleachers; a middle-aged man, alone, sat off to the side, eating roasted peanuts from a grease-stained paper bag. Curtis, taking his seat, looked at the program the woman had given him; it was a cheap, photocopied pamphlet, printed on shocking yellow paper. On the cover was the picture of a bear, its jaws open to reveal an astonishing row of teeth. Above the picture was a banner, which sported the words: "WILD ANIMALS! SAVAGE BEASTS!" At the bottom, a similar banner read: "ESBEN THE GREAT!" Curtis opened the pamphlet, only to have the inner pages go fluttering to the ground at his feet. He was just reaching down to retrieve them when the lights flashed in the tent.

The man who they'd just bought tickets from shuffled in and

surveyed the sparse audience. "Ladies and gentlemen," he said in a flat and unenthused voice, which seemed to sluggishly slide from one word to the next. "Prepare yourselves for the experience of a lifetime. Let the Gamblin Brothers Circus big top transport you to a place of magic and wonder." He stopped and picked at his nose, briefly studying his finger before wiping it on his pants and continuing, "They've traveled the world, from Siam to Siberia, tickling the fancies of tsars and sultans alike. Women and small children should be advised: What you are about to see will confound and astonish. The show everyone's been talking about . . ." He gave a halfhearted dramatic pause before announcing: "Esben the Great."

The seats rose up in an amphitheater-like fashion from a dirt floor that was the big top's stage. A bright red tent stood at one end; its flaps were thrown open suddenly, and out strutted a man in a felt top hat, candy-striped tights, and a black jacket with tails. He seemed to take a moment to glare at the ticket taker—his introduction had apparently lacked sufficient gusto—before smiling widely to the audience members. Curtis looked around him. There were only six of them.

Curtis heard Prue hiss, "Could that be . . . ?"

But they both came to the same conclusion simultaneously: The man made a low bow before dramatically flourishing his hands. They were, undoubtedly, very real hands, not resembling hooks in the slightest. The man, having finished his bow, waited patiently as an old woman, a latecomer, hobbled her way to her seat.

"LADEES AND GENTLESMEN," said the man, very loudly, in a voice tinged with an accent of indeterminate origin. "Thee danceeing monkeee." His words slurred together as if they were made of putty; it occurred to Prue that he might be drunk.

A young boy, perhaps Curtis's age, manned a station on the side of the stage surrounded by an array of instruments: a dented trumpet, a snare drum, and a penny whistle. At the announcement, he lifted the trumpet to his lips and gave a sorry fanfare.

The flaps of the canopy behind him were folded open again, and a darkened figure shoved two rhesus monkeys out into the lights of the big top. The two animals wore matching fezzes. They looked confused. In the time they'd taken to scurry to center stage, the ringleader had procured two hula hoops, which he was brandishing wildly.

"Thee monkeees will jump. Throo zhe hoooops!" The man walked with determination to where the monkeys stood and waved the hoops in their faces. "Jump!" he yelled. "Jump!"

They stared at the man, bewildered.

The man let out a string of curses in an unrecognizable language before walking sternly to the two monkeys and quietly berating them. He then returned to his original position and held the hoops aloft. "Jump, monkeees, jump!" he shouted.

One of the monkeys wandered to a hula hoop and lazily climbed through, one leg after the other. The other stared at something on the ground; whatever it was, it didn't survive much inspection before the animal had grabbed it with its thin fingers and popped it into its mouth. The boy on the side stage gave another splatty toot on his horn; the monkeys were ushered from the stage.

"This is depressing," Septimus whispered into Curtis's ear. Curtis could only nod.

"Did we get the wrong Esben?" he asked.

"Maybe Esben's coming out later," Prue whispered.

What followed was the most dismal display of a one-ring circus event that any of them had ever seen. The monkeys had been reluctant, but they had been more invested than the single wizened elephant, who lumbered onto the stage with all the enthusiasm of a kid going into the dentist's. The lions were positively narcoleptic and the "dancing squirrels" so hyper that they immediately dashed from the tent flaps to the exit in a split second, presumably freeing themselves to return to their brethren on the outside. Their trainer, a fat man in a too-small suit, ran after them, smiling all the while to the audience—though not before Prue noted that his hands were, in fact, very real. The ringleader was becoming increasingly frustrated and thereby increasingly sober at every disaster; he stamped his feet angrily as each one came to pass until, conferring with an offstage handler (real hands, no hooks), he decided to move directly to the main event.

Walking to the center of the stage, he addressed the audience (now down to five; the two teenagers had run off in a fit of hysterical laughter after the disappearance of the squirrels) in an ostentatious voice: "Ladees. And zhe gentlesmen. I preesent you: Esben the Great."

Curtis grabbed Prue's hand in anticipation.

The red tent flaps were thrown open, and in sauntered a very large black bear. He walked on all fours, as bears do, but not without some difficulty. It wasn't until he'd reached the center of the stage and stood, dramatically, to full height that Prue and Curtis saw why: In the place of his front paws were two golden hooks.

Curtis gasped; Prue let out a little cry. The man with the bag of peanuts turned around and shushed them.

"Esben weeel now show to yooo, his power of amazeeementt!" announced the ringleader as he rolled a ball toward the standing bear. Esben dutifully climbed onto the ball and proceeded to wheel around the stage, balanced precariously on his hind paws. The ringleader did little to direct this activity; Esben seemed to be fully in control of the performance himself. He leapt from the ball at the ringleader's shout and the audience, Prue and Curtis and the two adults, applauded loudly. Prue was still in shock from this sudden reversal in her expectations. They'd been looking for a man; of *course* he was an animal. The moles were blind and, Prue reasoned, apparently unaware of the distinctions between different species of Overdwellers. They had clearly not seen the importance of parsing out what *sort* of Overdweller he was.

A few passing carnival attendees had heard the applause; several more people had filed into the tent to watch the display. The bear, with some help from the ringleader, had managed to balance a wide tin plate on his left hook. With his other prosthetic paw, he was spinning it as it teetered on the curve of the golden hook. The ringleader, with a flourish, presented Esben with a metal dowel, which he placed on top of the spinning plate; another plate was put on the dowel's end and it, too, was set to spinning. The growing crowd hooted their approval.

"Pretty good," noted Septimus quietly.

The show went on like this, with Esben managing a series of incredible feats in an all-too-sentient way, as if he contained an intelligence uncommon among his species. While the audience crowed and shouted their amazement at the sight, however, Prue and Curtis watched the bear perform with a knowing recognition. He was a Woodian, all right. No doubt about it.

The show ended with an incredible sequence of death-defying stunt work from the bear, featuring a stack of overturned chairs, balanced one on top of the other; a fiery hoop; and a wire that extended from the ceiling of the tent to the ground. Climbing the chairs, Esben fixed his hooks to the wire and slid at a breathtaking speed down from the ceiling to emerge, safely, on the other side of the flaming hoop, to the spectacular shouts of the now half-filled house. The success of the routine allowed the audience to forgive the ringleader his previous failures; Esben had saved the show. The cast bowed to raucous applause—even Esben, much to the crowd's delight—before turning and jogging back through the tent flaps in the rear. The overhead lights came on; the ticket taker appeared and began to usher people from the tent.

They knew what they needed to do next.

The same man was idling by the gate that led to the backstage area. He saw the two kids with the pet rat approach and smiled. His front teeth were knobby little stumps.

"Well, if it ain't the two bear cubs, come to see their ol' dad."

Curtis scowled. "We're just really big fans."

"Will you let us go back and see him?" asked Prue, trying on her persuasive charm.

"They're packin' up," said the man. "Off to Pendleton. Or some such place. They ain't got time to chat with fans right now."

Prue, despite herself, said aloud, "He can't go!"

"It's really important that we see him," said Curtis, becoming very impatient. "It's a life-or-death situation."

"Lemme get this straight," said the man, eyeing his fingernails casually. "You need to see a bear. A circus bear. Because it's a life-or-death situation."

"It's a long story," added Prue. "But, yes."

"Please?" pleaded Curtis.

The man looked at them both, his eyes moving from one to the other. The tired and slack look on his face had been replaced by one of bewildered pity. "No," he said finally.

They walked away, despondent. The sounds of the carnival were dying away into the frigid night air as the barkers and the vendors closed up their stalls. A few raindrops had begun to fall. They landed noisily on the muddy, melting clumps of snow that still lay here and there among the dirt and tire ruts of the circus grounds. A few men could be heard shouting terse directions from within the big top tent. In a matter of moments, the peak of the tent tilted sideways, and the big top began to droop like a deflated balloon. A gaggle of riggers, greasy with sweat, attended to its disassembly, swearing and spitting with equal profusion. Prue threw her hood over her head and frowned.

"The whole thing, it's doomed," she mourned. "We're going to lose one of the makers." She was following Curtis, her face downcast, as he walked the length of the fence. She almost ran into his back when he suddenly stopped.

"Wait," he said. "Where's Septimus?"

The rat had been at his shoulder the entire evening; only now did he notice that Septimus's ever-present claws were no longer gripping to his coat.

A scream alerted them to his presence. Looking over, they saw the backstage guard they'd just been speaking to give out a quaking holler and begin dancing across the sandy ground like a puppet under the control of a caffeine-riddled handler. Curtis recognized the dance instantly: the top-hatted Henry had cut identical steps, the week before, in his escape from the captured stagecoach.

"There he is," said Curtis.

By the time they'd returned to the backstage entrance, the man was gone, having loped, screaming, all the way to the men's bathroom to try and remove whatever demonic ferret had snuck into his mackintosh. The way was wide open. Curtis gave a surveying glance at their surroundings before ushering Prue through the unguarded gate.

"Thank you, Septimus," she whispered.

A city of cages and crates made a kind of maze in the backstage area, all awash with the movement of frenzied crew members in black coveralls and work boots, tearing down and packing up the show's gear. So frenzied, in fact, that the activities of two twelve-year-olds in their midst never warranted a second glance.

They walked with a deliberate confidence, assuming that two kids crouching low and tiptoeing were more likely to be detected. The twin cages of the obstinate monkeys let them know they were nearing the animal pens. Turning a corner by a wooden-slatted crate holding a flock of jabbering peacocks, they saw, standing alone, a black metal cage with the word ESBEN written on a placard above the bars.

Arriving there, they peered into the cage. It was completely dark.

"Esben?" whispered Prue. She was mindful to not get caught trying to talk to a circus bear. Not only would that likely get them kicked out, but they ran the risk of being committed to some loony bin too.

Curtis elbowed her ribs and pointed into the back of the cage. There, in the darkness, two small eyes caught the light of the backstage floodlights. Glowing yellow, they stared straight ahead at the two kids. A small movement of the bear's arms created a glitter of reflection from his two hook prosthetics.

Prue shared a quick look with Curtis before turning back to the figure in the dark. "We know who you are. We know that you're one of the makers that the Governess hired to make Alexei. We know that you were exiled to the underground; it's super important that you come with us."

The bear, for his part, said nothing. The blackness of his fur camouflaged him to the dark. It was as if the shine of his eyes and the glint of his hooks hovered in the shadows in the back of the cage.

Curtis stepped in. "Long story short, Esben: We need you to come with us. We can get you back to South Wood. The Governess is long gone; we were there when she—" He hesitated before saying that she'd died—it hadn't exactly been the case. "Disappeared," was the word he decided on.

Still, the bear was silent.

"Why won't you talk to us?" asked Prue, feeling increasingly desperate. Some of the crates and cages behind them were being loaded onto awaiting flatbed trucks; a train could be heard in the distance, idling its engine. "We know you can talk. We know you're from the Wood."

Curtis tried flattery. "Nice work in there, by the way. Really impressive stuff. I think you've made the most of your, you know . . ." Again he paused, searching for the right word. "Disability."

The glowing eyes shifted to stare at Curtis; he thought he could read a growing anger in them. The bear's breathing had become more rapid. Curtis looked over at Prue to see that she was shooting him a disapproving look.

She cleared her throat. "We need you to come with us. We need you to come back to South Wood."

The bear let out a low growl. It seemed to issue from some deep part of his gut. His refusal to talk was disturbing to Curtis; for a moment he considered the possibility that they had the wrong guy, that the two hooks were only a coincidence. Maybe they were really just talking to a normal bear.

Prue continued, "Listen. We know that you were treated terribly. Believe us, we know what a horrible woman the Governess was. But she was crazy. She thought that what she was doing was best for the country. And maybe she was right. I'm from the Outside, but I'm half-blood. The Council Tree of North Wood has spoken to me; it's told me that in order to save the Wood, I need to find you and the other maker. We need your help. Desperately."

"You need to reanimate Alexei, the mechanical boy prince," interjected Curtis. He spoke with an urgency pushed along by the milling crew members, who would, no doubt, discover them momentarily.

With an explosive ferocity, the bear erupted into motion, throwing himself against the bars of the cage. He let out an enormous roar that flattened the hair on Curtis's head and caused Prue to let out a scream. They both fell back into the mud, their faces wet with the bear's spittle. A commotion arose from the workers behind them; they were alerted to the bear's anger and began running in the direction of the cage.

Curtis, at a loss for words, did something impulsive. As he watched the bear retreat back into the shadows, the air echoing with the shouts of the circus crew, he reached for the medal at his chest. It was the one that he'd been given by the moles, the one with the man giving the thumbs-up. The one that said ZEKE on the bottom. Pulling it from his chest, he stood up and set it between the bars of the cage and slid it toward the bear. Just as he'd done so, the men from the circus were upon them.

"What're you kids doin' back here?" one shouted.

"Who let you in?" yelled another.

The voice of the security guard, the one who'd been a victim of Septimus's gambit, rose above the rest. "Those are them kids! They musta snuck back!"

Within seconds, the rough hands of the workers were on their shoulders, and the two of them, Prue and Curtis, were being marched toward the gate. Prue gave a quick look over her shoulder and watched as Esben's cage receded into the distance. Before she and Curtis were rudely thrown through the gate of the fence and her line of vision was cut off completely, she saw a crew of men begin pushing the cage toward an awaiting freight car.

The sound of scurrying alerted them to Septimus's arrival. He leapt onto Curtis's shoulder, and once he was sure there were no Outsiders in earshot, he whispered to the two children, "What happened? Where's Esben?"

"He won't come," said Curtis.

"What?"

"That's it," said Prue. "He won't even speak to us."

"After all that?" hissed the rat. "I had to brave that guy's hairy back for nothing? Ungrateful bear."

The train gave a somber whistle; the three of them—the boy, the girl and the rat—made their way despondently back toward the heap of rubbish.

CHAPTER 23

Out of the Periphery; Unthank's Unwanted Visitors

If you'd been there to see it, you might not have believed your eyes. The placid line of trees, the lingering snow, the half-light of the coming evening. And then you might've seen a kid, no older than fourteen, with long, straight black hair and wearing both a uniform coverall and a focused expression, break through the trees. Her hand would be extended back, as if holding on to something from within the tree line. In a short time you would see that her hand was in fact holding on to another hand, this one of a young boy who gaped at the dim sunlight beyond the trees' veil like an animal emerging from its burrow.

Soon, more followed; a succession of children appeared from the woods. In the midst of the chain was an old, hobbled man who relied on the guidance of the children to show the way. After what might seem like an eternity, the last child emerged, this one only holding the leash of a small black pug. The girl's name was Elsie, and she'd returned to the Outside after what seemed like an eternity.

They all stood silently, blinking at the panorama before them: the weaving clusters of piping and conduit, the towering smokestacks, the clattering thrum of the Industrial Wastes. The twin spires of the railroad bridge could be seen some distance down the river's gorge. On the other side, they reckoned, was freedom. But first, they would have to cross the Wastes. With renewed energy, they began moving in that direction.

They traversed the margin between the chemical-tank-strewn flats and the wild, hilly green of the woods. This margin, a small patch of dirty grass, was wide enough to accommodate them in a line. They said nothing as they walked; Carol wore a wide, beaming smile the whole way. The bridge hove closer in their vision.

No sooner had they crossed over into the Wastes, the Railroad Bridge within reach, some of them still holding the hands of their neighbors, when a single figure appeared from behind a low, broken smokestack. He wore an argyle sweater and a goatee. He positioned himself between them and the tracks of the bridge.

"Hello there," said Unthank. "Welcome back."

The huddle of kids froze and gave a collective gasp of surprise.

Unthank guessed at the reason for their shock. He batted his earlobe; the kids felt at the yellow tags pinned to their ears. "As soon as you stepped out of there, I had you. You're all tagged. GPS locators. Simple stuff, really."

Rachel stood defiantly. "Out of our way, creep," she said. The kids behind her murmured approval. They were thirty-eight strong. Here, beyond the structure and confines of the machine shop, their resistance was unstoppable. The man had no control of them here.

"I'd expected you'd be a little more thankful," answered Joffrey. "At least one of my little concoctions seems to have done the job. I don't know how you did it, but I expect to find that out in short time. And, you should know, I'm a man of my word. Wealth, freedom. It's all yours. Just tell me which of you managed to get out first."

"No deal," said the girl behind Rachel. It was Martha Song. Unthank recognized her by her ever-present goggles. "We're not going to be your slaves anymore."

Unthank moved his lips into a smile. His body was framed by the exterior of the Unthank Home in the distance; faces could be seen at the windows, the faces of children, who were watching the proceeding standoff. "Come on," he said. "Where are you gonna go?"

The children didn't answer; the wind swayed the tall trees behind them.

"That's right," said Joffrey. "Nowhere. Now let's all forget our little squabbles and get back to the Home. Once we're there, I can take you each individually and see what sort of effect—"

"We said, we're not going," said Martha Song. "And you can either stand there and get pounded by a bunch of angry orphans or you can get out of the way."

Before Unthank had a chance to respond, two more men had appeared from the direction of the building. They looked as if they'd traveled from two distinctly different eras. One, athletic and broad-shouldered in a tight-fitting suit, wore the demeanor of the modern age; the other, wisp-thin, looked as if he'd fallen from some distant corner of the nineteenth century. The latter adjusted the little spectacles on his nose as he approached.

"What's going on here, Joffrey?" asked the larger one.

"My Unadoptables, Mr. Wigman," he said, not taking his eyes off the children. "They've made it out. Somehow." He repeated the last word again, this time more quietly. "Somehow."

Wigman seemed to study the children carefully, assessing the implications. It gave Elsie a moment to consider just how ridiculous they must look, all huddled around an old man with wooden eyes, all wearing identical dirty jumpsuits and yellow tagged earrings. She thought she saw some glimmer of charity appear on the man's face, some recognition of Unthank's endeavors having gotten out of hand.

"This is pointless, Joffrey," he said finally. The wind whipped at his tie; his perfectly molded hair seemed to ruffle slightly. "Let the kids go." Here he looked for backing from the man at his side, who'd been craning his head forward and adjusting his glasses all the while. He seemed to be taken by a certain figure in the group.

"Carol Grod!" the man shouted.

The old blind man perked up his ears. A scowl came over his face.

Both Unthank and Wigman turned and stared at Roger. "That's—him?" stammered Unthank.

Elsie looked up at Carol, analyzing the grim look on his face. "Who is that?" she asked, referring to this strangely dressed man.

"Roger Swindon, as I live and breathe," said Carol defiantly. "Children, meet the man who carried out the orders to have my eyes taken from me."

Roger seemed unfazed by the accusation. "That's the past, Carol. No sense in reliving old hardships."

"I'm not *re*livin them, Roger," replied Carol. "I live with 'em every day."

Roger smiled embarrassedly at Unthank and Wigman, who stood speechless at his side. He turned back to the group of kids. "Hand him over, kiddos," he said with all the charm of an impatient dogcatcher.

Unthank managed to snap out of his reverie. "That's Carol Grod, the machinist. The guy who made the Cog?" he asked, though it sounded more like a statement that he wished somehow proved false. He couldn't believe the serendipity.

"Yes, Mr. Unthank," said Roger. "One of them, anyway. That, right there, is one half of our ticket to success."

Wigman, having heard the exchange, had begun looking at the gaggle of children in an entirely different light. "Listen to him, kids," he said, fast making sense of the situation. "Give us the old man." He paused, considering his next words before deciding that threatening children was fairly acceptable behavior in the Industrial Wastes. "And no one gets hurt."

"You're the one who's gonna get hurt," said Martha.

The crowd of children murmured their determined consent.

Rachel walked to Martha's side and faced the men defiantly. "Thirty-eight to three," she said. "That's how I figure it. We're going to cross the bridge, simple as that. I don't think you'll be wanting to stand in our way."

Unthank swallowed nervously. Roger squirmed in his pointy black shoes, his eyes never wavering from the figure of the blind man. Wigman seemed unperturbed. He reached into his pocket and retrieved something that looked like a cell phone. Flipping it open with his thumb, he depressed a button, and suddenly the silos and smokestacks of the Industrial Wastes were ringing with the persistent, clamoring sound of a ringing bell. The children all threw their hands to their ears; the noise was near deafening.

Doors, once imperceptible, revealed themselves in their opening amid the tangle of rusted piping and wire; from each spewed an army of maroon-beanied hulks, their muscled shoulders near to bursting from their gray work shirts and overalls. They carried ratchets and hammers, wrenches and pipes. The protuberance of their chins, speckled with stubble, bore such a resemblance, one to the other, that they looked as if they'd been birthed from the same test tube. The giant men fanned out, and soon the pack of kids found themselves surrounded.

Addressing the kids, Wigman yelled over the clamorous sound of the clanging bell, which continued to ring unabated, even though the alarm had clearly been heeded, "You're in the land of the Titans, kiddies," he said. "No one threatens a Titan of Industry on his own ground."

❧

The rain was falling harder now; the last light of the day was dissipating westward. Prue and Curtis trudged despondently up the hill of junk away from the circus and the noises of its shuttering. Their hair was soaked through from the freezing rain; their clothes clung chilly to their prickly skin. Septimus stood at Curtis's shoulder, his fur so soaked with rain that he most resembled a used bath towel, wadded up on the floor of a water-wet bathroom. Prue didn't think she'd ever felt more defeated than she did now. Her heart felt like it had sunk as far back in her rib cage as it could manage, like a cat cowering from a vengeful owner. It seemed to weigh down her every step as she navigated the discarded television sets and box springs of the junk heap.

"I suppose we'll just head back to the moles," she said. "Without Esben. They'll be able to take us to South Wood, where we can try to find this other maker. Right?" It was like pulling a filled bucket from the depths of a well, so great was her effort in finding the will to speak about what lay ahead.

Perhaps, she reasoned, regardless of these apparent missteps, she was on the right path anyway. Perhaps the tree foresaw this hiccup—Esben's unwillingness, his implacability—and the dominoes would continue to fall in their favor. *Kismet*, was what her mother had once called such things. A kind of magic symmetry to the world. She wasn't sure, however, how long they'd be able to string such events together before something eventually went wrong. No, it was best that they just soldier on. Return to South Wood. Rally the people. Something was bound to offer itself.

Curtis remained silent; Prue assumed he hadn't heard her.

"I mean," Prue continued, "we'll have to see if we can just make do with one maker. Maybe one is enough after all; maybe we can be his eyes. What do you think?"

"I'm not going."

"What?" Prue stopped abruptly.

"I said, I'm not going." Curtis walked past her, making his way over the garbage-strewn ground. "I'm sorry. I made an oath. I have to go back to the camp."

"What are you talking about, Curtis? What about the tree?"

Curtis stopped and pivoted, glaring at her. "The tree! The tree! All this talk about the tree!" His voice was quavering with emotion. "I don't hear plants talk, Prue. For all I know, this is some weird hallucination you're having. And I've humored you this far. Find the makers? Reanimate the heir? What's all that supposed to even mean? How is that supposed to help anyone?"

Prue could feel tears springing to her eyes. "It is," she managed. "It is going to help things. I know."

Septimus had remained silent; he watched the two of them from his perch at Curtis's collar. The boy spoke again. "I told you, I made a vow. The longer I'm away from that camp, the more I'm going against it."

"So just like that. You're leaving me."

"Well, don't put it that way. I've been with you for a long time now. And all along, all I've wanted to do was get this thing taken care of so I could find out what happened to Brendan and everybody. That's where my, you know, allegiance is." He paused, as if measuring the impact of his next words. "Prue, maybe you should just go home. Go back to your parents. Maybe this whole thing with Alexei is just over our heads."

"Me?" Prue asked, taken aback. "*I* should go back to my parents? You're setting the standard here, Curtis. What about *your* parents?"

"I know, but—"

"But nothing," countered Prue. "I know what I have to do. The boy—the tree—told me. Everything else is unimportant right now. You know what? I haven't thought about my parents this whole time. For some reason, it's like my heart isn't in the Outside anymore. It's there. There in the Wood." She pointed angrily at the horizon to the west. "I'm a Woodian, Curtis. North, South, Wild. What I do now, I do for the tree. I've been called. Nothing can change that. You've got your oath and I have my calling. My life in the Outside is *over.*"

Curtis stared at her, unsure how to respond. "Fine," he said, after a beat.

"Fine," said Prue, battling the swelling emotion in her chest. "You go do your thing. Find your bandits. I'm sorry for whatever harm I caused you and your brothers and sisters. I have to do this." She turned and continued down the trash heap; the shack that housed the ladder to the underground was not far off.

Curtis remained. "Listen," he called after her, the defiance in his voice softening, "we'll reconnect in South Wood. How does that sound? Let me figure out what happened to the bandit camp; I'll stick around to rebuild if necessary. I'll send word when I can join you. The moles will help you out, I'm sure."

"I'll be fine," shouted Prue over her shoulder. "It's not like I needed you around when I was looking for Mac."

That last bit stung. Curtis watched his friend disappear around a pile of transistor radios. A clutch of rusted springs lay at his feet and he kicked them, angrily.

"Can I speak?" asked Septimus.

"Of course you can," responded Curtis.

"Don't be so hard on her," he said. "She's a lot more fragile than you think."

"Maybe so. But she definitely doesn't let on."

"Humans are weird that way. Something I've always observed." The rat smoothed back his whiskers, flicking water from the tips of his claws. "So what's the plan?"

"Back to the camp, find the survivors."

"In that case, we should get moving. We've got a long way to go before we're back in Wildwood."

Shoving his hands deep into the pockets of his pants, Curtis turned about and walked back toward the floodlights of the disassembling carnival. They would go over ground, he decided. He would walk through the Outside for the first time in a long while. They would cross the Railroad Bridge as he had so many months before; they would find their lost brothers and sisters. He was determined.

❧

On the other side of the ridge of trash, Prue stumbled in the dark to arrive at the little trough in the pile where the dilapidated shack stood. She found herself muttering to herself as she walked, mouthing words of self-affirmation. "I'll be fine," she said, and then, as if to reinforce it, said, "You'll be fine." A little bit later: "Curtis will be fine," along with its companion: "Of course he'll be fine. He's a big kid." She realized, then and there, that she was enacting a conversation between herself and some invisible guardian; she was acting as her own surrogate parent.

Had she really meant all that, back there? Had she really forsworn her parents? The thought, oddly enough, created very little regret in the cavity of her chest; the overwhelming power of her task and the tree's whispered instruction seemed to eclipse all other concerns. It felt as if she'd been slipped some powerful draft that had made her whole reasoning and perspective shift. Or, she figured, perhaps it was of her own making. Maybe this was what becoming an adult felt like.

Her mind was consumed by this new realization, this epiphany. As she grew closer to the shack, however, she saw that there was something very different about it; different from how she and Curtis had left it only a few hours before.

The door was open.

Indeed, it was so open as to be banging on its hinges, blown by the cold wind. Her mind flashed back to their first arrival; she was certain they'd closed it tightly before they'd left to search for Esben, for fear of someone finding the hole. They'd even put a spike through the latch to keep it closed.

That was when she began to hear the noise. It sounded like a broken, uncommon yell—a voice in a garbled dialect on a transcontinental phone call. She realized it seemed to be coming from her feet. She looked down to see a gray tuft of grass peeking up through a tangle of rusted wire. The sound grew in volume, its timbre more focused and intense.

Prue squatted down, her feet on either side of the tuft. *What is it?* she thought.

GGG.

She screwed up her brow and focused; the bit of grass seemed to be wanting to convey something—something of grave importance. Like a ship cutting through a dense blanket of fog, the little plant's desire to speak became more and more clear to Prue's mind.

GGGGGG!

What is it? she repeated. *What are you trying to say?*

Louder now. *GGGGG.*

It became clear that the grass was trying, to the best of its ability, to scream at her.

And then it broke through:

GO!

Prue nearly fell over, so great was her surprise. The plant had formed a cogent, single word in the center of her mind, its meaning as evident as if she'd been yelled at through a megaphone. It was the first time she'd ever heard the noises in her head coalesce into an intelligible thought. The grass made a kind of sigh, as if it were relieved that she'd finally understood what it was trying to say. It seemed so simple: She now realized it wasn't the plants who'd lacked the sufficient power to communicate clearly; it had been her own slow learning curve.

I've got to get out of here, she suddenly knew.

She began to walk away from the grass, which, lapsed back into wordlessness, was sounding a kind of howling moan. She searched her surroundings for a route of escape; a tunnel made by a pair of toppled car fenders suggested itself. Before she could arrive there, however, a dark shape stepped between herself and her target.

"Where to, little one?" asked the shape.

Prue froze.

The shape, black as pitch, seemed to undulate slightly in her field of vision; the evening's dark was pervasive now. The glow of the departing carnival, just beyond the ridge of trash, dimly lit the scene. Prue watched with horror as the shape convulsed before her eyes.

"Who's there?" she called out, though she knew the answer to her question.

"Just your old science teacher, Prue. Your old pal." The dark shape of Darla Thennis—neither fox nor human—seemed to spasm in between shapes, the movements making a kind of eerie quaver in the woman's voice. "Been some time, hasn't it? Now, I'm not one to hold a grudge, but you did a pretty bad thing back there at your precious bandit camp. A pretty bad thing."

Prue's eyes adjusted slightly to the dark; she saw two gleaming eyes peering out from the wobbly dark shape. "Just let me go, Darla."

The shape coughed a laugh. "Let you go? After what you did to

Callista? Poor, sweet Callista." The contortions ceased; the figure, caught between its two warring shapes, began to approach her. The nascent glow of a low moon, hidden by clouds, gave light to the horrible thing: It was undeniably the shape of a woman—she walked upright, though hunched—but her head had a distinctly canine shape. Twin fangs jutted over her lower lip; black fur, matted from the rain, covered her otherwise naked body. It was the most hideous sight Prue had ever witnessed; she recoiled in revulsion.

"What's the matter?" asked Darla. "Do I *scare you*?"

Prue began moving backward; a bent piece of rebar caught her boot heel, and she fell backward against the ground.

"You don't think, do you," said Darla, approaching. "I mean, it was smart of you, staying underground; very clever. But I knew you'd eventually come up for air. They all do. See, I've been doing this a long time now. I've killed a lot of things. Animals, humans. Yes, even kids. I take particular pleasure in the children, actually." She punctuated this statement with a wide smile before continuing. "In the process, I've come to learn folks' motivations, the things that drive 'em. I've also learned to be patient. Very, very patient. I figured maybe you were dead, sure. That was an awfully long fall you took. But it just didn't *taste* right." She was circling her now, toying with her. Her speech sounded like it came from someone who'd been in isolation for too long; it was half-crazed and weirdly cadenced. Prue scrambled backward, trying to push herself onto her feet. The uneven terrain of the trash heap was unforgiving. The fox-woman spoke on. "That's the only way to explain it. So I was patient. I didn't rush things. I knew, if you survived the fall, you'd pop up again." To illustrate the word *pop*, she made twin explosive gestures with her hands, spooking Prue. Her fingers were black with fur and topped by long, yellow claws. "And lookit that. You did."

"But how could you have known?" murmured Prue. Her fingers wormed their way to her knapsack; it still lay slung over her shoulders. She found the clasps mercifully undone.

"Good question," responded Darla, taking on her life-science-teacher tone. "Very adept. Passing grades, all around. You should know the answer yourself, Prue. Prue of the Council Tree, the Half-Breed Mystic, Wildwood Regina, *the Bicycle Maiden*. I have tricks. I have informers." Again, those fingers illustrated the words in little flicks and wiggles. "All over. Even here, in the vulgar Outside."

Judging from the bedraggled and half-shapen appearance of the Kitsune, Prue guessed that this assassin was well at the end of her rope. She looked as if she'd been driven mad. Prue couldn't decide if that was a good or bad thing. Her fingers continued their excavation of the knapsack's innards.

"Now," said Darla, "we can do this quick and easy or we can drag it out. The old lady, that miserable, magical hag, put up an *inconvenient* amount of resistance. I would prefer if we didn't have to play that little scene out." She turned her head, as if stretching her neck; she appeared to be practicing a few momentary exercises before her deadly work began. But before she managed to do anything further, she let out a shrill, harrowing scream.

Prue had stabbed her in the foot.

❧

They were called stevedores. This is what Unthank had called them when he stepped to the man in the tight-fitting suit and asked him, fairly petulantly, why they'd needed to be brought into things and weren't they handling this fine by themselves, thanks very much. Elsie had heard him. But regardless of their name and their strange, identical dress and comportment, they were moving slowly toward the group of Unadoptables in a way that could only be described as menacing. The stare-down between Unthank and the man who appeared to be his boss, Mr. Wigman, continued. It looked tense; Mr. Unthank seemed much put out by the stevedores' presence, as if their being there was somehow undermining his authority. The stevedores, for their part, played up their threatening ferocity by smiling coyly and smacking their lead pipes and ratchets on their palms as they walked. Elsie looked at her sister; Rachel was grimacing.

"What do we do?" hissed Elsie to her sister. There were many moments during this prolonged adventure she'd been having since her parents deposited her at the Unthank Home when she'd wished she'd had Intrepid Tina; this was decidedly one of those times.

"I don't know," said Rachel.

The children watched as Roger spoke to Wigman, his voice haughty and impatient. "We don't need the children, Mr. Wigman. We need *that man*."

Wigman, being petitioned from both sides, waved both Unthank and Roger away. "Listen, folks," he said, addressing the crowd. "It's starting to rain. It's getting dark." Both of these things were true; the light was disappearing to the west, and a chill drizzle was wetting the hair and maroon beanies of everyone present. "Let's all move this little conference back to the Unthank Home. No one gets hurt, no one has to do any hurting. Agreed?"

The stevedores had stopped their advance, though they continued to flaunt their weaponry in a decidedly threatening fashion. There seemed to be no avenue of escape. The stevedores outnumbered the Unadoptables—Elsie guessed there to be fifty of them. Finally, Carol spoke up from the center of the crowd. "Let's do as they say, children. No sense in resisting."

The children, their faces solemnly downcast, nodded consent. The dogs were released to the avenues of the Wastes; the stevedores began corralling the group of Unadoptables toward the drab gray building in the background. They followed the same gravel road as Elsie and Rachel's parents had driven when they'd first seen the Home. The building, its lights illuminating the windows from within, came closer into view. Faces were at the glass, watching the oncoming procession.

And then the windows began to break.

The contingent stopped sharply; everyone's heads swiveled in the direction of the breaking glass. Unthank moaned a loud "NO!" as several metal footlockers were vaulted from what would be the second-floor dormitory to land with an explosive crash on the ground below. The sound of a hundred voices joined together in a loud cheer could be heard emanating from now-empty window frames; more footlockers followed, through more windows. Then came a bed frame, lumbered to the wide windows by a pack of children who pitched it, with some difficulty, to the ground below. The mattress had been set on fire. It landed on the ground in an

The children of the Unthank Home for Wayward Youth were revolting.

eruption of sparks and broken glass.

The children of the Unthank Home for Wayward Youth were revolting.

The riot spread like a virus to the boys' dormitory on the third floor; glass showered over the ground below as more objects were thrown through the windows. A crew of boys, their faces wide and smiling, looked out from one of the shattered frames and taunted Unthank and the stevedores with raspberries and shouts of derision.

"Welcome back, Unadoptables!" shouted a girl from the second-floor dorm. Another yelled, "Here's your welcome home party!"

A window broke; out of it flew a rectangular box that hit the ground with a staticky *pop*. It was a loudspeaker; it continued to broadcast harsh bursts of static, like a disembodied head still imbued with a few last flickers of life. Then it lapsed into silence.

Unthank had grown ashen pale as he watched the agitation carry over to the tall windows of the machine shop. In a short matter of time, pieces of metal pipe, liberated from their machinery, were being launched through the glass as a wild conglomeration of children, girls and boys, convened in the shop and proceeded to tear it to pieces. The front doors were flung open and Desdemona, followed by Mr. Grimble and Miss Talbot, made her panicked retreat from the rebellion growing within.

"Bradley!" she shouted. "They are destroying it all! This is not how I wanted!" She ran as fast as her dress would allow toward the crowd of stevedores and their group of detained children. She was out of breath by the time she reached Wigman; she steadied herself on his thick arm. Unthank, still deeply traumatized by the scene that was playing out before him, shot her a bewildered glance.

"Bradley?" he asked. "You call him Bradley?"

Desdemona looked away; she pushed herself closer to Wigman, who put his arm around her protectively as he continued to stare, transfixed, at the ongoing commotion.

"Wait a second . . . ," Joffrey murmured. Puzzle pieces, long separated, began to find their way together in his mind as he stared at Desdemona and Wigman, cradled together. "It was you!" he finally yelled at Desdemona over the crashing of the insurgency. "You were the one who tipped him off! You brought him into this!"

But there was scarcely time for recriminations; orange flames were spitting from the topmost windows of the tall gray building. Through the emptied windowpanes, they could see that the children had built a great bonfire of chairs and tables in the girls' dorm and had quickly set it alight. By the time the flames began to find their way to the windows, the children of the Unthank Home had streamed from the open front doors and out into the gravel drive. Once collected there, they turned—they were easily a hundred strong—and began running pell-mell toward the Unadoptables and their captors. The flames issuing from the building's windows provided them an ominous backlight. That, combined with the look of absolute rage on their faces, gave them the likeness of furies released from the depths to wage chaos on the living world.

CHAPTER 24

Rebellion!

Darla threw her head back and let out a harrowing scream, a scream that seemed to straddle the gulf between the cry of a woman and the howl of an animal. It reverberated through the trough of garbage and rattled the screens of the discarded computer monitors and television sets. It pierced deep into Prue's eardrums as she used the creature's momentary distraction to continue her backward scramble up the pile of junk. She'd barely made it a few feet away when she saw Darla reach down to remove the blade from her foot. She made a pained grimace as she did so, eyeing Prue the whole time.

"You shouldn't have done that," the fox-woman said. "That's only going to make things worse." She threw the knife aside casually.

Prue risked a quick look over her shoulder; the crest of the hill of trash was maybe thirty feet away. The floodlights from the carnival created a kind of white lining along the top. Curtis couldn't have gotten far.

"CURTIS!" Prue screamed.

The lowing wail of a train engine overlapped her cry, obscuring it. The circus train was leaving, and the night was filled with the sounds of the engine's rattle and whine. She tried again, though her voice was hoarse from exhaustion.

"Oh yes," said Darla, approaching again. She favored her right leg now; dark blood seeped from the wound in her foot. "Please, bring your friend. He's next on my list. That'd make my job quite a bit easier." The rain was coming in thick sheets now, and Prue could feel the water pouring in streams from her brow. It dripped over her lips and into her mouth, which was slightly open as her breathing came in deep, heavy bursts. Darla's fur was oil-black and looked to have the consistency of oil, the way it clung to her skin, the way the water poured over it and fell to the ground.

"CURTIIIIS!" Prue screamed again.

Darla, comically, chimed in. "CURTIS!" she yelled, cupping her long claws around her mouth. "Come join the party!" She then cocked her head, saying, "Strange, he doesn't seem to be hearing."

"You won't get away with this. They'll come for you."

"And who's this mysterious 'they'?"

"Owl Rex. The bandits."

"I have some information for you. Owl Rex flew the coop." She chuckled at her own joke before continuing. "Totally MIA. As for your bandits, they were gone when we got to their little encampment."

"Gone?"

"I'd love to take credit for that, but there were only three of us Kitsunes and, what, a hundred bandits? No, no. They'd all disappeared. Lots of smoke and fire. No bandits. Someone else did that tasty bit of culling. You flatter me if you think that we three took out that entire camp." She laughed. "Shouldn't have said anything. Oh well, you'll be dead in a few seconds anyway."

Something cold and sharp jabbed at Prue's palm. Looking down, she saw it was a section of metal rebar, jutting up from the heap. She quickly slipped her fingers around it and pulled it free: It was a rusty three feet long and sat reassuringly heavy in her grasp. She swung it out in the direction of the approaching Kitsune, and the creature flinched.

"Put that away," Darla said.

"Leave me alone."

"I can't do that. I have a job to do."

Prue swung again. The bar whistled in the air before Darla's outstretched claws. "I won't let you. I won't. I'll stop you." The words were flowing from Prue's mouth in nervous fits. The pounding of her heart beat a kick drum in her ears.

The creature cracked a wide smile. Prue swung the bar again. Darla feinted right and pounced.

Prue leapt sideways, catching herself against the slope of the hill with her elbow. The hot weight of Darla's body collapsed onto her, and it crushed her to the ground. She felt the end of the rebar bite through the fabric of her coat at her waist; a blister of pain tore through her. She yelled out; she could smell the sour breath of the fox-woman above her.

Instinctively, she kicked and was surprised to feel her left boot find purchase on the creature's underbelly. The thing yelped; her weight lifted momentarily and Prue, the rake of the slope to her advantage, rolled away. The piece of rebar still clung to her side. It wasn't until she'd managed to get a few feet from Darla that she realized it had, in fact, pierced her skin. Blood was welling up in the space between her naked waist and the cotton of her shirt.

She began to run. Her ankle was stiff; she hadn't realized how little she'd been using it on their walk through the underground. The pain was now flashing anew. She could hear Darla righting herself behind her, cursing the girl as she gave pursuit. The shack in the center of the trough was only a handful of yards distant. She could make it, she thought. If only she had a little more time . . .

Darla's twin sets of claws seized her shoulders. The thick wool of her coat tore, and Prue screamed to feel the sharpness burrow into her collarbone. The full weight of the Kitsune's body was now bearing down on her back. Prue tumbled forward. Both of them hit the ground and rolled the final yards to the bottom of the trough. They came to a stop in a wide tussock of grass, landing in such a way that Darla was able to straddle Prue's chest, immobilizing her, as she lay pinned to the hard earth.

The Kitsune fought for breath, her chest heaving in rapid jerks. Her long arms, slick in black fur, lay at her side as her knees pressed painfully into Prue's shoulder. She spat angrily at the ground and abruptly slashed Prue across the face with her claws.

Three bright red welts instantaneously appeared on Prue's cheek. Tears streamed down from her eyes. "Please!" she shouted.

"Too late." She lifted her arm to strike again.

Please.

The grass responded. Little yellow tendrils shot up Darla's arm, ensnaring her. Suddenly, the Kitsune's midsection was so crisscrossed with the fibers of grass that she resembled some bizarre model of the human nervous system. She let out a scream; the grass began to wick its way up to her neck. Prue, surprised at the turn of events, was able to push her way from underneath Darla. She began crawling again toward the shack, now only feet away. The claw marks at her face burned; the wound in her side was tacky with blood.

The sound of tearing earth caught her attention, and she twisted around to see Darla rip free of the grass's clutches. She was doing it with some considerable effort, and her face was showing her very intense frustration. Prue looked down at the tufts of grass at her feet and thought:

Now.

At her command, the grass came alive and slithered about Darla's ankles and tangled between her toes. The Kitsune stumbled forward, shouting a string of petulant curses.

For now the trash heap was awake with the voices of the wild bracken. Every blade of flaxen grass had raised its voice to Prue, chiming in a cacophonous unison. And they were all looking to her for instruction. A thistle branch clawed at the creature's calves; more weedy grass grasped her ankles. A maple tree, lost within a stack of hollowed-out truck cabs, shook free and whipped its branches at Prue's pursuer. From below the earth, a bellowing noise arose as the ground began to break away and the roots of the plants, long buried beneath the heaps of trash, liberated themselves and redirected their strength to the destruction of the half-fox, half-woman.

In the spray of mud, dirt, and metallic detritus, Prue stood and commanded the plants like the conductor of a symphony.

Darla screamed in terror and despair as the roots at her feet began to drag her beneath the earth.

Prue then realized: She was going to kill this woman.

This moment's hesitation caused the voices of the plants to spiral into confusion. Prue, blindsided by her newfound power, had forgotten herself. Forgotten that the plants, in her control, were bent on *murdering* Darla. And while it seemed like the right outcome, considering that her own life was very much in danger, it still gave her pause. And it was that pause that threw her. Suddenly, she found she could no longer keep their chiming voices separate and, as a consequence, began to lose control of them. With a violent lurch, Darla broke free of her bonds and moved toward her target.

Before Prue could shake herself from her trance, Darla's fingers were around her neck and squeezing.

"You stupid child," said the creature, her long yellow teeth spotted with blood. "No more of your magics."

"Please!" Prue squeaked. She tried to commune with the plants, but the noise was just too wild in her head, a rat's nest of intersecting voices, all screaming and shouting. The grasses were seeping back into the earth; the tree swayed dumbly in the wind. Prue felt herself slipping from consciousness.

A darkness was descending over her eyes, a threadbare veil. The world was being erased from her vision. Her pain was disappearing; her body glowing with a quiet numbness. The noise in her mind receded to a static hum, and she closed her eyes. And that was when she heard:

THUNK

THUNK

They were two sounds that Prue would never forget; they would remain etched in her mind until her final dying breath—a breath she was not destined to breathe that day, nor any day in the very near future. But regardless, she would remember the sounds—and though she'd never actually witnessed such an event, she imagined they were not unlike the sound of a butcher's meat hook sinking, twice, into a heavy, cold side of meat. She was abruptly dropped to the ground, where she collapsed in a pile.

Opening her eyes, Prue saw Darla, still poised to attack, standing above her. The whites of her eyes—half fox, half woman—shone brightly. She mouthed a distressed and surprised gasp. And then she was lifted from the ground.

Below her was a massive—and very angry—bear. He was holding her aloft in the twin pincers of the golden hooks he wore in place of his paws. His head lolled back, and he gave a loud, expressive roar. Darla, writhing in his grasp above his head, screamed shrilly. Her body, crooked and contorted, seemed to metamorphose violently between her human and fox shapes as she lay punctured on the bear's hooks. Blood streamed down the bear's paws and spattered his face. Finally, just as Darla's body began to heave in death-shudders, the bear flexed his massive biceps and vaulted the body, now assuming its human form, across the junk heap to land with a hollow clunk on a pile of discarded toaster ovens.

❦

"My shop!" shouted Unthank, his voice brimming with anguish. "It's burning!" The orange light of the fire played on his face. It gave his goatee a devil-like cast.

He seemed to be more concerned with the destruction of the machine shop than he was with the pack of ravenous children, freed from their bondage, running toward him. Roger was keeping a keen eye on Carol, who was still in the midst of the protective Unadoptables. Desdemona clung to Mr. Wigman, who was quick to shore up his stevedores.

"Hold your ground!" he shouted as the hulking men prepared their makeshift weaponry. He had actually given seminars on the quelling of worker rebellions; he was somewhat in his native element. The fact that they were children did not seem to daunt him.

"You want us to, uh, fight 'em?" asked one of the stevedores.

"No, I want you to snuggle 'em," replied Wigman angrily. "Of course you should fight them!"

Elsie and Rachel found each other in the huddle and gripped each other's arms. That was when Martha let out a celebratory whoop and fired the first volley of the insurgency: She walked over to one of the stevedores, his attention diverted by the rapidly approaching gang of kids, and kicked him, hard, in the shin. He looked down at her, surprised.

"Why'd you do that?" he asked. So she did it again, in the other shin.

By that point, the rebelling children from the Unthank Home had reached the group on the road; they threw themselves into the horde with an unbridled relish, their teeth flashing and hands flying. The stevedores were trying to fend off the attacks of the children without doing bodily harm; it appeared that even these giant men, vicious by nature, recognized the dubious morality of the situation. Wigman, on the other hand, did not bat an eyelash: When a young boy leapt toward him, he grabbed the kid by the neck and threw him to the ground. As if to illustrate his contempt, he then stepped on the poor child's back.

"That," he said, "is how one stops an uprising."

And then he was dogpiled by a throng of kids.

Martha, her goggles engaged, was bear-hugging the upper torso of a stevedore while Carl Rehnquist had dived to grab his ankles. The man soon plummeted, with a howl, to the ground. They disarmed him of his pipe wrench, and Martha set about whacking his neighboring hulk in the shins. She seemed to be taking to the violence with enthusiasm.

In the chaos, Elsie felt Carol's hand at her elbow. He leaned low and hissed to her, "Get me away from that man!" He evidently meant Roger, who was presently approaching them with a look of intense covetousness etched on his face. She hollered to Rachel, "Let's get out of here!" Grabbing either arm of the blind man, they began to hustle

him away toward a small avenue between two chemical tanks.

"What's happening back there?" Carol asked as they slowly moved through the warring crowd.

"The orphans have escaped; they've set fire to the machine shop! The whole place is going up in flames!" said Elsie, aghast at the chaos around them.

"Good for them," said Carol, smiling.

A voice came from behind them. "Stop them!" it cried. It was Roger. Caught in the clamor, he'd climbed on top of a metal pylon and was pointing a bony finger at the escaping trio. A few stevedores heard his call and began to lumber toward them.

The children, for all their pluck, were no match for the stevedores. Perhaps it had been a hopeless endeavor from the beginning. Under Wigman's urging, the giant men began to lay into their young foes with a renewed urgency, and the orphans collectively decided to make a run for it. They were pressed into the gravel pathway that Elsie and Rachel were slowly walking, with the blind man steadied between them. The cascade of children, orphans and Unadoptables, fell over them; it was all they could do to stay upright in the sudden flow.

They heard Roger barking madly behind them, "Forget the

children! Get the old man! Get the maker!"

The tide of children had crested; only a few straggled behind, limping and nursing their bruised limbs, as they all made their way deeper into the heart of the Industrial Wastes. Elsie and Rachel tried to urge Carol on, but he was old and blind and his steps were slow and faltering. A discomfited look played across his face; the sound of the stevedores' loud footsteps in the gravel was growing closer.

Michael, his eye blackened and his coverall in tatters, stopped in his retreat to yell at them. "Hurry!" he shouted.

Elsie, desperate tears pouring down her face, yelled back, "We can't!"

"Carol, can you go any faster?" pleaded Rachel, her voice quick and frightened.

Carol shook his head dolefully. He stumbled a little, and the girls labored to keep him upright.

The sounds of the stevedores' boots grew closer.

A figure broke away from the retreating pack of orphans ahead of them.

It was goggled Martha, who grabbed Carol's arm from Elsie's grip and began to tug him, urgently, forward. She then yelled at Elsie and Rachel, "Get going! I'll stay with Carol. We can't let them get you guys, too."

The Mehlberg sisters stared at her, dumbstruck. The idea of abandoning the old man seemed impossible. Besides, wouldn't Martha also be captured? Martha guessed their feelings, shouting, "Better me than you. You have the whatever, the Woodsblood. You have to go."

"No, Martha," protested Elsie.

"Children," said Carol. "She's right. We can't afford to let them have you. Your gift is too great."

Rachel saw their reasoning. She grabbed Elsie. "C'mon, sis," she said. "It's true. We won't be safe with them. We have to go." It was the first admission she'd made regarding this extraordinary thing the two of them shared.

Martha smiled through the fear that was now descending on her face. "I'll be fine," she said. "I'll be with Carol. I'll look out for him."

And so the Mehlberg sisters broke away from the old man's side and ran, as fast as their feet could carry them, toward the busily escaping pack of children in the distance. Once they'd pulled far enough away, Elsie hazarded a look backward and saw the mob of stevedores fall on the old man and his young companion. Martha was whisked up in their strong arms, while two of the men roughly accosted Carol, pinning his arms behind him as the rest of the crowd arrived at the scene. But she couldn't watch any more beyond that. It was too heart-wrenching. She turned and faced the road ahead: a long, winding path that led farther and farther into the unknown pale of the Industrial Wastes. She ran as fast as she'd ever run in her life.

❧

The next thing Prue knew, she was lying cradled in what felt like a sheepskin rug. The far-off city lights reflected against the deep layer of clouds in the dark sky; the fall of rain had grown heavier, though she seemed to be sheltered from the worst of the weather by the body of the thing that held her in its arms. The face of a bear, its eyes weary and warm, looked down at her. She could feel the metallic chill of his prosthetics against her side.

"Esben?" she managed.

The bear did not respond. Prue's right side, just above her hip, felt like someone had taken a jackhammer to it; her face was laced with an intense, needling pain. A low whistle sounded from afar and the bear looked up, steam jetting from his wide nostrils. This noise was followed by the whine of a train heaving itself into movement.

"The circus," Prue managed. "They're leaving."

The bear only nodded; he shifted his arms under her body and carried her the few yards to a small lean-to made of corrugated metal. There, she was gently set down on a ratty blanket while the bear began stacking salvaged pieces of wood in the guttered fire pit.

"Why aren't you with them? Why aren't you going?" she pressed.

The bear paused in his labors, as if registering the girl's question, before continuing (somewhat awkwardly, owing to his hooks) to attend to the fire.

Prue groaned as she tried to move; the pain was immobilizing. She laid her hand gingerly on her hip and felt that her clothes were wet with her blood. The moments prior to her rescue came back to her in fits and starts—the sudden and tremendous power she'd had over vegetation, the chiming of their voices, the roar of the creature who'd been somehow stretched between the animal and human world.

"Darla . . . ," Prue sputtered. "What's happened to her? Is she dead?"

The bear only nodded.

"So you understand me. But you don't talk?"

The bear stared at her, hard. He set down the remaining bits of wood in his hooks and took a deep breath. He then spoke, in a low, sonorous voice that sounded to Prue as if it was being emitted from the exhaust pipe of a car that hadn't been driven in fifteen years. "No," he said, before clearing his voice and saying, "I can talk. Though truth be told, I hadn't expected I'd need to. Not till you came along."

"But why?" asked Prue.

"Because maybe sometimes folks just want to be the things that they are. I wanted to be a bear. Not a Woodian. Not an Overdweller. A bear. That seem strange to you?"

"No," said Prue. "Sorry." She paused as the bear returned to his fire making; a stack of kindling had been built, and the bear began to fumble with a box of matches. "Here," said Prue. "Let me help with that."

The bear, huffing a quick thanks, tossed the matchbox to Prue, and she held a lit flame to the crumpled paper below the kindling. Soon, a glowing fire radiated warmth into the modest lean-to. Prue watched the bear as the flames cast glowing shadows across his broad face. She tried to move into a seated position, but the pain at her side proved unbearable.

"Don't move," said Esben. "You're pretty badly worked over there. That was a nasty creature you angered. Not wise." Reminded, he began rifling through a duffel that he had strapped over his shoulder, pulling a worn T-shirt from within. "I'll see to those wounds. Best do it quickly."

"But why?" asked Prue. "Why'd you come back?"

As if in answer, he reached into his duffel and retrieved something else: Zeke's smiling face on the badge gave Prue, in her swimming vision, a cheerful thumbs-up. "A city of moles saved my life once; it occurred to me I had a calling to do the same for someone else." He put the badge down and, picking up the T-shirt, stepped over to where Prue lay. He began dabbing at the dark heart of the wound at her side with the cloth wrapped around his right hook.

"I've got some wrongs to right of my own, half-breed," said the bear. "And I figure falling in with you is the first step forward. No sense in running away."

The pain ratcheted upward; Prue grimaced and turned her head to the opening of the hovel. The rain was slashing sideways; the lights flickered against the haze of clouds. The last of the circus trains sounded in the distance, heralding its progression along the wide iron tracks that ran along the river and out of town. The circus was leaving, the ringleader having not yet realized that one of the animals' cages stacked in the middle car, the one formerly housing his star, lay empty. Instead, the star was here, in the trough of garbage, seeing to the health of this one injured child. Here, in this bent lean-to, where a fire burned quietly in the deep dark.

CHAPTER 25

Season's End

Listen.

The snow has stopped; the rain has begun.

Listen.

Through the checkerboard neighborhoods of his former world, the boy is walking away. He can hear the lowing of the train in the distance. The blackness of the night hides him. He is a stranger to the world. He is still wearing the outfit he wore at the beginning of his journey. The rat remains perched on his shoulder, his snout pointed ever outward, a sentinel on the bow of a storm-plowing ship. The boy is intent on one thing: to find his adopted family, the one to whom he'd given his oath, his vow. He silently curses himself for having disregarded that vow for so long. He will make it right, he swears. The trees loom far on the horizon, over the river and through the sleeping city. This is where he means to return.

Listen.

A man in a dirty and ash-smeared argyle sweater is kneeling in front of a building on fire, his plump tears making clean tracks down the soot on his cheeks. The smoke from the conflagration is billowing into the air; there are sirens sounding in the distance, but the man knows that it is far too late, the fire is far too progressed, and that the salvation of the building and all his beloved machines within is beyond reach. He can only kneel there, in the wet gravel, and watch the thing burn. He's been left by his compatriots: the woman in the gown, the man in the tight-fitting suit, the man with the pince-nez. They've left him to watch his building burn; they are walking away with a young, parentless Korean girl and the blind man whose side she refuses to leave. They have their quarry; they have no more need for the man with the goatee and the argyle sweater. He swears mightily under his breath; a deep vengeance is growing in his heart.

Listen.

Farther into this nest of silos and smokestacks there is a wide expanse of lonely, abandoned buildings, their windows empty, their roofs collapsed. It is a quiet place; no one lives here. Even those who toil inside the Industrial Wastes have no reason to tread in this desolate land; the avenues are pocked with potholes, the sidewalks splintered and broken. But now a group of tired children have entered it, searching for shelter. They have run a great distance to arrive here, their pursuers having given up the chase long ago. They walk with slow, heavy steps. They have lost two of their number, the Korean girl and the blind man, and their hearts are heavy at the loss. At the front of the pack are two girls, one older than the other, one with straight hair and one with curly. They are holding hands. The younger girl, the curly-haired one, is holding a doll that has been rescued from the burning building by one of the other children. The reunion was gleeful—she's only just stopped pressing the button on the doll's back and making her talk—but now she's fallen into a deeply thoughtful reverie as she considers what lies ahead. She looks at her sister; she is encouraged by the determined look on her sister's face. They have learned a strange secret about themselves, one that may lead them

to find their brother, long lost. But first, they've decided, they must save their friends. A building, its roof intact, comes into view of the crowd of children. It stands in the center of a large square. Seeing it, the children walk toward it, as if drawn by the building's gravity. Perhaps this will be their home.

Listen.

Far off, beneath a shanty roof made of discarded sheet metal, a bear is stoking a small campfire and warming the quiet body of a young girl. She is awake and staring at the flames. The rain is falling on the metal of the roof; it's falling on the heap of garbage beyond their vestibule. The girl is thinking of all that she must do; she is wondering at how impossible it all seems. She is wondering about her parents, about her brother. She is wondering about the words the plants spoke to her; how she was able to speak to them so clearly in return. But most of all, she is wondering about the iron-and-brass chassis of a mechanical boy who lies in state, a mausoleum his home, far away in a very different land. They have much work to do, the girl and the bear. But she is confident that their actions are correct. The tree has decreed it.

Listen.

Looming over the city landscape, the burning building, the forgotten trash heap, and the abandoned square is an expanse of deep green, of sky-tall trees and vast carpets of moss and fern. Inside, a world is alive.

In the southernmost region of this deep wood, a city sleeps. The windows on a mansion are drawn closed, and a quiet murmur descends on all the region's denizens, animal and human. Their daily struggle, the tenuousness of their lives in the vacuum of power that has remained in the wake of a revolution, can wait until tomorrow.

And over the spiny range of a mountain chain, beyond a patchwork of tidy farm plots, a massive tree, its gnarled limbs snaking against the cloudy black sky, sits rooted to the loamy ground. A young boy sits in meditation at its foot, communing with the tree's silent spirit. All of this: the boy and the rat crossing the Outside, the crying man in front of the burning building, the captive child and her blind friend, the lost children in search of a new home. The bear in the metal lean-to, the quiet, thoughtful girl pondering the road ahead, the sleeping town—all of this, he sees.

The snow has stopped falling; the rain has come.

Winter is passing.

A Spring will soon arrive.

The End

About the Author and Illustrator

COLIN MELOY once wrote Ray Bradbury a letter, informing him that he "considered himself an author too." He was ten. Since then, Colin has gone on to be the singer and songwriter for the band the Decemberists, where he channels all of his weird ideas into weird songs. With the Wildwood Chronicles, he is now channeling those ideas into novels.

As a kid, CARSON ELLIS loved exploring the woods, drawing, and nursing wounded animals back to health. As an adult, little has changed—except she is now the acclaimed illustrator of several books for children, including Lemony Snicket's *The Composer Is Dead*, *Dillweed's Revenge* by Florence Parry Heide, and *The Mysterious Benedict Society* by Trenton Lee Stewart.

Colin and Carson live with their sons, Hank and Milo, in Portland, Oregon, quite near the Impassable Wilderness.

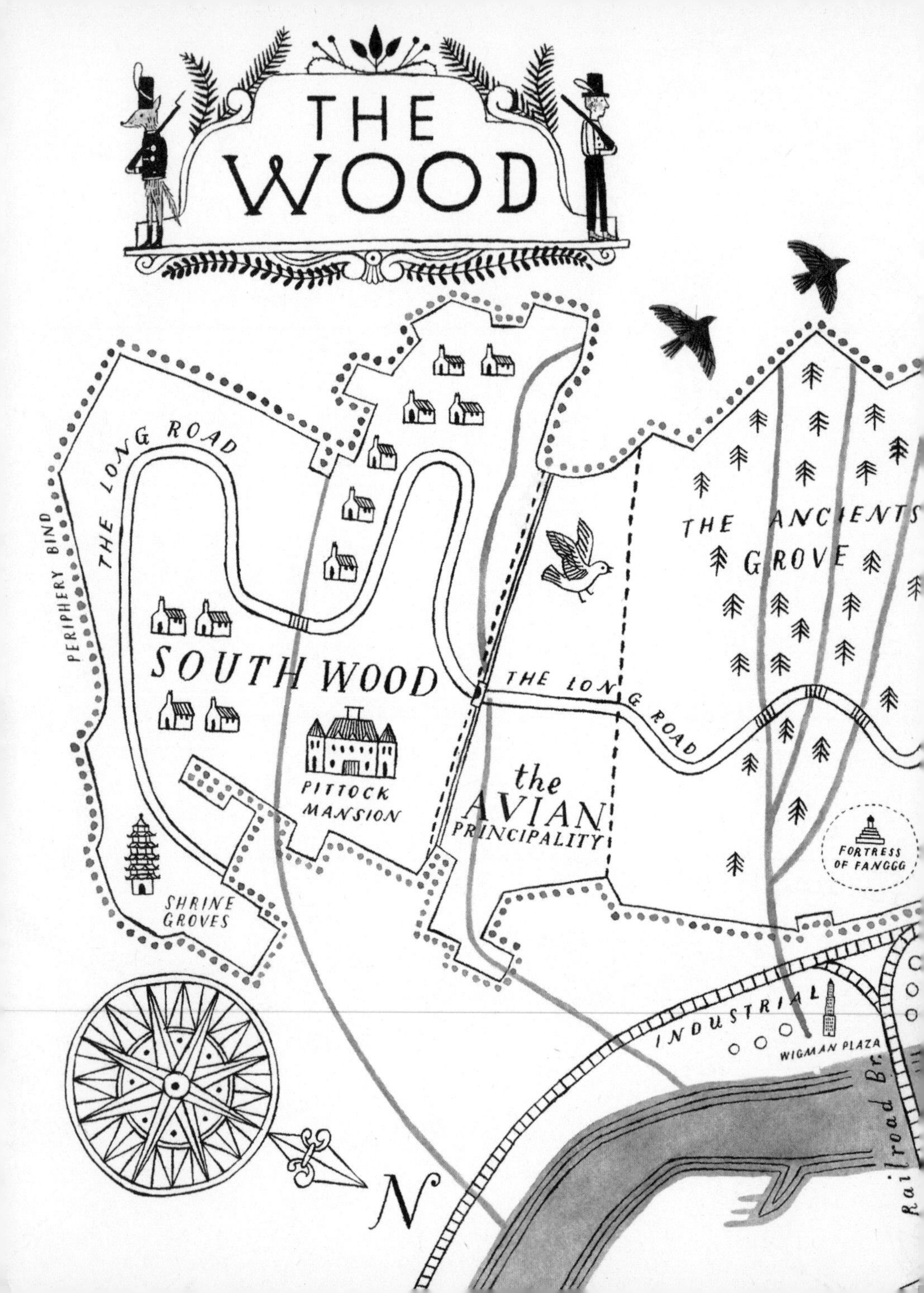
THE WOOD
THE LONG ROAD
PERIPHERY BIND
SOUTH WOOD
PITTOCK MANSION
SHRINE GROVES
THE LONG ROAD
the AVIAN PRINCIPALITY
THE ANCIENTS GROVE
FORTRESS OF FANGGG
INDUSTRIAL
WIGMAN PLAZA
Railroad Br.
N

BANDIT CAMP II
PERIPHERY BIND
THE LONG GAP
CAVERN POOL
NORTH WOOD
THE LONG ROAD
GREAT HALL
Gap Br.
THE COUNCIL TREE
WILD WOOD
CAROL'S COTTAGE
WASTES
UNTHANK HOME
WILLAMETTE RIVER
THE BLUFF
St. JOHNS
PRUE'S HOUSE

A Sneak Peek at

WILDWOOD IMPERIUM

THE WILDWOOD CHRONICLES, BOOK III

CHAPTER I

The May Queen

First, the explosion of life. Then came the celebration.

Such had it been for generations and generations, as long as the eldest of the eldest could remember; as long as the record books had kept steady score. By the time the first buds were edging their green shoots from the dirt, the parade grounds had been cleared and the May Pole had been pulled from its exile in the basement of the Mansion. The board had met and the Queen chosen; all that was left was the wait. The wait for May.

And when it came, it came wearing a bright, white gown: the May Queen. She appeared on horseback, as was tradition, wearing a blinding white gown, and her hair sprouting garlands of flowers. Her name was Zita, and she was the daughter of a stenographer for the courts, a proud man who stood beaming in the stands—a person of honor—with the Governor Regent elect and his flushed, fat wife and his three children looking bored and bemused, stuffed as they were into their little ill-fitting suits that they only wore for weddings.

But the May Queen was radiant in her long brown braids and white, white gown, and everyone in the town flocked to see her and the procession that followed. In the center square, a brass band, having performed *The Storming of the Prison* to satisfy the powers-that-be, launched into a familiar set list of seasonal favorites, led by a mustachioed tenor, who played up the bawdiest bits to the delight of the audience. A traditional dance was endured by the younger set among the audience, while the elders cooed their appreciation and waxed nostalgically about their own time, when they wore those self-same striped trousers and danced the May Fair. The Queen reigned all the while, smiling down from her flower-laden dais; she must've been only fifteen. All the boys blushed to make eye contact with her. Even the Spokes, the hard-liners of the Bicycle Revolution, seemed to drop their ever-present steeliness in favor of an easy gait, and today there were no words of anger exchanged between them and the few in the crowd who might question their fervor. And when the Synod arrived to rasp the benediction on the day, the crowd suffered them quietly. The rite was a strange insistence considering the fact that the May Fair's celebration had long predated the sect's fixation on the Blighted Tree; indeed, the May Fair had been a long-standing tradition, it was told, even when the Tree's boughs were full with green buds, before it earned its present name, before the strange parasite had rendered the Tree in a kind of suspended animation. But such was the spirit that day: Even the spoilers were allowed their separate peace.

By the time the festivities, the beribboned May Pole their axis, had spiraled out into the surrounding crowd and the light had faded and the men gathered around the barrels of poppy beer and the women sipped politely at blackberry wine and the dancing had begun in earnest, the May Queen had long been hoisted on the shoulders of a crowd of local boys and brought with much fanfare to her home, where, her now-tipsy father assumed, she was peacefully asleep, her white gown toppled in a corner, her braids a tattered mess, and her pillow strewn with flowers.

But this was not the case.

Zita, the May Queen, was climbing down the trellis from her second-floor room, still wearing her white gown and her wreath of flowers still atop her braided hair. A thorn from the climbing rose made a thin incision in the taffeta as she reached the ground. She stopped and studied her surroundings: She could hear the muffled, distant sounds of the celebrations in the town square; a few straggling partygoers, homeward, laughed over some joke on the street. She whistled, twice.

Nothing.

Again, she pursed her lips and gave two shrill whistles. A rustle sounded in the nearby junipers. Zita froze.

"Alice?" she asked to the dark. "Is that you?"

Suddenly, the bushes parted to reveal a girl dressed in a dark overcoat. Remnant pieces of juniper stuck obstinately to her short blond hair. Zita frowned.

"You didn't have to come that way," said Zita.

Alice looked back at her improvised path: a hole in the bushes. "You said to come secret."

Another noise. This time, from the street side. It was Kendra, a girl with wiry, close-cropped hair. She was carrying something in her hands.

"Good," said Zita, seeing her. "You brought the censer."

Kendra nodded, proffering the thing in her hands. It was made of worn brass, discolored from decades of use. Tear-shaped holes dotted the vessel; strands of gold chain clung to its side, like hair. "I need to get this back tonight," she said. "It's serious. If my dad knew this was missing. He's got some weird thing he has to do tomorrow." Kendra's dad was a recent recruit to the rising Synod, an apostle to the Blighted Tree. She clearly wasn't very happy about his newfound religiosity.

Zita nodded. She turned to Alice, who was still brushing needles from her coat. "You have the sage?"

Alice nodded gravely and pulled a handful of green leaves, bundled by twine, from a bag slung over her back. The earthy smell of the herbs perfumed the air.

"Good," said Zita.

"Is that all we need?" asked Alice, stuffing the herb bouquet back into her bag.

Zita shook her head and produced a small, blue bottle. The two other girls squinted and tried, in the half-light, to make out what was inside.

"What is it?" asked Kendra.

"I don't know," said Zita. "But we need it."

"And isn't there something about a mirror?" Again, this was Kendra.

Zita had it: a picture mirror, the size of a tall book. The glass sat in an ornate gold frame.

"Are you sure you know what you're doing?" This was Alice, fidgeting uncomfortably in her too-large coat.

Zita flashed her a smile. "No," she said. "But that's half the fun, right?" She shoved the bottle back in her pocket, the mirror in a knapsack at her feet. "C'mon," she said. "We don't have a ton of time."

The threesome marched quietly through the alleyways of the

town, carefully avoiding the crowds of festival goers on their weaving ways homeward. The red brick of the buildings and houses gave way to the low, wooden hovels of the outer ring, and they climbed a forested hill, listening to the last of the brass bands echo away behind them. A trail snaked through the trees here; Zita stopped by a fallen cedar and looked behind them. The lit windows of the Mansion could be seen winking in the distance, little starfalls in the narrow gaps between the crowding trees. She was carrying a red kerosene lantern and she lit it with a match; they were about to continue when a noise startled them: more footsteps in the underbrush.

"Who's there?" demanded Zita, swinging the lantern toward the sound.

A young girl appeared, an overcoat hastily thrown over flannel pajamas.

"Becca!" shouted Alice. "So help me gods, I'm going to kill you."

The girl look appropriately shamed; her cheeks flared red and her eyes were downcast. "Sorry," she muttered.

Zita looked directly at Alice. "What is she doing here?"

"I'd ask her the same thing," said Alice, her eyes not leaving the young girl.

"I know what *you're* doing," said the young girl.

"Oh yeah?" asked Zita.

"Becca, go home," said Alice. "Do Mom and Dad know you're gone?"

The young girl ignored her sister's question. "You're calling the Empress."

Zita's eyes flashed to Alice's. "What did you tell her?"

"N-nothing," stammered Alice. She glanced around at the gathered girls, hoping for some rescue. Finally, she frowned and said, "She heard us talking. Last night. She said she'd tell Mom and Dad if I didn't let her in on it."

"I wanna come," said Becca, still staring at Zita. "I want to see you do it. I want to see what happens."

"You're too young," said Zita.

"Who says?" said Becca.

"I do," said Zita. "And I'm the May Queen."

This seemed to silence the little girl.

"Go home, Becca," said Alice. "And I won't make you rue the day you were born."

Becca rounded on her sister. "I'll tell Mom and Dad. I swear to the trees. I'll tell 'em. And then you won't be able to go out for a week. You'll have to miss the school Spring Pageant."

Alice gave Zita a pleading, desperate look that seemed to say, Little sisters: What can you do? The May Queen gave in, saying to Becca, "How much do you know?"

The young girl gave a deep, relieved breath and said, "I heard about it before, but I didn't know anyone who'd done it. At the old stone house. Off MacLeay road. They say she died there." She looked from girl to girl, judging by their silence that she was true in her telling. "You say something? A chant? In the center of the house. And turn around three times. To wake her. Her ghost."

Zita listened to the girl in silence. When she'd finished, Zita nodded. "Okay," she said. "You can come. But you've got to swear you'll not tell a soul what you see. You swear?"

"I swear."

"Follow me," said Zita, and she continued walking. Alice, cuffing her sister on her head, took up the rear of the procession.

A clock struck the half hour, somewhere in the distance, and Zita quickened her pace. "Not long now," she said.

"Why the rush?" asked Kendra.

"After midnight, it won't work. It's got to start before the hour. The first of May, *too loo too ray.*"

Kendra looked to Alice for some sort of explanation, but Alice only shrugged. Zita had long been a mysterious force in their lives: Since they were little girls, she'd always had a kind of peculiar magnetism. An imaginative girl, she'd captivated her friends with strange drawings and poetry, with her long-standing fascination with the occult.

The forest grew wilder as they moved away from the populous part of South Wood and into the mangy scrub that bordered the Avian Principality and, beyond that, Wildwood. A path led through the undergrowth, and they followed it. Before long, the girls arrived at the house, or what was left of it.

It was a ruin, its stone walls worn down by the elements and nearly consumed by a thick blanket of winding ivy. Branches invaded the house where the roof had been, and thick swatches of moss lay in the chinks of the stone. The four girls walked cautiously into the center of the house, its floor long overtaken by the forest's bracken: a carpet of ivy fighting for dominion of the small enclosure. Whoever had lived here before had made do with very little: The house amounted to a single, small room. Two breaks in the rock walls suggested windows, and a door, its keystone long collapsed, led out into a dark empty expanse. Which is not to say that the house had remained entirely uninhabited all these years—empty tins of food, their labels sun-bleached indecipherable, littered the corners of the house, and the names and exploits of past explorers made a kind of diary on the inner walls: "OLD RED SLEPT HERE SOME." "TRAVIS LOVES ISABEL." "NOT REALLY NOW NOT ANYMORE." "LONG LIVE THE EMPRESS!" were all scrawled in chalk or paint or chiseled into the stone.

Zita looked at her watch; she nodded to the other girls. "Let's do this," she said.

As she'd been told, as she'd heard from the older girls in her class (who whispered around her in the back of the small schoolhouse classroom, who smoked illicit cigarettes in the schoolyard, and who sneered when she approached), as she'd finally learned when she'd got older: The Dead Empress was a ghost who inhabited the house, who'd lived in the house when she'd been cast out by the old government, centuries before, when the Wood was an Empire. And how the old government had sent knives to exact their final revenge, and she'd been cut down in the middle of the house, the small stone house, in front of her son and her daughter while her husband had been hunting in the forest. And then they had killed her children. And when her husband had returned and witnessed the horrific scene, they'd killed him too. It was said that they gave the two children and the man a proper burial, but the Empress they left on the floor of the house and set it afire, ensuring that her soul, after death, would never find rest.

Learning the story was like a coming-of-age benchmark for teenagers in South Wood; everyone knew it. However, very few acted on the promise of the story, the dark epilogue: With the right incantation, on the right time of the month, when the moon was full and the sky bright with stars, the Empress's soul could be called from her hellish purgatory to be witnessed by the living. Once she'd been called, though, there was very little information about what she would do: Some said she would do your bidding for seven days. Others swore she would administer revenge on whomever you named. Still others claimed only her shade appeared and wept for her murdered family, keening like a banshee. In any case, it was enough to drive the macabre fantasies of Zita and make her determined to bring the woman's ghost from the ether.

At Zita's instruction, the three other girls gathered around her in a tight circle in the center of the structure. She set the mirror at her feet. Taking the censer from Kendra, she opened it and filled the chamber with the sage leaves Alice had brought. The girls were silent as they answered Zita's instructions, staring at their friend with the quiet expressions of parishioners before a solemn clergyman. Finally, she produced the blue bottle from her pocket and proceeded to pour its contents into the censer: By the light of the lantern, held by Kendra, the stuff appeared to be a grainy, gray powder.

"Match," said Zita.

Alice brought out a small box labeled THE HORSE AND HIND PUBLIC HOUSE. Pulling a match from within, she struck it against the side, and the thing flickered alight. Zita took it from Alice and held the flame to the now-closed censer.

A light exploded from the object.

Kendra shrieked; Alice threw her hand to her face. Only Zita and little Becca remained calm as an eerie illumination blew from the little holes in the censer and flooded the ruined house like someone had tripped a floodlight. The smell of sage filled the air, sage and another scent that none of them could properly identify; perhaps it was the smell of water. Or the smell of air released from an attic room long closed off.

"Okay," said Zita, calmly. "Everyone join hands around me."

The girls did as they were instructed. Zita stood in the center with the glowing censer, thick tendrils of smoke now pouring from the teardrop-shaped holes in the brass. Taking a deep breath, she began her recitation:

On the first of May
Too loo too ray
Before the dark succumbs to day
When sparrows cry
Too loo too rye
We call the Verdant Empress

She looked at the small circle of girls surrounding her. Their eyes were tightly shut. The littlest, Becca: Her brow was furrowed in deep concentration. "Now we all repeat," said Zita, "after me."

And they did:

We call you
Verdant Empress
We call you
Verdant Empress
Verdant Empress
Verdant Empress

Then Zita spoke alone: "Now count off. I'm going to turn."

The girls hummed the count as Zita made slow pirouettes in the center of the circle.

ONE
TWO
THREE

Suddenly, the light from the censer was snuffed out, like a gutted candle flame.

The ivy rustled at their feet, though no breeze disturbed the air.

And then, issuing from the ground came the distinct sound of a woman's low, gravelly moan.

Kendra screamed and fell backward; Alice grabbed Becca and, in a state of absolute panic, threw her sister over her shoulder and stumbled for the house's doorway. Within a flash, three of the four girls had made a hasty exit from the house and were sprinting, screaming, through the encircling woods. Only Zita remained, transfixed, the extinguished censer swinging in her hand.

All was silent. The moaning had ceased; the ivy had stopped writhing. Zita looked down at the mirror at her feet. The glass was fogged.

Slowly, words began to scrawl across the glass, as if drawn there by a finger.

GIRL, it read.

Zita caught her breath in her throat.

I AM AWAKE.